MW00717183

stitch

gothika #1

sue brown
eli easton
jamie fessenden
kim fielding

Dreamspinner Press

Published by
Dreamspinner Press
5032 Capital Circle SW
Suite 2, PMB# 279
Tallahassee, FL 32305-7886
USA
http://www.dreamspinnerpress.com/

ISBN: 978-1-62798-833-9
Digital ISBN 978-1-62798-834-6

Printed in the United States of America
First Edition
April 2014

table of contents

The Golem of
Mala Lubovnya

kim fielding

~1~

THE FIRST thing he knew was the touch of fingers. Later he learned the difference between a scholar's gentle, hesitant strokes and a stonemason's calloused caresses, but in the beginning there were only fingers rubbing lines into the clay of his chest.

He opened his eyes and discovered the world.

It was only a small piece of the world, as he also learned later. Great wooden beams over him, and between them, smaller slats of wood in neat rows. He studied the pattern for a moment and was pleased with it. But then he saw the sparkle of dust motes in a shaft of sunlight, and he was so delighted he reached up to touch them. That was when he discovered his hand, and it was a wonder. His fingers were long and broad and pale, and they moved as he willed them. He played with them, making them dance along with the dust. He heard a sound like rocks tumbling down a mountainside and realized it was his own laughter, and he was so happy to be able to make the sound that he laughed some more.

"Golem!"

He turned his head and was astonished to see a man standing beside him. But of course—those fingers on his chest must have belonged to someone. The man was small, dressed in dark clothing and a dark skullcap, and his dark beard was threaded with gray. His eyes were wide. "Stand!" he ordered.

The golem slowly rose to his feet. Feet! They were large, and the toes moved nearly as nimbly as his fingers. He curled the toes under and stretched them out, and he pressed his feet more firmly against the floor so as to feel the splintery floorboards.

"Look at me," said the man.

The golem towered over him. Could easily have lifted the little man into the air and torn him in two. But the man glared at him fiercely and pointed at him with a finger still wet with clay. "Do you know who I am?" asked the man.

The answer required thought, which was also new for the golem, and clumsy. "My master?" he finally rumbled. He liked the way the sounds hummed and hissed in his mouth.

"Yes. I am Rabbi Eleazar of Mala Lubovnya, and I am your master. This means you will obey me in all things."

The golem nodded. He was glad to have a master, because the golem knew nothing and surely Rabbi Eleazar knew everything. "Who am I, Master?" he asked.

The rabbi shook his head. "You are not a who but a what. You are a golem. I made you in man's image but you are not a man. Just as men are made in God's image but we are not God."

A heaviness churned in the golem's belly as he looked down at himself. He had skin like his master's, two legs, a thick soft penis, a heavy scrotum. His broad chest was hairless, and letters were carved into his sternum. He couldn't read them. "I'm not a man?" he whispered, sounding like shifting sands. "Then what am I?"

"Golem."

It wasn't a nice word. The golem's legs felt weak, and he collapsed to the floor. He gathered his knees to his chest and closed his eyes. He wasn't real. He was nothing but an object made of clay and he had no family, no friends.

"What's wrong with you?" asked the rabbi. "Are you broken?"

The golem shook his head mutely. He was everything a golem ought to be. He didn't understand how he knew about things like family and friends, but various bits of knowledge rattled around in his head.

After a long silence, the rabbi sighed. "It's nearly dinnertime. You stay here and keep quiet. Tomorrow I will test you."

The golem's eyes were still closed, but he heard his master's footfalls on the floor, the creak and thud of a door, more footsteps descending stairs. And then he was alone in the silence. He sat until he felt cramped, and then he carefully stood. The light had begun to dim, and the air was chill on his bare skin. Remembering his master's orders, he tiptoed to the room's single window and peered outside.

The world was so much larger than he'd imagined! He nearly fell back in surprise. Peering through the rippled pane of glass, he saw the sky, huge and violet. Down below him—for his window was several stories up—were stone buildings. Most had red tile roofs and boxes of colorful flowers outside the windows. One structure was only partially complete, nothing yet but an open rectangle. The spaces between the buildings were paved with small blocks. Two cats, one orange and one brown, lapped at a small bowl. A trio of girls hurried by with their arms linked, a man carried an armload of wood into one of the buildings, and a black-and-gray bird watched from a nearby rooftop.

None of the other buildings were as tall as the one where the golem stood. He leaned his forehead against the dusty glass and watched all the activity, and he wondered whether there were other golems observing from other windows.

As the light continued to wane, several men approached the golem's building. He couldn't see them well from his angle, but he thought they entered through a door. He hoped they were coming to see him, to speak with him. They looked happy. But nobody came clomping up the stairs.

He padded quietly to the room's door and leaned his ear against it. At first he heard nothing, then the soft rumble of many voices speaking at once. When the speaking stopped, it was replaced by chanting. They were praying. He didn't understand the words, but he liked the sound of them—sometimes somber and sometimes joyous—and he liked the way the men's voices joined together into one complex tapestry. One voice rose above the others, however, clear and strong. The golem wished he could hum along, but his master had told him to be silent. Besides, perhaps prayers were meant only for real people. Perhaps a prayer from a golem was an abomination.

The golem curled up on the floor with his ear to the narrow crack under the door, and he listened until he fell asleep.

"YOU'RE IN the way," said Rabbi Eleazar. He stood in the doorway, the doorknob still in his hand, and he looked down at the golem. He had a pile of fabric tucked under his arm.

"I'm sorry, Master." The golem stood and backed away. Although morning light flooded his room, he rubbed his arms to chase away the nighttime's lingering cold.

Rabbi Eleazar held the fabric toward the golem. "Put these on. Make yourself decent." He shook his head. "I hope they fit. It's not easy to find something your size."

There were trousers, coarsely made and patched, too big around the waist, and falling barely below the golem's knees, but it was real clothing, and that felt good. He put on an equally well-used vest, which couldn't close across his chest and covered him only to the bottom of his ribs. But it had two shiny metal buttons, which the golem liked very much. He smiled at his master once he was dressed. "Thank you."

"Next time I'll bring you some rope to use as a belt. Can't have your trousers falling down." For the first time in the golem's presence, the rabbi allowed himself a small grin. "You'll be a shock enough to the congregation as it is."

"The congregation? Will I be allowed to meet them?"

"Not yet. If I'm lucky, never."

"Oh." The golem's excitement dimmed and his shoulders slumped.

If the rabbi noticed, he didn't comment. Instead he pointed to a jumble of empty sacks in one corner of the room. "You can clean those up today. Stack them neatly and place them on a shelf. And tidy the rest of the attic, so long as you can be quiet about it."

"Is that why you made me, Master? To clean?" The golem liked the idea of having a purpose. If he was meant to clean, he would do a very good job of it. He would make his master proud.

"No." The rabbi walked across the room to look out the window. He nearly had to stand on tiptoe to see outside. "There are... petty men out there. They're not even truly evil. Just selfish and greedy and a little drunk with power. Some of those men would harm my people. As if we were not citizens too, hardworking and loyal and as good as anyone else. I am hoping their threats are empty. Perhaps clearer, fairer minds will prevail. But so often it seems as if people are eager to hear the worst words, the most dangerous ideas."

Rabbi Eleazar fell silent and remained at the window for a long time, lost in thought, his brow furrowed. Eventually he turned to the golem, who'd been waiting patiently. "I fear my people are in danger, and that is why I made you. Tonight I will test you. If you are as strong as I hope, you will serve to protect us should the need arise."

At these words, the golem stood very tall and straight. "I will do my best, Master."

"Of course you will." The rabbi patted the golem's arm. It was the first time they'd touched since the rabbi had made him. The hand was warm, and now that they stood close together, the golem realized his master smelled of wool and fresh bread.

"Clean," said the rabbi, not unkindly. "And be quiet." Without another word, he left the attic. The latch seemed very loud when it settled into place.

There were a lot of bags. When the golem picked one up, bits of dried clay pattered at his feet, and he realized where the sacks had come from. They must have held the substance from which he was made. He imagined the rabbi digging at a riverbank, filling the bags, loading them into a cart and bringing them home, carrying them one by one up the stairs. Nothing but sacks full of damp earth that the rabbi had shaped and formed into the semblance of a man. Had he thought about the specifics of how his golem would look, or had he simply squished and smoothed until he decided it was good enough? The golem ran his fingers over his face, feeling his thick, dry lips, his wide nose, his hairless brow, his bald scalp. He must be very ugly.

He sighed loudly and began to fold the sacks into neat squares. He piled them on a shelf alongside a few dented tin boxes and a couple of chipped pottery bowls. When he found a broom tucked in a corner, he swept the clay dust into a little pile. But he wasn't sure what to do with it, so he ended up gathering the dust into one of the bowls.

After that, he looked for more things to clean. In the rafters there were cobwebs, which he vanquished. A thin layer of dust lay over everything, and he used one of the bags to wipe it away, with some success. He wandered to the window and dusted the glass, then realized he would need to wash away the grime. He had no water. Perhaps he could ask his master for some later.

He was still at the window when some motion outside caught his attention. Several men were working near the half-built house. Two of them chiseled large blocks of stone, while two others carried the blocks and set them into mortar that a fifth man had spread. All five resembled each other, although one was a generation older. A father and sons, perhaps. The golem wrapped his arms around himself, wondering what it would be like to have a family.

The golem soon forgot his cleaning as he fixed his attention on the masons. He was particularly interested in the one who set the mortar. He looked to be the youngest of the group. He had a short beard, and his dark hair was very curly. He was a little less burly than his brothers, all of whom were big men, but not as big as the golem. The youngest mason moved confidently, deftly, almost like a dancer, and unlike his brothers, he rarely seemed distracted by passersby. When a stout woman in a gray sweater and gray head scarf appeared with a basket of food, the youngest mason sat a little apart from the others, staring up at the clouds as he ate.

The golem watched the masons all day. When the sun angled low, the men packed up their tools and walked out of sight; the golem felt oddly lonely. He turned back to his own work, setting some broken chairs into a neat pile and folding wads of worm-eaten woolen fabric. When he couldn't find anything else to do, he hurried to the window again and was rewarded by the sight of the masons approaching his building. They were dressed in nicer clothes, and he could hear them laughing as they walked up the pavement. All except the youngest one, who trailed the rest and looked somber.

Not long afterward, the praying began. The golem loved it as much as he had the first time. He again sat very close to the door, not quite daring to open it a crack. But even through the heavy wood, he could hear the voices chanting together and the one voice that rose above the rest, soaring like a bird. The golem smiled.

Rabbi Eleazar came up the steps not long after the men had left. He carried a candle in a metal lantern. "Did you clean?" he asked, holding the lantern high. The light didn't creep very far into the room.

"Yes, Master. Except for the window."

"The window can stay as it is. Follow me."

If the golem had a heart, it would have raced as he trailed the rabbi. They went out the door—the golem had to stoop to fit through—onto a small landing and to a steep stairway. The stairs were so narrow that the golem's shoulders nearly brushed both sides. He had to concentrate on his steps as he descended; he didn't want to tumble all the way down. He might shatter, and he didn't know if the rabbi could repair him.

There were a lot of stairs. The golem didn't know how to count well, but the stairway twisted and turned several times until finally the rabbi opened a door and led him out onto the ground floor. They were in a large vestibule. It was too dark for the golem to see the details. But he could easily see a pair of double doors that stood open to a very spacious room filled with padded chairs. More chairs were arranged on a mezzanine. And in the center of the room was a raised dais with a large candelabra, a carved podium, and a painted and gilded cabinet with richly embroidered fabric covering the front.

"What is this place?" asked the golem in a whisper, because he wasn't sure whether he had permission to make sounds.

"The shul," Rabbi Eleazar answered.

"Do you live here?"

"Of course not. This is a house of worship. Nobody lives here."

Nobody except the golem. But he didn't count.

The golem was disappointed when they didn't enter the sanctuary. He would have liked to examine its details more carefully. Instead, the rabbi took him down a short corridor and out a door so small even the rabbi had to duck slightly. They were in a fully enclosed courtyard formed by the synagogue on two sides and two-story wooden buildings on the others. A cistern sat in the center of the cobblestone paving, and some small trees and shrubs grew near the walls. It was very quiet, although the golem could hear snatches of voices from somewhere else. Maybe inside the houses. The golem stood in the center and looked up at the deep black sky, wondering if it were possible to fall upward. He liked the way the breeze tickled the bare bits of his skin, bringing tantalizing whiffs of food and animals and growing things. He liked the feeling of the pebbly pavement under his bare feet. He wanted to touch the leaves of the trees, to taste the little puddle of water at the edge of the cistern, but he didn't dare.

The rabbi crossed the courtyard to a large wagon. "Can you pull this?" he asked.

The golem placed himself between the shafts and tugged. The cart came easily behind him, its wheels clattering on the pavement.

"Enough, enough!" said Rabbi Eleazar. "So you're as strong as an ox. But how much can you lift?"

The golem thought for a moment. Then he stooped to place his arms under the front of the wagon and straightened his knees. The cart rose into the air—a bit unsteadily because of its awkward shape, but without a great amount of effort on the golem's part.

The rabbi uttered an exclamation in a language the golem didn't understand. A brief prayer, maybe. The golem set the cart down again, taking care not to make too much noise. He looked at his master expectantly. He was enjoying this work—it felt good to be so useful.

"I have one more test for you. Come here."

In the corner where the walls of the synagogue met, there was a boulder nearly as tall as the rabbi. It was covered in moss and lichen. The golem wondered whether a stone could itch. His shoulders twitched in sympathy.

The rabbi picked up a hammer with a long wooden handle and a large metal head. He handed it to the golem. "I had to borrow this from Yitzak the smith, and I believe he was almost overcome with curiosity about why I might need it. Use it on the rock. Bring it down as hard as you can."

The golem hefted the tool in his hands. The shaft was smooth and solid. It felt good, but even better was when the golem lifted it high over his head. He wanted to utter an apology to the boulder, which had done him no harm, but he was afraid his master would be angry. The golem bunched his muscles, and with a satisfying grunt, he swung the hammer down with all his might. The head hit the stone, sparks flew, and the rock cracked apart like a great egg. The crash echoed off the walls.

This time there was no question the rabbi said a prayer. In the flickering candlelight, he looked equally gratified and horrified. "A mighty weapon indeed," he said to himself. "Let us pray we shall never need it."

He didn't say another word as he led the golem back indoors. The golem was deeply disappointed—he'd hoped to have more chance to investigate the world. But he didn't complain as they plodded up the stairs to the stuffy, dusty attic.

"Stay here and be quiet," said Rabbi Eleazar. And he left, shutting the door behind him.

~2~

THE GOLEM didn't like being alone in the attic. He had very little to occupy his time. In the evening, before the light left the sky, he would take the moth-eaten fabric from the shelf—it had once been curtains, probably—and make a bed for himself on the hard floor. In the morning he would replace the cloth on the shelf. He had nothing else to clean, no other chores. He poked around, but the room was filled only with broken and useless things. He discovered a few small holes at the base of the walls, but the mice were too scared of him to come out.

One afternoon he tried forming the leftover clay into a figure, a miniature replica of himself. But he had no way to moisten the dust, and it simply fell apart. Even had he been able to sculpt something, he would have had no way to bring it to life. He didn't understand how the letters engraved on his chest made him into something more than an inanimate statue, but still less than a man.

So that left him with two things to do. During the day, he stood at the window. The street below was quite busy, and he got little glimpses of people's lives. He watched them stroll by, sometimes in a hurry and sometimes slowly, sometimes alone and sometimes with others. Often they carried burdens such as baskets or parcels. Children ran by, laughing. Dogs and cats chased one another or lounged in patches of sun, and birds twittered from rooftops or pecked at crumbs on the ground. Most fascinating of all, however, was the construction project across the street. He liked to watch the men shaping and lifting the rocks, but he especially liked to watch the youngest mason lay the bed of mortar and fill the gaps between the stones. The man was so confident in his work, so careful and precise.

But the golem's favorite part of the day was at sundown, when he settled himself near the door to listen to the prayers—and especially to that one beautiful voice. The way the notes soared, the golem could almost believe they were intended to rise to the attic, to fill his ears with joy.

Once every seven days, the activity outside became especially frantic. Everyone bustled on those days, especially as the sun approached the horizon. Then great crowds entered the synagogue. Everyone was in their best clothes, and all their voices rumbled beneath him like stones rubbing together. The prayers on those nights were very loud, but even then the golem could make out that one voice among the others.

The next day there would be much less going on outside. The masons weren't there at all, which made him sad. So he was happy when the prayers began again, leading the congregation into sunset and beyond.

The golem didn't know how much time passed like this. The rabbi never came up to the attic, nor did anyone else. The golem wondered if he'd been abandoned along with the other unwanted detritus on the shelves. He was tempted to make noise—just a little—or to sneak down the stairs. But he mustn't disobey his master. He knew that.

One long, hot afternoon, when the air in the attic felt as thick as wool and even the youngest stonemason was sluggish at his work, the golem noticed something interesting. It wasn't a new thing, but he'd never before paid attention. While usually men walked with men and women with women, there were exceptions. Sometimes an elderly couple would hobble down the street elbow to elbow. Sometimes a young woman would smile at a young man. And on this stifling day, four women brought jugs of water to the masons and stood near them as they drank. The oldest woman was deep in conversation with the father, while three much younger women chatted with three of the sons. But the youngest son remained alone. When the old woman gave him a tin cup to drink from, he sat on the partially built wall with his back to the others and his face toward the shul. He looked sad, or perhaps just thoughtful.

The golem understood that as a thing of clay, his perception of emotions was poor. But there was something about the set of the mason's shoulders and the downward curl of his lips that reminded the golem of himself. The man was lonely, just like him, but the golem didn't understand why this would be so. The mason had family; he had the whole world to move about in. He didn't have to spend all day and all night in an attic without even somebody to tell him what to do.

It was both a mystery and a revelation: even surrounded by others, people could feel alone. The golem spent many hours pondering that puzzle, but he couldn't figure it out.

THE DAYS were growing shorter, and a chill had returned to the evenings. The masons had nearly completed the house's walls, which worried the golem. When they were finished, surely they would move on to another project somewhere else, somewhere outside his limited field of vision. That would leave him with only the prayers for solace, and they never lasted very long.

One afternoon the golem watched from his window as black clouds swept into the sky. All the people hurried to finish their tasks. In the buildings across the street, windows were shuttered tightly. All the masons left but one; the youngest, it seemed, wanted to finish setting a few more stones. He was covering them with heavy cloth when lightning began to crackle and thunder boom, and fat raindrops began to fall.

The golem had seen a few storms before, but none this fierce. He was frightened. Perhaps God had noticed the creature made of clay and decided he was an abomination. Perhaps God had sent the tempest to destroy him. The golem thought about himself, alone and unneeded in the attic, reduced to a pile of dust that would someday be swept away. If he were dust, he'd never again hear that voice lifted in prayer.

A bolt of lightning struck very close, and the thunder was loud enough to shake the building.

The golem wailed.

And as he looked out the rain-streaked window to the ground below, hoping for a final glimpse of the stonemason, he saw the man rooted in place. Staring openmouthed at him.

The golem rushed as far from the window as he could get. He backed into a corner—knocking over the broom—and sank to the floor. He huddled there with his face pressed against his knees. Now even more than the storm, he feared his master. If Rabbi Eleazar heard the noise the golem had made and discovered he'd allowed himself to be seen, surely the rabbi would be furious. Furious enough to destroy the golem.

The storm raged on, rain pounding the roof and wind making the window rattle, but the golem listened for the sound of footsteps running up the stairs.

Evening prayers began. The golem could hear the men chanting, but not that one wonderful voice. Perhaps this was a punishment for his transgression. He wasn't certain he could bear his existence if he was never allowed to hear that voice again.

The prayers ended, the storm waned into a soft patter of raindrops, and still the rabbi didn't come.

In the velvet blackness, it was difficult to find the old curtains and lay them neatly on the floor, but the golem managed. He took special care not to knock into anything and not to let his feet thud on the wooden floorboards. He settled down on his bed. But he couldn't rid himself of the vision of the stonemason looking up at him; the man's face lingered behind his eyelids like the aftereffects of a lightning flash. The man had looked astounded. But even then, and with his clothing soaked through, his curls dripping wet, he'd been handsome. In fact, the way his wet shirt had become almost transparent and clung to his broad chest only served to heighten the golem's attraction.

Without the golem's conscious intent, his right hand slid under the waistband of his trousers.

He had spent very little time thinking about his own body. Truly, he'd hardly thought of it as his own. He was a created thing. Property. His master could order him about at will, could destroy him as he saw fit. And while the golem had occasionally stroked the letters carved into his chest, he'd never explored the parts of himself that were covered by clothing.

Tonight, though, he allowed his hand to wander.

His belly was flat and uninteresting. But past that, he'd been made like a man. He didn't know why the rabbi had bothered with such details, creating a cock and balls proportionate to the golem's massive body. But now the cock leapt at his touch, lengthened, grew hard. He stroked it gently, using only his fingertips. His fingers were rough and raspy, like sand, but they felt good against the smoothness of his shaft. They felt very good. He rubbed harder.

A moan escaped his throat, unbidden, and he paused. He had already defied his master once tonight, making noise during the storm, and he dared not do so again. He should simply go to sleep. But he couldn't, not when he *ached* so. Instead, he stood and felt his way to the shelf where the empty folded sacks were stored. He took the top one and returned to his bed, where he wadded the bag into a ball and stuffed the rough, dry fabric into his mouth. With the hope that his sounds would be muffled, he began to touch himself again.

Very soon his movements became harder and faster. Usually he was cold, but now a spark lit in his center as if he'd trapped a bit of the lightning. He stroked his cock and the spark grew, warming him, making him tingle from scalp to toes. And as the feelings inside him intensified, it seemed as if he could hear the faint ghost of a singing voice and see a wet, upturned face with wide brown eyes. He could almost—almost!—imagine another hand on his skin, and the fleshly scent of sweat.

A storm broke within the golem's body. His torso bowed as his hips thrust upward; the back of his head thudded hard on the floorboards. For one brief moment, he felt real.

Afterward, he returned the sack to the shelf and settled on his side on the pallet. A light rain still tapped on the roof and window, but for the time being, the golem wasn't afraid. He knew now why people prayed—to thank God for the gifts he'd given them. Their songs were gratitude for life and love and joy. The golem had tasted only the faintest nibble of those gifts, but he was grateful for even that much. He wished he knew how to pray. But maybe it was just as well that he didn't, because then he'd be tempted to beg for a little more, for a few more bites of life.

The golem never dreamed. But that night as he fell asleep, his final thoughts were of a man standing in the rain.

~3~

A FEW more weeks passed. Rabbi Eleazar did not come to the attic, which was both a relief and a torment. The golem continued to spend his days watching the masons. The youngest man paused in his work several times each day to look across the street and up at the attic window. He gave no sign that he saw anything, but he would frown a little. He probably couldn't see through the glass since it was still grimy on the inside, and while the sky was bright, the attic was quite dark. The golem waved at him, even though he knew he was being foolish.

At night the golem had taken to removing his clothing completely so as to better explore his body. He found little creases and crannies that were especially sensitive to touch, like the lines where his legs joined his torso. He also felt as if something were missing, and he wished someone else would touch him as he'd been touching himself.

On a bright, blustery afternoon, the golem watched out his window as the glass rattled in its frame. The last of the bright leaves had fallen from the trees, and they now whirled and scurried down the street. Women tied their head scarves more tightly, and men held on to their hats. When a woman leaned out her window to flap a small rug, a passing donkey shied, causing its loaded cart to topple firewood onto the pavement. The donkey's owner yelled at the woman before stooping to gather the sticks; she yelled back. The golem smiled. He enjoyed watching the little dramas that unfolded outside his attic.

Just as the man was loading the last of the fallen firewood, a carriage turned the corner. It was a grand, gilded thing pulled by a pair of chestnut horses. The golem had never seen anything so fancy on the street, and perhaps neither had anyone else, because people stopped to stare. The carriage wasn't moving very fast. *Clop-clop* went the horses' hooves on the hard pavement, until the carriage halted in front of the shul. The golem had to crook his neck to see, and even then his angle was poor. He caught only a glimpse of a round, beardless man climbing out of the carriage and entering the front door.

Not long afterward, men came hurrying to the shul from every direction. Among them was the family of stonemasons. Loud voices rose to the attic—not praying but arguing. The golem stood near the door, wringing his hands, wondering if this was the danger Rabbi Eleazar had mentioned to him.

Those suspicions seemed confirmed when footsteps came from the stairway. The rabbi flung the door open, then recoiled slightly in surprise when he saw how close the golem was. He recovered quickly. "Follow me," he ordered. His face was set in grim lines.

Their progress down the stairs was quick. Emotions roiled inside the golem's head, and he couldn't identify them all. Better not to try, he decided. Better to simply concentrate on his master's orders.

But it was hard to concentrate on anything when they reached the large foyer on the ground floor and dozens of men gasped all at once. The golem froze. He wanted to bolt back to the safety of his attic, where there was nobody to stare and gape at him. Instead, he hung his head and gazed at the patterned stone floor.

"What is *that*?" demanded a loud voice.

"A golem," Rabbi Eleazar answered. "God has allowed me to create this creature to protect us. Blessed be the Lord." He muttered a short prayer, and several of the other men joined in.

Someone stepped closer. The golem glanced up and saw that it was the man he'd spied getting out of the carriage. His head was bare, unlike the heads of the other men the golem had seen, and a golden cross dangled from a chain around his neck. "It's certainly very large, Rabbi. A miracle indeed. But it can't protect you from the duke's soldiers, and it won't protect you once the people in the city take up arms against you. I'm telling you, Eleazar. You and your people must leave before things get any worse."

Leave? The golem imagined the street deserted. No more stonemasons or passersby, no more evening prayers. Would he be permanently abandoned in the attic, or would his master return him to nothing but globs of damp clay?

The golem couldn't see the rabbi's face, but he saw that the man's shoulders were set straight and firm. "We will not leave, Gospodin Novák. This has been our home for centuries."

"I know, I know. And I come to you now because we are friends and I respect you. You are a good man. But the plague has begun to spread again, already worse than last year at this time, and people whisper among themselves: *Why are the Jews not stricken as we are?*"

"We are not responsible for this plague! We have no quarrel with the gentiles, no reason to want them to die. All life is valuable to us, regardless of faith, and murder is a sin."

The hatless man nodded. "I know. I think even the duke knows this. But... he is also badly in debt." He shrugged. "If the whispers grow loud enough, he can easily stir people against you. And if you are accused of crimes or killed, he can seize your property. You know this, my friend. It has happened elsewhere."

"It will not happen here." Rabbi Eleazar turned to look at the golem. "Follow me. You will show Gospodin Novák what you can do."

The gathered men muttered excitedly and followed as the rabbi and Gospodin Novák led the golem out the large front doors, down a few steps, and into the street. Women and children came running up, exclaiming loudly, as the crowd arrayed itself in a large circle. One face near the front caught the golem's eyes: the youngest stonemason. His eyes were very round and his mouth slightly open. The golem gave him a small smile, but the man didn't smile back.

"Unhitch this donkey," Rabbi Eleazar commanded loudly. The donkey had been standing patiently, perhaps enjoying the respite from its labors. It didn't complain as its owner untied it and led it a few feet away. The rabbi turned to the golem. "Lift that cart."

The cart was large and awkward, but the golem got his arms underneath it and lifted. He was careful to not disturb the firewood. The burden didn't feel especially heavy, but the onlookers cried out in surprise. The golem looked at his master and waited for the next order.

"Carry it away." The rabbi pointed down the street.

The golem obeyed. The people backed away from him as he drew near.

"Bring it back," the rabbi called.

The golem spun around. He retraced his steps and replaced the cart exactly where he'd found it. It jostled a little as he set it down, jarring a few sticks loose. He picked them up and placed them back atop the heap.

"Yes," Gospodin Novák said, shaking his head a little. "It is very strong indeed. But I don't see that it's enough."

"Then I will show you more. And you will tell the duke what you saw. He will not dare to send his men against us then." Rabbi Eleazar looked around for a moment, until his gaze caught on a large tree. He pointed at a thick branch perhaps ten feet up. "Golem, break that off."

The golem was sorry to damage a tree, but his master had ordered him. He plodded over, again scattering the crowd. He leapt up, grabbed the branch with both hands, and pulled, breaking it from the trunk. Again, the people gasped.

"Break it into small pieces," said the rabbi.

The golem did, snapping the wood as easily as he might tear paper. It felt good to use his strength. For the first time, he wondered how much he was capable of. Without being told, he gathered the broken chunks of branch and set them in the cart.

But Gospodin Novák was still not very impressed. "Even with strength such as that, my friend, it cannot hold off dozens of armed men. Perhaps hundreds of them, if enough hearts are poisoned by the whispers. They will be armed."

"I know," Rabbi Eleazar responded. Then he turned to the youngest stonemason. "Jakob, fetch me your biggest chisel and your heaviest hammer."

Jakob. The golem smiled at learning the man's name. He wished he could say it aloud to see how it felt on his tongue and lips, how it tasted. But his master hadn't given him leave to speak.

Jakob hesitated a moment before running toward the nearly finished house. He returned soon afterward with the tools in his hands. He tried to hand them to the rabbi, but Rabbi Eleazar shook his head.

"No, no. You are much stronger than I. Golem, kneel."

The golem obeyed. His trousers were too short to cover his knees well, and the cobbles were very cold against his lower legs.

The rabbi nodded. "Jakob, with all your might, I want you to strike the golem's head with your hammer."

"I.... Sir?" Jakob looked suddenly pale and uncertain.

"Go ahead." The rabbi waved his hands. "As hard as you can."

For a brief moment, Jakob's gaze locked with the golem's. The man looked close to panic, and the golem wished he could say something to comfort him. Instead, he gave another small smile. Jakob had such beautiful eyes, very brown and deep as the starry sky.

Slowly, Jakob set the chisel onto the ground. As he walked closer to the golem, it took all the golem's willpower not to reach out and touch him. He wanted so badly to know whether those curls were as soft as they looked, whether the muscles on the man's chest felt as tight as his own.

Jakob grasped the hammer very firmly in both hands, briefly closed his eyes and opened them again, and swung. His aim was true. The hammer hit the golem squarely on the side of the head, making a sound very like that of the boulder the golem had split. But although the golem was rocked slightly to the side, and although he uttered a cry at the pain, his head was not damaged.

Dropping the hammer noisily onto the street, Jakob turned to Rabbi Eleazar. "That blow would have shattered stone."

The rabbi nodded. And for the first time, Gospodin Novák appeared truly shaken. But perhaps the rabbi thought his friend needed more convincing. "Golem, stand. Jakob, drive the chisel into the golem's chest. As hard as you can."

As the golem rose to his feet, Jakob backed away. "But…. Rabbi. The hammer hurt him."

"You won't damage him."

Jakob shook his head. "But he feels pain."

"He is not a person, son. Please. It is important that the duke realize what a mistake it would be to rise against us."

Jakob's movements were even slower this time, but he picked up the chisel and again approached the golem. He didn't raise the tool right away, though. He was a tall man, the golem now realized, although still at least a foot shorter than the golem himself. So Jakob had to tilt his head back to look up into the golem's face. The golem smiled at him again and gave him the tiniest of nods, encouraging him to listen to the rabbi. The chisel would hurt, but it was the golem's job to protect the people.

"I'm sorry," Jakob whispered so quietly that surely nobody but the golem heard him.

At the kindness of those words and the sadness in Jakob's eyes, something warm swelled within the golem. It was as if something within him was singing in joy and gratitude, because for a moment at least, Jakob had *cared* what the golem felt. When Jakob lifted the toothed chisel and jammed it into the golem's chest, the blade bit deep and pain bloomed, but the golem hardly noticed.

Jakob pulled the chisel away and dropped it next to the hammer. The wound in the golem's chest sealed immediately, leaving no scar.

"So you see, Gospodin Novák?" Rabbi Eleazar said.

"I see. And I will most certainly tell the duke. But Eleazar, he is a stubborn man and his debts are very large. I do not know if he will be reasonable."

"Then I will pray that his heart is softened and his mind sees what is best."

Gospodin Novák nodded and made a slight bow to the rabbi, who nodded back. Then Novák climbed into his carriage. His driver hupped at the horses, which trotted away through the parting crowd.

Voices erupted. Nobody quite dared to approach the golem—nobody but Jakob, who remained standing quite close by. The others rushed the rabbi, asking him questions, congratulating him, arguing with each other. After an existence spent almost entirely alone, the golem felt overwhelmed. He might have run away—back into the shul and up to the attic, shaming himself and his master—but Jakob was still very near.

"You were watching me," Jakob whispered. "I saw... I thought I saw, up in that window...."

His master was preoccupied, so the golem hazarded speech. "I'm sorry," he whispered back.

"You can talk!"

"Yes."

Jakob tilted his head a little and regarded the golem. "Why did you watch me?"

"I... I was alone. And you move so well with the stone. Like a dance." The golem didn't add that Jakob was beautiful, thinking the man would not want to hear such words from a monster like him.

Jakob chewed his lower lip thoughtfully and stroked his short beard. The golem wanted to say more—how Jakob's presence made his lonely days bearable, how he wanted to touch him, how sometimes he imagined Jakob's hands on his body. But again, the man would not want to know these things, so the golem remained silent.

After a few minutes, Rabbi Eleazar walked to the golem. "Enough.

The hour is growing late. Return upstairs. God willing, we won't need you again."

But the golem didn't want to go. "Please, Master. I can work. Whatever you tell me to do. I'll be good."

Rabbi Eleazar opened his mouth, no doubt to say no, but a woman had pushed her way close. She was middle-aged, tall and bosomy, and she wore an apron under her thick gray sweater. When the golem saw her eyes, he recognized them—they were the same as Jakob's. This must be his mother, whom the golem had occasionally seen carrying food or water to her family.

"Let us put that strength to use, Rabbi," she said. "It would be a shame to waste it."

"He was made to protect us."

"And he will. But who says he can't do some work at the same time? In fact, this will be better. If the gentiles see him laboring, they'll be reminded of his power."

The rabbi looked doubtful, but several men and women chimed in to support Jakob's mother, and at last he shrugged. "Fine. And who intends to employ him?"

There was a deep silence. The golem wondered if he disgusted these people or if they feared him. Perhaps they thought him too stupid to do anything but lift things or break them. He wasn't stupid, though. He could learn.

Jakob looked at the rabbi. "I can use him. I've been wanting to build myself a little house, but my father and my brothers are busy."

"Very well," Rabbi Eleazar said, and the golem wanted to leap with happiness. "But keep him near. And he'll spend nights in the shul."

"All right. Beginning tomorrow?"

"Yes." The rabbi brushed his hands together. In a loud voice, he said, "It will be sundown soon. The minyan needs to prepare for maariv service, as do I."

People began to wander off, still talking excitedly among themselves. Jakob lingered for a moment. His expression was troubled. But then he nodded slightly at the golem before collecting his tools and walking away.

The golem watched him for a few moments, then turned and followed his master back inside.

~4~

DESPITE THE golem's love for evening prayers, they weren't enough to calm his excitement. He paced the attic from end to end, replaying the afternoon's events, speculating as to what would happen the next day. He would be permitted out of the attic to work, and at Jakob's side! He squeezed himself tightly as if he might otherwise burst with pleasure.

The room grew too dark for him to see, and he settled down in his nest of a bed. But he couldn't fall asleep. He wondered if Jakob was also lying awake, thinking about him. The man hadn't seemed angry at having been watched. He seemed... curious, as if the golem were a puzzle he might like to solve. The golem vowed to work very hard, to make Jakob happy he'd requested the assistance. Maybe Jakob would even allow him to talk a little, to ask a few questions. There were so many things the golem wanted to know.

Alone in the dark and dusty attic, the golem whispered the mason's name. "Jakob. Jakob. *Jakob*." It was a good name, he thought. A strong name.

THE GOLEM awoke before the sun. He waited impatiently for morning prayers to finish. He always preferred the evening prayers anyway, because the man with the wonderful voice sang only then. The golem folded his bedding and stored it on the shelf. He straightened his too-short trousers and too-small vest. He rubbed the two metal buttons until they shone. Then he stood near the door and waited. Time passed very slowly; he began to wonder if Jakob had changed his mind.

Just as the golem started to truly worry, the door opened. "Come on, then," said Rabbi Eleazar. He looked a bit rumpled, as if he'd dressed in a hurry that morning. But the golem grinned and hurried to follow him down the stairs. If the rabbi hadn't been in front of him, the golem would have taken the stairs several at a time, leaping down like a goat.

Two old men stood in the foyer, frowning at him. One of them carried a thick book and the other had a walking stick, which he raised as if to protect himself. Neither said a word as Rabbi Eleazar opened one of the big front doors and motioned outward. "Obey Jakob as you obey me," he ordered. "While you work, he is your master."

The golem nodded enthusiastically.

Jakob waited at the bottom of the shul's front steps. He wore a thick cloak against the morning cold, and a heavy hat was pressed down over his curls. A large wooden box sat at his feet. He looked nervous and didn't return the golem's smile. He didn't speak either. He simply shrugged, picked up the box, and began to march down the street. People gaped as the golem rushed to catch up.

The box looked heavy. "Master? I can carry that for you."

Jakob flinched a little. "Don't call me that."

"I'm sorry. What shall I call you?"

"Jakob."

The golem sighed in relief. He didn't want to make Jakob angry before their day had even begun.

Passersby stopped in their tracks as Jakob and the golem walked by, and other people stared from house windows. Jakob looked steadfastly ahead, not even glancing at the golem. He walked until the street ended at a stone wall. Then he turned onto a street that paralleled the wall. The golem noticed that plants had rooted themselves in the small cracks between the stones. Maybe in the spring, some would flower. He thought it very brave of them to chance an existence somewhere so precarious.

An arched gateway led through the wall. There were heavy wooden doors to block the opening, but they were propped wide open. Judging from the weeds and bits of debris at their bases, neither door had been closed in a long time.

As soon as Jakob and the golem exited the town through the gateway, the road became packed dirt instead of cobbles. The golem liked the way the soil felt under his soles, although he couldn't help wondering whether the road minded being walked on. Did it hurt when metal-rimmed wagon wheels rolled over it, or when horses clomped their metal-shod hooves?

Very few buildings stood outside the wall, although a few small houses nestled among the fields. People worked in the plots, gathering the last of the season's harvest, and a few cows and goats watched curiously as the golem walked by.

Jakob turned off the road onto a narrow path that was hardly more than trodden grass. The path curved around a stand of trees, then rose up a small, steep hill. A space had been cleared atop the hill, and a few stones had been set around the boundaries of Jakob's future home. The golem wondered why Jakob wanted to live so far from everyone else, but he didn't ask. Instead he watched the clouds scud across the sky as Jakob set down the wooden box and removed his tools.

"I need more stone." Jakob pointed to the field below. "I was going to borrow a cart, but perhaps—"

"I can carry it!" the golem exclaimed. "I'm very strong."

The shadow of a smile flickered at the corners of Jakob's lips. "I know."

The golem ran back down the path toward the spot Jakob had indicated. Sure enough, a large pile of rocks sprawled untidily, as if the farmers had been too annoyed by their presence to bother stacking them neatly. No doubt the rocks would prove more useful in the walls of Jakob's house than scattered across the field. The golem hefted two of them—one under each arm—and rushed back to Jakob.

"Where would you like them, Jakob?"

Jakob's eyebrows were raised high. "You carry them as if they weighed nothing."

"I was made to be strong."

"Yes." Jakob shook his head slightly and pointed at a spot a few yards from the cleared space. "Put them there."

The golem obeyed. "Do you want them all?"

"Not all at once. I have to shape them before I can set them in place. Bring the biggest ones now so I can plan the base of the walls."

"Yes, Jakob." The golem hurried back down the hill.

Although he carried a great many stones, the golem never tired. He was so happy to be outdoors, to be working, to be helping Jakob—he thought that maybe the flexing of his muscles and the strength of his bones were his body's way of expressing joy, his own way of praying.

Jakob spoke very little. Most of his attention was on inspecting the stones, turning them this way and that—sometimes with the golem's help—reading them as if they were books. Sometimes he chiseled them, the sounds echoing brightly. The golem stole glances as he unloaded each new pair of rocks. Although the stones were large and rough and the tools heavy, Jakob handled them carefully. Almost reverently.

The golem had just brought up another set of rocks and was about to get more when Jakob held up a hand to stop him. "Lunchtime," Jakob said. "I brought bread and cheese."

"I don't eat."

Jakob blinked. "Never?"

"No."

"Then how do you survive?"

"I... I don't know."

After a moment's pause, Jakob shrugged. "Well, rest anyway. It exhausts me just to watch you work." He took a small fabric-wrapped bundle from his wooden box and sat on the ground with his back against one of the larger stones.

The golem hesitated a bit before sitting next to him. He hadn't noticed while he was working, but from this height, he could see the entire town laid out below. It looked neat and orderly. On the other side of the town, the road led to a larger city—also encircled by a stone wall and with a few pointed spires rising high. Beyond that, a green-gray river twisted like a lazy serpent. Perhaps the golem's clay came from that river's banks.

"What is that place?" the golem asked, pointing at the larger city.

Jakob had unwrapped his lunch and now tore a chunk from a small loaf of bread. He mumbled a quick prayer under his breath before answering. "That's where the gentiles live."

"You have separate towns?"

"Yes."

"Why?"

"I don't know. I suppose... people feel more comfortable living with others who are like them."

The golem nodded, although he didn't really understand. "Do they have golems too?"

Jakob gave a short laugh. "I very much doubt it. Nobody here has ever seen anything like you. We've heard stories, but... but we thought they were only tales told by old people to pass the long winter nights."

Those words saddened the golem, who'd held a small hope that there were others like him somewhere. "Maybe in other cities? Far away."

"Maybe. I've never been farther from here than two days' walk."

"And the world is very big, isn't it?"

"So I've heard. My corner of it is very small."

The golem looked out at the fields and towns spread beneath him and thought how much more there was here than in his dusty attic. He didn't say so, though. Instead, he watched as Jakob chewed a bite of cheese. He couldn't say why, but he was fascinated with watching those lips move, that throat swallow.

"I'm sorry." Jakob said after a while. "I didn't think to ask your name."

"I don't have one."

Jakob frowned. "If I'm going to work with you, I want to call you something besides just *golem*."

"Call me whatever you wish," said the golem, who was pleased to be called anything at all.

"Hmm." Jakob ate a few more bites. Then he turned to look directly at the golem, and his gaze settled on the golem's chest. "Move your vest, please. Let me read."

The vest only partially obscured the letters the rabbi had inscribed. The golem moved the fabric out of the way.

"*Emet*," pronounced Jakob. "I suppose that could be your name."

"Does it mean something?" The golem chewed his lip anxiously. What if it meant *monster* or *freak*?

But Jakob smiled gently at him. "It means truth. Which isn't a bad idea for a name, really. Better than my own, which is a lie."

"I don't—Jakob is a lie?"

"You don't know the Torah, do you? How would you. Jakob was the father of the Hebrews. He had twelve sons who became the twelve tribes of Israel. But me, I'll never be anyone's father."

It was the longest speech the golem had yet heard from Jakob, and it took him a moment to process the meaning. "You cannot have children?" asked the golem.

"I will not. And that *is* the truth, Emet." Jakob smiled, although his eyes were sad. He finished his meal without further conversation, stood, and returned to work.

Emet continued to haul stones. He was rewarded every time he reached the summit of the hill and Jakob gave him a small smile. As light as the rocks had seemed before, now they were no more burdensome than clouds, and Emet barely felt his feet touch the ground—because Jakob had given him a name. Just like a real person. And it was a good name too. While Jakob's name was as sharp and solid as the edges of his stones, *Emet* felt deep and rumbly.

Emet would gladly have continued to work until it was too dark to see. But well before the sun sank behind the horizon, Jakob gathered his tools and placed them in the wooden box. "You've done more today than my brothers could have in a week. At this rate my house will be built well before the worst of winter." He lifted the box and started down the hill.

"Why are you building your house here?" asked Emet as they descended.

"It's a good spot. My family's owned the land for generations because nobody wants to farm the hilltop. And I like the views."

"But why not live in the town? With your family?"

Jakob scowled. "My parents' house is too small for us all."

"Couldn't you add to it?" If Emet had a family, he'd never want to leave them, no matter how cramped they might be.

"It's not...." Jakob huffed impatiently. "We don't always get along very well. Mama and Papa expect me to marry as my brothers have, and... and I won't."

"Why not?"

"You ask far too many questions!"

Emet hung his head. "I'm sorry." He'd never before had the opportunity to ask anyone anything, and now he was getting carried away. He vowed to hold his tongue.

Neither of them spoke as they walked back to the town and entered the gate. Jakob took Emet to the foot of the shul's steps. "I have to go change for the maariv service," he said. "I'll fetch you again in the morning."

Emet had been afraid that Jakob would decide not to work with him anymore, so now he grinned. "Thank you, Jakob." He stood for a moment, watching Jakob walk away, then reluctantly scaled the steps to the shul's front doors.

~5~

JAKOB FETCHED Emet each morning for the next three days. They walked quietly out of town—Emet being careful not to bother Jakob with questions—and while Emet carried stones, Jakob shaped them and set them. The four walls of his house were soon evident, each rock nestled snugly against its neighbors and kept in place with mortar. It wouldn't be a large house. Only a single room, in fact, with the door facing the town. Jakob spoke infrequently, but he did mention that he planned to include a small porch adjacent to the front. "I want to plant a fig tree," he said. "And some grapes."

They rested each day while Jakob ate his lunch. Of course, Emet didn't eat. But he liked sitting next to Jakob and listening to him chew and breathe. Emet was a little worried over how fast the project was going. While Jakob might be pleased to have his house finished soon, Emet dreaded the day when the work was over. Yes, perhaps someone else would find things he could carry for them, but that someone else wouldn't be Jakob.

They finished work earlier than usual on the fourth day, although Emet didn't dare to ask why. "It's Shabbos," Jakob explained. "No work after sundown."

Emet's response was hesitant. "Until when?"

"Sunday. Just the one day for rest." Jakob set his chisel in the box before glancing at Emet. "What do you do when you're not working?"

"I sleep. I look out the window. I listen to the prayers."

Jakob had been about to lift the box, but now he paused to look at Emet. "You listen? Why?"

"Because the prayers are beautiful. I wish I could sing too. I wish God would listen to me." He shut his mouth quickly. Surely Jakob didn't want to hear him complain.

But Jakob didn't seem angry. "Why wouldn't God listen to you?"

"Because I'm only a golem."

"Even if you were a man, even if you could sing... God still might not listen. He doesn't answer everyone's prayers."

"Does he answer yours?"

Jakob shook his head.

That evening Emet listened to the voices in the chapel beneath him and wondered what Jakob prayed for. He seemed a kind man, a good man. He never raised his voice at Emet, never treated him poorly. He always thanked Emet for his labors and checked often to make sure that Emet wasn't overburdened. Jakob worked hard. His capable hands made stone do his bidding. But he was sad. Emet would have done anything to bring him happiness, but he didn't know how.

The next day seemed endless and empty. Where the attic had once been slightly confining, it now felt like a cramped cage. Emet longed to work outdoors, to have his brief chats with Jakob. He wondered what Jakob was doing all day, whether he spent the hours with his parents and brothers and, if so, whether he was happy in their company.

And that thought led to another: why wouldn't Jakob marry? People's habits and customs were still largely a mystery to Emet, but he'd gathered that they liked to be in pairs. He'd seen the way Jakob's brothers and their wives exchanged fond looks, the way Jakob's mother fussed over his father when she brought him lunch. Emet had seen pairings among the animals he spied from his window as well: birds that preened one another, cats that yowled as they mated. He thought he could almost understand why creatures did this, because when he looked at couples, he felt incomplete and unfinished. He yearned for a partner of his own, although he knew he'd never have one. But he didn't know why Jakob insisted on being alone.

On Shabbos afternoon, footsteps sounded in the stairway, and Rabbi Eleazar flung open the attic door and entered. He stopped in the center of the room and stared at Emet, who was hunched against a wall. "I have heard that you are working very hard," the rabbi said.

"Would you like me to work now, Master?"

"No. Nobody works today." He crossed the room, picked a piece of broken crockery off the shelf, and turned it over in his hands. "I wonder... how much can a golem learn? God created you for a specific purpose. Do we offend him if we use you for other things as well?"

"I like to work," Emet said quietly. "I think maybe it's good if I can help."

"Maybe. But maybe it is a great wickedness." Rabbi Eleazar sighed. "How am I to know? I am only a man. Ach, it was so much easier for the men in the Torah, who spoke with angels and sometimes the Lord himself. But I have no burning bush. I can only guess what is required of me, and sometimes I am afraid... I am afraid I am doing the wrong thing."

Emet's master seemed so small and lost. It had never occurred to Emet that the rabbi could be uncertain. He seemed so wise. "You care for your people," Emet said. "God must be pleased with that."

Rabbi Eleazar gave him a sharp look. Then he returned the pottery to the shelf. "I wonder sometimes if it isn't arrogant for any man to presume to know what God wants. And what are we to do when our hearts yearn for something we have been told we cannot have? Isn't misery a sin as well? Jakob, for example... ah, such a waste. He struggles to be such a good person." The rabbi glanced at Emet and seemed almost startled to see him there, as if he'd forgotten he wasn't speaking only to himself. He smiled wryly, shook his head, and wandered out of the attic.

That night, Emet listened to the havdalah service. As he pressed his nose to the crack under the door, he imagined he could smell the braided candles he'd seen Rabbi Eleazar holding the previous afternoon. He imagined the people gathered around the warm, flickering flames as they welcomed the beginning of a new week. And he could certainly hear their voices raised in song, especially the slightly mournful pleas that concluded the ceremony. It seemed to him that his favorite singer was especially gifted tonight, and especially sorrowful.

Alone in the silent darkness, Emet tried to picture what Jakob's house would be like once it was finished. Emet had never been in a home, so his imagination could go only so far. Still, he knew the little house would be cozy, the thick walls protecting Jakob from excessive cold and heat. Maybe Jakob would have lace curtains like those hanging in the windows of the houses opposite the shul. His tools would be placed on a shelf in the evenings, and at suppertime the place would smell of stew and fresh bread. On warm summer evenings, Jakob could sit on his porch and look up at the stars—or look down at Mala Lubovnya, where in the dark attic of the shul, a golem lay on a nest of old curtains and thought of him.

"DID YOU have a restful Shabbos?" Emet asked Jakob the next morning as they walked to work. The sky was gray, threatening rain, and the landscape had lost its color.

"I studied as always. While Papa and my brothers nap, I go to the shul and read the Talmud. I keep looking for answers there."

"Have you found them?"

"Not the ones I hope for."

A few goats eyed Emet hopefully as he passed. Most mornings he picked a few of their favorite leaves—those just out of reach on Emet's side of the fence—and fed the animals. He liked their strange eyes, and he liked to rub the hairs that grew between their horns. This morning, though, he found the plants wilted by the previous night's frost. He was sorry to disappoint the goats.

Emet picked up a pair of stones before heading up the hill. When he got there, Jakob was standing in the middle of his partially finished house, scowling at the sky. "I hoped we could get some work done before the rain began," he said.

Just then, a fat raindrop landed on Emet's head. "I can work in the rain."

"You wear so little clothing. Don't you get cold?"

"It doesn't matter."

Jakob shook his head. "Come with me."

They walked back down the hill and across the field. The rain began to fall in earnest, making Jakob bow his head and shiver. Emet moved around to Jakob's windward side, hoping his body would shield Jakob's a little. Jakob took them to a tumbledown structure that smelled of old hay. They sat in a corner where the remains of the roof were intact enough to shelter them, and they huddled close to each other, not quite touching. "This used to be a corncrib," Jakob explained. "It would have lasted longer if they'd built it of stone instead of wood. Let's wait a while to see if the storm passes."

Emet nodded happily, relieved that he wouldn't have to return to the attic right away. The drumbeat of the rain on the roof reminded him of music, although it was a much wilder tune than the prayers he was used to. "What do the words of the prayers mean, Jakob?"

"It depends which one."

"The last one from last night."

Jakob thought a moment. "Eliyahu HaNavi. It's a plea for the return of Elijah."

"Elijah?"

"The prophet. When he appears, we will be redeemed." Jakob must have read the blank look on Emet's face, because he sighed. "You know so little."

"I'm sorry," said Emet, ashamed.

"It's not your fault. In some ways you're like a small child who's never been taught anything at all. And… in other ways you are very like a man." Jakob shifted his body a little, increasing the space between them by a few inches. He picked up a small, smooth pebble and rubbed it with his thumb. "I'm sorry I hurt you, Emet. With my hammer and my chisel, I mean."

"I healed right away. You saw."

"Yes. But I caused you pain, and you didn't deserve that. You've never harmed anyone at all." His voice was so soft that Emet could barely hear it over the wind and rain.

"It's all right. You had to show that man how strong I am so the duke would be afraid of me." Emet considered for a moment before continuing, and decided to be honest. His name was truth, after all. "I *would* hurt someone if I had to. If Rabbi Eleazar commanded me to. If you— If your people were threatened."

Jakob turned and looked at Emet for a long time. "Why don't you leave? I wouldn't stop you. I couldn't if I wanted to—you're so much stronger and faster. You don't have to let me and the rabbi boss you around, and you don't have to lock yourself up in the shul. You could go anywhere. Conquer kingdoms."

"I don't… I must obey my master."

"Or what? Will you crumble to dust if you disobey? Will God reach down with his fiery arm and strike you from existence?"

"I don't know."

Jakob tossed the pebble away, out into the rain. "That's the difficulty, isn't it? We want so badly what we can never have, and we don't even know what the consequences of our disobedience would be."

"I don't want to go," Emet said very softly.

"But you do want something." Jakob shocked Emet by setting his hand on Emet's arm. It was the first time they'd touched—the first time anyone but Rabbi Eleazar had touched Emet—and Jakob's hand felt very warm and wonderfully rough against Emet's skin. "What do you want?" Jakob asked.

Emet's throat felt tight and it was hard to answer. "I want to be real. A man. I want... I want a house and friends and family. I want to work hard, and at the end of the day I want to sing my thanks to God, and then I want to go home and laugh with people who... who care about me." Oh, he wanted those things so badly that each word pierced more painfully than Jakob's chisel—but these wounds didn't heal.

Jakob squeezed Emet's arm before letting his hand fall. "Those are good things, Emet. They're not so different from my dreams. In my view, that makes you real—or makes me a monster. I'm not sure which."

"You are not a monster!" Emet said, appalled.

Jakob twitched his shoulders slightly. "I am... that I am." He chuckled humorlessly. And then, after a long pause where he slowly stroked his beard, he smiled at Emet. "But I can give you one small thing you hope for, at least. I can be your friend. If you like."

Emet smiled so widely his face ached. "Yes! I would like that, please. I don't... I don't know how to be a friend back, but I'll try."

Jakob squeezed Emet's arm again, very briefly this time. "Good. I could use a friend as well. What can I do to seal our friendship, Emet?"

Touch me, Emet wanted to say. But he didn't dare. "Could you tell me about Elijah, maybe?"

When Jakob smiled back, the corners of his eyes crinkled. "Of course. And since this rain doesn't appear to want to stop anytime soon, I can tell you more as well."

The rain didn't stop until it was almost time to return to town. Jakob talked and talked, telling stories about Elijah, about David who slew a giant and Moses who parted a sea, about Eve who spoke with a serpent and Solomon who was very wise. Jakob didn't seem to mind when Emet asked questions; he answered every one of them patiently and well. And when the rain slowed to a slight mist and they noticed the sun was getting low, Jakob looked as disappointed to be leaving as Emet felt.

They walked back to town, the cold mud squelching between Emet's toes. When they reached the shul, Jakob touched Emet for the third time, just a light tap on his elbow. "Good night, friend," Jakob said. "I'll see you in the morning."

~6~

"MY PARENTS tell me I'm foolish to be working in this weather," Jakob said as they walked toward town at the close of another day. As if to demonstrate what he meant, he waved a hand, causing the drifting snowflakes to swirl and spin.

"You are. I see you shivering as you work."

"Not much longer. Another week, I think, and the house will be finished enough that we can lay a fire inside."

Emet tried to smile at that idea—and he did sometimes daydream about being warm again—but he dreaded finishing the house. He and Jakob would undoubtedly have finished already if the days hadn't grown so short. "It's a very nice house," Emet said.

"It is. My finest work yet, I think. I'm going to carve an elaborate stone mantel that's far too grand for such a small shack. I may carve the ceiling beams as well, although I don't much enjoy working with wood." He grinned boyishly. "My little house will be fancier than the duke's by the time we're done with it."

We. Emet liked the sound of that. His fingers were much clumsier than Jakob's, but perhaps Emet could learn to do some carving as well.

They came to the field with the goats. During lunch that day, Emet had stolen a few crusts of Jakob's bread. As always, Jakob pretended not to notice. Now Emet gave the crusts to the hungry animals, who bleated their thanks after they ate.

"You're spoiling them," Jakob said, but he was smiling.

"They look hungry."

"They're goats. Goats always look hungry."

"They do seem to enjoy their food."

Jakob gave him a look Emet had grown used to—it meant Jakob was trying to puzzle something out. "You could try food sometime too, you know."

Emet shook his head. Jakob had offered before, and Emet had been tempted. But by now he'd learned that after humans ate or drank, they excreted, and Emet didn't think his body was capable of that. He pictured himself swallowing food and then having it remain somewhere inside him forever.

Jakob moved closer to Emet, so close they almost touched, and Emet could feel the radiant heat as if Jakob were a small fire. Jakob stuck out a finger and captured a single snowflake, which he held in front of Emet's mouth. "Try this at least," he said.

Obediently, Emet opened his mouth.

Even though the snow had probably melted already, Emet felt a dot of cold moisture on his tongue. It had no flavor. But Jakob's finger—ah. Jakob's skin tasted of stone and salt, and although Emet knew Jakob's fingers were very calloused, the skin felt smooth against his tongue. He sucked gently. Oh, that was very nice. A little bit of Jakob's body inside his own. Emet's cock grew as hard as when he stroked it at night.

With a noise somewhere between a groan and a gasp, Jakob pulled his finger away and took an unsteady step backward. His eyes were very wide and his cheeks were flushed. "No," he said, but Emet didn't know what he was denying. And then Jakob's gaze fell slightly and he moaned again.

Emet looked down at himself. His erection was clearly visible beneath the thin fabric of his trousers, and it fascinated him. He'd taken very little time to explore his body in the daylight, and he hadn't realized his arousal would be so visible.

"You can... you can...." Jakob swallowed loudly. "You are... complete."

Unsure what Jakob meant, Emet fidgeted. "Did I do something bad?"

"You... no." Jakob squeezed his eyes shut and kept them that way for what seemed like a long time. When he opened them again, his expression was somber. "Do you know about... about sex, Emet?"

"No?"

"In the stories I've told you, you remember how they lie together. Like Jakob with Leah and Rachel. And you remember the Song of Songs?"

Emet nodded enthusiastically. Jakob had recited the verses in Hebrew, which Emet didn't understand. But then Jakob had translated some of it: kisses like wine, eyes like doves. *I am my beloved's, and my beloved is mine*. The words were so beautiful.

Jakob ran his fingers through his beard, which was something he did when he was uncomfortable or deep in thought. "People... we find someone attractive. And we want, we want to lie with them. To have sex with them. Men want women and women want men. It's how babies are conceived. You understand?"

Emet did, although not fully. The Song of Songs spoke of one person's soul loving another. Emet had ached at these words, knowing he didn't possess a soul and would never possess love. But humans did; he knew that much. "Do you want a woman, Jakob?"

"No." Jakob's eyes filled with pain and anguish. "I want... men."

"Oh. Do you lie with them?"

"I can't."

"Why not?"

"It's wrong, Emet. Men cannot lie with other men."

Emet knew he wasn't very smart. Statements like this bewildered him. "Why not?" he repeated.

"It's wrong. An abomination. A grave transgression."

"But... why?"

"I don't know!" Jakob shouted loud enough that the startled goats ran away. "I ask myself this. Why would God make me this way if it is wrong? I pray—every morning and night I pray, Emet. I beg God to help me change, to stop these thoughts that linger in my head and these desires that kindle in my heart. But he forsakes me."

"You're a good man, Jakob. You are kind and clever. Surely God must love you."

Jakob shook his head. "Do you feel desire too, Emet?"

"Yes."

"I don't understand! You were created by Rabbi Eleazar, who is a pious man, and God gave you life. I was created by my parents, who are good and pious as well. And yet we have these... appetites. It's as if I was able to chew only the flesh of swine. It's forbidden, and I'd starve. I *am* starving."

Emet moved closer. After a brief hesitation, he settled his hand on Jakob's wool-clad shoulder. "You could lie with me, if you like. If my body allows it. I know I'm terrible, but I would try to be gentle. And I am not a man."

"You're certainly not a woman. And... I think of you as a man, Emet. Anyone who knew you would think of you that way." He stepped back a little, allowing Emet's hand to drop from his shoulder. He tilted his head to look up at the gray sky. Snowflakes landed on his eyelashes, making him blink. "It's late. We have to hurry." He turned his back to Emet and the goats and began to march toward town.

THE NEXT day was not Shabbos, but Jakob didn't come to the shul to fetch Emet, and Emet worried over this all morning. Maybe it was only the weather that discouraged Jakob. The snow had stopped, but the air was very cold. Everyone who walked down the street moved quickly, bundled in layers of bulky clothing. Jakob might have stayed at home today, where he could huddle by the fire with his family. Emet hoped so. He didn't want to imagine Jakob working alone on the top of the hill, too disgusted by Emet's offer to face him again.

He considered what Jakob had told him about desiring men and about such a desire being wrong. Emet was only a simple creature made of clay, and he didn't understand. It seemed to him if two people cared for one another—if they wanted to make each other feel good—such feelings were far better than disgust or hatred. Hadn't Jakob told Emet that being kind to others, treating them as you wished to be treated, was a mitzvah, a blessing?

The attic was so lonely. Emet wrapped himself in old curtains and told himself some of the stories he'd learned from Jakob. He was in the middle of Noah's tale—and trying to imagine what all those animals had looked like, crammed onto a boat—when he heard voices from the street below. He hurried to the window and saw a group of people gathered around a fancy carriage that he recognized as Gospodin Novák's. Novák himself was standing on the cobbles beside two other beardless men. Someone was shouting.

Emet had never before left the attic without Rabbi Eleazar's company. But he didn't like the yelling. What if someone was in danger? He dropped the curtains onto the floor and ran to the door. It wasn't locked. Even if it had been, he could have easily pulled it from its frame. He thundered down the stairs, his feet landing only on every third or fourth tread. He rushed through the empty foyer and out through the open front doors.

The assembled people gasped at his appearance. A few of them cried out in alarm, and several scurried farther away. But Rabbi Eleazar held his ground, as did the three men he'd been speaking to. Gospodin Novák looked nervous, and his companions, who had not seen the golem before, paled.

The sudden silence seemed oppressive. "May I help you, Master?" Emet asked.

Rabbi Eleazar was a small man, but he stood very tall and straight. "Wait beside me," he commanded. "So you see," he said to the men. "The golem is still here to protect us."

Gospodin Novák shook his head. "It cannot fully protect you, Rabbi. I'm telling you—the plague is terrible this year. Children are dying in their mothers' arms. And the duke spends his evenings gambling, falling deeper into debt. He's desperate, and the city is desperate too. I've seen them collecting weapons and making sure they're sharp. Leave here, Rabbi. Maybe when the weather warms, people will come to their senses and you can return."

"And where are we to go?"

"Zilnicza is only a few days' travel. The Jews there might take you in. Or perhaps Olodetz. They've a very fine synagogue—I've seen it myself."

"I've seen it as well. But Mala Lubovnya is our home. It always has been. We will not abandon it, not even until spring."

"Your golem can't save you all. I saw it lift a cart and withstand a few blows, but it cannot take on an entire city."

Emet tried to look fierce, but he knew Gospodin Novák was right. His strength was great, but not unlimited.

One of Novák's companions was a tall man with a thin face. His gray hair was long and straggly where it escaped from beneath his hat. He looked like he'd much rather be seated in a plush chair in front of a fireplace with a glass of wine in hand. "Look here. Have you asked your people what they want? Maybe they have more sense than you."

Instead of answering, Rabbi Eleazar lifted his arms toward the crowd. "What do you say, good people? Will you flee?"

The people muttered quietly. Then a woman stepped forward. Emet realized she was Jakob's mother. She planted her hands on her hips and glared. "My husband built my house with his own hands. My sons were born there. I'd rather die than leave it."

"You may very well get your wish," said the tall man.

She didn't back away. Within seconds she was joined by her husband and sons—including Jakob, whose eyes were wild. Other townspeople nodded their agreement. And to everyone's surprise— including perhaps his own—Jakob marched to Emet's side. "Emet— The golem has been working at my side for weeks now. I've seen what he can do. I trust him. I place my life in his hands."

Emet wanted to embrace him, but he couldn't even smile. He hoped Jakob somehow sensed his gratitude. And he hoped he could live up to such a great trust.

Rabbi Eleazar did smile. He faced Gospodin Novák and the other gentiles, but he raised his voice so the entire assemblage could hear him. "If anyone wishes to leave Mala Lubovnya, I will not stop him. I will even help him gather his belongings. And if he does not have a cart and cannot afford to buy one, I will give him mine. But I will stay here with the golem God has sent to protect us."

The tall man made a sour face, as did his companion, a young man in fine clothes who hadn't said a word. But Novák nodded slightly. "I cannot decide whether you are a very brave man, my friend, or a very foolish one."

"All men are fools, Gospodin Novák. Most especially those who think themselves wise."

Novák chuckled. "I hope your golem and your faith protect you, Rabbi. I hope they protect you all." He grunted and wheezed as he climbed back into his carriage. His friends followed, and the carriage rattled away.

None of the crowd dispersed. In fact, others showed up, until it seemed as if the entire town stood on the street, shivering in the cold and looking at the rabbi and golem with grim faces. Emet would have quailed under those staring eyes if Jakob hadn't been standing so close by his side, his head held high.

"Perhaps," said Rabbi Eleazar very loudly, "some of you would like to discuss this matter. Please come inside where it's warmer." He walked back inside the shul, followed closely by Jakob's family and

Emet. Most of the rest filed inside as well.

In the foyer, Rabbi Eleazar pointed at the stairs. "Return to the attic," he said to Emet.

Emet started to obey but was held back when Jakob grabbed his arm. "He's a part of this too, Rabbi. Let him join us."

"He's only a golem."

"He's more than you think."

The rabbi gave them both a long, considering look. "All right," he finally said.

For the first time, Emet was allowed to enter the large chapel. Women sat upstairs on the mezzanine with the younger children, while older boys and men filled the seats downstairs. Jakob was with his father and brothers in the very front row. But Emet was hesitant to sit—his clothes were too ragged and dirty for such a fine room, and he didn't feel as if he belonged in a chair. These chairs were meant for those who worshipped God; perhaps God would be offended at a soulless monster among them. So Emet instead chose to stand against a wall, and from that vantage point, he could see Jakob's face.

When everyone was seated and the whispering had settled down, Rabbi Eleazar addressed the congregation. He summarized the situation with the duke and the plague-ridden city folk, and he told a few dire stories of what had happened to Jews in similar situations in the past. He explained how he'd read ancient stories about golems and decided to try to create one himself. He described Emet's strength and resistance to injury. And then he allowed the people to ask questions and make comments.

After a while, Emet stopped listening. He didn't understand much of what people were saying, and anyway his role was clear: obey his master's orders, whatever they might be. He allowed his attention to focus on the room's furnishings and the faces of the congregation. And he especially watched Jakob and his family. The father and brothers barely glanced at him, but Jakob looked at him often, usually with a smile Emet couldn't help but return.

The conversation continued for a long time. Several people yelled and a few cried. But in the end, nobody seemed willing to leave Mala Lubovnya. Rabbi Eleazar stood in front of the dais where the Torah was kept in its decorated ark, and he nodded at his people. "Let us pray that hope and prudence will conquer fear and tyranny." He began to sing.

The rabbi's voice was loud but thin. It didn't matter, however, because the entire congregation joined him. That would have been lovely enough, as several hundred throats opened, several hundred tongues and lips moved in unison, and the notes bounced and thundered throughout the sanctuary like an ocean of sound. But then that one voice chimed in too, clear and pure, cresting the chorus like a wave.

Emet searched the crowd for the source of the sublime singing— and his legs nearly gave out when he realized it was Jakob.

Jakob sang with his eyes closed and his head thrown back. He was always handsome, but now he could have been mistaken for an angel as all his usual doubts and hesitancy fled his face, replaced by an expression Emet thought must be passion. People smiled at Jakob as he sang, but he didn't see them. His conversation was with God only, as Jakob thanked him and pled for peace.

Jakob had told Emet stories about souls. At the time, Emet had trouble understanding what a soul was, perhaps because he hadn't one of his own. But now he saw Jakob's soul very plainly. It was a thing of transcendent beauty.

Only when Emet's vision blurred did he realize he was crying. He brushed his fingers against his cheeks; they came away wet. He licked one finger—remembering the way Jakob's finger had so recently entered him—and tasted clay and salt. He could have crumbled to dust at that moment and been content.

When the prayers were over, the congregation slowly left the sanctuary. A few of them smiled at him as they passed, and he smiled back. Jakob was one of the last to leave. He didn't say anything to Emet, but he looked like he wanted to.

"So," said Rabbi Eleazar when everyone else was gone. "It seems you have joined the congregation. Do you understand what happens in this room?"

Emet nodded. "Yes. It's wonderful."

"Do you understand... God?"

"No. But I am grateful he allowed me to be created. I want to please him and protect his people."

The rabbi smiled. "Then perhaps you understand enough."

~7~

EMET WAS shy with Jakob the next day, too much in awe of him to talk as they walked to the hill. Jakob was quiet too; he seemed lost in his own thoughts. Even when they began to work, Jakob spoke only to issue orders.

During the previous week, a cartload of timbers had been delivered to the bottom of the hill. One of Jakob's brothers drove the wagon but remained seated and silent as Emet carried the big pieces of wood up to the house. When the wagon was empty, he drove away without a word. Emet lifted the timbers so Jakob could fasten them in place, and by the end of the day, the roof was formed. "That would have taken my family the entire week," Jakob said with wonder. "And we'd all have been sore afterward."

Once the roof supports were in place, Jakob showed Emet how to install the thatch. That job required skill more than brute strength and took them some time. After they eventually finished, they went inside and smeared clay daub over the ceiling. Emet thought the clay might have come from the same place he did, which made him happy—it was as if Jakob would always have a bit of Emet in his home.

Today the daub was dry. Emet helped Jakob smooth it out; then they swept the debris off the stone floor and scattered it outside. Many small tasks remained after that. They glazed the small windows, hung the solid door, and built a few shelves and cupboards. While Jakob worked on carving the mantelpiece, Emet assembled the boards for the front porch.

Woodworking was still very new to Emet, and he asked frequent questions. He was inside the house, asking yet again, when a woman's voice called from outside. "Jakob? Jakob!"

Jakob set his tools down very quickly. "Mama," he muttered. He rushed out the door with Emet behind him.

Jakob's mother stood a short distance from the house. Her head was tilted to the side as she inspected the structure. She wore several layers of sweaters and stockings and scarves, and a small wheelbarrow was at her side. "It is a very pretty house, Jakob."

Jakob embraced her. "Thank you, Mama."

"I am amazed by how quickly you've built it! You've worked yourself to exhaustion."

"I haven't. I had Emet's help." Jakob gestured in Emet's direction and then seemed struck by a thought. "I should introduce you properly. Mama, this is Emet the golem. My friend. Emet, this is my mother, Mrs. Rivka Abramov."

Emet had never been introduced to anyone before and wasn't sure what to do. "Hello, ma'am," he said softly as Mrs. Abramov peered sharply at him.

"Hello," she responded finally. "You have worked very hard for my son."

"I'm happy to help."

She nodded, then clucked her tongue. "And even a golem must be cold in such clothing, in this weather! I thought so yesterday when I saw you in the shul. So I've brought you something. It's not much—I had very little time, and we are not wealthy people." As Emet watched with curiosity and astonishment, she pulled something out of the barrow. It was a folded piece of fabric. At first he thought it might be a curtain for Jakob's house or perhaps a rug, but when Mrs. Abramov unfolded it, he saw it was actually an enormous cloak.

Mrs. Abramov flapped the fabric a little. "Ach, it's not such a pretty thing. If I had all winter, I could knit you a sweater. This is only bits and pieces of old clothing sewn together. You see?" She pointed to a dark-red patch. "This was a tunic Jakob wore when he was a boy."

Jakob grinned widely. "You've made him a coat of many colors, Mama?"

She flapped her hand at her son as if she were annoyed, but Emet saw the sparkle in her eyes. She walked to Emet and held the cloak out, and when he hesitated to take it—he couldn't quite believe it was for him—she clucked again and stood on tiptoes so she could settle it on his shoulders. It was heavy and warm, and it smelled like Jakob.

Emet wrapped the cloak around himself. "Thank you, ma'am. It's beautiful. Thank you so much."

"Ach, it's nothing. Just a rag." Her face glowed with pleasure.

Jakob watched the interchange with puzzlement on his face. Now he came forward to kiss her cheek. "That was nice of you, Mama."

"It's nothing. I brought other things too, for you. Some old household goods, which I thought you could use. A soup pot, bedding... remember that little green rug from when you were small? You used to trip over it every morning. You were such a clumsy child."

He grinned at her. "Thank you. Would you like to see the inside? It's not finished, but—"

"No. It's bad luck. You can have me for a proper visit when you're through with it. Go put these things away. I want a word with your golem."

Emet and Jakob exchanged uneasy glances, but Jakob nodded. "All right." He pushed the wheelbarrow to his porch, struggled to get it up the single step, and then brought it inside and shut the door.

"Emet is a good name," Mrs. Abramov said.

"Thank you. Jakob gave it to me."

"Hmm. You work well together, you and my son."

"Yes, ma'am."

She turned her head to gaze down the hill at the town. She had Jakob's eyes, but they were troubled. She crossed her arms over her ample chest, hugging herself. "Speak truly, Emet. Will you protect my Jakob?"

"I will."

"Why?"

"It's what I was made for. And... he's my friend. He treats me like a real person."

She looked back at him. "He treats you like a man."

"Yes."

"I love all my sons, as a mother should. But my Jakob, my Yankele, he's special. He almost died of a fever when he was a baby. And then he grew up so strong, and with a voice to make the heavens envious. But he's always so sad, my Yankele. So lonely."

Not knowing what to say, Emet only nodded.

She sighed. "Do you get lonely too? I know you're a golem, but you might have feelings too."

"I get lonely," said Emet.

"Yankele has always been the quiet one. Not like his brothers, always shouting over each other. If it weren't for his singing, there are times I'd have wondered if he'd lost his voice entirely. But lately... since he's begun working with you... he speaks more. Tells everyone how wonderful you are."

"I.... He does?" What was that fluttery feeling in Emet's belly?

She narrowed her eyes. "How far would you go to protect my son?"

"I'd do anything. I'd... I have nothing but my name and this cloak, but I'd give everything. I will crumble to dust before I allow him to be hurt."

"Good. This is very good. Yankele may need someone fierce on his side." She smiled. "Someone almost as fierce as me."

She reached up and briefly touched his face. She wore soft woolen mittens. She was the third person to touch him, and for a moment he thought he might melt from the tenderness of it. Then she dropped her arm and stepped back. "Tell Jakob to bring back the barrow tonight. And to hurry and finish so I can see his new house." She turned and marched quickly down the path.

"WHAT DID my mother have to say?" Jakob was just placing the rug near the fireplace. He'd already set the other things from his mother on the shelves. The few personal belongings made the house look like a home.

"She loves you," said Emet. "And she calls you Yankele."

"That's not the worst of it. She used to call me tsigele until I begged her to stop."

"Baby goat?"

"And my brothers would make meh-meh sounds at me behind her back."

Emet grinned. "You don't remind me much of a goat."

"Well, I'm glad to hear that." Jakob bent to straighten the rug a little more. When he stood straight again and glanced at Emet, he must have noticed something in Emet's face. "What?"

"She told me you talk about me."

Jakob's face reddened and he looked away. "What else would I talk about? I spend all my time with you."

"She said you tell them I'm wonderful."

"I… I never used that word." Jakob apparently decided his small stack of towels needed refolding. He turned his back to Emet.

Emet came a few steps closer. "Is it true, Jakob? Do you think so well of me?"

After a long silence, Jakob nodded. "I do," he said without turning around.

"Even though I'm a golem?"

"That's… that stopped mattering a long time ago, Emet."

Chewing his lip, Emet tried to frame his words carefully. "In the Song of Songs, they loved each other with their souls. But I think maybe… maybe it's possible for a creature without a soul to love. When I heard you singing yesterday, it was as if something stirred inside of me. A heartbeat with no heart. Is that what love feels like?"

"Love feels like a heavy stone in my chest, so heavy I can't breathe. But oh Blessed Lord, I can't live without that stone."

Jakob turned at last. His eyes glittered with unshed tears, and his hands opened and closed at his sides. "It's a transgression as great as murder, Emet."

"Love is a transgression?"

"I want to be a righteous man! I do. But I can't… I want you, Emet. I dream of you. I ache for you."

"Then lie with me, Jakob. Please." It wasn't only love that made Emet beg, and not only his desperate need to be touched. It was also the knowledge that his time with Jakob was short. The house would be finished. The duke's men would attack—or the duke would see reason, and Rabbi Eleazar would have no more need for a golem. It felt so unfair to be given such a short time in such a big world, but Emet wouldn't complain if he could only be close with his beloved just once.

Jakob threw himself so heavily against Emet that Emet rocked back a little. But he didn't mind, because now they could embrace, and now Jakob could rub his whiskers against the skin of Emet's chest. "Oh," Jakob moaned. "You feel so *real*." Jakob felt real too—solid and warm and more precious than any jewel.

Somehow they ended up lying on the green rug, their limbs entangled. The air was far too cold for Jakob to undress completely, but Emet happily removed his own clothing and let Jakob explore his body with rough fingers and soft lips. "Do I look like a real man?" Emet asked.

Jakob smoothed his palm over the letters inscribed on Emet's chest. "I've never seen another man naked. You're beautiful. But there are a few differences between us."

"Can I see?"

"All right," Jakob said, smiling.

Emet's large fingers were clumsy on the buttons of Jakob's coat and shirt, but eventually he managed to get them undone, and then he pushed the woolen undershirt up to Jakob's neck. Jakob's chest was muscular, with a triangle of dark hair. He gasped when Emet tentatively touched a thumb to a small nubbin of flesh. "I don't have these," Emet said, glancing down at his own blank chest.

"Nipples. They don't serve any purpose to a man. But... oh. That feels nice." Jakob writhed slightly as Emet gave each nipple a gentle pinch.

Emet was missing other parts as well. He had no navel, although Jakob did, and Jakob liked it when Emet dipped the tip of his tongue inside. A few minutes later, Jakob discovered that the cleft between the cheeks of Emet's ass was uninterrupted. Jakob unbuttoned his trousers, pushed them down, and showed Emet the tight little rosette between his cheeks. "May I touch it?" Emet asked.

"Yes. Please."

So Emet did, first with fingers and then with his tongue. He loved the way Jakob tasted, loved the scratch of Jakob's wiry hairs against his face.

Jakob spent a very long time playing with Emet's cock. He seemed to think it funny that Emet was circumcised. As far as Emet was concerned, Jakob could chuckle all he wanted, just so long as he continued to stroke like that with his calloused fingertips. And when it was Emet's turn to explore Jakob's cock—the silky skin and turgid veins, the slick smoothness of the flared head—Jakob emitted a string of satisfying grunts and groans.

"I'm not sure how to do this," Jakob said breathlessly. With his clothing still on but badly askew, he lay atop Emet's body.

Emet was so lost in sensations he could barely form the words to answer. "I think... think you're... doing well." If he had been capable of further speech, he would have told Jakob a golem *did* need sustenance after all, that every bit of contact between Jakob's skin and his was a delicious mouthful of a wondrous feast. But maybe Jakob knew this anyway, because he kissed Emet ardently and tried his best to touch every inch of him.

Emet's hand was bigger, softer; Jakob's was more clever. Both hands wrapped around the shafts of their cocks, pressing the lengths together. It was a far better thing than Emet's solitary touch as he lay alone in his attic. He tingled from head to toe and no longer felt the cold. Jakob cried out his name, and for a few endless moments, Emet was no longer a creature sculpted from clay but was instead a man of flesh and blood. "Emet!" Jakob shouted again, his voice ragged and hoarse, and hot liquid sprayed their bellies.

Their movements slowed. Jakob collapsed, still half atop Emet, and Emet pulled his new cloak over them both. Jakob nuzzled his face into the crook of Emet's neck. "God hasn't struck us down yet," he murmured. "But if he does, I think it was worth it. You're worth it."

Emet smiled and held him close. For the first time, he felt truly alive.

~8~

THE HOUSE was finished and Jakob had moved in, but he kept inventing excuses to require Emet's help. He needed firewood collected and carried and chopped. He wanted a low stone wall built around the top of the hill. A cistern needed to be dug and lined with rocks, and then—because little rain fell this time of year—he required many buckets of water to be drawn from the well in the center of Mala Lubovnya and then toted up the path.

Rabbi Eleazar was no fool, and he no doubt saw through Jakob's ruses. He'd lift an eyebrow and shake his head as Jakob explained his newest task, but then the rabbi would push Emet toward the door and say, "Work hard, Golem."

Emet *did* work hard. He moved boulders and dug holes and carried water. But only for part of the day, because before the sun dipped too far, he and Jakob would stoke the fire, strip off their clothes, and lie together in Jakob's bed. They discovered all the things their bodies could do together. And while Jakob still occasionally voiced his concerns about offending God, Emet was thankful for being made capable of such joy.

"You're a miracle," Jakob whispered to Emet one afternoon. Jakob was naked and sweaty underneath his thick quilts. Emet was naked too, and almost perfectly happy.

"I know," Emet said. "Clay that walks and talks. A miracle indeed."

"That's not what I mean. The Torah says all men come from Adam, and he was made of dust. So you're no more a miracle in that regard than I am, or anyone born of a man lying with a woman. I mean you're a miracle because you're so new, and you began so alone, yet you've taught me what love feels like."

"I do love you, Jakob."

"I know. You're a miracle *and* a blessing."

Emet still spent Shabbos and nights in the attic, but his room didn't seem as empty anymore when his head was filled with memories of time spent with his beloved. And when the minyan gathered at sundown to sing the evening prayers, Emet could listen to Jakob's voice and know that Jakob was singing not just for God but also for Emet.

The weather grew bitterly cold. Emet helped Jakob collect and deliver firewood to old people, some of whom complained it was the worst winter they'd endured, while others claimed the winters of their childhood were much worse. Mrs. Abramov trudged up the hill to inspect—and, happily, to approve—Jakob's house and to deliver a new sweater for Jakob and a thick quilt for Emet. "Ach, it's nothing," she said when Emet thanked her for the blanket. But he could tell she'd taken great care to embroider it with colorful flowers.

She also brought a huge pot of stew and dumplings because, she said, Jakob was likely to waste away without a woman to cook for him. "At least you keep your house tidy," she said as she inspected the shelves for dust.

"Emet cleans it for me. It keeps him busy."

"You're good boys," she said, which made Jakob laugh and Emet duck his head.

Then it snowed for two days straight. Jakob didn't come to fetch Emet, who fretted his way through a series of chores Rabbi Eleazar assigned him. "He's by himself, Master," Emet said as he moved the rabbi's ancient and enormous desk.

Rabbi Eleazar bent to pick up paper and other bits of debris that had no doubt accumulated behind the desk for decades. "Jakob Abramov is a grown man. He can survive a little snow. He built his house tight and sturdy, didn't he?"

"Yes."

"Of course he did. He's a fine craftsman." The rabbi peered speculatively at a broken quill pen. "He will be fine."

Emet worried anyway.

The weather turned unseasonably warm and the snow melted. Jakob returned for him, smiling broadly and mumbling a nonsense excuse to the rabbi about why he needed the golem's help. The rabbi sighed and flapped his hands at both of them. The road was a muddy, mushy mess, but neither Jakob nor Emet minded. They hurried up the hill and into Jakob's house, tore off their clothing, and tumbled into bed, where they made up for lost time.

The sun shone for over a week, the days grew longer, and the promise of spring was supported by little bits of green in the fields and on the trees. Jakob said he would have to return to his regular work when the building season began, and he promised to ask his father if Emet might join them. "We won't have so much time alone, but at least we'll be together. When they see how hard you work and how helpful you are, I think they'll welcome you." He grinned. "If Papa is reluctant, I think Mama might help me argue our case. He doesn't stand a chance against her."

But as it turned out, the promise of spring was false. The skies darkened and the air again chilled. Sleet fell fitfully for days, making the cobblestones hazardous, and people ventured out as little as possible. Emet and Jakob still walked to Jakob's house, but Jakob exclaimed when Emet got into bed with frozen feet, and the next day he presented Emet with a pair of shoes. "The shoemaker is my uncle. I had to beg him to finish them quickly, and he says they probably won't last long. But I can get you a better pair later. Do they fit? I had to guess your size."

Emet smiled as he put them on. They were small on him and pinched his toes a bit, but he was still delighted. "They're perfect, Jakob." Then he thought of something that made him frown. "You've given me so much, and your mother too, and I have no gifts for you."

"You've done a dozen men's work for me for months, Emet."

"That's my duty."

"But you've given me your love as well, and that's the finest gift I could ask for. I wouldn't trade a king's treasury of gold for it."

So Emet wore his too-small shoes and a patchwork cloak and felt better dressed than any nobleman.

"I DIDN'T hear you sing last night," Emet said as they walked up the hill. The clouds had fled, but the temperature was still very cold.

Little puffs of moisture escaped from Jakob's mouth when he spoke. "My throat was a little scratchy, so I decided to rest it. I didn't want my brothers reporting to Mama that I was hoarse—she'd smother me with ointments and teas."

"She told me you almost died when you were a baby."

"And she never lets me forget it!"

"I understand how she feels. If you were to become ill—"

"I won't." Jakob gave Emet's arm a light punch. "Don't you start smothering me too. It was a scratchy throat and nothing more. I probably howled too loud when we were in bed together yesterday."

Emet smiled at the memory. Jakob *had* been pretty loud. Emet hadn't been all that quiet either.

"Do you really have work for us today?" he asked. Rabbi Eleazar didn't even ask for an excuse anymore—he just ushered Emet out the door.

"Mm, not exactly. I had an idea, though."

If Emet had eyebrows, he would have waggled them. "Oh?"

"Not *that* sort of idea. Well, that too. But I thought maybe you might like to learn to read."

"Read?" Emet nearly stumbled with astonishment. "But I'm—"

"Only a golem. I know. Emet, you're as smart as any man I know. Much smarter than my brother Haskel, and even he eventually learned his letters."

They'd reached the top of the hill. Jakob opened the little wooden gate he'd attached to his stone fence, and Emet followed. They stopped just inside the yard, and Jakob reached up to caress Emet's cheek. He said, "You don't have to learn, but I thought you might like to."

"I'd... I'd like to try."

"Good."

Jakob turned to close the gate—then gasped. "What...."

Emet spun around, and what he saw made his belly clench. Mala Lubovnya was on fire. Not all of it, to be sure, but thick smoke rose from many of the houses.

"The duke!" Jakob cried.

Emet didn't bother with the gate. Instead he vaulted the stone wall with very little effort. He sped so quickly downhill that it was as if his feet barely touched the ground. At first he was dimly aware of Jakob running behind him, but Emet was much faster. He glanced quickly over his shoulder when he reached the town gate, but there was no sign of Jakob behind him. He could hear voices coming from the center of town—shouts and screams and people crying.

As he ran, he passed a few burning buildings and some shops with smashed windows. People were busily nursing the wounded. Since there was no sign of anyone with weapons, Emet continued toward the shul, which was just a block from the main square. He hoped Rabbi Eleazar would be there to give him orders.

But before he got to the shul, he came to the covered market and discovered an uneven battle. Old people and children huddled among the stalls, wailing, while men and a few women tried to fend off a crowd of strangers. The strangers were outnumbered, but they wielded swords, clubs, and spears, while the townspeople defended themselves with whatever they could grab. Bodies lay unmoving on the ground, and blood puddled on the cobbles.

Emet couldn't wait for someone to tell him what to do. He roared and charged into the melee. While the townspeople ran back toward the stalls, Emet grabbed the nearest man with a sword and tore off his head. It was an easy thing to do, killing a man. Plastering a ceiling was much more challenging. He lifted another man into the air and broke him over his knee like kindling. The others attacked him, and although steel bit into his body and heavy pieces of wood thudded against his back and head, he didn't slow. He didn't stop until every stranger lay unmoving.

Blood was everywhere, and the reek was indescribable. The townspeople continued to cluster among the market stalls. They stared at Emet with round eyes and snow-white faces.

Emet came back to himself enough to notice that there was no sign of his beloved. "Jakob!" he shouted. "Jakob!"

No answer came. But smoke from burning buildings still rose into the sky, and somewhere nearby more shouts resounded. Emet ran. He made several wrong turns—the sounds echoed and bounced confusingly off the stone buildings. But where a narrow street dead-ended against a wall, he found more people. They ran around and screamed, and the thick smoke made visibility poor. Emet nearly tripped over a man who knelt on the cobblestones, sobbing over the broken corpse of a woman in a gray scarf. The man looked up at Emet, his eyes wide with grief, and it was Emet's turn to cry out, because he recognized the man: Jakob's father.

"Jakob? Where's Jakob?" Emet asked.

There was no lucidity in Mr. Abramov's eyes. "They've killed my Rivka. My Rivka's gone."

Emet had no time for sorrow, not even for the woman who'd made him a cloak and a quilt. "Where's Jakob?" he repeated, shouting.

Mr. Abramov didn't answer.

A beardless young man lunged at them out of the chaos. His face and collar were splattered with scarlet, and he held a hatchet high over his head. But Emet plucked the hatchet easily from his hands and buried the blade deeply in the man's face. Emet viewed the world through a haze of red. Even his thoughts were red, his mind no more rational than Mr. Abramov's.

Several men charged Emet at once. As he broke one attacker's neck, he was pierced by sword and spear. He yelped at each fresh spot of pain—it seemed his body was nothing but pain now—but he killed them all. And then he cast around, desperate for Jakob. He would simply murder everyone until he found his lover.

Two figures lurched out of a burning house. Emet reached for them, intending to bash their heads together. As his hand touched one man's shoulder, however, his sensibility returned just enough for the familiar face to register. "Jakob!" he sobbed.

Jakob's face was sooty, streaked with tears and blood. His left arm hung at an unnatural angle; a gaping tear near the shoulder of his coat revealed a terrible wound. But with his right arm, he supported a nearly unconscious young woman. "Emet! Please! Inside."

So Emet plunged into the house and found more people—a crying baby, a man and a woman nearly overcome with smoke—and shepherded them to the door. He also found bodies, which he carried out without pausing to identify them.

The roof of the house collapsed, and the flames were too fierce even for Emet. He saw Jakob moving slowly around the street, trying to tend to his injured family. Emet was going to help, but more men came rushing into the street, each holding a weapon. Maybe they were coming for Jakob. Maybe not. Emet didn't wait to find out.

He raged through them as ferociously as the fire raged through the houses. He picked them up and dashed them against the ground, stomping the life from them. He snapped their backs. He tore their limbs from their bodies. He brought his fists down on their skulls, crushing them like stones.

He stopped only when his weapon-ravaged legs gave out, and he collapsed heavily onto his back.

"Jakob," he whispered when he saw who crouched over him a moment later. "You're hurt...."

"I'll live." Jakob settled his rough hand against Emet's cheek. "Oh, Emet. You're—"

"Golem."

Emet blinked to clear his vision. Rabbi Eleazar had somehow appeared beside Jakob. His hat and clothes were askew, his face and hands were covered in as much blood and soot as Jakob's. And his eyes were deep pools of sorrow. "So many dead," the rabbi said.

Jakob shook his head. "He was doing his job! He was saving us."

"I know. Ach, I am such a great fool! I should never have done this."

Emet didn't understand. Oh, he was so weary and he hurt so much. "Jakob?" he said. His voice was like pebbles shifting under a foot.

Jakob was looking at the rabbi. "Oh no, please, Rabbi! You can't! He loves—"

"I know," the rabbi interrupted. "I know, my son." He shook his head slightly and reached forward to unbutton Emet's vest. Those buttons had been the first belongings Emet treasured. He always kept them well shined. The rabbi's fingers were very thin and soft compared to Jakob's. Emet remembered the feel of them at his first awakening.

Jakob was crying. Emet wanted to cry as well, but he wasn't able. There was no moisture left in a body of dried clay.

"Emet means truth," Rabbi Eleazar said. "But if we remove the aleph, the word becomes *met*. Dead. I should have known from the beginning."

Emet hadn't known either. He'd never had the chance to learn to read. "Would you sing to me, Jakob?" he rasped.

As tears continued to course down his face, Jakob nodded. "Is there a blessing for this, Rabbi?"

After a brief pause, the rabbi sang. His voice was reedy, slightly off-key. But Jakob immediately joined him, and the prayer soared so high that even a broken creature made of clay could feel momentarily buoyant.

As Jakob continued to sing in Hebrew, the rabbi whispered the words so that Emet could understand them:

My flesh and my heart may fail,

But the rock of my heart and my portion is God forever.

When the dust returns to the earth that it was,

The spirit shall return to God who gave it.

Emet smiled at his beloved.

Rabbi Eleazar smoothed his palm over the aleph on Emet's chest, rubbing the inscription away.

The world crumbled to dust.

~9~

FINGERS TRACED across his chest over and over. Rough fingers—not a scholar's, but those of a man who worked with his hands. And the voice that chanted the blessings was rich and deep. "Blessed art thou, Lord our God." Emet knew those words even in Hebrew, because Jakob had explained them to him. He didn't understand the words that followed, but then the singing stopped, replaced by a hoarse murmur:

The Lord sends death and life;

He brings down to the netherworld and brings up from it.

He heals the brokenhearted

And binds up their wounds.

He will utterly destroy death forever,

And the Lord God will wipe away the tear from every face.

He opened his eyes to see wooden beams and smooth plaster. He recognized those beams. He'd hauled them up the hill and held them in place.

"Emet?"

Emet turned his head slightly. Jakob had new lines on his face, new depths of sadness in his warm brown eyes. But he was smiling hesitantly. "Maybe we should change your name. The word is different." He settled his palm on the center of Emet's chest.

"What does it say?" Emet was surprised when his voice was smooth instead of jagged.

"*Ahava.* It means love."

Emet looked down at his chest—and discovered a dusting of dark hairs and two pink nipples. He reached up to his scalp, where he found more hair, thick and soft.

"Jakob?"

"Can you stand?"

Emet could, although with some difficulty. He felt slightly dizzy, so Jakob helped hold him steady. And it was very strange, because although Emet was still taller than Jakob, he no longer towered over him. There was a strange thudding in his chest as well. A heartbeat!

"I don't understand," Emet said.

"Look at yourself, my beloved."

Taking a few moments to explore his remade body, Emet found more hair at his groin, on his arms and legs, and a coarse stubble on his cheeks. He had a navel now, perfect and round on his flat belly. "I'm... I think I'm hungry."

Jakob laughed. "Good! I have food to share."

"But I don't—"

"I didn't make you to protect anyone, Emet. I don't care how strong you are, and God forbid you should ever need to fight again. *I* made you this time, and I made you for love, from love. Not to be a golem, but to be a man."

Emet's legs collapsed and he fell to the ground. Jakob knelt in front of him. "Are you well? Have I made you properly?"

"I think so." Emet reached up to touch Jakob's left shoulder. "You were hurt...."

"I was," said Jakob gravely. "And I lost.... Oh, Emet! Mama's gone, and two of my brothers, their wives.... But I am alive, and now so are you."

Jakob rose, held out a hand, and helped Emet stand. Then Jakob picked up a patchwork cloak from his bed and settled it on Emet's shoulders. It was a little too big now, but Emet didn't mind.

"Mala Lubovnya?" asked Emet.

"Come see."

They walked across the room and out the door, onto the tidy front porch. The sky was a soft blue and the air was balmy. Inside the town walls were a few gaping holes among the buildings. But most of the town still stood, and the only smoke was friendly little wisps from fireplaces.

"Mala Lubovnya is still there," said Jakob. "You saved us. Almost everyone in town lost someone they loved. But the shul is still there. The minyans pray every morning and evening; the congregation gathers every Shabbos. And the gentiles have mourned their dead as well."

"I killed…. Jakob, I killed so many."

"A great transgression, for which we will pray forgiveness. But here beats the heart of a righteous man." Jakob turned to press a hand against Emet's chest.

Emet stood silently for a long time, thinking about this. His body felt far weaker than before, far more pervious to damage. Yet he felt more whole. "What did you do?"

Jakob smiled. "I told you. I made you with love. It says so, right on your chest. I took your dust and I moistened it with my own blood and tears and seed. I made you to be a man, not a tool or a weapon. I sculpted you far more carefully than ever I've shaped stone. And I shared myself with you to bring you back to life. Can you feel it?"

"Your soul," Emet said with wonder.

"Our soul now. Bound together."

With a throat-wrenching cry, Emet threw his arms around Jakob. They embraced so tightly neither could breathe well, and perhaps they each shed a few tears.

After they'd parted—only a little; never far again—Emet smiled. "Can we eat now?"

"We can! And then we will have to pack. Are you ready for a journey?"

"A journey?"

A shadow of unhappiness chased a little of the joy from Jakob's face. "We can't stay here. Not with what you've done, and not with what we are."

"But your house! Your beautiful home!"

Jakob shrugged. "We can build another. Perhaps not so easily, now that you're only human, but I haven't lost my skills, and you're still strong. I've nothing much here aside from sad memories now. We can go anywhere, Emet. We can see the world. And my true home will always be here." He returned his hand to Emet's chest, which felt perfect.

"Will you teach me to read and to pray?"

"I will teach you everything I know, and we can learn the rest together."

Jakob took Emet's soft hand in his hard one and led him back into the house. As Emet watched, Jakob gathered the ingredients for a feast. And when the meal was ready, together they sang their thanks.

KIM FIELDING is very pleased every time someone calls her eclectic. She has migrated back and forth across the western two-thirds of the United States and currently lives in California, where she long ago ran out of bookshelf space. She's a university professor who dreams of being able to travel and write full time. She also dreams of having two perfectly behaved children, a husband who isn't obsessed with football, and a house that cleans itself. Some dreams are more easily obtained than others.

Kim can be found on her blogs:

http://kfieldingwrites.blogspot.com/

http://www.goodreads.com/author/show/4105707.Kim_Fielding/blog

and on Facebook:

https://www.facebook.com/KFieldingWrites.

Her e-mail is dephalqu@yahoo.com, and she can be found on Twitter at @KFieldingWrites.

By KIM FIELDING

NOVELS
Brute
Good Bones • Buried Bones
Pilgrimage
The Tin Box
Venetian Masks

NOVELLAS
Housekeeping
Night Shift
Speechless

Published by DREAMSPINNER PRESS
http://www.dreamspinnerpress.com

Watchworks

jamie fessenden

London, 1900

HARLAND WALLACE stood at his second-floor bedroom window, watching as the coach pulled up in front of his Chelsea townhouse. The coachman jumped down to extend the footstep and open the door. The gentleman who stepped down was well turned-out and appeared young, though he moved with a certain stiffness, as though he suffered the effects of an accident or a childhood illness. He walked with the aid of a cane.

Harland waited until the man had been admitted to the house and Harland's butler came upstairs to present his card. *Mr. Luke Prescott.*

The visitor had been shown to the sitting room, though he was still standing when Harland entered. He was indeed young, perhaps in his twenties, and extremely handsome—one might even say "beautiful." He was very pale, with delicate features and a mouth as curved and sensual as a woman's. His hair was flaxen blond, short and combed back from a high forehead, and the eyes he turned upon Harland were wide and a startlingly vivid sky blue.

"Mr. Wallace," he said, smiling faintly and transferring his silk hat to the crook of his left arm, his left hand being occupied with the handle of his cane. He extended his gloved right hand and Harland moved to take it quickly, to avoid forcing the man to come to him. "I'm Mr. Luke Prescott."

"Mr. Harland Wallace."

"Please forgive the cane," the man said. "My balance is poor."

"Not at all. Shall we sit down?"

"Thank you, but I shan't take much of your time." There was something odd about the man's face. As strikingly beautiful as it was— Harland was troubled by how mesmerized he was by the man's features—his brief smile failed to move the rest of his face. No small crinkles about the eyes, no expansion of the cheeks. It was disturbingly still. "I am here on behalf of my employer, Dr. Mordecai Steward. He wishes to see you on an urgent matter, but I'm afraid he is unable to leave his house. He was hoping you might be persuaded to stop by."

"Might I ask what this is pertaining to?"

"I'm afraid I've been instructed to direct all questions to my employer."

"I am puzzled as to why the doctor should seek me out," Harland said. He gestured at a display case in one corner of the room. It contained some of the more elaborate watches he'd designed, along with others he'd collected over the years, including some particularly beautiful pieces he'd found during his travels in Germany and Switzerland. "He is aware that I am a watchmaker?"

"Indeed. Dr. Steward spent a considerable amount of time inquiring about skilled members of your profession in Great Britain and the Continent before deciding to approach you. He is looking forward to making your acquaintance."

Harland was flattered that Dr. Steward seemed to hold him in such high regard, but it also gave him pause. What could be so precious to the doctor that he would conduct such an exhaustive search? A family heirloom in need of repair, perhaps? Even that would hardly be deemed urgent. "I hope Dr. Steward finds me up to his expectations."

"I'm sure he will." Prescott withdrew another card from his waistcoat and extended it to Harland. "I've written our address on the back of his card. It's not far from here."

Harland took the card. The front was simple and elegant, with Dr. Steward's name embossed in a clean, legible typeface. Harland turned it over and saw the handwritten address of a townhouse in South Kensington. "Very well, Mr. Prescott. I'm intrigued. Will tomorrow morning be convenient?"

Prescott nodded and gave him that odd smile. "Quite. We look forward to seeing you, Mr. Wallace."

He took his leave, and Harland fretted for a few minutes about whether he should offer assistance. But though he relied upon the cane and walked stiffly, Prescott seemed able to navigate the hall and the front steps well enough. The coachman helped him up into the coach, and they drove away.

THE TOWNHOUSE of Dr. Steward was located in a block of nearly identical white-brick townhouses in a quiet neighborhood. Harland stepped down from the cab and paid the driver. The front door opened almost as soon as he'd knocked and a rather severe looking butler admitted him.

"Good morning," Harland said, "I believe Dr. Steward is expecting me. I'm Mr. Wallace."

"Yes, sir. Right this way, please."

The butler took Harland's coat and hat. Then he led the way to a side door and opened it, addressing someone inside the room. "Mr. Wallace has arrived, sir."

"Show him in, please, Bradley."

The parlor was dark, with walnut wainscoting and crimson wallpaper with a patterned silk trim, and a carpet of red and green. The chairs were of the same color scheme—dark walnut wood, upholstered in crimson. Though it was still light outside, the heavy curtains had been drawn and the gas lamps lit. A blazing fire made it extremely warm in the room, no doubt for the comfort of the gentleman seated near it, whose legs were covered in a knit shawl despite the fire.

Dr. Steward was quite elderly, his body seeming shrunken and withered with age. At one time, he might have been an imposing figure. He had a high forehead, now largely devoid of hair, and a strong patrician nose. The gray eyes that regarded Harland seemed to be sizing him up with a keen intelligence.

Mr. Prescott was standing beside Steward's chair and said with a nod in his direction, "Mr. Wallace, permit me to introduce my employer, Dr. Mordecai Steward."

"I'm honored to meet you, Doctor."

"Mr. Wallace." The doctor made a slight gesture toward Prescott. "You may leave us, Luke. Please wait outside until I call for you."

An odd thing occurred when Prescott attempted to leave the room. The butler was still standing in the doorway, as if awaiting further instruction, and when Prescott approached, Bradley continued to look past him, as if he wasn't there. He made no move to step aside, and Prescott was forced to turn sideways and slide past to go out into the hall.

The doctor frowned slightly at this but merely told the butler, "Bradley, will you please bring tea for our guest."

"Of course, sir."

The butler left, closing the door behind him.

"Please have a seat, Mr. Wallace. You may take one of the chairs away from the fire, if you wish. I realize not everyone enjoys roasting as much as I do these days."

Harland took a chair and the doctor asked him, "So, what do you think of Mr. Prescott?"

Harland was so taken aback that he merely blinked at the man for a moment. "I'm sorry?"

"Forgive me for being blunt," the doctor said, "but I dislike idle chitchat. I sent Luke to you so that you might observe him and see his condition."

"Observe… his condition?" Harland had to force himself not to fidget with the hem of his waistcoat. "I'm sorry, Dr. Steward, but perhaps there's been some sort of mistake. I'm not a doctor. I have no idea how to evaluate Mr. Prescott's medical state."

"I don't expect you to know anything about medicine, Mr. Wallace. I mean, how does he *appear* to you? Does he seem like a normal man?"

"I'm afraid I don't know how to answer that question."

Fortunately, they were interrupted by the return of the butler and a chambermaid with their tea. But it was a short diversion. After Bradley had poured for each of them, and then departed, Dr. Steward said, "When I was very young, my father took me to see a friend who had assembled a fascinating collection of automata—toys that moved under their own power. There were animals and people, some very elaborate. I absolutely fell in love with them."

"I felt the same way, the first time I saw a very elaborate German clock," Harland volunteered.

Dr. Steward nodded. "Quite. But you see, I was disappointed by their imperfections. They moved so stiffly. So I began to design my own. I made it my life's work, in fact, along with medicine."

"That's fascinating," Harland said, though he didn't really think so. But he felt one must indulge the elderly in their ramblings.

"My early experiments were crude, of course, but I soon surpassed the toys I'd been so taken with. As a schoolboy, I built a small dog that appeared quite lifelike. It ran about the house, navigating by means of lenses in the eyes, focused upon selenium wafers—are you familiar with the work of Charles Fitts, Mr. Wallace?"

"I'm afraid not."

"Well, I shan't bore you with all of the details of my experiments and inventions over the years. They made it necessary for me to acquire a considerable amount of knowledge in a wide variety of studies— electricity, hydraulics, pneumatics, physics, and of course mathematics...."

"Of course."

Dr. Steward leaned forward and with excruciating slowness lifted his teacup to his lips. His hand shook so much that Harland worried he might spill the hot liquid in his lap. But he managed to take a sip and lower the cup back onto its saucer without mishap. "All of this leads to my purpose in bringing you here."

"I had assumed," Harland said, "that you had a watch in need of repair. But now I suspect it may have something to do with one of your inventions."

"Quite so. As you've no doubt observed, my hands are no longer as steady as they were. My last attempt at repair work was a dismal failure. I merely damaged the mechanism further in my fumblings. So I began this lengthy search to find someone skilled in working with minute mechanical parts—a man at the top of his profession, and with an honest and discreet reputation. For reasons which will become clear to you, I do not wish this... invention... to be gossiped about. You must give me your word, Mr. Wallace, that you will discuss it with no one."

Harland felt very uneasy making such a promise when had no idea what he was promising to keep secret. What could possibly warrant such a pledge? A toy dog? Some other innovative automaton? Was Dr. Steward afraid someone would lay claim to his invention? But surely he would have patented anything he felt it necessary to protect.

Still, Harland's curiosity was piqued. He could hardly leave after all this buildup without seeing the invention. "I give you my word, Dr. Steward."

"Excellent!" The doctor picked up a small handbell from the stand beside his chair and rang it. The door opened and Prescott entered. "Luke, would you be so good as to show Mr. Wallace your left hand?"

"Of course, sir."

Harland felt immensely uncomfortable as Prescott stepped toward him, removing his glove at the same time. If the man was injured or possessed some deformity, there would be little reason for Harland to look at it. He was generally squeamish about such things. It took all his willpower to keep his outward appearance calm as the hand was brought close for his inspection.

What he saw was more horrifying than he could have imagined. Underneath torn flesh, there lay not muscle and ligament, but what appeared to be metal rods. When the ring finger flexed slightly, one of the rods seemed to contract, and Harland realized it was actually sliding into a slightly larger metal tube, while behind it, a complex assortment of incredibly tiny, interlocking brass gears whirled about for a moment. But there was clearly something wrong, for an ugly clicking sound came from the mechanism, faint enough to have been muffled by the glove, and the gears rocked as if jolted. The finger stopped flexing, as if it were unable to move any farther.

Speechless, Harland lifted his gaze to Prescott's face. It must have been the cold chill of fear creeping into his brain that distorted his vision, for as his eyes beheld the man's face, Harland imagined he saw the cold, inhuman mask of a life-size doll—porcelain or painted wax—just before he fainted.

HARLAND AWOKE to find himself lying on a sofa in a different drawing room than the one he'd had his conversation with Dr. Steward in, but there was little doubt it was in the same house. The Morris-style wallpaper wasn't identical, but it was very similar. And the color scheme was still crimson and dark walnut. Again the curtains were drawn and the gas lamps were lit, but the fireplace was cold.

There was a damp cloth folded neatly upon his forehead, and Harland lifted a hand to remove it before tentatively sitting up.

"Mr. Wallace?" a voice said—that of Mr. Prescott. Harland was reluctant to look in the direction of the voice, in case the… hallucination… he'd had might turn out to be real after all. But he forced himself to turn his head.

Prescott sat as far away from him as the room permitted, in a chair by the door. He was sitting rather stiffly, his gloved hands in his lap. His face… well, from this distance, in the dim light of the gas lamps, his face appeared normal again. Quite handsome, in fact.

"Bradley and Dr. Steward's valet carried you in here," he said. "The doctor felt that you would be better off in a cooler room. I would not have felt it wise for me to... be the first thing you set eyes on when you woke. But Dr. Steward ordered me to come check on you."

Harland attempted to laugh it off. "That's quite all right. I don't know what came over me."

"One of the maids was tending you until I entered. I'm afraid none of the staff will remain alone in a room with me."

Harland had been about to place the cloth in the small bowl of water he saw on the table near the sofa, but this made him hesitate, the cloth momentarily forgotten. Truth be told, *he* would prefer not to be alone with Mr. Prescott. But he told himself he was being cruel. What he'd seen a short time earlier.... Dr. Steward's invention was no more than a mechanical hand, similar to those sometimes worn by men who'd suffered amputations in battle or other circumstances. Far more sophisticated than any Harland had ever seen, of course. But for people to avoid Prescott's presence due to his affliction was terribly unfair, and Harland was ashamed of himself for fainting. "Please forgive me," he said awkwardly. "It was... very warm in the drawing room. I feel like a complete fool."

Prescott regarded him silently for a long time. Then he stood, slowly and stiffly, leaning heavily upon his cane. "I shall tell Dr. Steward you've recovered. Alas, his health requires that he be kept warm...."

"I understand," Harland said. "Please permit me to join you. I feel fully recovered."

He followed Prescott across the hall to the doctor's drawing room. Once again, he felt the oppressive warmth of the fire as they entered, but he was certain he could endure it. The fire hadn't been the cause of his distress.

"Ah, Mr. Wallace!" the doctor said happily upon his return. "How are you feeling?"

"Quite well, thank you. Though frightfully embarrassed."

"Not at all."

Harland attempted to put on a professional demeanor, clapping his hands together, as if he couldn't wait to begin. "Now, then. Am I correct in assuming you'd like to engage my services in repairing Mr. Prescott's damaged hand?"

"That and more," Dr. Steward replied. "But perhaps we've all had enough excitement for the present. Might I suggest we go into the details tomorrow morning?"

Harland wanted to protest that he was completely recovered, but then it occurred to him that his host might be tiring. "Certainly, Doctor. Tomorrow would be fine."

He took his leave and, Bradley being oddly absent, Prescott escorted him to the door. The man was unable to assist Harland with his coat, but it wasn't difficult for Harland to manage on his own. As he retrieved his hat, Prescott surprised him by putting a gloved hand on his arm. Almost immediately, he withdrew it, as if realizing Harland might be bothered by the touch. Harland smiled at him in an attempt to undo some of the embarrassment he must have caused by his reaction earlier.

"Please come back, Mr. Wallace," Prescott said earnestly. "I beg you. The… situation is becoming more urgent every day."

Though his handsome face was still oddly impassive, he sounded distressed, and his startling blue eyes were pleading. Harland could not help but be moved. He told himself that what he felt was merely compassion. If the doctor had created a functional prosthesis to replace the hand Prescott lost, it would be agony to watch it fall into disrepair as its creator grew too decrepit to maintain it. What Christian man could turn his back on someone in this predicament if he had the power to help?

But too, Harland was disturbed by a resurgence of the old stirrings he'd felt in his youth—feelings he'd hoped he'd left behind in boys' school. As much as Prescott disturbed him, he also intrigued him in a way that was perhaps better left unexplored. It was, at best, inappropriate to dwell upon the sensual curve of another man's mouth. Harland forced the thought from his mind.

He smiled and gave Prescott a cheerful nod. "Rest assured, Mr. Prescott. With some guidance from the good doctor, I'm confident I can make the repairs. I will return tomorrow with the necessary tools for the job."

HARLAND DID return the next morning, his leather tool case in hand. If anything, Bradley seemed even more dour than he'd been the day before as he led the way into the same drawing room, where Dr. Stewart and Mr. Prescott were conferring about some matter. But Harland quickly forgot about the servant as the doctor greeted him.

"Mr. Wallace! You've returned!"

Harland nodded, holding his tool case in his gloved hands. "As promised, Doctor."

"Excellent. Please have a seat. Shall I ring for tea?" The butler had departed without a word.

Harland settled into a chair but shook his head. "Please don't trouble yourself on my behalf," he said. "I'm most anxious to learn more about the mechanism in Mr. Prescott's prosthesis."

Steward and Prescott exchanged a look that Harland couldn't interpret, but then the doctor smiled and said, "Luke, would you please open the curtains so Mr. Wallace can have better light?"

While Prescott was attending to that, Harland made a gesture as if to lay his tools upon the inlaid top of the coffee table. "May I?"

"Of course."

The leather of the case, when opened like a book, provided protection for the table so that none of the metal files or calipers would scratch it. Harland withdrew a monocle from its protective silk cloth and placed it in his right eye. "Would you mind sitting here, Mr. Prescott?" he said, waving a hand at the chair beside him, which would allow for the easiest access and the best light.

Prescott perched on the edge of chair, looking very stiff and formal. He removed the glove from his left hand and extended it.

For the first time, Harland took the hand in his own without gloves. The "skin" on the hand was disturbingly cool to the touch and felt a bit too much like human skin for his comfort. The effect was that the hand felt lifeless. When he turned it over to examine the palm, he saw that, although the major lines of the hand were present, giving it the appearance of a human hand at a glance, the tips of the fingers had strangely regular "fingerprints." They were formed of small concentric ridges, similar to the fingerprints on Harland's hand, but with no variation from finger to finger.

"Unfortunately," Steward said, "there have been some areas in which I simply had to rely upon the expertise of others. The skin was one such area. It was designed for me many years ago by a dear friend who worked with chemicals, Parkesine, and rubber. It consists of layers of silk, in different weaves, each saturated in some sort of artificial resin."

"It's very soft for a resin," Harland commented, prodding the palm of the hand with his fingers. Even Parkesine, he knew, was rather hard. This material flexed and bounced back into shape, just as a flesh and blood hand would do, and his poking caused the fingers to flex in a disturbingly realistic fashion.

"I'm afraid I don't know the formula, and my friend is no longer with us."

"Can it be repaired?"

The doctor shook his head. "Alas, no. It will have to be stitched together. I do have a small supply of it in my workroom, but we must be very conservative with it."

Harland glanced up to find Prescott watching him intently. Once again, he was struck by the perfection in the man's features, as if he were a life-size china doll, and part of Harland wondered if it were possible that Prescott's face could be made of the same material as his hand. Fortunately, the thought did not produce the same embarrassing reaction it had the previous day, and Harland quickly put it out of his mind. He was being fanciful. Prescott merely had very attractive features, and it would not benefit anyone for Harland to dwell on them.

He turned the hand over again and peered closely at the mechanism underneath the skin.

"YOU HAVE exceeded my expectations, sir!" Steward exclaimed, obviously delighted, as Prescott flexed the mechanical hand, testing the range of motion of each finger.

It had been an exhausting couple of hours. The mechanism had proven to be ingenious and quite the most complex thing Harland had ever worked with. Though the doctor had offered guidance, much of it had been a journey of exploration, delving into the intricacies of the gears and springs and tiny pneumatics. It had been indescribably beautiful. Harland was awed by Steward's genius. But his brain felt like a bread pudding—complete with brandy butter—and he wanted little at the moment but to sleep. "Thank you, Doctor. I feel honored to have had the opportunity."

Prescott looked at him with a small, almost shy smile, his eyes lit up with delight. "Oh, Mr. Wallace…!" He seemed at a loss for words, but the childlike joy in his expression forced Harland to look away or risk blushing.

"A job well done," Steward said. "But it is my hope, Mr. Wallace, that you will continue to assist us."

"Certainly. If the prosthesis breaks again—"

Steward waved a hand dismissively. "You misunderstand me. Your services in the continued maintenance of Luke's hand would be much appreciated. But surely you've noticed that he has difficulty walking?"

Harland glanced at Prescott, uncomfortable discussing his difficulties so openly in front of the man. "Forgive me, Mr. Prescott. I merely assumed an injury…."

"I'm afraid… both of my legs are mechanical, Mr. Wallace." He sounded apologetic, as if he were sorry to embarrass Harland with these intimate details. It disturbed Harland that he found this endearing.

"Oh." Harland looked away and busied himself packing up his tools. "Of course, I would be happy to help in any way that I can…."

"Perhaps later in the week?" the doctor persisted.

Harland did have a business to attend to. He couldn't spend all his time here, as fascinating as it was to poke into the doctor's inventions—and as much as part of him continued to be drawn to Prescott. But he did have time later in the week. "Would Friday morning be suitable?"

"That would do nicely," Steward replied happily.

Once more, Prescott escorted him to the door. And again, he stopped him with a hand on his forearm. This time, he appeared to be less afraid of rebuke, for he left it there a moment longer and pulled it away without hurry. "The doctor doesn't always think of these things…. His profession, of course. But I'm concerned that… in order for you to work on my hip…. Well, you understand…."

He gave Harland a pleading look, and then Harland *did* understand. In order for him to work on Prescott's hip, Prescott would have to remove his trousers. Depending upon where the damage was, things might get quite intimate. The thought made Harland blush a bit, and he desperately hoped it wasn't visible in the dim light of the hall.

"Of course, Mr. Prescott," he said. "It can't be helped. But we're all professionals." At least, he and the doctor were. And despite the fact that Harland had no medical expertise, Prescott was, in an odd sense, still his patient.

Prescott looked as though he had more to add, but after struggling with it for a bit, he merely smiled gratefully. "Thank you for understanding, Mr. Wallace. I look forward to seeing you."

FRIDAY WAS a miserable day, gray and raining. If Harland hadn't already given his word, he never would have gone visiting in this weather. Even traveling by coach, he arrived wet, dripping water from his coat and hat in Dr. Steward's entryway. Bradley seemed even more disapproving than usual as he took Harland's wet things.

"I'm sorry to say that Dr. Steward is under the weather this morning," the butler said.

"Should I come back another day, then?"

"The doctor has asked that you be taken to the workroom, so you may attend to your work there." Harland noticed that neither Prescott nor the nature of Harland's work were mentioned. Was the butler uninformed? Or was this another manifestation of the aversion the staff appeared to have toward Prescott?

Harland followed Bradley down the hall to a room he hadn't seen before. The butler opened the door and stepped back into the hall, telling him, "Here you are, sir. I shall send the maid with tea shortly. If you require anything else, please ring."

And then he left, as if he wished to be away from the room as quickly as possible. Harland entered to find Prescott sitting as he always did, perched on the edge of his chair in an almost feminine posture, his hands in his lap. He was without a coat today, though he wore a paisley waistcoat in hunter green over his shirt, and he had dispensed with his gloves. The injured "skin" on his left hand had still, to Harland's knowledge, not been repaired, but it was now discreetly covered by a bandage.

"Good morning, Mr. Prescott," Harland said, closing the door behind him. He noted that the room had a table off to one side, large enough to accommodate a man lying down. It was upholstered in leather, with a padded headrest and a ridge at the other end. Above the table, four Welsbach mantle lamps adorned the wall, hopefully providing enough light for Harland to work by. Beside the table was a workbench with various tools, and vise grips to hold components steady.

Prescott stood and came forward to greet him, walking with the aid of his cane. "Mr. Wallace. I apologize that the doctor cannot join us this morning. It was his hope that what you learned on Wednesday might enable you to work without his assistance."

"I shall do my best." He extended his hand to Prescott and was surprised at the feel of the man's right hand. It seemed cool, not unlike the artificial left hand. But Harland released it after their handshake and suppressed the impulse to examine it more closely. "Before we begin"— and before they were both subjected to what promised to be a very awkward and distracting situation—"perhaps you could describe the injury to me."

"It occurred when I fell on the front steps last December," Prescott said. "There was no visible damage, but clearly something is damaged inside the mechanism."

"Very well." Harland fished around for something else to forestall the inevitable—something he realized he was dreading, not merely for the embarrassment it might cause him and Prescott, but for the stirrings in his groin that grew stronger every time he thought of Prescott disrobing. Of course, the man might be... damaged. That seemed likely, in fact. The injury that cost Prescott two legs—and a hand—must have been quite horrid. The transitions between flesh and prosthetics might not be pleasant to look upon. Harland would have to be very careful how he reacted, in order to spare Prescott further embarrassment.

They were distracted by a soft knock on the door and a woman's voice saying, "Your tea, sir."

Harland bade her come in, but there was no response. Puzzled, he went to the door and opened it to discover that a tray containing a teapot and a single cup and saucer—clearly Prescott had not been taken into account—and a small plate of cucumber sandwiches had been left on the hall carpet. "What the deuce...?"

"I'm truly sorry," Prescott said as Harland carried the tray inside and set it upon a marble side table. "The staff will not enter a room with me in it unless the doctor is present."

Harland was appalled that the mild-mannered Prescott had to endure such indignities in his own household. Certainly he had no intention of drinking tea while Prescott went without. He returned to the door and closed it. The key was in the lock, so he turned it. "Perhaps we should simply get down to business."

"Of course."

Harland felt like a lecher, watching Prescott undo the buttons of his trousers and drop them. He clearly had difficulty bending at the knees, so Harland felt compelled to remove his shoes for him and help him step out of the trousers, rather than force Prescott to struggle with them. That left him in his socks and drawers from the waist down. There was little reason to remove his socks, but his cotton drawers extended down to his ankles and clearly would be in the way. Prescott unbuttoned them and let them fall.

His shirt and waistcoat hung low enough to cover his manhood, but Harland was nonetheless embarrassed to be crouching in front of him, helping Prescott step out of the undergarment. It was incredibly clean, as if it had only recently been removed from the laundry. Though it was vulgar to even think about, it did seem odd to him that there were no stains or discolorations on the fabric.

When he stood, Prescott was watching him with his characteristic impassive expression, but the corners of his mouth quirked up in a shy smile.

"Do you…. Will you need assistance getting up on the table?" Harland asked.

"No. The doctor would never have been able to lift me onto it—not in recent years. The table tilts."

And so it did. Harland found a lever that caused the end with the ridge to drop nearly to floor level. This enabled Prescott to step onto the ridge and lean back against the table. He handed Harland his cane. When Harland tilted the table back into a horizontal position, his "patient" was lying full-length upon it. "Clever," he said with a smile.

Then he noticed the seams, and his smile faltered. As with his hand, Prescott's leg prostheses were extremely lifelike. At a casual glance, they appeared no different than living human legs, albeit completely devoid of leg hair. However, there were several barely detectable seams in the artificial skin. It made sense, of course. It would have been impossible to effect repairs if the skin was one single sheath covering the entire leg. But it was unsettling, all the same. Harland would have to peel the skin away in order to get at the underlying mechanisms, and the thought made him squeamish.

"Where do you think the problem is located?" he asked.

"My right hip."

"Roll over onto your left side, please," Harland told Prescott. "Facing me."

The man did as Harland asked, and of course it was impossible for his... anatomy... to remain in place when he did so. It wasn't unusually large, but it still flopped obscenely against the back of Harland's hand where it rested at the edge of the table, causing him to jerk back involuntarily.

"I'm sorry," Prescott said, adjusting his shirt to cover himself.

"That's quite all right. I was... startled."

There was nothing Harland could do about the fact that he would have to touch Prescott's hip, however. He placed his hand on it and was surprised to find it warm. For a moment, he wondered if he were touching actual flesh—Prescott's body had to begin somewhere—but no. There was a seam just an inch above where his hand lay. Unable to stop himself, Harland slid his hand downward over the hip and onto the leg. He noticed that it grew cooler as he descended. He slid his hand back to the seam and traced it with a finger, until he encountered hair toward the front of Prescott's body—pubic hair. With a start, Harland yanked his hand away again.

"The seam follows my inguinal ligament," Prescott said.

"Your what?"

"That's what the doctor calls it. The crease between my stomach and my pelvis."

"Ah. Yes. I see that." What was disturbing Harland more than the touch of pubic hair was the involuntary swelling it had caused in his own trousers. He'd never thought of himself as... that type of man. It was true that he'd avoided women, preferring to live as a bachelor. But that didn't necessarily make him a mandrake, did it?

He had no choice but to return to his examination of the seam and hope he could prevent himself from becoming fully aroused. It would be impossible to hide that in the trousers he was wearing. But it wasn't going to be easy. As he followed the seam around to the back, he saw that it cut down alongside Prescott's buttocks and under them, following the crease there. Part of him was tempted to ask Prescott what the doctor's name for *that* crease was, but he thought better of it. The mere thought of being that close to Prescott's arse was making it difficult for him to breathe, and he felt his groin stiffening further.

"What's the best way to open the seam without damaging it?" he asked, attempting to focus on his task. His voice sounded ragged with arousal to his ears, and he prayed that Prescott didn't notice.

"It can be rolled down."

He did so, wincing when a slight tug with his fingers popped the seam open, exposing a dark gray substance underneath. Prescott apparently felt nothing, because he lay calmly on the table, his head resting on the headrest. He would be unable to see much in that position, but his blue eyes watched Harland with interest, as if gauging his ability to do the job.

Harland continued to roll the artificial skin down over the thigh, accidentally brushing his fingers against Prescott's scrotum in the process. A faint intake of breath made it apparent that Prescott had noticed, but both men pretended nothing had happened. When the skin was down to Prescott's knee, Harland realized that the gray material underneath was some kind of rubber, molded into pieces that resembled muscles. They were easily removed, and the gears and hydraulics they'd been protecting were indeed very similar to those in Prescott's hand. Harland felt reassured.

He also felt relieved that he could concentrate on something other than those tantalizing brushes against Prescott's anatomy.

It took longer without the doctor's guidance, but after what must have been hours of experimenting—asking Prescott to flex his leg and knee and foot, while observing the behavior of the mechanisms—Harland was finally able to determine what the primary cause of the problem was. One of the hydraulic pistons had a bent rod. Nothing more. Yet this had nearly crippled poor Prescott for months.

When he was certain he wouldn't be causing irreparable damage, Harland removed the piston and asked Prescott, "Are there replacement parts available?"

"I believe so," Prescott replied, "but I'm not certain where the doctor keeps them."

Waking Dr. Steward was probably out for the moment, so Harland set about repairing the piston, if he could. He anchored it in one of the vise grips and, using a pair of pliers, managed to bend the rod until it was straight again and slid in and out of its cylinder smoothly. Then he replaced it, put all the rubber padding back in place, and unrolled the artificial skin to cover everything up again. As he smoothed out the seam, he couldn't help but notice that Prescott's member was swelling as much as his own.

He finished quickly and turned away, embarrassment causing his neck and cheeks to flush. "Why don't we see if that does it? I'll help you down."

He didn't need to tilt the table again. Prescott sat up and scooted forward until he dropped off onto his feet. Then the man took a brief walk around the room, still naked from the waist down. It was somewhat improper, but since he would simply have to remove the trousers again and climb back onto the table if something was still malfunctioning, there was little sense putting them back on for the moment. His shirt hung low enough to cover him, but there was some obvious tenting in the front. Harland's manhood was likewise misbehaving, and Prescott had to have been aware of it. But they both pretended not to notice.

The leg repair appeared to be a complete success. Prescott walked a bit stiffly, but he assured Harland that he'd always walked that way, even when his legs had been at their peak performance. He positively beamed at the Harland as he moved around the room. "Thank you, Mr. Wallace!" he exclaimed. "You have no idea."

Harland found his childlike giddiness endearing, but when Prescott executed a small jump and caused his shirttails to flap up and reveal more than was proper, Harland hurriedly retrieved the man's trousers and undergarments.

"Let me help you dress," he said, wishing for a glass of water. His mouth had suddenly gone dry.

Prescott needed little help with his clothes. He perched on the edge of one of the chairs in order to slip his underwear over his stocking feet and pull them up past his knees. Then he did the same with his trousers. Inching them up his thighs and over his buttocks—one garment at a time—by rocking back and forth was a more arduous process, and Harland felt he was witnessing something private that he really shouldn't be watching. But Prescott seemed unselfconscious. When he had his trousers up at last, he stood and accepted Harland's assistance fastening his suspenders. He smiled at Harland, looking at him intently with eyes full of emotion. "Mr. Wallace… may I count on you, in the future?"

Harland shook his hand and smiled back at him, meeting Prescott's eyes as long as he dared. "You may, Mr. Prescott."

"Thank you."

Harland was exhausted, so he took his leave. Out in the hall, he encountered the butler, to his annoyance. His few encounters with Bradley had given him a dislike of the manservant. He allowed Bradley to retrieve his hat and coat, however, and responded politely to Bradley's inquiry into whether he'd had a pleasant afternoon. To his surprise, the butler said, "It's come to my attention, sir, that the maid who brought you tea left it on the carpet outside the door."

Harland felt uncomfortable responding, but really he had little reason to cover for the woman. Her behavior had been appalling. "I'm afraid that's correct."

"I do apologize, sir. She has been reprimanded."

"I see," Harland said noncommittally.

"Unfortunately, some of the staff have a rather irrational fear of the… invention."

Harland took his hat from Bradley and hesitated a moment. He knew he had no right to discipline another man's household staff, but he was unable to stop himself from saying, "The *invention*, Bradley? Are you referring to the prosthetics Dr. Steward constructed for Mr. Prescott?"

"Somewhat, sir…." Bradley appeared to be holding something back.

"Mr. Prescott is to be pitied for his infirmity, Bradley—not feared."

"'Mr. Prescott,' sir?" Bradley blinked at him, as if he couldn't comprehend. "I was led to believe that sir examined it."

"*It?*" Harland was extremely close to losing his temper.

"Forgive me, sir," Bradley said. "But surely sir has noticed that this 'Mr. Prescott' is a machine?"

"Mr. Prescott has prostheses, Bradley, but it's absurd to call him a 'machine'! He is still quite human."

"Ah. I believe I see where the miscommunication lies. I'm afraid, sir, that no part of the… I believe Dr. Steward prefers to call it an 'automaton'… is human."

IT WAS impossible. Harland had been attempting to dismiss Bradley's ridiculous statement on the coach ride from South Kensington to Chelsea. But every time he'd convinced himself that it was nonsense, odd things came to mind—the fact that Harland had been unable to discern the difference between the artificial "skin" below the seam at Prescott's hip and the supposedly real skin above it, the disturbing appearance of Prescott's face, as if it were a mask....

Prescott's face wasn't completely immobile, of course. It moved around the mouth and eyes. The man's eyebrows were part of what made his eyes so expressive. And Harland had spent little time examining the skin on Prescott's hip, buttocks, and groin, because he'd found it too arousing to do so.

That brought up other things Harland found disturbing. He disliked thinking of himself as a mandrake. The very word disgusted him. But even the memory of trailing his fingers through the hair at Prescott's groin was causing a stirring in his loins. Then again, wasn't Prescott's obvious reaction to Harland's touch proof that he was a man? Never mind what it might say about his inclinations. Surely a machine could not....

And even if it were possible for a machine to appear human on the surface, how could it talk and appear to think, as Prescott did? The very idea was absurd!

It was all making Harland feel ill. At dinner that evening, he found himself without an appetite and ate so little that he had to feign a stomach ailment to avoid insulting the cook. It wasn't far from the truth. He retired early—with a glass of hot barley water the cook foisted upon him—hoping sleep would soothe his troubled mind, but it eluded him. The image and feel of Prescott's smooth, sensuous buttocks plagued him, until he was finally forced to take himself in hand. Afterward, he was disgusted—both by the thought of reacting this passionately to another man, and by the possibility that he was reacting not just to a man, but to a *simulacrum* of a man.

Spent, Harland was able to at last drift off to sleep, but his rest was disturbed by confused nightmares, none of which he could remember the next morning. He desperately wanted to question Dr. Steward. Had the man deceived him about Prescott's... nature? Or had Bradley been passing along a bit of malicious gossip? Thinking back over the conversations he'd had with the doctor, Harland was unable to recall him ever referring to Prescott as a "man." But of course one would assume that to be the case.

He waited as long as he could stand it before sending a messenger to the doctor's house, inquiring if he was recovered enough to receive visitors. The reply was no, but the doctor would inform him when he was. There was little Harland could do but wait. He could hardly discuss the matter with Mr. Prescott.

It was three days before he received a message inviting him to South Kensington. Little had changed in that time. Harland was still eating little, and his staff had begun to nag him about seeing a doctor—something which amused him, even in his distracted state of mind. He'd also been tormented by thoughts of Prescott and visions of him naked and aroused, causing Harland to masturbate more often than he'd done since he was an adolescent. He hadn't had a strict upbringing, so he felt less disgust about the physical deed than others might have, perhaps. But his thoughts during it were repugnant to him once he was spent. He wasn't certain if learning the truth about Prescott would lessen or increase his distress.

He sent a message to the doctor, specifying a time of arrival—after luncheon, of course, and well before afternoon tea—and requesting that Mr. Prescott not be present. He felt a twinge of guilt, as if he were betraying the man after they'd had a rather pleasant day together, but then, that was the issue. When he arrived and Bradley had shown him in, Harland was pleased to find the doctor had complied with his wishes. Prescott was absent.

"Your work on Friday was excellent, Mr. Wallace," Steward said congenially. He appeared even more frail than during their last conversation, and Harland hoped he wasn't taxing the man unduly. But his questions could not wait.

"Thank you, sir."

"The leg seems to be working perfectly. Luke was most pleased. Which reminds me—I've made certain he now knows where all the components I have on hand are located. It never occurred to me that he wouldn't know, after all these years. But I suppose he was used to waiting while I fetched them...."

Harland listened patiently while the old man rambled on. But as he was uncertain about his continued involvement in Prescott's... upkeep... he wasn't convinced any of this information mattered now. Eventually, when Steward seemed to be finished, Harland said, "I've come to ask you about Mr. Prescott."

"What about him?" the doctor asked. "Did he behave badly during your time with him?" It seemed an odd question to ask of an adult man. But then, Prescott appeared young enough to be Steward's son, or perhaps even his grandson.

"Not exactly. But you see... in order for me to adjust his leg, I had to peel down the artificial skin on it."

"Of course."

"There was a seam following the contours of his hip. I naturally assumed that this would separate the artificial skin from his real skin. Truthfully, I had expected to find straps of some sort...." He looked at the doctor hopefully, as if he might volunteer the information he was looking for, but Steward merely watched him curiously. "I don't wish to pry, but it seems like something I should know."

"What?"

Harland sighed. "How do Mr. Prescott's prostheses attach to his body, doctor?"

"I take it you didn't ask Luke to undress completely?"

"Of course not. It was hardly necessary for him to remove all his clothes to provide me with access to his hip and leg."

The doctor looked amused. "I suppose. But it would have answered your question."

"Perhaps, but it didn't seem appropriate at the time."

"Why don't I call Luke in here and have him undress for you?"

Good Lord! Harland felt himself turn scarlet. "No! Please. I see no reason to embarrass Mr. Prescott."

"I doubt Luke would be embarrassed. He's had to do that a great deal, as I've perfected his mechanisms over the years."

"I'm afraid *I* would be. Please remember that I am not a doctor."

Steward raised his eyebrows at him, as if he felt Harland was being unreasonable. "What you would have seen for yourself, had you asked him to undress, Mr. Wallace... is that Luke is flawless, apart from the seams you've observed."

"How is that possible?" Harland asked, a feeling of dread filling his chest and making it difficult to breathe. "The artificial skin is lifelike in appearance, but… it isn't *skin*. There must be places in which there are transitions from that to real skin.…"

"No, Mr. Wallace, you've observed for yourself that the skin on both sides of the seams is the same."

Harland was on the verge of panic. He realized he'd made a mistake in coming here. He no longer wanted his suspicions confirmed. He wanted the doctor to tell him this was all a miscommunication, that Prescott was as human as either of them. "Surely it cannot cover his *entire* body.…"

"It does."

Harland sat in silence for a very long time, and the doctor merely watched him without interrupting his swirling thoughts. At last, he asked, "Is there… any part of Mr. Prescott… that is flesh and blood, doctor?"

"No, Mr. Wallace," Steward replied calmly. "I tried to tell you this on your first visit, but there was all that fainting business. Luke is an automaton. The most sophisticated one ever built."

Harland felt like fainting again, but his stubborn brain wouldn't cooperate this time. It left him awake to deal with the horror of what he'd just been told. He stared blankly at the garish green-and-crimson carpet and said, "He isn't… alive.…"

"Not in a strictly biological sense. But I maintain that biological life is not the essential aspect of a man. What makes a man is *consciousness*—awareness of his surroundings—and the ability to *think* and *feel*."

Harland looked up at him slowly. "How can a machine do any of those things?"

"I confess I'm uncertain whether Luke is truly conscious. He exhibits behavior that suggests it. But feelings.… Those came first in my experiments. Feelings are, at their simplest, extrapolations of the pleasure and pain felt by the body, abstracted and applied to models we hold in our minds. Luke can 'feel' through myriad minute sensors placed throughout his body. They sense pain, pressure, temperature, balance.…" Harland had encountered small disks on the surface of the mechanisms in several locations. They appeared to correlate with metallic spots on the underside of the "skin," so he'd carefully worked around them. "I even gave him extra touch sensors in his sexual organs, to mimic the same functionality in the human body."

Harland must have looked shocked, because the doctor chuckled and shook his head. "No, Mr. Wallace, I have never used Luke in that manner. I did once pay a young woman to spend time with him—to test that particular functionality. He reported that it all seemed to work correctly, but I don't think he enjoyed it much. The woman's body was too alien to him. I believe he found her a bit repulsive."

Harland could no longer listen. His brain was screaming at him to get out of the house and run as far and as fast as he could to escape this madness. Fortunately, the doctor ended the conversation at that point.

"I'm very sorry," the old man said as he leaned forward stiffly to pick up the bell from the table and ring it twice. "I'm not currently up to long conversations. These few words have already tired me. Might we take up our discussion again in a day or two?"

As Bradley entered in response to the doctor's bell, Harland took his leave and slipped past the butler. He walked quickly to the door but stopped, his hand on the doorknob, when he heard Prescott say behind him, "Mr. Wallace? I wasn't aware you were visiting."

Harland stopped and turned around very slowly. Prescott was smiling and his eyes seemed lit up in delight. But Harland couldn't bring himself to say anything to him—to this artificial mockery of a man. Something in his eyes must have given him away, because the light in Prescott's eyes faded and he glanced away.

"I see," he said.

Bradley had closed the door to the parlor and they were alone. Despite himself, Harland felt his heart aching in response to the sadness and loneliness that came over Prescott's features. Involuntarily, he walked nearer, until they were standing eye to eye in the front hall. Then he cleared his throat and said quietly, "Mr. Prescott. Forgive me... but I should like to touch your face a moment."

Prescott looked back at him, his eyes full of resignation. Silently, he nodded his assent.

Harland removed his glove and hesitantly lifted his hand until his fingers brushed against Prescott's cheek. As he had feared, it was cold. The work he'd done on Prescott's leg and hand had made him familiar with the feel of the synthetic "skin" covering those appendages, and that was what he felt now.

Prescott's entire face was synthetic.

Harland slowly withdrew his hand as a cold chill crawled up his spine and made the hair on the back of his neck feel as if it were standing on end. He could not avoid looking into Prescott's eyes, seeing the anxiety there.

"Please," Prescott said. But he fell silent after that, as if he had no idea what to say next.

Without a word, Harland spun about and left the townhouse.

SEVERAL DAYS went by, during which Harland attended to work he'd put aside for far too long while caught up in Dr. Steward's… project. During this time, he had horrifying dreams in which he saw Prescott standing in his bedroom, gazing out the window. He approached the man from behind and called his name, but there was no response. At last, he reached out to touch Prescott's shoulder, and the man turned. But when he did, Harland saw that his face was nothing but a mass of brass gears and copper wires.

Or worse, he would dream that Prescott was lying on his bed, apparently naked, though his body was covered in a linen sheet. These dreams were always disturbingly erotic in nature, and Harland felt his breath quicken as he approached the bed. Prescott smiled up at him with his perfect, china doll face and lifted the sheet to welcome him. But what lay under the sheet wasn't a beautiful male body. It was a hideous array of tubes and pistons, sparking and belching steam.

Harland frequently awoke screaming from these nightmares.

He could not get Prescott out of his mind. No matter how much he told himself the man was nothing more than a machine, it was impossible to think of him that way. He often found Prescott's beautiful face coming to mind when his thoughts were idle, or the perfection of his "body," of his… "manhood." Harland felt he must surely be ill. A healthy man would never have these thoughts about another man, let alone a mockery of a man made from metal, rubber, and resins. In daylight, when his will was at its strongest, he banished his daydreams and concentrated on his work or forced himself to read a book. But at night, lying in bed and waiting for sleep to take him, he was powerless to keep his mind from turning to fantasies that shamed him in the light of morning.

When two weeks had passed since he'd last visited Dr. Steward's residence, a message was delivered to Harland's townhouse. It read:

My Dear Mr. Wallace,

I hope this letter finds you well. I have grown concerned that so much time has passed since our last meeting. I would very much like to invite you to discuss our business arrangement at your earliest convenience.

Sincerely,

Dr. Mordecai Steward

Harland was tempted to go. It was absurd how much he longed to see Prescott again, even knowing what he did now. But his mind revolted at the thought. His fascination with Prescott had become a sick addiction. The best thing for him would be to stay away and never see that abomination again.

He sent a reply with the messenger, telling Dr. Steward that he was uncertain when he would be available. But of course, that would not resolve the problem, and he was unsurprised when another letter came from the doctor that afternoon, asking Harland to please contact him as soon as his schedule would permit a visit.

A week later, another message arrived, apologizing for the doctor's impatience, but reminding Harland that his health was failing. Harland again put him off with vague excuses about his schedule. He had to wonder just how long he would keep up this game. Until the doctor tired of inquiring? Until the man succumbed to his illness? It made Harland uncomfortable to think part of him was hoping for that eventuality. The decent thing to do would be to tell the doctor plainly that he would no longer work with Prescott. Yet when he sat down to write a letter to this effect, Harland stopped halfway through and tore it up.

The matter was decided for him two days later. Steward's message boy arrived panting, apparently having run most of the way. The letter he carried stated:

Dear Mr. Wallace,

Please forgive me for pressing the matter, but the situation has become urgent. Luke has been injured, and I am simply not capable of handling the matter myself. I beg you to come at once.

Most Sincerely,

Dr. Mordecai Steward

It was absurd that the words "Luke has been injured" should evoke such a strong feeling of fear in him—fear for Prescott—but he found himself telling the boy he would come at once.

WHEN HE arrived at Steward's residence and Bradley took his coat, Harland could not escape the feeling that the butler was disappointed in him for responding to the doctor's summons. There was nothing overt in his manner or the few words he spoke to Harland, but something in his eyes....

Harland found the doctor in his sitting room, as usual. The old man seemed to have grown smaller since the last time they'd met, and when he spoke, it was barely above a whisper. "Mr. Wallace, thank you so much for coming."

Harland was still uncertain exactly why he *had* come, but he smiled politely and said, "Of course, Dr. Steward. I was sorry to hear the situation has grown so dire."

"Forgive me," Steward said, "but I am not up to conversation. Luke is waiting in the workshop. He can inform you of the details."

"Of course, Doctor."

Bradley told Steward, "The nurse will be in shortly, sir." Then he escorted Harland to the workshop and left him there with little more than a curt bow. "Sir."

Harland entered, part of him afraid to see for himself how serious Prescott's injury was, and another part of him frightened by the prospect of seeing Prescott at all. But Prescott was sitting upon the workbench with his shirt off, looking as beautiful and perfect as he always had, and Harland felt the knot in the pit of his stomach unraveling itself. Then he mentally chastised himself. *Why should I be relieved that he doesn't appear seriously injured? He—it—is merely a machine!*

It was difficult to remember that when Prescott smiled at him and said, "Mr. Wallace! I'm delighted to see you again."

"Mr. Prescott. I understand...." He balked at saying "you," as if that would grant the automaton some measure of humanity that wasn't warranted, but it was simply impossible to avoid addressing Prescott directly. "...you've been injured."

Prescott didn't get off the table, which caused Harland to wonder if he'd done something to his leg again. But Prescott held out his left hand and said, "I grabbed a hot poker."

Harland closed the door behind him and approached, holding his bag of horological tools. He set the bag upon the table and took Prescott's hand in his, disturbed that the feel of Prescott's cool synthetic skin still quickened his pulse. But the sight of Prescott's palm made him cringe. It wasn't blistered, as one would expect of human skin, nor reddened, but the skin had melted on either side of a horrible, blackened tear. There was a soft, gray rubbery pad underneath, like the thicker pads Harland had seen under the skin on Prescott's leg. Thankfully, that wasn't damaged, beyond a shallow imprint from the poker, and likewise the mechanisms in the hand were undamaged. But the skin was beyond repair.

"I'm afraid, Mr. Prescott—"

"Please," Prescott interrupted. "I would like it if you called me Luke."

Harland regarded him thoughtfully. Then he said, "How is it you can 'like' anything? I've seen how your physical mechanisms work. They are works of genius and immensely complex. I would have thought them impossible a few months ago. Yet I can see how they work and understand them to some degree. But to give the appearance of thought...."

The smile on Prescott's face faltered, and he gently pulled his hand away from Harland's grasp. He said nothing as he placed the hand in his lap and shifted his gaze to the Oriental carpet.

"The automatons Dr. Steward spoke of the last time we conversed," Harland went on. "I've seen something similar. One used a cylinder like the one in a music box to guide its movements and give the appearance of autonomy. But that's all it was—appearance. Like a magician's trick. The automaton could not in actuality *think*. Yet you are so much more sophisticated than that. I still cannot fathom how you mimic human speech and actions so perfectly."

Prescott continued to stare at the carpet as he responded, "The doctor told me once that my brain was composed of several thousand thin sheets of silk, hand-painted with gold circuits and embedded with silicon wafers so small that it would take a watchmaker to sort them all out."

"I should like to see it," Harland said.

A look of what could only be fear passed across Prescott's face as he raised his eyes to Harland's. "It's all sealed together with resin. The layers cannot be peeled apart without destroying them."

The look in his eyes cut through Harland like a knife. He was forced to place a reassuring hand on Prescott's wrist. "I shall let it alone, then."

Prescott's soft sigh of relief disturbed him. *Can he really feel? It's impossible!* Yet Harland was afraid to test his assumption.

"I suppose this... unique situation would make it acceptable for us to use first names," he said. "I will call you Luke, if you will call me Harland."

Luke smiled bashfully at that and glanced away. "Thank you, Harland."

"Luke." Harland returned the smile briefly, but then he frowned as he ran his thumb over the damaged skin of Luke's palm. "I don't know what I can do to repair this," he said. "The mechanism isn't damaged. Merely the skin."

"I can show you where the replacements are kept," Luke suggested.

"Very well."

He helped Luke off the table, seeing little point in lowering the table with the lever when it was a mere few inches. Even so, he hadn't anticipated how intimate it would feel to have Luke's hands upon his shoulders, his hands on Luke's hips, and his palms against Luke's naked skin. He knew it wasn't actually skin, of course, but he'd grown so used to the feel of it that his mind played a cruel trick on him and made it *feel* like naked skin under his hands. Far worse, his body responded to the touch in a highly inappropriate manner, and he prayed that Luke wouldn't notice. Perhaps he shouldn't care if an automaton observed him stiffening in his trousers, but he was nevertheless embarrassed and glad to break the contact when Luke's feet touched the floor.

Luke led him across the room to a tall mahogany wardrobe against the far wall—one of four, placed side by side. It was locked, so Luke drew a ring of keys out of his pocket and selected one, saying, "There are only two sets of keys for the wardrobes—mine and the doctor's. Perhaps we could have another set made for you."

When he opened the doors wide, Harland could see instantly why the contents of the wardrobe would be so closely guarded. It was full of body parts. Luke's body parts, to be more precise. Though just the skin—hands and feet laid out on display racks like empty gloves and stockings, two dress forms with sections of buttocks and male genitalia attached, and stacks of thin wooden drawers with labels such as "Upper Right Arm" and "Lower Left Leg." The genitalia made Harland blush, but he found the face far more disturbing. There was only one, suspended on the back wall of the wardrobe, attached to a form that preserved its shape. Two similar forms were on the wall beside it, made of wood with several small metal nubs on their surface, but they weren't covered in the artificial skin. The solitary face was identical to Luke's but for one grisly feature—the eye sockets were empty. It looked as if a surgeon had removed the skin and mounted it, and it filled Harland with horror.

"I feel a bit lightheaded," he said. There was a chair to one side of the wardrobe and he dropped into it, forcing himself to look elsewhere in the room, while he took slow breaths to calm himself.

Luke approached him, looking distressed. "Shall I fetch some water from the kitchen?"

Had he asked if he might ring for some water, Harland would have agreed. However, he realized Luke was unable to do that. None of the staff would respond to his summons. That thought forced Harland to rouse himself. He stood and said, "No, thank you. I'm fine."

He approached the wardrobe again, determined not to show further signs of distress. He avoided looking directly at the face but turned his attention to the hands. They did appear very much like gloves, although the synthetic skin was a bit thicker than leather. Only one pair remained, with an additional left hand. Harland wondered what happened to the other right hand skin.

"I damaged my hand with a pot of boiling water seven years ago," Luke observed, apparently sensing his curiosity. Then he added wistfully, "I must be very careful now."

Harland nodded, and then a thought occurred to him. "What about that gash you received on the back of your right hand?"

Luke held up the hand in question, so that Harland could see that it still sported a bandage on the back of it. "It doesn't seem worth using up the one I have left to replace it," he said.

"I see."

Harland lifted one of the left hand skins up gingerly and carried it over to the worktable, where the light was better. He set it off to one side and said to Luke, "Will you allow me to lift you back onto the table?"

"Of course."

It was disconcertingly like going in for an embrace. Luke was looking directly into his eyes with a serious expression as he placed his hands upon Harland's shoulders, and once more Harland felt as though he were holding a partially naked man as he placed his hands on Luke's waist and lifted him into position. The heaviness of his breath afterward wasn't entirely due to the strain.

Luke held out his left hand, and Harland saw the thin line of the seam between the hand and the forearm. He gently popped the seam open and separated it, folding the skin down as if he were removing a glove. He'd expected to be disturbed by the sight of the mechanical hand underneath, but he was not. In a way, it was very beautiful. Luke flexed the fingers slightly, and Harland watched the exquisitely smooth movement of the pistons and gears with fascination for a moment. Then he picked up the new molded hand skin and carefully stretched the wrist opening in order to slide it over the hand.

When it was done and the seam had sealed itself—the material along the seam adhered to itself somehow, without forming a permanent bond—the hand was nearly indistinguishable from a real human hand. Harland smoothed down the skin carefully, until he realized he'd been doing it for longer than necessary, and his touch was now more caressing than practical. He released Luke's hand and asked, "How does it feel?"

Luke flexed it. "Very good."

"How did you come to burn it?"

"I picked up a hot poker from the fireplace," Luke responded, as though the answer should be obvious.

It *was* obvious, but that wasn't quite what Harland had meant. "You didn't know it was hot?"

"I knew," Luke said. "That was the reason I picked it up."

"I don't understand."

"I picked up the poker to burn my hand."

Harland blinked at him in surprise. "Why on earth would you do that?"

"I hoped you would come if I was injured." There was no hint of guile in his voice or in his expression when he said this. If anything, he seemed delighted. "And you did."

It was true that Harland had needed something drastic to bring him back to this house, but he disliked being manipulated. And the smile on Luke's face angered him. "According to the doctor, these skins cannot be replaced, and what we see in that cabinet is the last of them. You cannot afford to deliberately destroy one. What were you thinking?"

"I needed to see you."

"There was no need to see me. You were uninjured!"

His harsh tone caused Luke's smile to fade. "Please don't be angry. The doctor has been so ill lately... and I've been so lonely...."

"Lonely!" The feeling of horror Harland had barely been keeping at bay welled up within him. "You can't be *lonely*! You can't feel anything! You're a *machine*!"

Luke stared at him open-mouthed for a long moment, and then he slowly crumpled, lowering his eyes and hunching over, his shoulders sagging. He placed his repaired hand in his lap and rubbed the back of it with the fingers of his other hand.

At last he said in a very small, quiet voice, "I'm sorry."

Harland began to say something—something about talking to the doctor about this when he was feeling better—when he noticed Luke's cheeks were wet. He was crying.

He can't cry! It seemed impossible. What use could there be for an automaton to cry? *Perhaps it's merely a mechanism for lubricating the eye, so the lids can close smoothly,* he told himself. And that seemed a likely explanation. But it didn't matter. The sight of Luke crying was immensely disturbing. To all appearances, Luke was in his midtwenties and too old to be openly crying in front of another man. But he'd never been to school and had the lovely experience of being publicly humiliated for doing so.

"Please," he said. "Don't do that."

"Don't do what?"

"Cry."

Luke attempted to wipe the tears off his cheeks, but that merely served to make him look more vulnerable. "I thought you liked me."

He's a machine! I can't have hurt his feelings!

But even as Harland cursed himself for being a fool, he reached out and gently brushed Luke's cheek with his index finger. "I'm sorry, Luke. I do like you. Please don't cry."

DESPITE THE fact that there was little reason for him to come to Steward's townhouse if Luke was in good repair, Harland had been unable to escape without promising to return twice weekly—every Tuesday and every Friday. It wasn't the doctor who'd exacted this promise, but Luke. No matter how often Harland reminded himself that Luke was an automaton, his mind persisted in the belief that he was… if not human, then at least conscious and feeling.

Worse, Harland could not quench his physical desire for Luke, even after seeing the complex arrangement of gears and pistons and circuitry that made up his body. Harland continued to have intensely erotic dreams about Luke, of lying with him naked on the Oriental carpet in the workroom. But the dreams frequently turned nightmarish, with Luke's body falling into pieces like a china doll just as Harland climaxed. He awoke to find himself spilling his seed into the bed linens, at once aroused and confused and terrified, his heart pounding in his chest.

Still, he found himself enjoying the visits. He had the opportunity to speak briefly with Dr. Steward on his next visit about his concerns that simply keeping Luke company, when there was nothing in need of repair, seemed an abuse of their business arrangement. However, Steward dismissed this.

"I will pay you for your time, of course, Mr. Wallace."

Harland suddenly felt very uncomfortable. "That is not my concern, doctor. Luke... the automaton doesn't require anything from me at present—"

"He requires companionship," the doctor stated flatly. "I'm afraid my failing health no longer allows me to spend much time with him."

"I confess I'm having a difficult time with the concept of... the automaton... requiring anything so... emotional."

Dr. Steward regarded him thoughtfully before lifting a glass of water with a shaking hand to take a sip. "Mr. Wallace, it would require days to describe the complex mechanisms underlying what motivates Luke—weeks. Suffice to say, he has the ability to feel pleasure and pain on a physical level, and he has the ability to model that in his mind. Once these physical sensations become abstracted to a certain degree, and associated with, say, another *person* in his mind, then they effectively become what you call 'emotions.' You do him—and me—a great disservice by insisting that he cannot feel lonely or need human companionship."

The problem, Harland knew, was not that he couldn't believe Luke had feelings, but that he was *afraid* to believe it. "Very well, Doctor. If you wish me to act as a companion, I will do so."

Dr. Steward smiled. "Excellent! You may of course wish to take the opportunity to familiarize yourself with the contents of the other wardrobes. They contain replacement parts for all of Luke's systems."

Being a companion to Luke was far from a hardship. He was a pleasure to talk to. The doctor had apparently spent many long evenings giving him a rudimentary education in a number of fields of study, as well as the social niceties. He had little interest in politics, and Harland was unable to engage his enthusiasm on that topic, but he enjoyed hearing about the year Harland had spent traveling across the Continent. Luke longed to see the world outside London, since he'd never been permitted to leave the townhouse except for the shortest of errands, usually accompanied by the doctor. These excursions had all but vanished now that Steward was ill.

Luke was also fascinated by mythology, and many of their afternoons together were passed with Harland regaling him with the adventures of Hercules or Icarus or Persephone. Harland brought in the Mercier translation of *Twenty Thousand Leagues Under the Sea*—his grasp of French was poor and Luke's appeared to be nonexistent—so he could read it aloud on some afternoons. Luke listened intently, fascinated by such things as oceans and sharks and giant squids. Verne's description of the *Nautilus* provided Harland with the opportunity to inform Luke on the history of submersibles, though he found that only mildly interesting. What interested him was exploration. Perhaps, Harland thought, when they finished this novel, they could move on to Verne's *Journey to the Center of the Earth*.

HARLAND HAD learned, over the course of these visits, that Luke's body—and mind, for that matter—was powered by rows of nickel-cadmium batteries stored in his arms and legs, as well as several locations in his torso. They required charging every night in order for Luke to function.

One morning, after Bradley had silently removed his coat and hat—the butler rarely spoke to him these days, unless Harland directly addressed him—Harland entered the workshop to find Luke sitting on the sofa... completely nude. Some mechanical monstrosity Harland had never noticed before was belching steam in the corner. Harland stood in the doorway in shock a moment, before he came to his senses and hurriedly closed the door behind him. He locked it for good measure.

Luke seemed to find his distress amusing, because he smiled broadly and said, "Good morning, Harland," as if nothing were amiss.

"Good morning," Harland replied. He took a few steps into the room. "Might I inquire as to why you're naked?"

"I'm sorry. Is it upsetting you?"

What it was doing to Harland was arousing him, and *that* he found upsetting. "You haven't answered my question."

"The cable that charges my right leg must have been loose last night," Luke said. "It was barely responsive when I awoke." Luke did not "sleep" as a human would, Harland knew. But when his systems were charging, his body was largely dormant. "I reconnected it, and it appears to be charging now, but it will take several hours."

There was a thick cable leading to the sofa from the steam-driven machine in the corner, which Harland surmised must be an electrical generator.

"Do you always remove your clothes when you charge?"

"Yes," Luke answered matter-of-factly. "It's easier to reach the connectors that way."

As Harland drew near, he could see that Luke's right leg had the skin rolled down slightly on the inner thigh, up near his groin. It would indeed be difficult to reach that spot with clothing on. His manhood was casually pushed aside to make room for the electrical connector, and Harland felt himself flush at the sight of it. He forced himself to look away.

"Shall we pick up where we left off?" he asked, holding up his copy of the Verne novel.

"Please."

He read for perhaps an hour, doing his best to keep his eyes focused on the pages of the novel and avoid staring at Luke's naked body. Despite the fact that the seams were now clearly visible, Harland was still enthralled by its perfection. The situation was made worse by the fact that both he and Luke were becoming aroused. While it was somewhat possible for him to disguise his own arousal by crossing his legs, he suspected Luke was nonetheless aware of it, and there was no hiding Luke's arousal. If the young man—Harland had abandoned the conceit of referring to him as "it" or "the automaton"—seemed unconcerned about it, but Harland found it far too distracting. He eventually gave up his attempts to read and closed the book.

"Is something wrong, Harland?"

"Luke... I understand that you don't feel embarrassment at being naked," Harland said awkwardly, "but even in front of a doctor or in a sporting club... one doesn't allow himself to...." If he hoped for Luke to fill in the obvious, he soon realized that wasn't going to happen. Luke hadn't the faintest idea what he was referring to. "It isn't considered proper for a man to be obviously aroused in front of another man," he finished.

Luke appeared to consider this. "Not even if we'd like to have coitus?"

Harland's eyebrows nearly crawled up into his hairline. *Is he propositioning me?* It was possible, considering Luke's lack of experience in these matters. Harland suddenly felt faint, and was glad that he was already seated. "That isn't something two men... would generally do together...."

"The doctor explained that to me," Luke said, "after my wretched experience with that woman." He screwed up his nose as if he smelled something unpleasant. "It felt somewhat pleasant in my genitals, but I didn't like the way she felt against my body and in my hands—too soft and... she didn't hold her shape well."

Harland found his description humorous, but Luke clearly did not, so he avoided smiling.

"I told the doctor that, if he wanted me to do it again, it would have to be with a man."

"I assume he ruled out that possibility."

To Harland's surprise, Luke shook his head. "He simply said it would be more difficult to arrange and perhaps a bit dangerous."

"One would think," Harland said, though he really had no idea. The thought of propositioning a man in a back alley somewhere and possibly being beaten or knifed for his trouble—or arrested—terrified him. "Is that all he told you about it?"

"He said it was something only a few men enjoyed doing with other men. But you...."

He seemed to think he'd said too much, and he allowed his last sentence to trail off. But Harland's heart was in his throat. Had Luke perceived something about him that even he was only vaguely aware of, that only haunted him in his dreams? "What about me, Luke?"

Luke stared hard at the carpet as he replied, "You become aroused when you touch me, and when I'm naked, you have difficulty looking away from my genitals."

Harland swallowed hard, finding his throat incredibly dry. He wished desperately for a glass of water, but that would require him to ring for a servant, and the last thing he wanted was for another person to enter the room at this moment. Perhaps he should leave, tell Luke he was being absurd, order him to never speak of it again. But Luke deserved a better response than that. "I suppose I do. I'm very sorry."

"If I'm likewise aroused by you," Luke said, "doesn't that mean we're attracted to each other?"

"I suppose so."

"Then why should you be sorry?"

Harland sighed and set the book down on the table beside him. "Society—other people—would not approve."

Luke leaned forward and gazed earnestly into Harland's eyes. "Harland... outside this door, everybody but the doctor hates me. I've overheard the servants talking about how I should be smashed into pieces and burned. What I do in this room... with you... won't affect that."

Harland felt nauseated by the thought of any harm coming to Luke. And perhaps that was what overrode his fears about what discovery could do to *him* and to the business he'd spent his life building. He glanced at the door, and then because he didn't trust his memory, he got up and walked over to make certain it was locked. It was impossible to hide his arousal while he did this, but there seemed little point.

He went back to stand in front of Luke and asked him, "What would you like us to do?"

Luke gave him a delighted smile, like a boy being offered a present. "May I see you without your clothes? I've never seen anyone, apart from myself in the mirror."

"You saw that woman," Harland pointed out, though he began to remove his tie. It would be difficult to get his clothes back in order without his manservant to assist him. He worried that he might leave the workshop looking obviously... disheveled... and give the servants more to gossip about. But it was evident that Luke dressed himself daily, since none of the servants would assist him. Harland would simply have to depend upon him.

"I saw very little," Luke said. "It had to be dark, so she wouldn't see my seams."

"I see."

Harland removed his tie and set it on the sofa. Then he removed his jacket and set it beside it. As he unbuttoned his vest, he asked, "Do you know how to... pleasure yourself?" He mimicked the motion in front of his crotch, which was tenting in a way he would have found highly embarrassing mere moments earlier.

"Yes. Would you like me to do that?"

It was making Harland uncomfortable to be the only one doing anything. "Does it feel good when you do it?"

"Of course."

"Then yes, I would like you to do that while I remove my clothing."

Luke laughed and began to stroke himself while he watched Harland undress. It was positively the most lewd and indecent act Harland had ever witnessed, and he found himself panting heavily with desire. At that moment, it didn't matter to him that he could see every seam in Luke's artificial body, and that an exact duplicate of Luke's beautiful face resided in a wardrobe not twenty feet from where Harland stood. It didn't matter that Luke was a machine. Harland wanted him as he had never wanted another human being.

After he'd removed his vest and lowered his suspenders to remove his shirt and undershirt, Harland sat down on the sofa to remove his shoes and socks. He'd never been aware of just how many layers of clothing he wore until he was in a hurry to remove them. At last he was able to stand again and slip both his trousers and his undergarments off in one motion. His manhood jutted out before him like the prow of a ship, bobbing as he stepped out of his things.

"May I touch it?" Luke asked.

"Of course." Harland stepped closer and allowed the young man to reach up and caress him. His touch was cool, as Harland had known it would be, but gentle and sensual enough to make Harland shudder. "You may do whatever you like," he offered.

Luke leaned forward and pressed his cheek to Harland's manhood, which throbbed at the touch. "I don't know what else to do," he said.

"Would you like me to teach you?" Harland was not overly experienced in such matters, but he had learned a thing or two from his fumblings in back rooms in boarding school.

Luke pulled away from him and looked up into his face. "Yes, please."

There was one thing in particular that Harland wanted—needed—to do. He placed a gentle hand under Luke's chin and leaned down until their mouths met in a kiss. Luke's lips were warmer than he'd expected, and moist, but he didn't move them under Harland's lips. At least, not at first. Harland persisted in sliding his lips along Luke's and nibbling at them gently, until Luke tentatively began to kiss back, mimicking his movements. When Harland pulled away, his entire body inflamed with by the touch of those lips, he asked breathlessly, "Did you like that? Or were you simply copying what I was doing?"

"Of course I copied you," Luke said. "But I liked it. Can we do it again?"

Harland obliged him. The cable charging Luke's leg was awkward, so he asked if it could be removed for a short time—Luke wouldn't have to use that leg for what he had planned. Once that was out of the way and the skin folded back into place on Luke's thigh, Harland climbed on top of him so that they could rub their bodies together and caress whatever was within reach of their hands and fingertips. Luke's body was warm under his, because it was more difficult for heat to dissipate from his core than from his extremities. But the technical explanation no longer mattered to Harland, and truthfully, it wasn't so different from the way heat was distributed in the human body. He simply chose to enjoy the sensation of it pressed against his flesh as they kissed.

When Luke moaned—a very human sound—Harland couldn't resist breaking the kiss and asking him in a breathless whisper, "Does this feel good to you? Is it what you'd hoped for?"

He was very much afraid Luke was merely mimicking his own behavior, cold and calculating like a machine. But Luke smiled up at him, and the expression he wore seemed blissful. "Very much. Nobody—not even that woman—has ever touched me all over my body, for no other purpose than to make me feel good. I don't ever want it to stop."

"I confess, my motivations aren't entirely selfless," Harland admitted. "I rather like touching your body."

Luke laughed. "Then please continue."

Harland obeyed, exploring every inch of Luke's body. He found himself doing things that would no doubt disturb him when he was less aroused—licking the seams that separated Luke's appendages from his torso, for instance. He had no wish to pop them open, but instead felt the need to show Luke that he accepted them and all they symbolized. He also found himself exploring Luke's fundament, inserting a finger to plumb its depths. He was disappointed to discover that it wasn't very deep—certainly not deep enough for the base act that had flashed through his mind as his finger slid inside—and Luke reported no particular sensation associated with the penetration.

The same could not be said of himself. Harland's explorations of Luke's body had put him in a position which placed his private parts within Luke's easy reach, and to his delight, Luke felt the need to explore as well. When he inserted his finger into Luke, the young man did the same to him. It hurt a bit, but the pleasure was far stronger, causing Harland to moan.

Luke laughed. "Yours is much deeper than mine," he said, sliding his finger in as far as he could manage.

Harland gasped, disgusted with himself at the same time he wished Luke could go deeper. "Yes, it's... very deep. Do you know what humans use it for?"

"Yes," Luke replied. "Elimination. The doctor gave me some anatomy lessons."

"It's rather disgusting."

"Not to me."

"I'm glad of that." It made Harland's wanton desire for more than Luke's finger a bit easier to accept, though he was still horribly embarrassed.

"The doctor told me about buggery," Luke continued, shocking Harland with the crude term. "When I told him I would rather be with a man than a woman, he told me that some men might want me to bugger them. Would you like me to bugger you?"

Harland was silent for a very long time, while Luke's finger continued to move gently inside him. He'd never done anything like that before, and though he could not deny that the sensations he was feeling now where nearly overwhelming his inhibitions, the disgust he felt whenever Luke used that filthy term was too strong. "I... I think not," he said reluctantly. "Perhaps some other time."

They returned to kissing, while Harland rubbed himself on Luke's body. It wasn't long before he was bucking his hips and panting heavily into Luke's mouth. Luke lifted his pelvis and writhed underneath him, moaning in response. They spent at the same moment, or at least Harland spent, spilling his fluid between their bodies while giving out one last strangled cry. Luke appeared to reach climax as well, gasping into Harland's mouth and clutching at his body for one endless moment, before collapsing into blissful exhaustion beneath him.

But when Harland lifted himself to examine the results of their lovemaking, he was surprised to discover that only his seed lay between them.

"Did you climax?" he asked.

"Yes," Luke said sleepily, and there was little doubt in Harland's mind that he was sated. Harland was a bit disappointed that he hadn't spilled the way a human man would, but that would have made little sense. Tears may have had a practical value for Luke, but semen clearly would not.

"Did you enjoy it?" Harland asked.

"More than anything I've ever done before."

Harland smiled. "I think I can say the same."

But in the dark recesses of his mind, the joy he'd felt in Luke's arms was tainted by feelings of disgust—that he could have done these things with a man, and furthermore with a "man" who was in fact not a man at all.

HARLAND AVOIDED going back to Steward's townhouse for the next week. It wasn't anything deliberate on his part—he was simply busy with other jobs. Although, if he were being honest, the thought of returning to the townhouse filled him with unease. He was perhaps easily distracted from his visits by things that might have been scheduled for another time. But he knew that, if he were to return, there would probably be a repeat of what had happened the last time. And the thought made him very uncomfortable.

He could no longer deny his desire for Luke. But outside the doors of the workshop, that desire seemed unhealthy and disturbing. He could not blame Luke. He had been created as a unique creature, and as such, he had no others like himself at which to direct his passions. But Harland was flesh and blood. There had to be something... twisted... diseased in his nature for him to be so strongly drawn to Luke.

It wasn't his intention to stay away forever. He knew that Luke needed repairs now and then, and Harland had promised to look after him. But perhaps if he kept his distance for a short time, his inflamed passion would subside and he would be better able to perform his duty.

A letter arrived from the townhouse on the ninth day, when he'd failed to show up for the second time. To Harland's surprise, it was not from the doctor, but from Luke. It read:

> *Dear Harland,*
>
> *Your continued absence is beginning to worry me. Are you ill, perhaps? Please let me know that you are well, and when I might expect to see you again.*
>
> *Your Dear Friend,*
>
> *Luke*

The desire to rush to Luke's side was nearly overwhelming. But it was the sheer strength of his need that frightened Harland enough to resist. While the messenger waited, he penned the following response:

> *Dear Luke,*
>
> *I am well, thank you, as I hope are you. Business has kept me away for a few days, but I shall see you soon. I promise. Please give my regards to the doctor.*
>
> *Your Friend,*
>
> *Harland*

It was distant but not utterly cold. Harland simply needed more time to sort himself out. He would have to go back eventually, perhaps even later in the week. He sent his reply and prayed that Luke would not be hurt by it.

Three days later, however, another visitor arrived at his door—a solicitor by the name of Mr. Dargan. It was with some trepidation that Harland invited the man into his sitting room.

"I'm afraid I'm the bearer of bad tidings, Mr. Wallace," Dargan said. He was a frail man, stooped and pale, with an agitated demeanor. He held an envelope in his hands that he continually rubbed and crinkled between his thumbs and forefingers.

"Would you like some tea, Mr. Dargan?" Harland offered.

"No, no thank you. I've come to tell you that an acquaintance of yours and a client of mine, Dr. Mordecai Steward, passed away a couple of days ago."

Harland felt the blood drain from his face. "Oh. That is… dreadful news, Mr. Dargan." He was thinking of Luke, however. Without the doctor, he would be lost. "Two days ago, did you say?"

"I'm afraid so."

That would have been just after Luke sent the letter. Why hadn't he sent another message with this news? Surely he hadn't felt that Harland had completely abandoned him.

"I understand you were a good friend of the doctor's," Dargan was saying.

"I… had a business arrangement with him."

Dargan looked surprised. "Oh? I was led to believe you were a close acquaintance." He opened the envelope with slow, quivering fingers. "He left you a considerable sum of money, as well as the entire contents of his townhouse." Dargan withdrew a stack of papers from the envelope, as well as another smaller envelope. This one was sealed. "The doctor met with me several weeks ago to draw up the paperwork. He also instructed me to give you this."

Dargan extended the envelope.

The envelope contained a key ring with several keys, and a short note:

My Dear Mr. Wallace,

The contents of this envelope may come as a shock to you, as I don't know whether I shall have time to discuss the matter of my will with you before my passing. In any event, please accept these keys to my townhouse and various cabinets contained within, of which you will know the purpose. I have made these arrangements in the hope that you will look after our mutual interests. Please, Mr. Wallace, I am depending upon you.

Yours,

Dr. Mordecai Steward

Harland fingered the key ring, while in the back of his mind a voice screamed, *What has become of Luke?* "Mr. Dargan," he asked, "do you know anything about a young man named Luke Prescott?"

Dargan shook his head. "No, sir. I cannot say I do."

"He wasn't mentioned in Dr. Steward's will?"

"No, sir."

"Has anyone been to the townhouse since the doctor passed away?"

Dargan looked uncomfortable being put on the spot like this. "I understand that the butler made arrangements for the… doctor to be… removed. Then the staff appears to have vacated the premises."

"The townhouse is empty?"

"It would seem so. I went to the house yesterday, but it was locked and nobody responded to the bell."

Harland felt a cold hand creeping up the back of his neck, and his breathing was becoming labored. "Didn't you have a key?"

"No, sir. Not without opening the envelope with which the doctor entrusted me."

HARLAND WENT to the townhouse alone, terrified of what he might find there. He opened the front door with one of the keys Mr. Dargan had given him and entered the front hall. The lighting was dim, so Harland couldn't see it at first. Then his eyes adjusted and he nearly screamed, but his breath caught in his throat.

Scraps of clothing, torn into shreds and tossed about the hall. In and of themselves, they were little enough, but Harland recognized them as Luke's. They appear to have been torn off and strewn about, but Luke wasn't there.

"Luke!"

There was no answer, so Harland checked the sitting room, where the fireplace now lay cold and the heavy curtains kept out nearly all light. Harland crossed to one of the windows, his shoes crunching on a small porcelain figurine as he walked across the carpet. When he drew back the curtain, the light revealed that the room had been ransacked. Most items of value had been stolen—by the staff, Harland suspected, since he hadn't yet discovered signs of a break-in. He satisfied himself that Luke wasn't lying behind one of the sofas and went back out into the hall.

In the shadows at the far end of the hall, outside the workshop door, he discovered Luke.

He lay there completely motionless, collapsed in front of the door in a heap, like a horribly mutilated corpse. He was naked, apart from the torn remnants of some of his clothing, and covered in scuff marks from the boots that had obviously been kicking him as he attempted to crawl to safety. He was covered with spittle. His member had been torn off, leaving a gaping hole out of which rubber tubes jutted. But the worst was his face. Some wretched monster had taken a hot iron to it, leaving one entire side melted and scorched, and one of his beautiful sky blue eyes shattered from the heat.

Harland wanted to be sick. His stomach heaved, but somehow he willed himself not to vomit. Instead, he knelt down beside the pathetic ruin of Luke Prescott and reached out to touch him gingerly on the shoulder. "Luke," he said in a voice that quaked with fear. "Please...."

There was no response.

Harland sat on the carpet beside him for a long while, stroking Luke's hair, and trying to rouse himself to begin the long arduous task that lay before him.

But he could not stop crying.

THE SAVAGES who'd beaten, humiliated, burned, and mutilated Luke hadn't found the key to the workshop. Harland would uncover it later in the remnants of Luke's trousers. They had apparently not considered it worth their time to break down the heavy wooden door. *Thank God*, Harland thought, as he unlocked the door with one of the keys on the ring Mr. Dargan had given him and found the room untouched. He carried Luke's still form into the room and laid him out on the worktable, and then removed the shreds of clothing that still clung to him—the waistband of his trousers, his tie, the cuffs of his shirt, his stockings....

His leg didn't lie correctly on the table, confirming Harland's suspicion that Luke had taken a tumble down the stairs—shoved, most likely. The image of Luke attempting to crawl away as his attackers unleashed their hatred upon him made Harland's gorge rise, but he forced himself to focus on the job at hand.

He found a pot for water in the kitchen, along with some clean rags, so he could bathe Luke's body and at least remove the saliva and scuff marks and... good God... there were *teeth* marks! The skin was strong and hadn't been breached in many areas, but it took a lot of scrubbing to remove some of the scuff marks, and he had to be careful not to wear the skin down in those places.

He prayed that Luke was unresponsive because his batteries had completely discharged while he lay on the hall carpet for two days, unable to reach the haven of the workshop. The horrible image tormented him as he worked—decades later, it would still come to him in his nightmares—but he feared something might have been damaged in the fall, something he could not repair.

He removed all of Luke's skin, so that he might work unhindered by it. Especially that melted, burnt face. He couldn't bear to look upon it. The eye, he was relieved to discover, could be easily replaced by one he found in the wardrobes, and he did so. When he was finished, Luke lay before him, stripped of his illusion of humanity. There was no denying that this skeletal frame covered in pistons and hydraulics and gears was a machine. Yet something in Harland's vision had changed. Luke looked beautiful to him, even like this. And Harland knew now that no one else would ever look as beautiful to him, not until the day he died.

There were several connectors for the recharging cable at various locations in Luke's body. Harland found the one closest to the head and plugged it in. The other end was already connected to the steam-powered electrical generator in the corner of the room. When he lit the pilot, it took several minutes to heat the water in the generator's reservoir, but eventually steam began to cause an internal rotor wrapped in coils of wire to spin.

Nothing happened. Harland should have known that it would take hours to charge the batteries he'd connected, and Luke would require several of these locations in his body to be charged before he could function, yet still he felt a wave of despair threaten to overwhelm him. Part of him had hoped Luke would immediately open his eyes and speak to him.

He pushed his feelings aside and settled down to work.

IT WAS an arduous undertaking. Luke's knee had broken in the fall, and although the framework of his leg was intact, several components were bent or broken. Harland found some replacement parts in the wardrobes, but now that he desperately needed them, he could see just how few of them remained. He was forced to scavenge some parts from the broken knee he was replacing and bend others back into shape as best he could.

Other parts of Luke's body were in better shape—some denting here and there from the blows he'd received, some jammed gears and flywheels—but there were so many repairs to be made, Harland despaired of ever completing the work. The day faded into night, and another day dawned.

He found tea and some bread in the kitchen—most of the food had been stolen—and that was his first meal since he'd arrived yesterday afternoon. He finally had to give in to his exhaustion and have a lie down on the sofa. How long he slept, he had no idea, but he woke to the sound of a human voice, speaking incoherently.

"Haaa-uuunnhhh...."

He bolted upright and looked around him. The sound was repeated, and he realized it was coming from Luke. He scrambled over the top of the sofa and rushed to the table, where he found Luke looking up at him with eyes that were lucid and focused. But when he tried to speak, his skeletal mouth was unable to form words.

"Don't speak," Harland told him. "Just a moment."

He went to the wardrobe and delicately removed the last remaining skin of Luke's face from its form. Then he carried it back to the worktable and told Luke, "Keep still."

It wasn't difficult to put the skin in place. It had been designed with tiny magnetic disks on its inside which lined up with similar disks of a reverse polarity embedded in Luke's facial structure. It merely required Harland to line everything up carefully, and then the magnets latched on to one another.

"Harland," Luke said softly.

Harland was unable to stop himself from kissing Luke tenderly on the mouth. Then he said, "I'm sorry, Luke. I'm sorry I wasn't here. I should never have let this happen." He saw a tear—his own tear—fall onto Luke's perfect cheek.

"I knew you would come for me."

"I don't know how," Harland responded, unable to prevent the tears from coming now. "I've been so horrible."

"You said you liked me."

"I do like you, Luke," Harland said adamantly. "My God, when I thought I'd lost you…. I've been such a fool for denying how I feel about you. I *love* you. Society be damned! You're the most important thing in the world to me."

And then Luke began to cry too, but he was smiling.

IT WAS only possible to charge one of Luke's systems at a time, and they'd all been thoroughly discharged, so it was a very long process to bring him back to "life." They spent the time with Jules Verne, and only when that novel was finished was Luke willing to talk about what the servants had done to him as they left the townhouse for the last time.

It had happened more or less as Harland had pieced together. As soon as the doctor's body had been removed, Mr. Bradley paid the staff their wages and told them their services would no longer be required. Then there was an argument about the amount being paid out to one of the kitchen staff, who felt she deserved more for her years of service, and someone brought up the possibility of "it" inheriting the doctor's estate.

Luke had been attempting to remain out of sight in the sitting room during all of this, but a couple of the younger boys felt it necessary to drag him into the front hall. Luke tried to tell them they could deal with Mr. Bradley for any wage disputes, but when he tried to go upstairs, one of the boys ran up to the landing and shoved him backward. The tumble down the stairs shattered his knee.

When the others saw him on the floor, it unleashed something in them and they began to shove and kick at him, and finally their contempt for him "masquerading" as a man and "putting on airs" led to them tearing at the expensive clothes he was wearing. He was stripped naked and beaten while Mr. Bradley looked on, heedless of Luke's pleas for help.

"I knew they hated me," Luke went on quietly, "but I thought their respect for the doctor…." He trailed off, falling silent for a long time, before continuing. "I tried to reach the workshop, though I knew it was hopeless. One of the boys spread my legs and pulled at me with both hands… tore it off, while the others laughed. Then the housekeeper brought out one of her irons…." He seemed to notice the horror in Harland's face and said, "I didn't feel pain. I'm not designed to."

He was lying, Harland knew. Dr. Steward had told him that Luke *could* feel pain. And the horror of it was almost too much to bear. But if Luke wanted to protect him, Harland would pretend to believe him. "Thank God!"

"But I was frightened," Luke went on. "Terrified. If they had broken open my head… they could have utterly destroyed me."

"Luke…. Luke…. Luke…." Harland couldn't think of anything to say beyond that, so he merely held Luke's hand and kissed it over and over again. Then at last, he said, "Nothing like that will ever happen to you again. I won't allow it!"

"Don't leave me here," Luke said, fear in his eyes.

Harland thought of Luke alone in this large townhouse, and his insides clenched. What if someone had held onto a key? Would they come back to steal more and find Luke there defenseless? Even if he had the locks changed, Harland knew he would never feel comfortable leaving Luke alone.

He would have to find a way for them to live together. Always.

London, Five Years Later

THE PACKAGE arrived via messenger, addressed to Mr. Harland Wallace and sent from Munich, Germany. Luke accepted it and carried it inside, but once the delivery boy was out of sight, he gave up all pretense of being a proper butler, tossing the package onto an upholstered chair in the hall and giving Harland a kiss instead.

"That might be important," Harland chided him, leaning over to retrieve the package.

"It is," Luke said. "It's the brass gears from Herr Baier."

"Ah. So it is." The elderly watchmaker was one of many contacts Harland had been reaching out to in Britain, the Continent, and the New World, in order to have custom parts made for Luke. The special skin was still a problem, but he had sent small samples to some chemists he'd located, in the hopes that they could find a way to reproduce it.

Luke really was a very poor butler. But then, he only needed to convince the occasional visitor and two women who came in for a few hours a day to clean and do the cooking. Harland had reduced his staff as much as possible, fearing that live-in servants would soon notice something odd about Luke. And if not something about Luke in particular, then the fact that Luke spent all his nights in Harland's quarters.

Harland missed Flannagan, his old manservant—Luke wasn't particularly skilled with a tie—but it was a small price to pay for the privacy he and Luke now enjoyed after Mrs. Carmichael went home in the evenings.

He kissed Luke again but broke off when he remembered dinner would be served in less than an hour. Fortunately, the cleaning lady came and left in the early morning. "It's no good getting stirred up," he said regretfully. "We'll have to wait until evening."

"As you wish, sir."

Luke gave him a cheeky grin and slid a gloved hand up the back of his thigh to cup Harland's buttocks. Luke had found several uses for that particular bit of Harland's anatomy—uses which had made Harland a bit squeamish at first, but which he now enjoyed thoroughly.

He moaned slightly and gazed into those startling blue eyes. It was pointless telling himself that they were made of glass. He could see the desire in them and the love.

Luke was real in every way that mattered.

JAMIE FESSENDEN set out to be a writer in junior high school. He published a couple short pieces in his high school's literary magazine and had another story place in the top 100 in a national contest, but it wasn't until he met his partner, Erich, almost twenty years later, that he began writing again in earnest. With Erich alternately inspiring and goading him, Jamie wrote several screenplays and directed a few of them as micro-budget independent films. He then began writing novels and published his first novella in 2010.

After nine years together, Jamie and Erich have married and purchased a house together in the wilds of Raymond, New Hampshire, where there are no street lights, turkeys and deer wander through their yard, and coyotes serenade them on a nightly basis. Jamie recently left his "day job" as a tech support analyst to be a full-time writer.

Visit Jamie: http://jamiefessenden.wordpress.com/

Facebook: https://www.facebook.com/pages/Jamie-Fessenden-Author/ 102004836534286

Twitter: https://twitter.com/JamieFessenden1

By JAMIE FESSENDEN

NOVELS
Billy's Bones
By That Sin Fell the Angels
Murderous Requiem
Screwups

NOVELLAS
The Christmas Wager
Dogs of Cyberwar
The Healing Power of Eggnog
Saturn in Retrograde
We're Both Straight, Right?

Published by DREAMSPINNER PRESS
http://www.dreamspinnerpress.com

Reparation
eli easton

Reparation was inspired by two of my favorite gothic novels--
Frankenstein and *Wuthering Heights.*

~1~

EDWARD OPENED his eyes and looked up into a hazy purple mist that was struck through with flickering tongues of lightning and swirled into eddies by the wind. *A storm. I'm outside and there's a storm coming.*

That was his first conscious thought. And then he remembered everything. He was lying on the rocky ground and he tried to sit up, but his right leg screamed in pain. His hands curled into fists at the agony, and he dropped back to the ground. He turned his head, looking for....

The coach. It lay on its side like a dead beetle, its shiny, cream-colored fiberglass splintered and cracked, its undercarriage still smoking from where something—probably a rock—had struck it. *Oh gods. Please, no.*

They'd been on their way back from a wedding, that of the Carlson's firstborn son and heir. The Carlson farm was two hours away by coach, and they had lingered overlong. Anese had been reluctant to leave. She'd clung to the rare social gathering like a child to a favorite toy at bedtime, and guilt had robbed Edward of the will to force her out the door. On the way home, the storm had come up from nowhere. Signis had pushed the coach too fast, trying to outrace it. They'd nearly been home, and then—then there'd been a terrific grinding crash as something hit their undercarriage and—

Anese. Edward gritted his teeth and forced himself to move. He crawled on his elbows toward the carriage, dragging his howling agony of a leg behind. The wound was pumping out blood. He could feel it, hot and slick, soaking into his pants farther and farther down his leg. Moving only made it worse, but what did it matter? Whether he moved or not, he was a dead man.

The rocky surface of the road dug brutally into his elbows and knees as he crawled. Kalanite, the lovely lavender rocks that made up the planet's surface, were harder than a priest's conscience. No wheeled vehicle could survive long; only hydraulic hovercraft travelled the roads of Kalan—or crashed here.

He reached the coach and pulled himself up the undercarriage, then pried open the door that now faced the sky. He'd been flung from inside, so the door must have opened and snapped shut again, ejecting him into the air at some point in between. It might have been an amusing image, were it a children's game. It wasn't.

The emergency face masks hung inside the door. Edward felt for one and grabbed it, pulling it off the wall. He got it over his head and breathed deep, feeling the sick lightheadedness caused by the spores begin to fade.

He had not lain there long, then. And the growing wind of the storm helped, blowing the spores away. By all rights, he should be dead already. Invigorated by the filtered air, Edward pulled himself up farther to peer into the coach.

Anese was lying against the far door. Both of her small, white hands lay palm up in her lap as if in supplication. Her eyes were closed, her young face as blank as a winter's dawn. Her neck was bent awkwardly and unnaturally to the right.

Edward closed his eyes, breathing harshly and trying to swallow his gorge. His wife was dead. Poor, pretty Anese. She had never loved Kalan, nor Edward for that matter, had never quite fit in here, had wanted so much more from life than he could offer her. At least it looked like she hadn't suffered.

And Signis? Edward pulled himself away from the coach door and slumped down against the undercarriage. It was hot and burned his back. He managed to pull himself a foot away from it. And when he collapsed to the ground, weary and weak from pain, he could see as a worm might, eye level with the ground. In the distance was a heap in cheerful livery, tossed like a broken puppet and unmoving. Signis, his adjunct, had been with the family since Edward was a boy. Edward relied on him. The strings of marriage were to be respected, but on Kalan, the ties of mutual need and cosurvival were rooted deep and red. The loss of his right-hand man cut Edward to the quick. He gasped at the raw sting of it and rolled onto his back, not wanting to see the body anymore.

The wind was picking up now, its light chattering building into a moody, swooping howl as the storm swept closer. He'd loved that sound as a boy, bundled up warm in his room. He'd imaged the wind was some gigantic creature that stalked the Kalanese moors, maybe seeking a friend. He'd been a fanciful child—and a lonely one. *I'll be your friend,* he'd told the wind, reaching out a hand to lay it against the thick, shuddering glass of his bedroom window. *I'll be your friend.*

Perhaps it was suitable, then, that he would be part of the wind at last. A true storm could sweep away picks and plows, even coaches if they were foolishly left outdoors. It would surely sweep his body away, tossing him along the rocky surface of Kalan and picking him up again. Would he be smeared like liniment across the hectares of Parmeter?

Oh, Kalan. My extravagant, harsh, and wretchedly beautiful mistress. You have done me in after all. Edward pulled off the air filter and gasped in the humid air of the storm. The spores or the blood loss would kill him before the wind gained enough strength to take his body. He was not ready to die; he wanted life in this moment more than he could bear. But if he must die, he would prefer it to be quick.

The mist swirled above him, the curls made lavender by the light reflecting up from the rocks. The eddies grew like waves dashing against the cliffs as something parted them—and then he appeared, huge and looming, his shoulders massive, his face lost as he was backlit against the sky.

For one insane moment, Edward thought: *It is the wind.* As if his childhood fancy had come to life. The creature squatted down, his face and shoulders coming into focus, his hair wild in the storm. And Edward recognized him.

It was one of the recons. The one called Knox.

Edward stared up at the monolith, too weak to move. Knox's eyes surveyed him head to toe as if assessing a bit of scrap metal. The recon could easily crush the remaining life out of him. He certainly looked the part. But recons were programmed against violence, Edward reminded himself. And when Knox gently took the air filter from Edward's hands and pressed it against his face, there was tenderness and compassion in his eyes.

A trick of the light was Edward's last conscious thought as he slipped into darkness. ·

~2~

LIFE IS sacred. Life is sacred.

Knox heard the words over and over in his head as he cradled the master to his chest and stumbled through the mist toward the house. The words were not part of what he thought of as his *must dos*. He knew what those felt like: cold and frozen, like a knife in his mind. This, this was a deeper imperative, born of some moment of personal conviction that he no longer remembered.

Life is sacred.

The other two were dead—the mistress and the one called Signis, who ran the factory. But this one, the master, was still warm and soft. His heartbeat was thready but determined, like a mouse Knox might hold in the palm of his hand, frightened but suffused with life.

He pictured that small creature, willing its heart to beat on as his heavy boots ate up the rocky ground. The master was so very young—too young for that heart to stop beating. The wind gusted and screamed and tried to drag Knox off his feet. It would be easy to get lost in this mist, but he had an image in his mind of where the house was and he headed for it doggedly. Finally, just when he was sure he was off course, the lights of the windows appeared, playing hide-and-seek with the vaporish mist.

At the door, he shifted the master's weight, cradling it in his left arm. It was awkward. The master was not heavy, but he was tall. Knox turned the door handle. The wind screamed in the entryway and then he was through, pushing the door shut behind him. A small woman, round as a fat sausage, bustled into the room.

"Oh lords! Oh heavenly stars!" She stopped in horror, staring at Knox and the bundle in his arms. Knox was aware of the picture he must make, saw it in the terror in her one good eye—the other was shot through with mist of its own. Knox knew her, but only from a distance: she was Moll, the cook who made the pans of food Signis delivered to the recon barracks.

He forced speech. He disliked speaking and had little need for it. His tongue felt thick in his mouth and his voice sounded foreign to his ears. "Accident. The coach. Need help."

This was sufficient to set the little woman in motion. She moved as if to take the master from his arms and then realized the futility of this. She changed direction and led Knox, with hand motions and soft words, as though he were a dangerous animal, up the stairs to a bedroom. Knox laid the master on the bed. His right pant leg was soaked through with blood. Too much blood. His face, always pale next to his brown hair, was now white.

Moll hovered over the master as if unsure what to do. "I must call the doctor."

"Won't come. Storm," Knox said roughly.

Moll looked frightened. She covered her mouth with her hand as if to stifle a sound. "Where is Signis? He'll know what to do."

"Dead. Mistress too. Coach overturned."

"Oh lords, no." Moll's one good eye glistened with moisture. "Oh, poor Edward."

Knox could have turned around and left. He'd delivered the master to the house. Nothing compelled him to do more, nor even to have done that much. But that voice inside him spoke again. *Life is sacred.*

An image appeared in his mind of the master, sitting tall on his mount against the stark beauty of the purple rocks and the orange Kalan sky. That first week after Knox had arrived, the master had watched him harvest the lichen, had gotten down off his pony to show him how to marry the blade to the rock, how to carefully pry up the preternaturally green clumps so they slipped up the suction hose as intact as possible, preserving the spores. The master never raised his voice, never beat them. His face was noble, handsome, and kind. And if his eyes shied away from making contact, from really seeing Knox, it was no more than Knox deserved.

If the master died, what would become of them?

Knox stripped off his heavy coat. "Hot water, medicine, bandages. Get these things."

Moll hesitated. She wanted to throw him out, Knox could tell. Her face held a look of disgust. But perhaps she decided he was better than nothing, for she finally nodded and left the room.

Knox stripped the master quickly, rending his clothes as if they were paper. Pale skin emerged, perfect skin, cold from the want of blood.

Knox did not allow himself to dwell on it or on the uncomfortable sense of wrongness of being in the big house, of touching the master this way, as if Knox were someone, as if he were not just a slab of meat meant for labor. He ripped the bloodied pant leg carefully, pulling the fabric away and discarding it. He averted his eyes, did not look at what lay between the legs before he gently rolled the master onto his stomach so he might see the wound.

A long gash split the skin and meat at the back of the thigh. It still oozed blood, but slowly now, the bright flow thick as syrup.

Do not die.

Knox searched his mind in frustration. Sometimes skills would come to him when he needed them, like nuts that had been squirreled away just below the surface of his consciousness. He did not remember how he knew these things. He looked at the gash now, willing himself the skill to attend to it.

He *did* know. He had not the skill of a doctor. He couldn't repair the torn muscles in the leg nor transfuse blood into the body. He knew these things were possible, but beyond him. However, he knew enough—*emergency first aid*, his mind labeled it—to make a modest effort. The wound had to be cleaned and disinfected, strongly disinfected. He should search the wound for debris and then stitch up the skin (*sterile needle and thread too, if you can get it*). It might not be enough to save the man, but it was better than nothing. His fingers prodded the wound. The blood seemed to be coming from the ravaged tissue, not from an artery. That was good. He did not have the skill to repair an artery.

Moll returned. Her face was red from tears but she had a first aid kit, a kettle of boiling water, clean rags, and a bottle of disinfectant. She handed him the kit and poured the steaming water into a basin, then splashed disinfectant into it. "'Tis spore killer. The wound has to be soaked with it, and any other small cuts besides, or he'll die."

She faced him with sort of zealous protectiveness as he opened the kit on the bed and dug out what he needed.

"Please don't hurt him," she said stiffly.

"I will not." Knox's voice was so strange and rough. He felt a pinch of longing for another voice, one refined and capable of inspiring confidence, but he could not say whose it was.

As he worked, Moll watched him, every swab, every stitch. Neither of them said a word.

~3~

EDWARD AWOKE to the mournful cry of the howling wind. The windows shook. The sound and vibration of it felt like safety, felt like home. He opened his eyes.

He was in his bed, in his pajamas. He reached down to his leg instinctively and felt the bandaging around his thigh and the tight, pulling pain of the wound underneath. He'd survived, then. The doctor had been called, and he'd been treated. There was an enormous sense of joy; he was not dead. And then he recalled that Anese and Signis were not so lucky.

The door opened and Moll bustled in. "Yer awake!" she said with relief.

"Yes, much to my surprise."

Moll smiled, but it faded quickly as darker thoughts intruded. There was a glass of water on the nightstand and she handed it to him. "Drink a bit now. I'll fetch ya some nice hot tea in a minute."

Edward took a sip, and then, surprised at the dryness of his throat, finished the glass. But he grabbed at her skirt before she could go.

"Signis? I saw him fallen on the road, but…."

She shook her head, lips invisible in the hard pinching of her face. "He didn't make it. Nor the mistress, the gods grant her swift renewal. They be in the cellar. That… creature fetched them, and I laid them out best I could." She wiped at her eyes.

A heavy grief burned in Edward's chest. He swallowed and blinked rapidly. "The doctor was here?"

She shook her head. "No, Sir. I sent word, but the storm hasn't let up enough for a soul to come."

"Then how—"

"He did it. That… recon. Brought ya in and doctored ya too. Never heard of such a thing in my life."

That surprised Edward. He frowned. "Do you mean Knox? Where is he now?"

Moll looked torn. "I hadn't the heart to send him out to the barracks in this wind, had I? Not after he went out there and... and brought them home. He barely made it back that time. And too, I didn't want to be alone with ya, in case...."

"You did right," Edward reassured her.

Moll looked relieved. "Put him in the old butler's room in the attic. He sat with ya for hours, porin' over that." She pointed to a thick volume on the table, one from his father's library. Edward recognized it. It was a volume on home medicine, one of the many such survival volumes that came in handy on a place like Kalan.

He met Moll's eyes in surprise. She just shook her head as if she had no idea what to make of it either. "Never heard of such a thing. Well, ya up to some broth? No, never mind. Yer having some, will or no. 'Tis good for the blood. Don't make me force it into ya."

Edward smiled. "You won't have to hold my nose, Moll. I'm hungry enough. Put some bits of meat in it, will you?"

Grunting with satisfaction, Moll left.

Edward lay back on the pillow and closed his eyes. His mind began to puzzle over the trouble he was in. His coach was ruined, so he had no way to get out in case of an emergency. His adjunct, Signis, was dead, leaving a critical job on the farm unfilled. His wife, Anese, was gone. Though they'd never been in love, he would miss her company in the long, bitter evenings—the music, the chatter, the card games, her warmth in the bed. He'd miss Signis's company as well. The three of them had been a small enough household as it was, not the large, bustling family most farms raised. And now he was alone, alone with a two-thousand-hectare farm to manage. Alone except for an old, one-eyed cook and five recon labor slaves who kept to themselves out in the barracks. At least, they usually did.

The next Federation transport would not arrive for six months.

His mind flirted with despondency. He'd worked so hard since Father and Jeb had been killed. He'd taken a wife, courted and contracted from off-world. He was determined to have children and raise the farm back up, even though it was not his natural inclination. And what had come of it? He was now in worse shape than ever. He didn't think he could bear to marry another off-worlder. Anese had come to

Kalan full of hopes and dreams—and she'd hated it. Hated the long storms and the winters. Hated how far they lived from their neighbors. Hated the harsh Kalan landscape. She'd seemed to feel it was all beneath her, even Edward. He could never do that again. And Kalanese brides... they had disadvantages of their own. But that was a longer-term problem. The immediate crisis was this: how would he manage the farm without Signis?

He heard a sound and opened his eyes. Knox stood in the doorway, leaning against the frame on one shoulder, looking at Edward. For a moment, Edward had a fanciful image in his mind of some childhood fable he'd read of a colossal being holding up the universe on his shoulder.

Knox was massive, easily the biggest humanoid Edward had ever seen in person. He was six feet six at least and built to proportion, wide and muscled. His hair had grown long in the year he'd been here, dark as a miner's heart and hanging down around his face like a curtain, as if such a huge being could hide himself behind a few strands of hair.

Knox had arrived two transports ago. One of Parmeter's older recons had died suddenly. An immune system fever, the doctor had said, parts of the body rejecting what it perceived as foreign tissue. It could happen at any time with a recon, though the drugs they took made it a rare occurrence. Edward had placed the order for a new one, and when Knox had been assigned to him off the shipment, he'd first felt pride and pleasure—Knox was the biggest recon Edward had ever seen, clearly a magnificent specimen, one who would provide ample muscle for the farm. But then, looking at the recon's face, came uneasiness. Something about the creature unnerved Edward. His massive size, yes, but also... his face was *attractive*, rough and masculine but not brutish like most recons, and not as old. And his eyes... there had been something intelligent and piercing in those eyes, even then. But Edward had pushed aside his innate reaction—the recons were never comfortable to be around. He worked with Knox as he would any other slave, teaching him how to harvest the spores. Knox had taken to it quickly, spoke little, and caused no trouble. Edward had never heard him speak except for the occasional monosyllabic yes or no.

Knox was watching him now with those unnerving eyes.

"Come sit down." Edward waved to the chair.

Knox hesitated, then did as he was told. He sat down, his eyes lowering subserviently to his lap. Edward's heart pounded. He'd never had a recon in the house before, nor could he ever remember a time from his childhood in which that had happened. But he could not ignore the fact that this one had saved his life. He owed Knox some courtesy.

"Thank you for bringing me in from the storm."

"I would not let you die," Knox said, looking up at him fiercely, as if affronted.

Oh. He could speak, then, and well enough.

"Moll says you tended to my leg."

"As best I could."

"Did you learn how from that?" Edward motioned toward the medical book.

Knox glanced at it. "No. Later... I looked at the book. Afraid of infection. Wanted to know what to do."

Edward studied Knox's face for signs of untruth. But the creature just kept his gaze fixed on his lap.

"So you do know how to read, then?"

"Yes."

"Did they teach you that at the recon factory?"

Knox looked up, a bit defiantly. "No."

Edward nodded. "And do you remember other skills from... before? Like how to patch my leg?"

Knox looked back down into his lap and frowned as if he didn't understand.

Edward rubbed his chin thoughtfully. He hadn't known it was possible for recons to have such skills. Then again, he had never tested them, never asked them to do more than harvest the lichen or move boulders or bales. Still, if any of the other recons could read, he'd be surprised. There was definitely something different about Knox.

The stubble of several days' growth grated under Edward's fingertips, reminding him he'd been out of it for some time. He suddenly felt tired, exhausted by the burden of knowing the farm could not go on without him, not even for a day. And now he was without an adjunct and incapacitated besides. How would he be able to ride his pony with this leg? Supervise the recons? And do Signis's job of managing the processing of the lichen at the same time?

The wind made the windows shudder, but it was lessening even now. The recons, like everyone else, had been holed up through the storm. But soon it would be over and they would need to get back to the harvest.

He looked at Knox and hesitated. He thought about asking for help. But even if Knox could read, how could Edward trust a recon to manage the valuable spores safely and well? The system he'd grown up with his entire life rejected such ideas. Recons were brute labor, nothing more. Nothing more, *ever*. Knox was deceptive because he didn't have the facial scars some recons had. He was not physically hideous like many of them. He almost looked....

Knox looked up and met his eyes. *He almost looked human.*

"Well, I thank you again, Knox. And thank you for bringing...." Edward's voice cracked. "For bringing in the bodies of my wife and Signis. Now you may go. Make sure Moll feeds you."

"I should go to the barracks," Knox said flatly.

"When the wind dies down enough that it's safe, you may do so. Don't risk yourself. We're short enough hands as it is."

Knox nodded and left.

Edward forced himself to push the blanket away and swing his legs over the side of the bed. The wound in his thigh shot agony down through his foot and up into his groin. *Hells.* He pulled a mirror out of his bedside drawer and managed to snake down his pajama bottoms. He unwrapped the bandaging around his thigh, pulling it away gingerly, and used the mirror to get a look at the wound. It had been stitched up. Knox had done a decent job of it too. The skin was red and tight but it didn't look infected. Still, it was a bad gash, long and deep, and it seemed to be impacting his muscles and his mobility, at least for the time being.

Dear lords—what was he going to do?

~4~

THE DAY of the funeral was as breathtakingly stark and beautiful as any fall day on Kalan could be. The storms always left Kalan as fresh and unspoiled as a newborn. The sky was a deep, bottomless orange. The ragged landscape was brilliant with color as if it had just been painted—the lavender of the rocks, the green of the lichen, the black of the borderlands, the gray of the occasional twisted Anderoak. The everlasting mists had been blown away and, for a few days at least, the inscrutable land was bared like a woman dropping her veil.

Though post-storm days were work intensive, still a dozen of Edward's neighbors came, one family driving over two hours by coach. He would have been touched—*was* touched—except he couldn't escape the feeling they were here as much to take his measure and decide what to do about him as they were to offer their condolences. The farmers on Kalan, like the planet, were tough and fierce, concerned, ever and only, with the spores.

Edward insisted on taking the front position on his wife's pallet even with his bad leg, though they had to go slowly and haltingly as he limped. Three of his father's closest associates, all dressed in their best black pants, long-tail suit coats, white cravats, and black air filters, acted as pallbearers. Behind them came four more men bearing Signis.

Most cultures burned their dead, but it was tradition on Kalan to bury them. It was a matter of returning the resources to the planet. Some believed such remains fed the very rocks of Kalan and made them fertile for the lichen. Edward thought that was an old wives' tale, but he nonetheless liked the idea that, when he died, he would be placed in the rocky ground of Kalan, that his body would become part of the very fabric of the planet, that the place that had birthed him would swallow him back up again.

The recons had dug the twin graves side by side, a massive amount of labor even with the electric rock slicers. The five of them stood now, in a solemn line, up on a high mound where they were silhouetted against the sun.

Knox was among them, his tall, broad form clearly towering over the rest. During the service, performed by the local magistrate, Edward could not stop his eyes from wandering to the silhouetted figures. Knox made Edward's stomach twist in a hot mix of reactions—confusion, curiosity, fear, and gratitude among them. And perhaps there was something else too, something he would never admit to anyone.

Wood was rare, so the bodies were taken off the pallets and laid in their graves, wrapped in their shrouds and nothing else. Edward took pads of lichen from a bucket in his gloved hands and strewed them over the corpses—*for quick regeneration.*

He did not cry as he bid his companions a final farewell. The loss was beyond tears.

INSIDE THE house, Moll served refreshments while Edward stood in the parlor receiving condolences. He tried to hold it together and appear calm, but inside he alternated between feeling numb and feeling frightened of the dire nature of his situation. But he was hopeful when William Trenton pulled him into the library to talk.

William was of an age with Edward's father, or had been before Father had died. The man was weathered and hard and a de facto leader in their community. He'd raised three sons, two of them now living off-world. He clasped Edward's shoulder.

"'Tis a hard, hard thing, Edward. You've had more than yer share of sorrow."

It didn't seem all that long ago Edward had buried two other bodies together: his father and his older brother, Jeb. Had it been six years? It felt like yesterday. He wouldn't let himself become self-pitying, though he supposed he had cause.

"I will survive it," he said firmly.

"No doubt, no doubt," William agreed while nevertheless managing to convey extreme doubt. "Well." He cleared his throat. "The offer I made when yer father and brother passed still stands. Yer not cut out for this life, Edward. That's not to belittle ya, son, just the truth. Sell the farm and get out while ya can."

His tone was sincere and final. Edward clenched his fists and bit back a quick retort.

It was easy for Trenton to say—*sell and get out while you can.* He'd always lusted after Parmeter, one of the richest spore farms on Kalan. He'd tried to get his hands on it by marrying off one of his daughters to Jeb, and then, once Jeb was dead, to Edward. Unfortunately, his daughters were unattractive and churlish besides. And Edward knew allowing Trenton into his life as father-in-law, or in any capacity whatsoever, would put an immediate end to his autonomy.

Edward couldn't sell. He would not be the son of Parmeter who failed, who ended the line, who allowed the farm that had been in their family for six generations to pass out of their hands. The families of Kalan had too many privileges—they did not have to send their sons to military service or pay duties to the Federation. The spore labor was subsidized and the revenue was generous. And their children were welcome at the most prestigious academies. Besides, Edward did not like being dismissed as weak and incompetent. He hadn't liked it when his own father had done it, and he damn well wouldn't accept it from William Trenton.

"What I'm in the market for at the moment," Edward said with a tight smile, "is a new adjunct. I can pay well."

William looked regretful. "Aye, there's the thing. I've been talkin' with the others. Regretfully, there's not a soul qualified to be an adjunct who isn't already employed, not 'til the next transport."

Edward nodded stiffly, upset but not really surprised. The people who lived on Kalan worked hard. And anyone not absolutely needed was already off-world in schools or working on freighter ships. There were no idle hands waiting to be tapped.

"Howsoever, I've been talkin' with Carlson. Ya know he's a hundred hectares that edge my farm, and we've both bit more labor than we can use in winter. If he and I share a recon, we can spare one for ya. I know it's not what ya need, but it's a pair of hands."

Edward felt humbled. Perhaps he had misjudged Trenton. "I— thank you, William. That is most appreciated."

William patted his arm. "Wish it could be more. Remember my offer, Edward, if things get too bad." The magnitude of the challenge that lay before Edward was underscored by the grim set of William's face. "May the gods be with ya."

EVEN WHILE planning the funeral and informing Anese's family about her death, Edward had been unable to get Knox out of his mind. The giant lingered behind Edward's eyes like the aftermath of a bright flash—the huge, rough bulk of him, the tenderness in his eyes as he'd plucked Edward from the storm.

Edward had done some research on the interspace. Of course, the information on the official page of FedTech was nothing he hadn't already known, but he could use the reminder of exactly what Knox was.

Recons, or Reconstitutes, were cyborgs that were part robot and part human. The human parts of recons came from condemned Federation prisoners. The practice had been instigated over a hundred years ago by a prison reformer. All resources were valuable and limited, and as much as possible, everything was recycled and reused. Why not humans? Unlike most people, who lived to a ripe age, prisoners were often young when they were condemned to death. It was a shameful waste to burn the bodies. Then, too, what a fitting way for the condemned to repay their debt to society—by being useful after death. And the sale of them helped pay for the prison system. The program had been widely applauded.

A recon, like a regular cyborg, could not be more than 80 percent human—because then they would, by law, deserve human rights—but most of them were much less. FedTech guaranteed a recon could not become violent—the cyborgs had strict programming against it and against any behavior that was directly related to their former crimes. Nevertheless, they were not intended for household use. They were made for manual and factory labor.

The farms on Kalan used recons because they were Federation subsidized for the mining of the spores—they were cheap. And the planet's harsh conditions required tough and expendable laborers.

But the FedTech site did not explain exactly how the recons were made. Edward had never thought about it overmuch. Each recon came with a bundle of paperwork Edward dutifully filed away in his office. It included heath records and schematics in the event a recon needed doctoring or mechanical work. He pulled Knox's file and spread it out on the table.

Knox. It gave Edward an uneasy feeling to see the details of Knox's body laid out before him, as though the recon were a machine he owned and he was looking at the blueprint. Knox was 80 percent human, unusually high for a recon. His entire body, save the liver, was from one prisoner. His brain was from another. His liver from a third. The 20 percent of his body that was artificial consisted of reinforced titanium joints—knees, elbows, wrists, ankles—and the spore filtration system embedded in his lungs. He'd been engineered for Kalan.

Unfortunately, the file did not give the names or histories of the prisoners used to make Knox. But that was not surprising. They'd already paid the ultimate price. Their crimes did not carry forward to the new entity. Even so, they had been condemned to reconstitution, so Edward knew their crimes had been severe: murder, treason, arson, serial rape, sabotage—something heinous. It was frightening to contemplate but it gave Edward a needed dose of reality. He could not afford to become sentimental about Knox, even if he had saved Edward's life.

Most recons were not very bright. Edward had always thought their brains must be damaged in the process. They took simple orders well enough, but in their off hours they watched endless movies on the vid con in the barracks or played simple card games with each other. They were childlike, in a way. Knox was different. Knox... remembered things. He seemed to have an unusual level of intellect.

It was all rather fascinating, really. Edward had always had a curious mind and a fondness for strange stories. But he was no scientist. He was a farmer, one who was short critical labor. And that was the filter through which he contemplated the enigma of Knox. If the conclusion he came to was one that also followed a small quiet compulsion within his heart, he was able to honestly tell himself he had no choice.

AFTER HIS neighbors had left, Edward asked Moll to go to the recon barracks and fetch Knox. It was embarrassing to be so helpless that he had to ask his arthritic old cook to do such a task. But his leg was aching after exerting it all day, and he just couldn't walk that far. He waited for Knox in the library.

Moll ushered him in. Knox was wearing his rough gray longcoat, a garment that helped break the wind. His hat was in his hands. He stood just inside the doorway and looked at Edward, then down at the floor, which he seemed to study with silent fascination. Moll hovered.

"It's all right, Moll. You can go back to the kitchen."

She gave Edward a look, as if pleading with him not to do anything rash, but she said nothing. She left them alone.

"Please come sit down, Knox."

Knox looked at Edward then, his expression unsure. Edward just waved at the other chair in front of the coal fireplace. Knox walked over, reluctantly, and sat on the very edge of it. He made the chair look like a child's toy.

Knox's eyes were cast down at the hat in his hands. Edward was in no hurry to speak, giving himself one last chance to change his mind as he studied the recon. Knox had a high forehead, its paleness accentuated by that thick black hair. His nose was slightly flat and flared. His lips were full, the bottom one thicker than the upper. His chin was wide and square, rough with stubble and ruddy from spending long hours in the elements. There was something about him that made Edward want to stare, something mysterious and compelling, brutal and beautiful, like Kalan herself.

Edward supposed it made sense that, when a condemned prisoner had such a body as this, so strong and well-formed, they would use it whole as much as possible. What had this body done in its first life? Had it been a rebel solider, a Goliath of the opposition? Or perhaps it had simply been a bar brawler, violent and crude.

But the mind... inside that skull was a different person entirely. Edward found it hard to imagine. What would it be like to wake up and find himself conscious in another's body? Was Knox even aware such a thing had happened? What had the man been like who had once possessed that brain? What were his crimes?

Still, Knox did not raise his eyes.

Edward licked his lips nervously. He picked up a book off the side table and opened it to a page he had marked. He handed it to Knox. "Read this aloud, please."

Knox glanced at him questioningly but took the book. He held it gently in those large hands.

"*Parmotrema psilocybin kalanis* grows only on the planet of Kalan in the Hebredis system. The plant, a distant relative of lichen and fungi, thrives on the unique mineral composition of Kalanite, the hard rock that makes up the crust of Kalan. It produces colonizing spores that are harvested for the production of life-saving pharmaceuticals. The plant—"

"That's enough," Edward interrupted. His pulse beat rapidly with a mild kind of shock. Knox's reading voice was a bit halting, but Edward suspected that was because he rarely spoke. He pronounced every word correctly and without stopping to think about it, even the Latin. Edward didn't think the same could be said for any of his fellow farmers.

Knox carefully closed the book and held it out. Edward didn't take it, forcing Knox to look up and meet his eyes. There was a high color on Knox's white cheeks—embarrassment? Annoyance? Pride?

"Keep it, Knox. I want you to read the entire thing and remember what it says. The book will teach you about the lichen. Do you think you'll be able to retain what you read?"

Knox nodded, putting the book on his lap. "Yes. 'Checking a wound for spore infection, step one: Remove any bandaging and examine the wound. If a spore infection is present, the wound will feel warm to the touch and be red and swollen. If there is a yellowish or green growth at the wound site, the infection is advanced. Step two: Check the patient for fever. Even a slight elevation of temperature can indicate an immune system response to infection. Step three: Check for swelling at the lymph system closest to the wound. If swelling is present, this indicates the spores are spreading in the body and treatment is no longer possible. The closest lymph system for the legs is in the groin.'"

It took a minute for Edward to understand what Knox was talking about. Then he remembered the medical book Knox had been reading after his injury. Knox was showing Edward he remembered what he'd read.

"That's... that's very good, Knox. Good. Now I want you to read *this* book. It's very important. Because I want you to try to understand what we do here, the purpose of this farm, and the life cycle of the lichen."

Knox looked up at him, another question forming on his brow. But he looked down again instead of asking it.

"Can you tell me what my duties are on this farm?"

Knox worried at the hat in hands. "You... manage the harvesting of the lichen."

"Can you be more specific? You've observed me in the field. What exactly do I do?"

Knox thought about it for a long moment before speaking. "You ride over the farm and say where the lichen is ready to harvest. You test it—with your fingers."

Edward nodded. "That's right. Go on."

"You tell us where to harvest and watch us. We must cut the lichen away carefully and not leave waste. You tell us where to use the spray on the bare rocks to grow more lichen. The lichen is your... responsibility. You own the farm. It is all your responsibility."

Knox stopped abruptly, as if he feared he'd said too much or said the wrong thing. He didn't look up. Edward stroked his chin with nervous fingers, feeling prickles of both excitement and, if he were honest, fear.

This man was a manager of some sort in his previous life, a leader. No common worker takes such a long view.

"And do you know what Signis did for the farm?"

Knox frowned a little. "He worked in the factory. But I don't know about that."

Edward wasn't surprised. The two oldest recons worked in the factory on processing days, but Knox never had.

Edward tented his fingers together and made up his mind. When he spoke, it was with conviction. "There is no one available on Kalan to take Signis's place, and I cannot run the farm alone. I need to ask for your help."

Knox looked up at him quizzically but said nothing. He did, however, give a single jerky nod.

"I always preferred to be outdoors, myself, to work directly with the lichen. But with my leg, it's not practical for me to be on a pony all day, at least not for the next month or so." Edward sighed deeply. "So... I thought we might try this: I can train you to recognize when the lichen is ready to be harvested, especially if you read that book. But I'll probably have to go out with you in the mornings at first, make sure you know where to work. Most of my time I'll spend in the factory, doing Signis's job. Which means you will need to oversee the other recons, make sure the harvesting is done correctly and that none is wasted. And at the end of the day, you'll bring the lichen to the factory. Now. Do you think you would be able to do that?"

Knox blinked rapidly as he looked down into his lap. The color on his cheeks deepened. Edward wished he knew what was going through Knox's mind. Did anything at all go through a recon's mind?

"If... if you tell the others they must follow my orders, I think I can. I will try, sir."

"I will tell them, of course. And if you have any difficulties with them, you must come to me."

Knox didn't say anything.

Edward leaned forward and spoke firmly. "You need to understand—all the farms on Kalan have spore sensors that tie into a central console. You know those white boxes on poles we have around the farm?"

Knox nodded.

"If too many spores get into the air, that means we're not doing our job right and we'll get a warning on that system. I'll be fined. And if I get too many warnings, they can even take the farm away from me. That's why we *have* to keep up with the spore harvest. Do you see how important it is?"

"Yes."

"Good." Edward leaned back. "We have a new recon arriving tomorrow. He's on loan from a neighbor's farm. He can take your place on the crew."

Knox nodded. He stood up slowly but remained at his chair, as if asking permission to go.

Edward didn't give it to him. He looked beyond Knox at the window. It was a nervous gesture, wanting the reassurance that the farm was still out there and that, for now at least, all was still well. But it was night and he could see nothing beyond the heavy, fortified glass, not even swirls of mist. What he could see was the reflection of him and Knox—Knox, like a giant with his back to the window, towering, and Edward himself sitting in the high-backed chair, looking like a boy playing at being a land owner. He wasn't sure which of them was odder.

"I don't think it's wise for you to remain in the barracks. Since you will now be overseeing the other recons, you need to distance yourself. Go and gather your things and return within the hour. You'll move into the room in the attic that Moll gave you before. You can start reading the book tonight."

Knox breathed in a sort of gasp and got very tense. "I don't.... It is not my place to live in the house." His voice was rough with fervor.

Edward took a sip of his drink. "Do you have programming that forbids it?"

Knox thought about it and slowly shook his head. Edward was relieved. He wasn't sure what limitations the factory put on the recons.

"Very well. I'm sorry if you don't like leaving the barracks, Knox, but I've explained my reasons. Until the transport comes, we must all make sacrifices. Please do as you're told."

Knox gave a nod of acquiescence and then fled the room.

Edward had a profound stab of doubt. What was he doing, inviting a recon into his home, giving him managerial duties? This could end very badly for all of them. And yet... he had to try. Something told him Knox would not hurt him; hells, the recon had saved his life. And he believed Knox was up to the task, at least if he could get past his own submissiveness.

Still profoundly uneasy, Edward finished off his drink and stood. His eyes went to the bookshelf. He walked over and took the medical book down from the shelves. He searched the index for "spore infection" and found the page.

Checking a wound for spore infection, step one: Remove any bandaging and examine the site of the wound. If a spore infection is present, the wound will feel warm to the touch and be red and swollen. If a yellowish or green growth at the wound site is observed, the infection is advanced. Step two: Check the patient for fever. Even a slight elevation of temperature can indicate an immune system response to the spores. Step three: Check for swelling at the lymph system closest to the wound. If swelling is present, this indicates the spores are spreading in the body and treatment is no longer possible. The closest lymph system for the legs is in the groin.

Hells. Knox had quoted it almost word for word.

KNOX FOUND the shiny black duffle bag he'd arrived with under his bed. He pulled it out and began putting his things into it. He didn't have much: a dozen articles of clothes, work pants and shirts, undergarments designed for warmth. He had a few items he'd been given at the factory for grooming—a comb, a razor, a mouthbrush and powder, soap. He had no photographs, no books, no music, no money, no papers.

For a moment, he stood at his bunk, looking down into his bag. He remembered these things, remembered a time when he'd had such things on a tablet and a com device. He felt disoriented for a moment, his breathing quickening, and he felt certain he was leaving things behind, *important things*. It took several moments before the confusion and sense of panic cleared and the present settled back down firmly in his mind.

No, he was a slave. He had some clothes and some items for grooming; that was all he owned. He was forgetting nothing. The knowledge made him feel a little sick. He wiped at his mouth, took one last look around his bunk, assuring himself it was really empty, and then he headed for the door.

The other recons—Gibbon, Smenk, Core, and Cray, were silently playing cards at the table as they usually did at night. He felt their eyes on him, maybe wondering what had happened. He did not speak to them. He just left.

I'm sorry if you don't like leaving the barracks, Knox, but I've explained my reasons.

The master thought he did not want to leave the others. Knox didn't care about that. He felt nothing for the other recons, rarely spoke to them. He sometimes watched the vids with them in the evenings but otherwise he kept to himself. With nothing to keep him occupied, Knox spent many hours on his bunk just staring at the ceiling, his mind fuzzy and drifting.

No, he didn't like the barracks, but he was invisible there, nothing was asked of him. He did not belong in the house.

The idea of living in the house upset him. His feelings were a muddle. Something about penance, something about being unworthy. He did not deserve it, felt uneasy in the luxury, as if his filth might rub off on the finery. And there was fear too; a fear of awakening things better left quiescent. Being in the house, being with the master, made Knox remember things, *feel things*. Even the short time he'd been around the master when he was wounded had disturbed Knox's peace of mind. Having remembered he could read, Knox longed for a book. Having been in the master's presence, been spoken to, *thanked*, made Knox long for more of such contact in a frustrating and futile way. It was better not to remember, not to feel. It was better to lie on his bunk and stare at the ceiling, his mind blank. Oblivion was better.

I am not a man. I am not a man.

He did not want hope; did not want consciousness.

Eventually the master's leg would heal and the transport would come. Signis would be replaced, and Knox would be back to labor. What the master asked of him was unfair—to act like a man for a short time only and then to sink back into being nothing. Oh, cruel fate.

What fates impose, that men must needs abide; It boots not to resist both wind and tide.

The words came to him, he knew not from where. But they were true; Knox could not resist, neither the winds of Kalan, which had tossed the master's coach and wrecked his world, nor the sucking tide that seemed to be pulling Knox into the master's orbit.

He'd seen the despair on the master's face when he'd woken up to the damaged leg. He'd seen the same look at the funeral, and he'd seen pity on the faces of the others. The other farmers in their fancy suits, they looked at the master the way they might look at a dog who'd been hit by a car and lay bleeding at the side of the road, feeling sorry for it but not moving to do anything to save the wretched creature or put it out of its misery.

I need your help. Knox could not turn his back. He would help, no matter what it cost him. The master was so young and he was... good-hearted. *Lovely. Sweet.*

No. Knox would do as he was told. But he would not allow himself to get attached, not to any of it, not even to his own reason. He was not worthy to even think such thoughts about the master.

Inside the house, Moll's lips were pinched tight, her face ugly with dislike for him. She said nothing as she led him back up to the attic, her manner icy and cutting as the wind.

"There's a bath down the hall," she instructed flatly, as if he hadn't stayed there before. The bed had been freshly made and there were clean towels folded on top of it.

Knox stood there clutching his bag to his chest, his eyes on the floor. She huffed and left.

He sat on the bed, its frame creaking under his weight. *Gods, this body!* He thought of it as *this body*, as a separate thing, not *my body*, though he could not have said why. This body always loomed over everything. It created a weird sense of dislocation. Now, as he looked at the book in his hands something crawled under the surface of his mind—another book, another bunk. But the hands were not the same and those knees did not tower over the floor as these ones did. He looked up at the window, half-expecting to see the black and stars of deep space. But there was only the planetary darkness of Kalan, interrupted by the wisps of mist that caressed the face of the glass.

Sighing, he opened the book and started to read.

~5~

THE NEXT morning, Edward woke Knox with a tap on his door and they went out at first light. Edward mounted the pony, but the saddle rubbed the back of his thigh directly over the wound and he couldn't stand it. After a few minutes of trying to work out a system, the saddle was removed and a blanket placed on the pony's broad back. Kalanese ponies were stocky and wide, their feet well shod and their sense of balance ideal for picking their way over the rocky ground. Edward sat with both legs on one side—he could lean on his right hip that way and keep his weight off the left. Knox led the animal slowly by its reins.

It took twenty minutes to get to the area that was due for harvest. The mists were mild today and the visibility was good. The bright, fluorescent green of the lichen could be spotted from far off. When they reached the area, Knox helped Edward down from the horse, his strong hands grasping Edward's waist and lifting him. Edward put his hands on Knox's arms in surprise, and neither of them moved when his boots touched the rocks.

Knox looked down into Edward's eyes, his face concerned. "Can you stand?"

Edward nodded, not trusting his voice. Knox's large hands burned through his coat and Edward felt a sudden, unexpected flush of arousal. He pulled away abruptly, nearly unbalancing himself, and limped over the rocks. He tried to squat down at a likely looking clump of lichen, but his leg would simply not bend like that. In a heartbeat, Knox was there, grasping his elbow. Edward had no choice but to lean on him and squat down on his good knee, keeping the other leg straight out in front of him. Knox squatted too, as sturdy as a mountain in his solid boots. He held Edward's arm in a sure grip to keep him balanced in the awkward position.

Edward pushed aside the unwelcome reaction of his body with some annoyance. He ran his hand above the dense green lichen. Beneath his palm, the tiny spores—thousands of them, with round tops the size of a pinhead and hairlike stems—rippled from the mild disturbance his hand created in the air.

"Do you see them?" he asked, his voice tinny through the filtration mask.

"Yes," Knox said, his eyes fixed on the spores.

"You can't see them from a distance because they blend in completely with the lichen. When the lichen gets about this green, it's usually a few weeks before the spores appear, and they appear overnight. You've only got a week to harvest them, maybe another day or two if the wind is low. Once they loosen up, the wind takes them."

Knox nodded. "I read about the sporing period, but I would not have known to use my hand to see them as you did."

"Try it," Edward urged. "But be careful not to actually touch the spores. The area must be as undisturbed as possible during harvest."

The hand that was not holding Edward upright extended, and Knox ran the flat of it above the spores. They rippled as though they were alive, looking like the sinuous movement of a snake. This seemed to upset Knox, for he frowned as if thinking of something unpleasant.

"What is it?" Edward asked.

Knox shook his head. "Nothing." Then, in a tight voice, "This feels familiar to me."

"Well, I should hope so. You've been working with the crop for a year."

Edward made a move to stand, and Knox rose to his feet, pulling Edward up with him. He kept hold of Edward's elbow, for which Edward was grateful because his leg was hurting badly. He gritted his teeth and stood still until the pain subsided.

"I told you how important it is to keep up with the harvesting." Edward nodded toward one of the spore sensors on a white post that were placed around the farm. "If we let too many spores get airborne, and there's no storm to excuse it, we'll be fined—and worse."

Knox grunted in acknowledgement. He looked worried, but then, Edward was too.

"You should know the size of a plot by now, Knox. It generally takes four days to harvest one plot, then the rocks are sprayed for two days. We don't need to disseminate new spores because—"

"The spores are virulent," Knox said. "No matter how careful the harvesting, there are always enough spores in the air to reseed the plot."

"Yes, that's right. That's from the book, isn't it? Did you read more of the book last night?"

Knox nodded.

"Good. Very good, Knox. Your job while the recons are harvesting is just to make sure they stay inside the ripe plot and use the harvesters the right way. All of the recons have been here awhile, so they shouldn't need to be told, only kept on task."

"Yes, sir."

Edward felt an uncomfortable trickle of fear and dread at leaving the harvest in Knox's hands, but he had no other option and there was nothing more to say.

"We should go back to the factory. I'll talk to the recons this morning and then you can bring them out to harvest."

"Yes, sir."

Knox helped Edward limp back over to the pony, then he lifted Edward onto the back of the animal. Again, Edward felt that heat suffuse his body from the feeling of Knox's large, firm hands. And when Knox steadied his hips on the blanket, the meat of his palm rested on the tops of Edward's thighs. Knox did not look up but waited, eyes downcast, as if needing permission to release him.

Or maybe he likes touching me too? Edward thought, then chiding himself for thinking it. "I'm all set," Edward said briskly. Knox let him go without looking up and began to lead the pony back toward the house.

Edward cursed himself. There had to be something sick inside him for him to react physically to Knox like this. Knox was Edward's slave and not entirely healthy of mind either, or so it seemed to Edward. While he obviously had an innate intelligence, he still seemed lost at times. And that didn't even touch on the fact that he was *not human*. But Edward's body didn't know any better. It was reacting to the touch of a large, virile, attractive male. It felt like forever since Edward had been with a man.

Growing up on Kalan, homosexuality was not an option. He'd known that with every fiber of his being, and he'd never told anyone about his unusual desires. In the privacy of his own room, he got relief and knowledge on the interspace, but never, never on Kalan. And then he'd been sent to the academy. As a second son, one his father didn't especially care for, Edward had never been meant to inherit the farm. So he'd gone off-world to learn a trade. Things were different there, at that elite boys' school. Homosexuality was not exactly the norm, but it was tolerated under cover of dark. There'd been a boy, Javel, who'd returned Edward's glances, and they'd met secretly in the bathrooms at night. They'd both been curious and eager, and they'd tried everything at least once. Gods, how heady were those fumbling touches, furtive kisses, and silent ejaculations!

But when Edward's father and brother were killed in a pirate attack on Kalan's spaceport, any chance of Edward's living off-world came to an end. He knew he had to do his duty and take a wife, have as many children as possible. There could be no man in Edward's future on Kalan. And even if he could risk it, it was most certainly inappropriate with a recon like Knox.

Oblivious to Edward's inner turmoil, Knox pulled him steadily on.

IT WAS almost sunset when Knox brought the harvesting machines into the factory, and they were emptied into the holding bins. Edward looked the batch over with trepidation. The slabs of lichen that had been scraped off the rocks and sucked into the container looked much like they always did. He didn't see an unusual level of damage to the spores or any large amounts of debris or lichen that was not ripe. The weight was a little low for a day's take, but not by much. For a first effort, it was better than Edward could have dreamed possible.

Knox stood silently, waiting for Edward's judgment.

"It looks good, Knox. Excellent work," Edward said through his spore filter. Knox gave a single nod and left.

That night, Edward dined alone while Moll delivered a tray up to Knox's room.

AT THE end of the week, they had enough lichen to process a batch. Edward worked the bundling machine all day with two of the oldest recons assisting while Knox took the others out to the field to spray the harvested rocks with a sticky-sweet substance that encouraged airborne spores to adhere and grow. The bundling machines removed debris and pebbles and bundled the lichen spore-side down into bales, which were then stacked in the drying room to cure. By the end of the shift, with a week's spore harvest safely bundled, dated, and stored, Edward felt an unaccountable sense of relief. The week's take was within parameters for this time of year, and the farm's spore warning system had not triggered, not once.

They had done it.

They were not completely out of the woods. If any of the machines in the factory went down, Edward didn't think he could fix them. Signis had been the mechanical one on the farm. And Edward still had to take care of the books and other assorted duties that were less urgent. But as long as they could keep up with the harvest, they had a chance—gods, they really did have a chance of making it.

That night, Edward was in a good mood as he went downstairs for dinner. He wanted to celebrate. He sat in the dining room, at the head of an empty table for ten, as Moll brought him his plate. He took a bite. He could hear himself chew, it was so quiet. The bottle of wine from the cellar he'd decided to open mocked him, sitting so full on the table.

He threw his napkin down in disgust. "Enough of this," he said out loud.

He stormed out of the dining room as fast as his bad leg would carry him, then limped up the stairs and up the stairs again. When he reached the door to Knox's room, he hesitated only a moment before knocking loudly.

Knox opened the door, looking concerned. "What is it?"

"What is it? This is ridiculous, is all!" Edward replied, his voice edged with frustration. "We're stuck here together all winter, and you eat in your room and I eat alone in the dining room like an idiot. I insist that you join me."

Knox's face paled and his eyes fell to the floor. "If you order me to," he answered flatly.

"I do order, damn it! Now come downstairs."

Edward turned and limped back down the stairs. He heard Knox follow quietly.

In the dining room, Edward waved at the chair to his right and told Knox to sit. Moll came out to check on him and took a step back in surprise.

"You won't be serving Knox in his room tonight," Edward said firmly. "Bring his plate in here."

"But I—"

Edward glared at her, in no mood to be gainsaid. Moll gave a brief courtesy and left, but it was clear she most strongly objected. She returned with Knox's plate and a glass of water and put them down with an angry clang. Edward ignored her and she returned to the kitchen.

Knox stared down at his food like a child being punished. Edward sighed. He took Knox's water glass and held it out. "Drink. Drink it all."

Knox looked at him questioningly, but he took it and drained it.

Edward, still buzzing on his anger, filled the glass with expensive wine. "There," he said, placing it by Knox's plate. "That's more civilized."

Despite his bravado, he had a glimmer of doubt about giving alcohol to an enormous recon, but he pushed it away. Knox had proved himself capable of bringing in the harvest. Surely he could handle a glass of wine, especially with his bulk.

Edward sat back down and picked up his fork. "Now. Tell me how the week went. Did you have any trouble with the recons?"

"No, sir." Knox's hands were in his lap. He made no move to eat his food.

"Please eat with me," Edward insisted quietly.

Knox licked his lips as though nervous, but he picked up his fork and took a bite.

"I would appreciate your company, Knox, because, you see, I get very lonely when there's no one to talk to. This silent house drives me mad. I'm a social person, which may tell you how well I'm suited to life on Kalan."

"I am not fit company for you," Knox said with conviction. But he took another bite.

For some reason, that made Edward smile. Maybe it was the absurdity of it all. "Well, you're what I've got. And I'm what you've got. And that's the way of it," he said cheerfully.

Knox was silent for a minute, and then, "Why do you not have more family? I know the accident killed your wife and Signis. But…."

"Why isn't there anyone else?" Edward carefully cut a piece of meat, watching it get smaller and smaller under his knife. His voice was cold. "My mother left my father years ago—just took a shuttle off-world, and that was the last I heard of her. My father and brother were at the spaceport when it was bombed in a pirate raid. That was almost six years ago now."

Knox put down his fork and knife, looking a little green. He started to get up. Edward grabbed his arm.

"No, please stay. I'm sorry for being maudlin. I can't much stand myself when I get that way. Let's talk about something else."

Knox hesitated for a long moment, his body stiff with tension, but slowly he relaxed under Edward's hand and sat back down.

"What do you think of Kalan?" Edward asked, trying to steer the conversation to something harmless.

"It is very beautiful. And very barren."

"Yes," Edward mused. "That says it all very succinctly, doesn't it? Of course, I've lived here all my life, so it's hard to be objective, but I did spend two years off-world at school...."

Edward chatted about his school days, about the green world the academy had been on and how much he'd loved it, loved the long walks in the pure atmosphere with no need for an air filter.

Knox seemed to listen to him very carefully, as if filing the information away, but he didn't say much, nor did he ask any more questions.

Moll served them dessert, still looking right put out at Knox's presence, but Edward found he was extremely glad for it. "I would like for you to join me every evening, Knox."

"I am not good company. I don't... remember very many things. I have nothing to talk about."

"We can fix that," Edward said determinedly. He scooted back his chair. "Come on."

Knox followed Edward to the library. Edward began perusing the shelves. "That book on the spores was all well and good, but would you like to read something just for the pleasure of it?"

Knox nodded slowly. His eyes went to the shelves, and they held an interest and excitement Edward had never seen in them before.

"Excellent. Let's see. Do you like novels?"

Knox thought about it. "Yes, I think I do."

"How about I give you a few of my favorites?"

Edward got a little carried away. He kept seeing titles he liked and pulling the books off the shelves, and soon even Knox's considerable arms were beginning to sink under the load.

Knox looked at the latest as Edward added it to the stack. "Johansen Rider?"

Edward paused. "Yes. Do you know him?"

Knox frowned. "I… don't know. A starship crashes. There are big animals."

Edward was delightfully surprised. The book was one of his childhood favorites. "Yes, that's right! What else do you remember about it?"

Knox concentrated. "Nothing. It's gone."

"It's all right, Knox. But maybe you'd like to read this one first."

"Yes. Thank you." Knox looked at Edward and smiled.

It was the first time Edward had ever seen Knox smile. It should have looked awkward on that big, rough face, but it didn't. It looked spontaneous, real, and even a little rakish, the way his grin tilted to one side. It gave Edward a strange feeling in his stomach.

Whose characteristic is that lopsided grin? Edward wondered. *The body's or the mind's?*

Knox tried to resettle the embarrassment of riches in his arms. "This is enough."

Edward laughed. "I'll say. I guess I overdid it. You can just choose which of those you want to read. I don't expect you to read them all."

Knox nodded and turned for the door, as if to leave. The prospect of yet another long evening alone did not appeal to Edward.

"Would you… like to sit down here and read this evening? I can make a fire." Knox didn't answer right away and Edward felt like a fool, begging a recon for company. He really was beyond ridiculous. "It's all right, Knox. You can go up to your room if you prefer."

Knox set his stack of books down carefully beside a chair and took up the book by Johansen Rider.

Stupidly pleased, Edward placed some coal in the fireplace and set it to burning, then closed the smoke screen. He settled into his chair and pulled a tablet from the drawer of the chairside table. It was his habit to check the interspace news for the day before he allowed himself to pick up his book. He brought up the keypad to type in the name of his favorite news site and heard a strange moan from Knox. He looked up to see Knox's face had paled, and he looked like he was about to be ill. He tore his eyes away from the tablet in Edward's hand with a whimper of fear and stared at the fire.

"Knox? What's the matter?"

Know shook his head, not answering.

"Is it the tablet?"

Knox didn't answer, but he looked petrified. His book slid from his lap to the floor and his hands were clenched on the arms of the chair, white-knuckled and shaking. Concerned, Edward got up and crossed the room. He quickly put the tablet in a desk drawer.

"It's gone," Edward said, sitting back down. He leaned forward and watched Knox worriedly. "Knox, I put it away." He gently touched the recon's knee.

Knox glanced at Edward's hands, as if not trusting it was truly gone. But when he saw that it was, and his darting eyes did not find it in the immediate vicinity, he visibly relaxed. He took a deep breath, his face red. "I'm sorry. I will go to my room."

Knox seemed humiliated by the incident, but Edward didn't want him to go. If they left it like this, the shame of what had happened would only grow in Knox's mind, and he might be unwilling to sit with Edward again. Edward wasn't sure what had happened, but it had to have something to do with a bad memory, or perhaps recon conditioning. Had Knox been conditioned against using a tablet? If so, why? Were all recons forbidden from using electronics to limit them to manual labor? Or was it just Knox? Had his crime been something related to computers?

"Please stay." Edward pressed on Knox's knee more firmly as he started to rise. "I was just going to check the news, and it's always the same anyway. 'The great Federation,' blah, blah, blah. I'd rather read a book." He forced a smile.

When Knox seemed less about to bolt, Edward leaned back into his chair and took up his book, hoping Knox would do the same. After a moment, Knox picked up the Rider book off the floor. But he didn't read long before speaking.

"I... remember having such a device once. I don't know why I...."

He sounded confused.

Edward put his finger in his book to hold his place and looked at Knox curiously. "How did it make you feel when you saw it?"

Knox worried his lower lip. "Frightened... like if I got close... something about stinging.... I kept thinking of Silantran wasps...."

"Gods, that is frightening! I've seen news reports on those. Not a pleasant way to die. But there are no wasps on Kalan, don't worry. And I won't bring the tablet out again."

"But... why do you not read on it? Why do you have books instead?" Knox waved at the room.

"Ah." Edward sighed. "Because this is Kalan. The winds can knock out the interspace and power for days, even a week or more. The core functions of the farm are run off an underground grid. That's so we can communicate with each other in an emergency and keep the spore filters and the factory controls running no matter what, but nothing can keep us on the interspace. And during storms is when most people actually *have* the time to read. Anything that can be kept offline *is* kept offline, that's our motto. We're rather survivalists here on Kalan."

Knox seemed to want to say something else. From the dubious look on his face, it was probably to insist again that Edward would be better off without his company. But he swallowed it. He was not, Edward thought, at heart a whiner or even much of a talker. Edward rather liked that.

Knox offered Edward another small smile, and then he started reading.

~6~

A HALLWAY corridor, green tile—cold and sterile. His heart hammered in his chest. His own breath sounded harsh and panicked in his ears, and fear coursed through his veins. He could not seem to get control over it, could not banish it. It was the pure flight-or-fight terror of the physical body. But he steeled himself not to show it, not to give them the satisfaction.

A heavy door—the surgery ward. One of the guards opened it with a thumb scan. He was forced inside, the guards holding his shackled arms.

They presented his paperwork to a man at a desk. The man never looked him in the eye. While they waited for it to be checked and double-checked, his legs nearly gave out from under him and they had to hold him up. His breathing grew louder until it was like a horror soundtrack in his ears, his body's terror infected the mind.

I will show no fear.

They led him into a small room and stripped him. They pushed him into a shower. The spray stung, a mix of water and disinfectant. He tried to make himself enjoy the sensation of the water hitting his back, for it would be the last time he ever felt it. But he was too afraid and the acrid disinfectant stung his nostrils and throat.

Dear gods, please let me wake up from this nightmare.

The water turned off. He was handed a towel, and he dried as best he could, his hands shaking badly. He expected to be handed a robe, something, anything, but he was not. Instead he was forced back into the corridor, naked and still a bit damp, and down to another room.

As the door opened, he thought he would be sick. Inside was a table made of cold, hard, shiny silver metal that glinted like a knife. On the table were clamp restraints for the ankles and wrists.

He couldn't help it. He turned to run, his bowels turning to jelly, but the guards were ready for him and they grabbed him firmly on either side, holding his arms.

I will not scream. I will not beg.

He didn't. He kept his mouth firmly clenched shut. But he could not stop his body from stiffening or his heels from trying to dig into the floor. The guards had to drag him toward the table. In an obviously coordinated move, one guard shoved at his middle so his butt hit the table while the other grabbed his legs and pulled them out from under him. In moments, his hand shackles were gone and he was flat on his back on the table, wrists and ankles secured.

He closed his eyes and tried to get himself under control. He was going to die; nothing could change that. There was no point in making a spectacle of himself while doing so. He was an officer. He had his pride.

To be sentient, conscious of the self, was a precious gift but also a curse. An animal led to slaughter didn't know what was happening, had no awareness of its own mortality. But a man... a man knew. He didn't want to die, but he particularly hated to die like this, not in battle, but at the icy, clinical, disinterested hands of his enemy.

The table was hard and cold under his bare back, buttocks, thighs, and calves. A clean drape was laid over his groin but even that was not a comfort, its starched surface scratchy on his skin. Oh, to be warm in a nice bed one more time, to open his eyes to a new day, one full of possibilities instead of terror.

The room grew quiet. He was left alone to wait, to wait for the executioner and the final injection.

KNOX SCREAMED and opened his eyes. He flailed with the bedcovers, fighting to get up, to get out, to get free.

He was out the door of his room and pounding down the attic stairs before he realized where he was. He slumped down at the bottom of the staircase that led to the attic and covered his mouth, trying to stifle his own soft cries.

The lights in the hall came on, and Edward appeared, dressed in a robe. Knox shrank against the banister, hiding his face in his hands.

"What is it, Knox?" Edward's voice was filled with distress.

Knox took a deep breath, trying to get ahold of himself. It was just a dream. No, not that. "I remembered. When they... when they killed me."

"Oh." Edward took a shaky breath. He sat down on the step next to Knox. Edward said nothing more, but his hand rubbed Knox's shoulder.

Knox realized he was sobbing, and he wiped his face with his hands.

Realization came slowly, but it came. He'd known he was a slave, that he had been made somehow, that he was not on the same level as humans. He remembered the recon factory but only vaguely, like a dream. His mind had been so fuzzy then. But he remembered what they'd told him. He was built to serve. He was to do labor and be quiet and never expect anything more. That had been drilled into him.

But now... now he knew where he'd come from and why he had skills he did not remember getting, why he felt so odd in this body. His fingers raised tentatively to the back of his head. His fingers waded through the thick hair there and found the scar that ran from the top of his head to the base of his neck. He swallowed a cry. He brought his hands down and looked at them.

Oh, horrible! Oh, horrible! Most horrible!

He had only dim recollections of his own body, the one he'd had before—thin and pale, a little fragile. It had probably been burned to ashes or perhaps cut up and sewn onto other tissue, his life's blood given away. The thought filled him with panic, as though he'd been ejected from a space ship and floated in space alone, doomed to a slow death as his air supply depleted. Though of course it was not the same. This body was fully capable of sustaining his consciousness. He tried to calm himself down.

"You didn't know?" Edward asked quietly. He was still rubbing Knox's shoulder. The contact helped Knox feel less like he was flying apart, and he got ahold of his emotions, stopped his tears. He shook his head.

"I've looked at your file. Your brain is from one person and your body almost entirely from another. And, of course, they added the spore filtration system to you so you could work on Kalan, and they reinforced your joints."

"Why do you tell me this?" Knox asked, his voice rough.

"I... I guess I thought it might make you feel better to know. Surely it's better to know exactly what's what, and then you can accept it and move on. Your brain is intact, Knox, and you're more intelligent than any other recon I've ever known. That's a good thing, isn't it? That your mind survived what was done to you?"

Knox looked at Edward, wondering if the man thought his words made any sense whatsoever. He'd survived what had been done to him? Had he? Or was he only just conscious enough to feel the horror of his fate, like a brain in a glass box?

"Do you… remember everything from before? Do you remember who you were?"

Knox thought about it. There'd been glimmers before today, and the dream had told him he was a prisoner, gave him words like "officer" and "enemy." But he didn't really know. He shook his head. "No."

"That's all right," Edward said, as if he meant it. "It's really not important anymore."

The words did make Knox feel better. The dream, and what it meant, still clung to him. But sitting on the stairs in a warm house with Edward beside him, so concerned and generous, was… soothing. There was nothing here to threaten him, no immediate cause for alarm, and his body could only hang onto the fear for so long. He felt his terror leach away.

Edward seemed to grow tired of rubbing his shoulder, but instead of releasing him, he slid his hand down and put it over Knox's clenched hands. After a moment, Knox opened his hands and Edward's slipped into one of his, not intertwining the fingers, just palm to palm, like… like a child's hand. Or a friend's.

Knox knew he didn't deserve Edward's kindness, and even thought he was taking advantage of the lonely young man. He should tell Edward a recon did not deserve to be talked to, touched. But he couldn't make himself push away the offer of friendship. It felt too wonderful, like feeling the sun on his face after a lifetime of darkness.

They sat like that on the stairs for a while, until Knox had relaxed so fully that exhaustion crept back in.

"It is not dawn yet," he said. "You should go back to sleep. I'm sorry I woke you."

"Yes." Edward released his hand and stood up. "You get some more sleep as well. Good night, Knox."

~7~

THEY MADE it through the fall burst of burgeoning spores as the lichen did its best to outrace time. Then winter settled in, the storm season arrived, and the ripening slowed. In the winter, storms could last for a week or more and be severe. And when it wasn't storming, there often was not as much to harvest because the storms would take any spores that were even close to ripe and the lichen reproduction grew lazy.

Edward got used to the procedure in the factory, getting more efficient and less stressed about it each week. The recons moved through their actions without a word or issue, or at least none Knox shared with Edward. And they never once triggered the spore alarm. Things would have been remarkably well if only Moll had given up being quite so hostile. She treated Knox with an impervious chill and several times had "spoken" to Edward about her concerns—a recon should not be in the house, should not be at the dinner table, should not be conversed with of an evening. What would people say?

So far, Edward had put her off. Though her attitude troubled him, he had no choice but to use Knox as a foreman, and he was not willing to give up Knox's company.

In fact, Edward took great pleasure in their evenings. After dinner, Moll would retire to her room and Knox and Edward would sit in the library and read and talk. Edward found he and Knox liked the same books—adventures, classics, and dark romances. Knox had spoken only haltingly at first, and with much prompting from Edward. But his speech had grown more fluid and free, until now it seemed they both enjoyed discussing the books as much as reading them. Often Edward would read a passage aloud that he particularly liked, and sometimes Knox would do the same.

Edward found it fascinating what Knox would come up with in these discussions. He had a strong grasp of philosophy and moral issues, things like love and duty and honor. And sometimes, though very rarely, he would remember things from his past life.

One night they were discussing a novel that was set onboard a space station, and Knox said, "I think I lived in space."

"Truly?"

"I think I lived in space for some time. I remember a porthole on a spaceship. I think it was in the room where I slept. I remember the stars outside and planets too. Beautiful planets."

"I always wanted to spend more time in space," Edward said with a rueful smile. "I only travelled to and from my school once each way but it was really an experience. Do you remember any of the places you visited on the ship?"

"No." Knox's eyes were far away. "But I think I lived on a planet that was green once. I think about green things."

Rather excited, Edward got up and pulled down one of his favorite photo books. It was of other worlds. "Like this?" He opened the book to a stunning scene of verdant green, with ferns and trees and lush forest surrounding a lovely turquoise bathing pool.

"Yes, a little," Knox said, looking at it. "Not these." His finger circled the giant ferns. "But it was a place as green as this." Knox trailed his fingers over the image. "It makes me feel... sad. Like it is gone."

"You mean you're homesick?" Edward clarified.

Knox shook his head doubtfully.

"Keep the book and look through it. Maybe you've been to some of these worlds, and you'll remember."

Knox took the book, but he didn't look at it then. He set it on the table. "Also... I remember this body."

"What do you mean?"

"I remember seeing this body. In a cell. The man who had it, he yelled a lot. He cursed and ranted day and night, kept us awake. He would hit the bars until his hands bled, and once he hit them hard with his head."

Knox's fingers went up to his forehead and tentatively traced a small scar.

Edward swallowed nervously. "So you watched the man... the man who had this body. You were in prison with him, then? You had a cell near his?"

Knox just looked at him.

"Are you sure it was the same man?"

Knox nodded slowly, looking very grave. "He was unbalanced in the mind. He would take his clothes off. I saw his tattoos. They are on this body."

Knox said it as a fact, but Edward's mouth was suddenly dry. "You... you have tattoos?"

"This body does."

Edward's mind was caught in a loop. He knew what tattoos were, of course. He'd seen them in vids. But he'd never seen one in the flesh. It was not the sort of thing the Kalanese did. He struggled with his curiosity and something... more dangerous. He could ask Knox to show him the tattoos. After all, Knox was technically still a slave. He had to do anything Edward said. If Edward asked him to strip so he might satisfy his curiosity, Knox would. The thought of it, of Knox stripped of his clothes and standing naked in this library in the dancing firelight, made something low in Edward's body clench and demand.

But... Edward would never do such a thing. They were sitting in the library like two gentlemen. A gentleman did not ask another to bare himself. While the idea of them being friends, gentlemen, might be an illusion, Edward found it was one he truly did not want to break. So he firmly put aside the idea.

"I see. What do the tattoos depict?"

Knox pointed a finger and circled his left bicep over his clothes. "Here, a hawk—angry, with its mouth open." He drew a line across the top of his left shoulder, then his right. "Along the back, a rope with knots here and here." He pointed to the far side of each shoulder.

"Goodness."

"Here...." Knox circled his heart, or perhaps his left nipple. "... a heart in a wire cage. Drops of blood come down here...." He trailed his finger downward toward his left hip. He paused with his finger poised, as if he were going to continue. But he blushed and slowly lowered it.

Of course, that only set Edward's imagination on overdrive. Did the body—Knox's body—have tattoos around the genitals? What would they be like? Such thoughts made him wonder, suddenly, what Knox's cock and balls looked like. Was he as large there as he was everywhere else? Edward shivered.

He looked up to find Knox watching him curiously.

Edward scrambled to recall where the conversation had been going. "So… you saw this body when you were in prison. He was unstable, you said."

Knox nodded.

"Do you know his name?"

"No."

"What about… what about *you,* your mind? Have you remembered anything more from before? Besides the idea that you were on a spaceship?"

Knox looked down at the floor, his face pensive. "I…." He shook his head. His voice was rough. "I get flashes of memory… I see a man."

Edward leaned forward. "Yes? You can tell me, Knox. I won't judge you."

KNOX LOOKED into Edward's expressive brown eyes and wondered. He'd been having increasing flashes of scenes *from before*, and they both upset and aroused this body. It was because of his proximity to Edward that he was remembering these things. Edward, with his kindness and his sweet smiles, stirred up feelings and thoughts that were painful in their intensity—and in their futility.

"I see a man. His hair is brown, like yours, but not as dark." Knox reached out and carefully touched a lock of Edward's hair. Edward's eyes went round but he didn't pull away. Nevertheless, Knox made himself draw his hand back. "He is… fit. Handsome. Sometimes I see him laughing or angry. And sometimes…."

"Is this man you?" Edward asked with interest.

Knox shook his head. "No. He looks *at* me. He was someone I was close to."

"Ah. A brother perhaps?"

"No."

"Someone you worked with?"

"I think he was my lover," Knox said simply. Sometimes these memories would flash through his mind when he was with Edward— brief seconds of seeing another face. But mostly they came when he was in bed at night. He would be half-asleep and reach for someone, someone naked and warm, someone whose body had given him pleasure. When he woke up like that, aroused and wanting, he would have to touch this body to put an end to the ache the memories created in him.

Knox suddenly registered the look of shock on Edward's face. *Oh.*

Edward's expression moved between confusion and distress. "Do you... do you think you might have been a woman before?"

"No! I was not a woman." Knox knew that much at least. He remembered being dragged into the shower, then into the room with the table where they killed him. His body was not as large as this one, but it was definitely male.

Then he suddenly felt ten ways a fool, and frightened too. He had not remembered.... He'd not remembered some cultures didn't accept men loving men. He should have never opened his mouth. "I'm sorry if I offended you. It... it must not be a true memory," Knox stammered. He stood to go.

"Wait, Knox," Edward pleaded. "Please, sit down."

Knox sat down, but he was shaking. He stared into the fire. He should not let himself get lured into telling Edward things, to the illusion they were friends. He was too damaged. He didn't remember all the correct social cues, the things that were safe to say and the things that were not. He could feel the weight of Edward's eyes on him.

"You were a man who... slept with other men? Before?" Edward's voice was soft and rough.

Knox pressed his lips tight and said nothing.

"Don't be afraid." Edward touched his hand. Knox didn't move and couldn't look at Edward. Edward didn't say anything for a long time. And then: "I had a lover in school. His name was Javel."

Knox looked at Edward, surprised.

Edward smiled a little, as if in sympathy. "I told you I wouldn't judge you. What do you remember about this man? Were you life mates?"

"I don't know. But he is very familiar." Knox hesitated. "I think he was dear to me." He couldn't explain how frustrating it was not to be able to remember more, not to know more about this man who might have meant so much to him once upon a time, in another life.

Edward nodded, looking down at his hand, which was still on

Knox's, his thumb rubbing lightly. Slowly, he took it away. "I'm sorry. I can't imagine how hard that must be."

"But you lost your wife."

"I do miss Anese, and I feel terrible that she died. But I never loved her like that. The marriage was arranged for us. I didn't even meet her until she came to Kalan for our wedding."

Edward had leaned far forward in his chair, elbows on his knees, and he was so close. Knox could still feel the weight of Edward's hand touching his, even though he'd removed it. *Edward had taken a male lover.* The thought swam around and around in Knox's mind, opening up some doors, closing others, and stirring up painful feelings and questions. He felt this body stirring and commanded it to stop.

Edward was watching him. He attempted a lighthearted smile. "It's an interesting philosophical question, isn't it? What determines who you are attracted to? Is it the body or the mind?"

"The mind," Knox said at once. He did not even have to think about it.

Edward swallowed, the smile slipping away under some heavier emotion. His eyes lingered on Knox's face, and his gaze grew heavy with desire. The blood inside Knox's body thudded faster and faster until he was swollen tight and throbbing. Edward wanted him; Knox could see it on his face. He wanted Edward, but he was confused about what was expected of him. Too much was expected of him and that both frightened and angered him.

"Is that why you brought me into the house?" he asked roughly. "Am I to service you as your slave?"

"What?" Edward sat up abruptly. "N-no. Knox, I... I would never ask that of you." Edward got up and paced, obviously upset.

Knox knew he had made a mistake, but he wasn't sure exactly where it lay, nor did he have any idea how to fix it. Angry and frustrated with his own limitations and awkwardness, he stood up quietly and left the room.

THAT NIGHT, Edward lay awake in bed for hours. He was upset with himself for asking Knox those questions, for pushing. What had he been hoping to hear? That Knox's memories somehow cleared him of all wrongdoing? That his death sentence had been undeserved, that he'd been falsely accused? It was an unlikely hope. And anyway, what did it matter now? Whatever crime the man who'd once had that brain had committed, Knox was no longer that man—not physically and not mentally either. At most, his memories were flickers of light on a screen, nothing more.

Edward wondered why he felt so compelled to dig into Knox's past. Why couldn't he stop thinking about the recon? Why couldn't he simply accept Knox for what he was and not expect more of him, expect him to be *human*, expect him to fill the gaps that were aching in Edward's life?

Because he's capable of it, just as he's capable of being your foreman.

Some instinct in Edward believed that, was drawn to something buried deep inside Knox like a hidden treasure. But Edward knew it was possible he was only seeing what he wanted to see because he was so lonely. Yet Knox was already proving to be better company than Anese and Signis had ever been, more interesting to talk to, drawing Edward's attention like a moth to the flame.

That's because it's sexual. You're attracted to him, to his body.

It was true. As much as Edward enjoyed their conversations, he did lust after Knox in a most craven and carnal way. If he was honest, he'd felt the attraction at first sight, when he'd been assigned Knox off the transport, but it had only been a vague murmur then. Now, after spending so much time with Knox, it was a dull roar. He was drawn to Knox's presence, to that large, muscular body, to the rough, masculine beauty of his face, to the intelligence in his eyes, to the dark, enigmatic mystery of him. And tonight he had let it show. The thought of what Knox had accused him of—it was humiliating.

Is that why you brought me into the house? Am I to service you as your slave?

Gods, what those words made Edward feel! Ashamed, abashed, and yet hotly desiring too. But the tone of Knox's voice, his anger, made it clear Knox did not feel the same.

Edward said a silent prayer of thanksgiving to the gods. Yes, thank the gods Knox's mind did not run like that, that Edward would be saved from himself. Because if Knox wanted it, if he ever moved to touch Edward, Edward knew he would not have the willpower to resist. And something like that could very well prove to be a fatal mistake here on Kalan. They were alone, and that lulled him into a false sense of privacy. But Edward knew they were not unwatched.

Plagued by these thoughts and by the restlessness under his skin, it was nearly dawn before Edward finally fell asleep.

In his dream, there was a body above him—muscled, naked, sweaty, and laboring in passion. He reached up to grab strong arms, trying to get closer. He ground his hips upward. *So hard, need it so bad.* He could feel the man's cock, huge alongside his own as Edward strained for release. The promise was intense but the friction maddeningly light. The room was dark and outside he could hear the tormented howl of the wind. He could not see the man's face.

More. Closer. Please.

On and on the dream went, Edward grinding upward, *so close,* but never able to quite get enough. He suddenly saw, in the dim light from the window, a design on the man's chest—a heart in a wire cage. It dripped down on him as if it was real, *drip, drip,* the blood splattering on Edward's chest as the body above him worked and plunged. Edward was so insanely hard by now, he *had* to come. *If I can get myself under that drip, the force of it hitting my cockhead might make me release.* He did not even care it was blood. He just needed to come. He tried to maneuver his hips up.

But the man's cock suddenly wrapped around Edward's like a prehensile tail and *grabbed* his shaft, preventing him from moving. It squeezed him tight. Edward bowed up in ecstasy. *Yes, yes, touch me, oh gods, squeeze me harder.*

Just as he was about to come, one of the arms he was clinging to so fiercely began to give way. It came off in his hand like a doll's arm. And still the body above him writhed, and still Edward thrust up, needing to come. He cast the arm away and clung to the shoulder on that side. Then the other arm started to crumble in his grasp and the blood dripping from the chest gushed more and more. *Oh gods,* his lover was falling apart in his hands, and—

Edward awoke in horror. He sat up, breathing in panicked gulps. He was alone. The man... Knox... was not coming apart. There was no blood. It was just a dream. Just a dream. Despite the fear and the panic, Edward's cock was turgid and throbbing painfully in his pajamas. He groaned and fell back to the mattress. He rolled onto his stomach and stuffed a hand beneath him and into his underclothes. He couldn't even bring himself to care that he would make a mess and Moll would know. He thrust and thrust again, grabbing the bed sheet tight with his other fist.

Knox.

He thrust and groaned until he came and came into the bedclothes, the pleasure shuddering through him.

~8~

KNOX KNEW he'd hurt Edward that night by the fire, that night when the desire had been written on Edward's face and Knox had accused him... of what? He could not even remember now why he'd been angry or what he'd accused Edward of. Something about planning to force him to have sex because he was a slave? It seemed very foolish, in hindsight. Edward had always been kind; he wouldn't force Knox to do anything he didn't want to do.

Now Edward was careful to appear friendly but distant. The workdays were shorter, the winter dark came early, and the evenings in the library were long. They continued to read and discuss books, and sometimes they played chess on a board. Knox found he remembered the rules and the strategy. He let Edward win sometimes. It seemed like the polite thing to do.

Edward's eyes now rarely lingered on Knox for more than a few seconds at a time, not when Knox was looking back.

Knox noticed Edward's awkwardness, but his mind was occupied elsewhere. Inside, Knox was changing. The responsibility of managing the spore harvest, being in the house, reading, and, most specifically, Edward's company and the dialogue they shared, these things all required him to be more—to be human, intelligent, thoughtful, civilized, self-aware. As the days grew shorter, the sun ever more pale and weak, and the winds harsher, the fog in Knox's mind was clearing too, just like the Kalanese mist. The mental fuzziness lessened day by day, and so did the panicked sense of disassociation. The thread of terror over what had happened to him—that he had been condemned, murdered without emotion or qualm, and his brain put into another man's body—gradually dulled, like any other horror of the past. The periods when he felt like a stranger in this body grew more and more infrequent.

Knox spent hours in the evening, when he should be sleeping, staring at the mirror in the bathroom at his face, at his eyes, finding himself inside this great, powerful shell.

One night after a shower, he stood in front of the mirror naked and explored himself—his large and muscled arms, his hands—wide-palmed and shorter-fingered than his own, he thought, but not ugly. His chest and stomach were muscled and ridged and bore a light mat of dark hair. He memorized the colors and lines of his tattoos. He explored his cock, which seemed to be the most alert part of this body. Its demands were becoming more frequent and more aggravated the better Knox felt. The cock was long and thick and the foreskin encased it completely when it was flaccid. It rose easily and often, and the pleasure it gave him when he stroked it was intense, its seed copious and milky white. This body was younger than the one he had left, he was sure of it, definitely stronger—and more coarsely sensual, more virile.

When he stroked that cock he sometimes saw it as someone else's, as if he were touching another man, and sometimes he was able to feel it was his own. He tried to think of the male lover he sometimes had memories of, but that was too far away and too vague. His mind had one subject it returned to at such times: Edward.

Edward was so young. Knox guessed he was no more than twenty-five. He was too young to be left alone with a responsibility like the spore farm, young to have to shoulder the entire weight of a family's legacy, young to have lost mother, father, brother, wife, work partner.

As Knox's facilities become sharper, he could see, understand, more about Edward. There was something strong and good and optimistic at the core of him. He was kind, intelligent, and curious. No matter how tired he was, he loved to stay up late talking like a little child who refused to go to bed when there was something more interesting to do. And he was beautiful. He had a smooth jaw, long lashes over expressive brown eyes, full lips, and a small nose. He was sweetly handsome as only a young man could be. It was those lips and eyes Knox thought of as he touched himself, and of Edward's body writhing beneath him, his hard cock in Knox's hand.

Though Edward tried to hide it now, Knox still sometimes caught him looking at night in front of the fire or in the factory as he unloaded the harvesters. Edward lusted after this body, big and masculine as it was. Knox rather thought the man he'd been before would have lusted after it too.

And this body lusted after Edward. Knox knew he could take the young man easily and that they would enjoy the pleasures of the flesh together. But something held him back. It was not only that he knew that to have relations with a recon would shame Edward should anyone find out, something he would protect the young man from if he could. But also… while Knox's mind was healing itself in some ways, he still could not remember who he'd been before or what he had done. There were blocks in his mind that prevented it, and when he tried to push past them, intense headaches would quickly overwhelm him. Still, he had a very bad feeling in the pit of his stomach—one he recognized as guilt and shame. Whatever he'd been or done, if Edward knew, he would hate him. Knox believed this. He kept his distance.

ONE NIGHT, Knox was awoken by a shrill cry that seemed to weave in and out of the howl of the wind outside. He sat up and listened, wondering if he had dreamt it. But the sound grew clearer and he realized it was coming from inside the house. It was not a human voice; it was an alarm. Knox got out of bed and quickly pulled on his work pants and laced up his boots as fast as he could. He wore only a thin sleeveless undershirt on top, but he didn't bother to find something better. He raced downstairs.

Edward's bedroom door was open and the room was empty. On the ground floor, the alarm clamored relentlessly. He found Edward in the library on the console. Moll was beside him, dressed in her hair pins and robe. Edward looked at Knox with wild eyes but he spoke calmly.

"It's the house air filtration system. It's gone down. I—I don't know how to fix it."

Without thinking, Knox strode over to the console in great steps. *The air filtration system.* It rang alarms in his head that were more worrying that the audible one. In a spaceship, such a system was life or death. Here on Kalan, it would keep the house free of the spores so Edward and Moll could breathe. They needed filter masks whenever they went outside.

"Where are your masks?" Knox asked, even as he crossed the room.

"Yes," Edward blinked in surprise. "Moll, go get the masks from the kitchen."

Moll hurried to obey.

"I don't know what to do, Knox," Edward said, the panic escalating in his voice as he tried taping keys on the console. "It's flashing yellow, which means imminent system failure, but I don't know what to do!"

Knox reached out. He was only going to touch the flashing screen, try to get a better look at the system error. But suddenly his mind, which had been dulled from sleep and then distracted by the crisis, shifted into gear, and he *saw* the console keyboard. He was close to it, only a foot or so away, and the pain and panic knifed into him with angry severity as if he'd touched a live wire. He suddenly saw the keyboard crawling with large and deadly-looking wasps, swarming over and under Edward's hands as he tried punching keys.

Knox screamed and scrambled backward.

"Knox!" Edward shouted, his face a mask of fear. "Knox, please! I need your help!"

But Edward's voice was muffled and remote, baffled by the sound of the alarm and by Knox's rising terror. He turned and fled. He found his way to the front door somehow, tore it open, and ran into the night. Behind him, he could hear Edward screaming something about the wind, but then it was gone and there was just the black night, Knox's pounding feet, and the wind ripping at him with icy, demonic fingers.

He didn't know how long he ran or how he managed it. The rocks were ragged under his boots as he stumbled forward in the dark. The wind buffeted him first one way and then another, whipping his hair into endlessly changing contortions and often blinding his eyes. By some miracle, he didn't fall and break a leg. But when the rocks grew from mere boulders to jagged pinnacles beneath his feet, he fell, hard, face first.

The glassy rocks cut his hands, chest, face, tore through the tough fabric of his pants. He knew then where he was—these were the black rocks of borderlands, the natural strata that ran between the Kalanite that was such an excellent host to the lichen. Lifeless and sharp, the black rocks flaked in slivers like knives and chewed into him.

The pain finally brought him back to himself, overcame the internal panic. He howled, his voice snatched and dispersed by the wind.

He managed to crawl to his feet, causing more cuts as he did so, and he carefully picked his way off the black rocks. Exhausted, bleeding, and bruised, he realized that he was outside in the dark and the wind. He started back toward the house, head bowed against the oncoming gale.

EDWARD WATCHED Knox tear out of the house and he cursed his ridiculous solitude as never before. Whatever they'd done to Knox to keep him away from computers, it was some heinous programming. He'd been out of his mind when he'd run out, into the *dark*, into the *killing wind*. And Edward could not go after him. He had to stay here and get this damned filtration system fixed or they could die.

Edward slammed the door shut against the wind and the spores as Moll ran in from the kitchen. She wore one filtration mask and carried another one.

"He's out there?" she asked, her voice hollow through the mask.

Edward nodded, upset. He put the mask on and went back into the library.

He still had no idea what to do with the system, but the sound of the alarm was driving him mad and the console was not responding to any of the keys he hit. He could get on the grid and ask for help from his neighbors, but between the dead-of-night hour and the wind, it was unlikely anyone could come to his rescue. He stared at the flashing yellow warning, his eyes hot.

How had he ended up here? Why had his father and brother died? Why had Signis not trained him on the system? Why had *Signis* died? Why did his one helpmate, Knox, who had more than enough intelligence to help him figure this out, have to be a recon who ran screaming at the mere sight of a computer?

For a moment, the self-pity swamped him. He felt Moll's hand, shaky, on his arm, offering him strength. He took a deep breath and fought down the emotion. Right. The air filtration system had not failed *yet*. He just had to get this damned alarm to go off so he could think clearly and try to figure out what the warning lights were telling him.

He knew his father had always warned about a hard reboot of the system, but Edward didn't think he had a choice. Praying he wasn't making things worse, he opened the clear cover over the master power button. He pushed and released it.

The console went black at once; the siren cut off as if it had never existed. Edward's ears rang in its absence. The faint white noise of the air filter system, so prevalent he never noticed it, shut down, making the house eerily quiet. And then the console flickered as it rebooted. After several anxious minutes, a prompt appeared: *Unauthorized system power down. Reboot all systems?*

Edward typed Y for yes and watched the system restart itself. He heard the air filtration system kick back on. When the main console screen reappeared, there was no error, and all systems were green.

Oh thank the gods. Edward slumped back in the desk chair and pulled off his mask.

Moll pulled hers off too. "Oh, Edward." She still sounded frightened.

"I'll send out a message first thing in the morning, see if we can get someone to come check the system."

She nodded, her lips pressed tight. "What about *him?*"

Knox. Edward felt his a stab of fear in his gut. "I have to go look for him."

"Oh, not in this wind. Edward, ya can't!"

He didn't bother to waste energy arguing. He knew Moll didn't like Knox and probably wouldn't care if he died out there. Edward just pushed himself out of the chair and jogged upstairs. He pulled on his heaviest clothes and boots. Back down in the entryway, Moll was waiting for him.

"Please, please think about this! I just checked the sensors. The wind speed is sixty. Ya can't go out in this! He's just a recon. He's not worth it." She dragged on his arm, her old woman's face harsh with determination.

"Moll, I need Knox to help me run the farm and... he's my friend. I've got to try!"

Edward shook her off and grasped at the front door. When he pulled it open, he nearly tripped over Knox, who was just coming up the steps.

"Knox!" Edward screamed, the wind battering him even here, at the door. Knox was bleeding from a dozen cuts on his chest, arms, and face. He was only wearing a thin sleeveless shirt, now ripped and bloody. But his eyes were his own as he stared down into Edward's, not those of the panicked animal he'd been earlier.

Edward grabbed him and pulled him inside. Between him and

Moll, they managed to get the door closed. Knox collapsed on the floor inside the doorway.

"By the heavens, Knox!" Edward wasn't sure if he was relieved Knox was alive or upset that he was so cut up and bloodied.

"I'll fetch the disinfectant," Moll tsked. She was shaking her head as she left, as if the whole world had gone mad.

"Are you all right?" Edward asked Knox, a ridiculous question, yet Knox nodded.

"Yes. Nothing is broken."

"Thank the gods. Come on, let's get you upstairs. We have to wash out every single one of those cuts."

Edward helped Knox to his feet and then tried to put an arm around his waist to help him up the stairs, but Knox pushed his hands away as if to say that he could do it.

On the way up the stairs, Edward stayed behind Knox. He could see tears up and down his trousers and, through them, bloody cuts. "You hit the borderlands," Edward said, upset.

"Yes."

"Hells, that rock is like cut glass."

Knox said nothing more. On the second floor, he paused, as if unsure if he should continue to the attic, but Edward was having none of it.

"You need to soak in the tub. The only one is mine. Come on."

When they got to the bathroom, Edward turned the taps to hot and began to fill the bath, but Knox just stood there, looking down. He held out his hands, palms up. He had a gash along the back of one hand that dripped onto the floor.

"Oh my heavens," Moll said with an annoyed huff as she appeared in the doorway. She had the medical kit and the large bottle of spore-killing disinfectant. "He's blood from head to toe!"

Edward took the supplies from her and set them on the floor. "Thank you, Moll."

"I'll do it," Moll said crisply, trying to shove Edward out. "I can wash them cuts as well as anyone. Don't look like any of them will need stitchin' or likewise anythin' fancy."

Edward held his ground. "*No.* I don't think he'd be comfortable with you doing it. You'd best go."

Moll's mouth dropped open and her face grew distressed. "Edward, please. It's... not right. Ya mustn't do this by yourself. It's not yer place, and it's... it's not right!"

Edward understood what he saw in her eyes, and knew her fears were not really about the task being below his station. She saw through him. And she was right. His stomach burned with shame, but he clenched his jaw stubbornly. "Moll, go to bed. I'll take care of it." His tone brooked no argument. He saw the resignation come into her eyes, resignation and a hardening too, a hardening against him. He didn't care. "*Now*, Moll."

She left, shutting the door quietly behind her. Edward turned to Knox, who was watching him with dark, intent eyes.

"You probably remember from when I had my cut," Edward said, trying for a casual tone. "Any opening in the skin has to be washed thoroughly with spore killer. It stings like hell but it must be done. If there are spores in the wounds, they can embed into the body and, well, it's not pretty."

Edward tried to smile encouragingly at Knox, but he was shaking. The hot water of the bath was making steam rise in the room. Edward adjusted the water temperature and then poured a liberal amount of the disinfectant into the water. He stepped closer to Knox and his fingers tugged at the bottom of what was left of Knox's shirt. It didn't have buttons and needed to come off over the head. Knox raised his arms and Edward pulled it up and off. As Knox's chest came into view—muscled, lightly hairy, and with the caged heart tattoo—*he was undressing Knox*—arousal bit deep into Edward's lower belly, sudden as the strike of a snake. He sucked in his cheeks to muffle a cry.

Knox said nothing, but his gaze never left Edward's face. Edward's heart was trying to push its way out of his chest as he dropped his fingers to the button of Knox's work pants. In his peripheral vision, he could see the blood still dripping from Knox's hand to the floor, and it reminded Edward of his erotic dream, the blood dripping from the tattoo. He could see that tattoo now, and the peaked nipple to the left of it. Edward was not a short man, but Knox was taller still by a good head and his bare chest was so close.

Edward managed to open the button and, his fingers visibly trembling now, he tugged on the zipper. His hand brushed against a very large erection straining behind the fabric. He gasped and froze, his knees going weak as desire slammed into him. Knox closed one hand over Edward's elbow to steady him. The other hand closed over his own, still immobile on the zipper tab, and helped him tug the zipper down. Edward shut his eyes, a moan emerging, unwelcome, from his throat. When the pants were open, Knox pushed Edward's palm against the pulsing flesh inside. His hand wrapped around the hard cock of its own accord. He moved closer, desperate to rut his own erection into Knox's thigh, desperate for everything.

And then he realized they couldn't do this.

"*Ah*! We... we can't. We have to get your cuts cleaned," Edward panted. He forced himself to let go and take a step back. He cursed his timing as he opened his eyes and saw the naked hunger on Knox's face. He wanted nothing more than to let Knox completely possess him this very second, but the cuts had to be tended to. It was life or death. "Please get in the bath," he whispered.

Knox grunted and dropped his gaze. He shoved down his pants and stepped out of them. The sight of his cock, hard enough to stick up toward his belly, thick and heavy and veined, made another moan rise in Edward's throat. He swallowed it. Knox turned toward the bath. "I can do it alone."

"No," Edward said firmly. "I won't breathe easy until I know every cut has been scrubbed."

Knox stepped into the tub. His back was a marvel—huge, sculpted muscles, a firm ass, and the rope tattoo that lay across the top of his shoulders. As he sank into the water, Edward remembered to speak a warning. "It's going to sting."

But he was a little late. As the water hit the back of Knox's legs, he bowed up and hissed in pain.

"I know. I'm sorry." Edward grabbed a rough cloth and knelt beside the tub. "The sting fades, but we might as well get it all over with at once. Can you lie back completely?"

Knox glared at him. "That's easy for you to say."

Edward couldn't suppress a smile. "Get everything in the water now and the pain will be gone in five minutes, I promise." *Well, except for the scrubbing part.* "And close your eyes tight. If the disinfectant gets in them it will *really* hurt."

Knox sank down in the tub, his knees bending and coming out of the water. He went under, his eyes squeezed shut. Edward saw a shiver of pain race though him but he stayed down. Edward began to work the cloth at the cuts on his arms. Then Knox came up, gasping.

"Ow!" he bellowed loudly.

"Hang on. Here!" Edward grabbed a towel and gave it to Knox so he could rub his eyes enough to open them.

Edward couldn't help but notice that, although Knox's erection had flagged, it had not completely vanished. He steeled himself to ignore it, though, as he squirted disinfecting soap onto the cloth and scrubbed all the cuts he could see on Knox's arms and chest, then moved around to his back. He could tell when the overall sting of the spore killer began to fade and the pain of the pressure he applied to each cut took the forefront. But Knox stoically bore it all.

"Stand up," Edward ordered when he'd done all the cuts on the upper body.

Like a giant rising out of the sea, the great body stood up, displacing the water, rivulets running down his torso. This put Knox's cock almost level with Edward's face, an ungodly temptation, but he willed himself to ignore it. He ignored the magnificent body in front of him too as he scrubbed at the cuts on the thighs and knees and then, grabbing Knox's hips and urging him to turn, at the gashes on the backs of his legs.

None of the wounds were bad enough to need stitching, nor were they bleeding anymore. Already the spore killer had begun to dry out the tissue in the wounds. Even the gash on the back of his hand, which Edward tended to gently, was no longer dripping blood.

When Edward had scrubbed the last cut, he couldn't help but stop and stare in appreciation at the firm waist, the curve of the broad back, the lavish expanse of shoulders, and the rounded muscles of Knox's ass. It was truly the most beautiful body Edward had ever seen or could even imagine. He dropped the cloth in the water and ran his fingers lightly over one hip.

Knox started a little. "Am I done?" he asked, his voice rough.

"Y-yes." Edward's voice cracked and he cleared his throat. "If you dry off, I can put some ointment on—"

Knox turned and stepped out of the tub. One look at his face and the words dried up in Edward's mouth. *Oh gods.*

~9~

KNOX KNEW he wasn't fully in control of this body at the moment, but he didn't care. The lust that had been growing for Edward for weeks, made thick and rich as honey by deepening affection, had reached critical mass. There was no way he could resist this temptation—being touched and unclothed by Edward, seeing that beautiful face racked with desire as Edward saw this body naked for the first time, the sexual need that poured off him in waves. This body wanted to answer that trembling plea with every single, solitary fiber.

Knox was going to take him.

He stepped out of the tub and ignored the towel Edward scrambled to grab. Still wet, he took Edward by the hips and lifted him up so that they were eye-to-eye, then pressed him back against the bathroom wall. Edward groaned and surrendered without a shot fired, his mouth going slack, his eyes half-lidded and soft focused.

"*Knox*," he whispered. There was a tiny spark of fear in those eyes, but there was also a thrill and a need so harsh it contorted Edward's panting lips

"Tell me to stop," Knox said fiercely.

"No! Gods, don't stop. Please." Edward grasped Knox's forearms in desperation.

"Are you certain you want this? Even knowing what I am?"

Edward's eyes widened and he hesitated, but only for a second. "You are... my friend. My only friend," he whispered, with shaky, heart-wrenching sincerity.

Knox lost his breath in the ache that filled his chest, threatening to crack him in two with longing. It was hope and the memory of what it meant to be loved, and it was the debilitating knowledge that any such hope was illusionary. He was not a creature worthy of love. But he *could* have this, this moment of touch and pleasure with this man, and he would have it.

Knox pressed himself against Edward, pinning him to the wall with his entire body. Edward was dressed for the outdoors and his heavy clothes felt rough and thick and heavenly against Knox's skin. He even welcomed the way the fabric abraded his cuts, making him feel everything more keenly. His cock, heavy and hard, pressed into Edward's belly and found an answering ridge that sent a thrill of excitement down Knox's spine. His hands rose to touch Edward's face with a gentleness that contrasted with his aggressive posture and with the lust he knew must be showing on his face. He ran his thumb over those full, soft lips.

Edward opened his mouth and licked at Knox's thumb. He pressed his hips up. *"Please."*

Knox gave in. He captured Edward's mouth—invaded and plundered. Edward made soft sounds as he kissed back. He wrapped his arms around Knox's shoulders and held him tight, so painfully tight.

In an instant, the cloth between them, which had felt so sensual against his naked skin a moment ago, was now an annoyance, a barrier between Knox and what he craved—Edward's skin, to touch that body, to sink into it.

Knox pinned Edward with his chest and made enough space between them to get his hands on the fastenings of Edward's pants. The hooks surrendered to his fingers and he pushed the cloth down, exposing Edward's cock. Edward tried to press it up into Knox's hands, needy and whimpering, but Knox was intent on his task. He pushed the pants farther down and, when he encountered the tops of boots, he pulled away from Edward's greedy mouth and barked an order. "Give me your foot."

Bereft of Knox's mouth, Edward attacked his throat instead, licking and sucking as he raised his foot as best he could in the tangle of his pants. Knox grabbed his heel and pulled off one boot, then its mate, and finally the pants were gone. Knox ran his hands up the backs of Edward's thighs to his buttocks, being careful of the nearly healed gash. The skin was soft and cool against Knox's injured hands. Edward responded by lifting those long, pale legs up and around Knox's hips. The urge to sink his cock into Edward's sweet body right there was almost overwhelming.

Knox groaned. "I don't want to hurt you." He put a hand on Edward's chin and gently lifted it, then couldn't resist kissing those swollen lips.

"You won't. I've done this before, and I want you. But first take me to bed. I want to touch you and taste you. I want everything. *Please, Knox.*"

Knox put his arms under Edward's buttocks and turned them both. He managed to open the bathroom door with one hand and carried Edward to his bed. Knox laid him down and pulled the sweater and shirt over his head.

Now. Now Edward was naked before him. Without his old-fashioned landowner's clothes, Knox could finally see him clearly, even in the low, yellow light of a single lamp. He was lean and hairless, with well-defined shoulders, chest, and arms. His skin was as pale as Pravalean snow, flawless. A fine, dark trail began below his belly button and descended to curly hair at his groin and the jutting desire of an engorged cock. His bullocks were high and tight, a succulent little mouthful.

Knox rumbled in his throat as he feasted on Edward with his eyes. It had been so long since he'd seen a beautiful man like this one, aching and hard with wanting him, and it was a sight he might never see again—he'd learned to count on nothing.

"Knox," Edward breathed. He arched his hips, his cock jutting straight up, and Knox couldn't resist. He leaned forward and took it into his mouth to the hilt.

Edward screamed, a deep, wonderful sound that merged with the howling wind outside into something primal and erotic. Knox hummed, his eyes rolling back in his head with the pleasure of having a man in this mouth, *his mouth.* Edward began to thrust, unable to control himself. Already he was so hard his shaft was rigid and taut against Knox's tongue, almost painful as it struck the back of his throat. But Knox was glad for the aggression. He craved it. The power that was wrapped up in this body was tensed and ready to break free, and he wanted it wild. He pulled off slowly, sucking hard until Edward's cock popped from his mouth. Then he grabbed Edward's hips and threw him higher on the bed. Knox crawled forward on his knees and grabbed Edward again, pinning his back to the headboard this time. His moves were rough but not rough enough to hurt.

Edward's eyes were wide with shock and lust. "Yes, yes," he chanted, putting a hand around Knox's neck and pulling him in with surprising strength. Their mouths clashed, raw and frantic, and Knox sought warm flesh, running his hands over smooth skin everywhere he could reach. When he finally touched Edward's cock, Edward gasped and pulled away.

"Want you inside me *now*," he panted, his voice surprisingly dark and wicked.

Edward's words hardened Knox further until he was so turgid he thought he might burst open from the pressure. Before he could move to obey, Edward pushed him hard, forcing him back, and crawled on top of him, attacking his neck and chest, biting and licking. Knox grabbed Edward's hips and ground up into the space behind his balls, wanting entrance more than he wanted to breathe.

Edward rose up and was silhouetted in a flash of lightning from outside. He reached over to the bedside table and grabbed a bottle of skin lotion. He pumped a handful from it and slicked Knox's cock.

Oh gods. The feeling of Edward's slick grip going up and down his shaft nearly drove Knox out of his mind. He hissed and cursed when Edward's hands left him bereft.

"Be patient," Edward growled. He reached behind himself with those long fingers, preparing himself to take Knox's cock.

"Yes," Knox groaned, unable to keep his hips from moving in time with the thrust of Edward's hand. He was about mad with need by the time Edward rose up on his knees and positioned himself. The boy's face was stony with determination, his eyes blown with lust.

They both paused, frozen by the significance of this moment. Knox went rigid, fighting the compulsion to thrust deep. He could feel the resistance of Edward's ring as he bore down to no avail. Then something gave way, and the head of his cock broke through into a sucking heat. Edward cried out, either in pleasure or in pain. He lowered himself slowly, slowly. Sweat popped out on Knox's brow with the agony of remaining passive, of needing to wait. And when Edward's ass finally touched Knox's thighs, Edward braced above him, his head thrown back, Knox had to touch. He took Edward's cock in his hand. It had softened a little at the pain and so he worked it, rubbed a thumb over the tip to collect a drop of fluid and then spread it under the head. He spat into his hand and massaged that sweet cock with his fingers and thumb, grunting at the pleasure of each touch and stroke as if it were his own flesh. His own member throbbed in sympathy deep inside Edward's tight heat. Soon, Edward was completely rigid again, gasping and moaning steadily.

He leaned back on his hands and thrust up into Knox's hand, his channel sliding up and down Knox's painfully hard shaft.

Knox's control broke. With a bellow, he grabbed Edward's hips and rolled them both. He got onto his knees, still buried deep, pulling Edward's hips up with him. With his thighs spread and braced and one arm secure under the small of Edward's back, Knox began to thrust. Edward's shoulders were still on the bed, and he placed his feet on the mattress to push back against the momentum. He gave off a continual stream of moans and pleas for Knox to take him harder, for *more*. Knox obliged, slamming into him, even as the lightning from the window lit up the room and cast his heaving shadow across Edward's torso. He spit on his free hand again and fisted it over Edward's cock, letting the lunging of his own member drive Edward's in and out of his hand.

Edward panted and groaned, so low and deep it seemed to come from his bones. He planted his feet more firmly on the bed and grasped the bedclothes with both hands. He whispered encouragements and demands, completely unconscious of what was pouring out of his mouth.

It was a moment Knox wanted to hold onto forever. But seeing Edward lost in passion was so arousing to his mind and the sensations on his cock so intense, Knox couldn't last long. He was not alone. Edward's panting grew desperate and he stiffened, screaming, "Now!" The fist through which he was slipping grew slick with jets of semen. His channel squeezed Knox painfully tight, forcing his orgasm to boil up inside him. It seemed to originate from every part of him, body and mind, drawing all of him in to one singularity of pleasure before bursting forth like an exploding star.

When he could breathe again, Knox lowered Edward gently to the bed and collapsed beside him. Edward was immediately in his arms, soft and damp and loose limbed with satiation. He felt and smelled so sweet, Knox could not resist nuzzling into his neck. *Oh, if only I could truly have this. Sweet Edward.*

"Hells, I have never felt anything like that," Edward breathed in wonder.

"This body has its advantages," Knox murmured, knowing for certain his old body could not have done that.

"It's the most wondrous body I've ever seen," Edward said frankly. He nuzzled further into Knox, his face rubbing along the hairs of his chest. "Knox...." His voice sounded thick with emotion, and he hesitated.

Don't say it, Knox thought. *Don't give your heart to me. For as much as I'd treasure it, I don't deserve it and it would ruin you.*

To keep the words from being said, either by the too-generous Edward or by his own weak tongue, Knox kissed him. He kissed Edward until there were no more words waiting between them. And then he kept kissing him until they were both hard again. Edward explored him this time, made a study of this body as thorough as the one Knox had made in the privacy of his own bathroom. When Knox couldn't take it anymore, they brought each other to completion with their mouths, more slowly this time and with agonizing tenderness.

~10~

OH, WHAT a beautiful, terrible vision. Their ship sat just above the sensor line, above the ability of any human eye to see them from the ground. Looking out the porthole, he studied the lavender-and-green expanse of land, the swirling of what looked like clouds from this height but were really banks of mist. The spaceport was barely a blemish on the lavender sea of rock and the enormous swatches of neon green of the lichen, but it glinted, making a fine target.

"Trevellyn, we need those shields down," a masculine voice reminded him over the comm.

Trevellyn turned to the young man sweating over the console. The cadet looked up in frustration. "I—I'm sorry, sir. I've tried everything, but I can't log onto the Kalan system."

The boy was young and earnest. For a moment, Trevellyn allowed himself to feel regret that this boy would probably not live long. But then again, he had little to live for.

"Let me try."

The boy rolled aside as Trevellyn leaned over the console, fingers dancing on the keys.

Intelligence had given them information on the firewall the station was using. Trevellyn tried scripts to exploit several vulnerabilities he knew existed in the software. But he found they'd been patched. Someone was on the ball. The grid was tight.

He sighed in frustration and wracked his brain. He recalled a worm program he'd used years ago on a predecessor of this firewall. The undocumented backdoor the worm took advantage of had likely been patched, but then again, it wasn't a widely known exploit. He quickly typed the script, digging hard into his memory to recall the exact syntax.

"Trevellyn, status!" the commander ordered over the comm.

"Working on it," he answered calmly.

"Time?"

"At least ten minutes, but—"

The console in front of him dinged and gave him a prompt. Root access.

"Commander, I'm in!"

"Thank the gods! We've spotted something on radar and we're out of time. Get those shields down now."

"I'm on it."

He typed on the keyboard, fingers flying. He didn't know this system, but he'd seen those of other spaceports. If he could just find the building's maintenance system.... He was still working when the commander came on again, sounding breathless. "Federation ship approaching. We're going to have to pull out. Trevellyn!"

The console in front of him blinked—Shields down.

"Shields are down, Commander. Go now!"

He went to the port window, his hand clenched into fists with the suspense. They'd worked and planned so long for this. There was a streak to his right as the missiles were launched, and then, ten seconds later, the spaceport below was obscured by billows of smoke. Oddly, there was no sound, not here. But down there, far below him, was fire and death and chaos.

All life is sacred.

EDWARD WOKE up to a sudden movement. He sat up to see Knox lurch naked from the bed and run into the bathroom. A second later, he heard the sound of retching.

"Knox?"

Edward scrambled from the bed and followed. He paused in the bathroom doorway, wanting to give Knox space if he needed it. The huge man was crumpled at the commode.

"Are you all right?" Edward asked, worried the flight into the dark last night had harmed Knox more deeply than he'd realized.

Knox clung to the commode a moment longer, then reached out and pulled the handle. The air stank, bitter and acrid, but Edward didn't care. He only wanted to comfort Knox. Knox looked like some ancient painting of a martyr—head slumped in defeat, naked, pale, and covered with red cuts. It made Edward feel a trickle of fear. He wet a cloth at the sink and took a step toward Knox, but the recon scrambled back against the wall on his ass and held up a hand. "Don't come closer."

"Knox, what is it? What's wrong? You're scaring me."

When Edward made no further move to approach him, Knox lowered his hand. His face was gray and contorted with some strong emotion, his eyes red. "I had a dream... a memory. From my old life." His voice cracked.

A chill swept through Edward as if an icy finger had been laid on his neck. He was naked too, he realized, and he suddenly felt terribly vulnerable. He wrapped his arms around himself. *Gods, no. Don't let it be bad.*

"W-what did you remember?" Edward whispered.

Knox blinked rapidly, his mouth twisted. His eyes were filled with self-disgust. "I was on a spaceship. It... attacked Kalan. The spaceport. We fired missiles. I... I was the one who broke into the spaceport's system and lowered the shields."

Edward took a step backward, horror sinking into him. "What? N-no. That can't be. It was just a dream, a nightmare! Because of what I said, about my father and brother. You just—"

Knox shook his head. He looked wrecked. "No, Edward. I was there. They called me Trevellyn."

Trevellyn. The name rang some dire bell in the back of Edward's mind. He hadn't followed the trials much, not like everyone else on Kalan, most everyone thirsty for the blood of the pirate raiders. But for Edward, still mourning father and brother, the reminder had been too painful. Even so, the name felt familiar and ugly, like a name he might have absorbed in a book of deadly snakes.

"No," he whispered again, shaking his head.

Knox squeezed his eyes shut and covered his face with his hands. "Gods forgive me. I'm so sorry, Edward."

He sounded anguished, but it barely registered. Edward turned and stumbled back to his bed. He sat down heavily, staring into space, feeling a terrible numbness spreading through his limbs, his lungs, his heart.

He didn't know how long he sat there before Knox appeared again, dressed and hovering in the door of Edward's room.

"If I thought it would make things right, I'd walk off into the storms. But you still need my help. I'll move back to the recon barracks and get you through until the transport comes. And once you've replaced me, I'll do whatever you decide. If you want to sell me or... or execute me, I will comply."

Edward didn't answer; he only turned his face pointedly aside. Knox made a small sound and walked away. When Knox had gone, Edward shut the door and locked it. Then he fell into bed and sobbed as he felt his heart breaking, the pain nearly unbearable.

Why me? What did I do to deserve all of this? I only wanted to love someone. Only a recon, a being that no one else wanted. Can I not have even that? Why must everyone be taken from me?

He cried until the pull of sleep dragged him into desired oblivion.

EDWARD LAY in a depressed, semiconscious daze for hours. He finally dragged himself to the bathroom. He stared at the tub where Knox had been laid out, naked, the night before. He looked in the mirror, face impassive, as he took in the slight marks of lovemaking on his neck, on his chest above one nipple, the faint bruises on his hips from where Knox had held him. He felt the stretched ache of his anus and the dried remains of their passion flaked on his skin. Even while he felt as emotionally numb and blank as scorched earth, his body trembled as though with a fever. He set about rinsing the bath over and over to erase what he imagined were lingering traces of Knox. And then, finally, he filled it and sank into the water. He scrubbed himself roughly, removing every bit of the recon from his skin.

Last night, he'd had a lover. Today he had nothing.

Moll had knocked several times and Edward had ignored her. When he went downstairs, dressed for the day at nearly sundown, she was not pleased to see him.

"Did he hurt ya?" she demanded, white with anger. "He's moved off back to the barracks, you lie in bed all day.... What did he do?"

"Nothing," Edward said.

Moll clearly wanted to hold her tongue but failed. Her face was ugly with disgust. "Ya let him touch you, didn't ya? That... thing, that creature. Ya wanted it."

Edward was shocked she would say such a thing. He could feel his face turning red. "Knox is back in the barracks, and he'll never step foot in this house again, Moll. That is all you need to know. And it isn't, and it never was, your business! I am master here."

Moll looked away but her mouth was still pinched in anger. "Ya should never have let him inside in the first place, not a recon. Your father was right about you. And to think of the times I've defended ya like a son! Oh, why did Anese have to die?"

Edward just stared at her in disbelief. *Not another one. Not Moll too. I can't bear it.* "I'm sorry if I've disappointed you," he said tightly. "I'm doing the best I can. Now I have to go out to the factory and make sure the harvesters are emptied."

Edward turned to put on one of the filter masks that hung by the back door.

"I'll have dinner waiting for ya when ya get back," Moll said as he left the house, her voice softening a bit.

Perhaps it was an olive branch of sorts, or perhaps it was pity. Neither was sufficient to erase the sting of yet another betrayal.

EDWARD HAD stayed abed all day, something he'd never done before. Fortunately, it was not a processing day, and the work he should have done could be shunted to tomorrow. Knox was waiting with the harvesters in the factory hanger. They appeared to be full as usual.

Edward said nothing to him, nor did he look Knox in the eye. He put on the extra protection of a factory mask and gloves and did the minimum he had to do to empty the harvesters of the lichen—rich with spores as it should be—and put it in the storage tanks for later processing. Knox used the air spray to clean out the harvesters for reuse the next day. When they were done, Knox waited, legs slightly spread, hands behind his back, eyes downcast.

Edward could not look at him without still finding him handsome, without feeling the warmth of wanting him, and he *loathed* himself for that, despised his own weak nature.

"Leave now. I'll lock up," Edward said coldly. Knox left.

THAT NIGHT, after picking at his supper, Edward sat alone in the library. He checked the console—all the systems looked fine. He sent out a general SOS to his neighbors for someone to come do maintenance on the air filtration system, explained the alarm that had gone off the night before. He didn't get an immediate reply.

While he was waiting for one, he was drawn to the interspace. He hesitated, but it was like pushing at a juicy wound. He could not resist. He did a search on the terms "Kalan" and "Trevellyn." Photos flooded the screen. A sound of distress left Edward's throat.

Comm Officer Levi Trevellyn, captured by the Federation in a pirate attack on Kalan along with the entire crew of the raider *Barstock*. They were tried as a group for the murders of over fifty Kalanese who died in a raid on the Kalan spaceport and for the attempted theft of billions of *dragers* of pharmaceutical spores for sale on the black drug market. All were condemned to death.

Edward shut his eyes, his fingers trembling on the keyboard. He opened them again. The face was only vaguely familiar, but Edward had seen it before on the news. Trevellyn was a lean man, no larger than Edward. He looked to be in his forties but with a world-weariness that said he'd been through much. He had a fine, noble face, long, dirty-blond hair, and piercingly intelligent gray eyes. It was a good face, one Edward could find appealing if he were not bound by his very blood to despise it.

Did he see Knox in those eyes? He couldn't tell.

If you play with the devil, boy, the bill always comes due.

It was something Edward's father used to say. He was always quoting pithy things like that. Always had a strong, masculine saying that was just right for demonstrating how Edward was weak. There'd been no love lost between them. His father was a hard man, a true Kalanese farmer. He'd doted on Edward's older brother, Jeb, who was a "fine figure of a man." Not like Edward, who was too soft, too needy, too shy, too sympathetic to others.

Why didn't you take me with you, Mother? Why'd you leave me here with him?

After his mother had fled Kalan, supposedly to visit her family but then never bothering to return, Edward had lost the only person in the household who understood him. But Edward had his out. He'd been allowed to go off to school, have dreams of a different life, until that attack on the spaceport put an end to all of that, forced him to return. But even if Edward had never been that close to his father or to Jeb, he was still bound by all that was sacred and right to avenge them if he could, and maybe to avenge his own wasted life too.

What irony had brought Knox here? Were the gods having a laugh? Or perhaps it was no coincidence. Perhaps the Federation had its own sense of poetic justice—to put the killers from the *Barstock* to work doing slave labor on Kalan, to break their backs harvesting the spores they once tried to steal, to be worn down and worn down and finally erased once and for all by the punishing winds of this place.

"I hate you, Trevellyn," Edward said out loud, staring at the images on the screen. But no matter how many times he said it, he could not for the life of him make himself *feel* it in his numb, cold heart.

He closed the interspace browser and checked for replies to his SOS. There were none.

~11~

THERE WAS a storm coming. It was going to be bad, Edward had said, the worst of the year. That's what the forecasters were predicting. When Edward had told Knox about the storm and told him what they needed to do to prepare, it was the most the man had spoken to Knox in a fortnight. Edward had hardly looked at Knox since the night they'd made love, since the night Knox had remembered he was responsible for the deaths of Edward's family. Knox understood he'd hurt Edward badly and that Edward bore the pain alone. That was so very, very unacceptable, but there was nothing Knox could do to change it.

When he moved back into the barracks, the other recons just stared at him as though he were some species they didn't recognize. They went out of their way to ignore him, walking around him if he were in the way in the barracks, ignoring him if he spoke to them. They obeyed him in the field, treated him as foreman. But they could not figure out how to respond to him in the barracks, so they simply didn't.

It was strange. Before Knox had spent that time in the house, before Edward, he'd been like these recons. Maybe he'd never been entirely like them; he remembered thinking them dull, even then. But he knew he'd spent long hours staring at the ceiling above his bunk and not thinking of anything at all, not *wanting* to talk or think, just wanting to be left alone.

He could not achieve that same place of forgetfulness now. His mind worked and worked like an engine trying to turn over. He wanted, *needed*, to remember more about who he was, about Trevellyn, about his family, where he came from, the spaceship, why he'd done what he did. But the edges of that dream were sharp and bright like the borderlands. He couldn't see beyond them.

He no longer had flashes of memory in which he saw that man, the man who must have been Trevellyn's lover. Instead, he saw Edward— Edward as he tried to undo Knox's trousers in the bathroom, the look on his face as he touched Knox's cock and closed his eyes tight against his own rapturous response. The way he'd looked spread out naked on his bed. The way Edward had explored this body in the dark, as if he wanted to spend hours touching, tasting. And he saw Edward in the evenings too—the bright and eager inquisitive look on his face as they talked. Knox missed that friendship most of all.

To escape the churning of his mind, he wrote. He'd asked Edward if he could take some paper and pencils from the factory office, and Edward had merely nodded. So Knox took them and he spent the evenings in the barracks writing page after page. He wrote down every scrap of memory fragment he'd had, even the description of his death on that steel table. He wrote down every word he could remember Edward saying to him, every look, every touch. He listed the books Edward had given him to read and what he'd thought of them. He wrote down what they'd eaten in the dining room of the house. He even started making records of the harvesting—the weather, how well the recons had worked, the take weight at the end of the day. He wrote everything and anything in a frantic flood of dashed-off letters. It was as if these memories, too, would be taken from him if he didn't write them down.

He wrote long apologies to Edward that he never showed him. He wrote poems to Edward's beauty. He put the pages under his mattress and never said any of this to Edward.

KNOX AND the other recons closed all the heavy metal shutters over the windows on the house and the barracks and bolted them. The window glass was strong enough to survive most storms; not the one that was coming. They worked sunup to sundown in the fields for four days straight to harvest every spore they could before the storm. Edward processed several batches in the factory.

The day the storm was to arrive, someone knocked on the barracks door just before sunrise. Knox answered it. The wind was already blowing fast enough to have a faint, eerie sound, and it whipped Edward's hair around his mask as he stepped inside.

The recon barracks didn't have an air filter because the recons had their own built in, so Edward didn't remove his mask. He set down two heavy, covered buckets.

"Fresh food for a few days at least. And you should have plenty of stores of emergency bars. Water too. Have you checked?"

Knox nodded. "Yes. We've enough for more than a month."

"Good. There'll be no work this morning. It's upon us already. It'll be impossible to leave the barracks within a few hours. Don't let anyone go out until the storm's passed. I'll come and knock when it's safe to leave."

Knox just looked at Edward. He had a terrible ache inside. Even though he'd accepted that Edward didn't want to see him anymore, and he knew he deserved it, he missed Edward's company with a deep, hollow craving. And it was so hard to let Edward board himself up into that house with no one but Moll to look out for him in such a vicious storm. Knox swallowed down his protectiveness. It was a bitter, bitter taste.

As if reading his mind, or maybe by some miracle having similar thoughts of his own, Edward looked torn, like perhaps he wanted to say something. Maybe he'd invite Knox into the house for the storm. But in the end, he said nothing. He only turned and opened the door.

"Please be safe!" Knox called after him. He braced himself in the doorway, holding the door wide, as he watched Edward struggle up the path to the house.

THE WIND, dear gods, the wind. It had been gaining in force until it screamed like a dying rabbit as it ripped along the contours of the Kalanese landscape. In the barracks, the five recons played cards over and over at the table, never speaking a word, their attention completely rapt. Maybe it helped them shut out the storm, kept them calm. But Knox was going out of his mind.

He kept thinking about Edward, Edward alone in that house with Moll. Of course, Moll wouldn't hurt Edward, as much as Knox disliked her and she disliked him. But she'd be no help either if something went wrong.

What could go wrong? That house had withstood storms for hundreds of years; the shutters were fastened. Yet Knox couldn't let it go. His body and mind were reacting primitively—outside was danger. He needed to be with the one he loved, needed to make sure Edward was safe. It made no sense but Knox couldn't shake it.

The one he loved. He did. He did love Edward. And he didn't regret it, even though he never expected to have that love returned.

He could not help but go to the door and listen; for what, he did not know. But on one such trip to the door, the wind dipped down for a brief respite and he could swear he heard something, something in the distance. Before he could be sure, the wind was howling again.

I imagined it. There was nothing there, only the echo in this head of the wind.

But he couldn't ignore the seed of dread that had settled in his stomach. He stood, his ear plastered to the door, waiting for the wind to die down again. Finally it did, and he heard it—faint, but it was there. The air filtration system alarm.

Knox backed up from the door in fear. "Oh gods!"

The recons, as a unit, looked at him blankly as he stood there pacing and panicking. Then they went back to their game.

There was nothing for it—Knox had to get to Edward. He tore open the trunk at his bed and put on two heavy sweaters over what he was wearing. He put on his work boots and took his protective longcoat and buttoned it up to the neck.

One of the recons stood in front of the door, waiting for him. It was Cray, one of the older ones. He shook his head slowly. "Go out there, you die."

Knox huffed in frustration. "I have to. I have no choice. Close the door after me."

Cray stared at him and then moved, as if unwilling to challenge whatever fate decreed. Knox went door and stood, taking deep breaths and trying to plan some sort of strategy. The house was due north by about eighty yards. If he ran when the wind dropped, stayed low to the ground when it was at its worst, perhaps he could make it. He had to make it.

He waited, his hand on the door, until he heard the wind die down again. Then he flung the door open and ran for all he was worth.

He hadn't made it ten yards before the wind swept back up with a gust. It nearly lifted him off his feet, so he dropped to the ground and pressed tight, covering his head with his arms. Gods, it was strong! It dug into him, trying to get its claws under him, to roll him. And once started, he knew he would roll over and over along the ground like a leaf until he was battered and bloody and far from the house. He gritted his teeth and used all his strength to resist, pushing his body into the rocky ground. The wind whipped his hair in fury at being denied and grit tore at his exposed hands, his throat. After what seemed an eternity, the wind died down a bit and he stood up and ran.

Sprinting, dropping, clinging…. It took forever to get to the house. But finally he was there, the big back door looming over him. It wasn't a very protected space; the wind cut along the sides of the house like a river rushing around a rock. Knox lay on the ground at the door and raised his fist to pound. Again. Again. The spore alarm was loud here and it cut through Knox like a dissecting blade.

Finally, he heard a voice on the other side, screaming to be heard. "Who is it?"

"It's Knox! Let me in!"

But Edward didn't. He didn't open the door. Knox laid there, hopeless. What did he do now? Work his way back to the barracks? Leave Edward to his fate? He lifted his fist and pounded again. "Edward!" he screamed.

"Wait!" he heard, faintly.

He waited. Edward hadn't left the door, he was right on the other side. And Knox understood. The next time the wind dipped, the door yanked open, and Edward was pulling him inside and slamming the door shut behind him.

THEY SAT on the kitchen floor, getting their breath back. The alarm screamed relentlessly. Edward was wearing one of the filtration masks. His face was pale and his eyes large and dark with resignation. Knox attempted to tame his own hair, which was all over his face and crazy from the wind. The backs of his hands, he noted, were raw and abraded. He coughed and then was suddenly hacking, his lungs burning like fire.

Edward came over and lightly rubbed Knox's back. "Breathe. Just try to breathe slowly."

Knox did. After a while, the coughing subsided—and Edward was beside him, an arm around his shoulder. He didn't remove it.

"I… heard the alarm," Knox rasped.

"From the barracks?"

"Yes."

"And you went out in that storm. For me." Edward said it flatly, studying Knox's face.

Knox couldn't help it. He took Edward's hand in his and looked into his eyes, willing Edward to see his sincerity. "I'd do anything for you, Edward. My life… it's not important."

Edward's face crumpled, and he threw himself into Knox's arms. "I don't care! I don't care what you did in your old life, Knox, you're a different person now. I've tried to hate you, but I can't! I don't want to. I forgive you, and I don't want to die without you."

Knox held him tight, reveling in the feeling of Edward in his arms and trying to comprehend the man's generosity of spirit. It was humbling. Edward's forgiveness, the return of his affection, flooded Knox with joy and relief and pleasure so raw it could only be love. How ironic that he'd found it only now, here on Kalan, that he'd had to be cut up into pieces and put back together again to find it. Maybe there was simply more room in this oversized heart.

He stroked Edward's hair. "Shhh! You're not going to die."

"I'm afraid I am." Edward pulled away. His voice was thick and he wiped at tears that wet the black rubber of the mask. "The air filtration system's gone completely red; it's not just a warning this time."

"But you have masks."

Edward shook his head. "A fully charged mask lasts about six hours. There are four in the house, but the chargers are dead too. I've about twenty-two hours of mask time left and this storm is not going to subside for at least three days, more likely a week."

His eyes, as he looked at Knox, were bleak. And not just bleak with fear, but something far more devastated. Fresh tears welled up. "I think… I think it was sabotage, Knox. When I woke up this morning, Moll was gone. Someone must have picked her up in a coach. And then the system went down and the chargers too."

Knox still didn't understand. He shook his head.

"Don't you see? They want me dead. They want this farm, and they don't think I'm fit to run it. They're right, I'm not strong enough. And I don't fit in here. I've failed at everything."

"Stop it!" Knox grabbed Edward's arms and shook him a little. "You work harder than anyone I've ever seen to keep this farm going. They want what's yours because they're greedy. I could see it on their faces at the funeral. And if you don't fit in, it's because you're better than this place, Edward. Your mind and your heart are too big for this narrow life."

Edward didn't look convinced, but he seemed less defeated than he had a moment ago. He took a deep breath and shrugged. "It doesn't matter. I can't fix the system. I've tried rebooting the console a dozen times, and every time it goes right back into red alert. I don't know what else to do."

Knox knew what to do, but he wasn't sure he could. He wanted to. More than anything, he wanted to save Edward. But he wasn't sure if all the will in the world would be enough.

So he pulled Edward in tight and held him, soothed him, kissed his hair, his eyes, the parts of his cheek he could reach around the mask. Edward reached up to take it off.

"No," Knox said, stopping his hand.

"I have to kiss you, Knox. The spores won't kill me right away. You have to breathe them for a while, and the house has been pretty tightly sealed."

Knox wasn't sure about all of that, but he knew he couldn't stop Edward if he was determined, and he wanted to kiss Edward one last time too. "Let's get away from this back door at least. It's been opened."

Edward nodded. Ignoring the infernal shrieking of the alarm, Knox pulled Edward to his feet and they went into the library. Knox shut the door and Edward pulled off his mask.

"One kiss," Knox whispered, as he pulled Edward into his arms.

They kissed long and hungry and slow. Edward's arms were around Knox's shoulders, still holding the mask, and he was standing on his toes. Knox's cradled him, strong and sure. The way their bodies felt pressed together, and the slick suction of their mouths, aroused them both. But there was no need to go anywhere or do anything more than to stretch out this moment and take comfort from one another. Finally, Knox's concern about Edward being out of the mask forced him to break away.

He gently took Edward's hands from around his neck and pressed the mask back to his face. "Please."

Edward put it on.

"I'm so sorry, Edward. For what I did—lowering the shields on the spaceport. I don't know why I did it. I haven't been able to remember anything more."

"It doesn't matter. You're not that person now," Edward insisted, as if willing himself to believe it.

But Knox wasn't sure that was true. He felt a little more like Trevellyn every day, his mind a little sharper, his vision of what it meant to be a man clearer. He thought of that part of his mind as Trevellyn, even if he didn't remember anything more about the man. But he didn't say any of that to Edward.

"I'm going to try to fix the system," Knox said.

"But… you can't even get near the computer."

"I know. They've programmed me with an aversion. I've got to try to break it. If I can get over the fear, I should be able to find out what's wrong and fix it."

Edward shook his head, but there was a new spark of hope in his eyes. "Do you really think you can? The last time this happened, you went out of your mind. If you run out into the storm now…."

"I have to try. I need you to talk to me. Stay with me."

Edward nodded. "If you start to feel like you're losing yourself, back off. Promise me."

Knox squeezed Edward's hand in lieu of promising anything. He knew what was at stake and what he was willing to risk. He turned to the console and looked at it. Already, even from across the room, there was something horrible about it, something cold and glaring and *wrong* that sent a trickle of fear through his bowels.

But he took a deep breath and stepped closer. Closer. Closer.

It got really bad at about three feet. There was a sense of something about to sting him. He couldn't stop a wince or a reflexive swatting at the air in front of his face. He gave a cry of alarm.

"It's okay, Knox. There's nothing there," he heard Edward say from just over his shoulder. His voice sounded a little off.

Knox gritted his teeth and took another step forward. The keyboard was in reach now, sitting on the hard, white counter. It seemed to be waiting for him, deadly and yet compelling like a hypodermic filled with a drug he craved, one that would kill him the moment it entered his veins. And then he saw something crawling over the edge of the keyboard—shiny black eyes large as raisins, a red streak above the eyes, black gossamer wings, a stinger long and thick attached to a pulsating green sac under the wasp's belly.

Knox gasped and took a step back. He felt a hand on his arm.

"Knox, there's nothing there!"

The voice was muffled by the blood coursing in Knox's ears. His breath was gasping, panicked. *Gods,* he had to run. That thing... at any moment it would fly at him, sting.... He could already imagine his hands swelling, his throat closing up. *No air. No air.*

"Knox! There's nothing there! See?" Knox couldn't tear his gaze away from the keyboard, barely registered the voice shouting at him. But then something broke his line of sight. A man—Edward. He stepped up to the keyboard and ran his hands along it. His eyes pleaded with Knox. "Love, there's nothing there. Oh, Knox."

He sounded so despairing. And his hand, it ran right over where the wasp had been—had been and was no longer. Knox gaped, his eyes searching the keyboard, the counter. It was gone.

He swallowed, his heart pounding. Right. He remembered now. He had to touch the keyboard. *Why?* He had to touch the keyboard because.... *Because if I don't fix the system, Edward will die.*

Edward was looking at him, his eyes damp and red, his jaw firm. "Knox, you're safe. There's nothing here," he repeated again and again.

Knox made himself take a step forward. Something in his head screamed and raged. There was a pain as though the flesh of his brain was being torn in two, like a temple veil. He cried out, reached out for Edward's hand on the keyboard. Misunderstanding, Edward started to move back.

"No! N-need you there," Knox said, or tried to say. His voice sounded garbled, the words all mixed up from the storm in his head. But Edward stayed, one hand resting on the top of the keyboard, the other grasping Knox's arm.

"I'm right here. There's nothing there. You're safe. There's nothing there."

Knox clung to the words like a beacon in the dark. He reached for the keys slowly, slowly. His hands trembled and, in a blink, the wasps were back, three of them now, crawling up as if from under the flat keyboard, crawling onto the keys, crawling over Edward's hand.

Knox hissed, his eyes flashing to Edward's face. Edward was not reacting to the wasps.

"There's nothing there, love. Please!"

Knox couldn't bear the sight of those things crawling on Edward, even though part of him understood they weren't real, they were a projection his mind was putting up. So he closed his eyes. His fingers reached and Edward took one hand, than the other, and gently laid them on the keys.

For a long moment, Knox stood, his eyes squeezed shut, teeth clenched, his fingers resting on the cool, rounded squares. The first few moments were agonizing, waiting to be stung, convinced he would be stung. It was like holding his hand as an axe hovered over it, ready to descend and cut it off at the wrist. His heartbeat raced so fast he thought he was going to have a heart attack. But Edward was gently rubbing his arm and Knox held still. He held, goddamn it.

After a long while, when no sting came, Knox's panic began to ease. His heart rate slowed, and he became aware of the steady rub of Edward's thumb on his forearm and the soothing sound of his voice. "You're doing great, Knox. You can do this. You're so strong and brave. You came through that storm for me. I know you can do this."

Edward was just speaking whatever came into his mind, nonsense babbling, Knox knew that, but he still found intense joy in those words. *He thinks I'm brave, that I'm a man, that I'm worthy. I owe you, Edward. My life, my blood. I don't want to fail you.*

The thought gave him the courage to caress the keys, just a little. They were starting to feel familiar under his fingertips. His movements grew larger, circling his fingers on the keys, his eyes still squeezed shut.

This. He remembered this. This was his instrument, wasn't it? His weapon. His canvas. This was more familiar to him than the face in the mirror. This was *Trevellyn*, part of the very fabric of his brain. *Oh yes. This. I know this.*

"You're doing great, Knox. You're doing so well." Edward's voice was rough with stress and relief.

Gods, what Knox must have looked like just now, lost in that panic. He wanted to say something, to reassure Edward. He was feeling better, he was. He could do this. But still, his throat was tight and no reassurances would come.

He opened his eyes to look at the screen—and the world fell apart.

Trevellyn.

He looked at the screen where video after video displayed atrocities, eye-witness testimonies from a dying world. His fingers danced over the keys, desperate, seeking, Espazia, Trent Glom, Portcalus, Greenbeck. Continent after continent, city after city—starvation, panic, bloated bodies stacked in the streets.

They'd only been gone nine months, a trip to a neighboring system to get supplies the Federation had blockaded. Then they'd heard, on their return voyage, that the blockade had been lifted. At first the messages from home had been elated, optimistic. Then several garbled messages had arrived telling them to stay away, to not come home. And then... silence.

Now they sat above their home world, Nobira, and watched the comm videos in utter shock and horror. The last postings had been over a month ago, a lone cameraman stumbling through a city of the dead. Now there was nothing but a digital flatline.

Two billion. Two billion souls.

Even from the upper atmosphere, they could see it, the familiar browns and grays and sage greens of their beloved world taken over by a putrid, neon green.

Mother. Father. Janek, Dazy, my friends, my lover. Gone. All gone.

"NO! NO, no, no, no, no!"

Edward watched Knox collapse at the console, slipping to the floor of the library, his face in agony, sobs heaving in his chest.

"Knox! What is it?" Edward dropped to the floor. He tried to hold Knox, but he shuddered violently and pulled away.

He'd been doing so well, or so it had appeared. He seemed to gaining the upper hand on his aversion. And then suddenly, his eyes had opened and he'd stared at the console screen like it was the face of hell. He'd gone pale all over, trembling, and then collapsed, screaming out as if anguished.

Edward tried again to soothe Knox, rubbing a hand over his back as he huddled, curled in on himself with some internal pain.

"It's all right. You don't have to try it anymore," Edward promised, his voice rough with emotion. "They made you this way, Knox. It's not your fault."

Gradually, Knox's wracking sobs—so anguished Edward could

almost *see* his heart breaking—weakened and then trailed off into big, wet breaths.

"It's all right," Edward kept saying as he stroked Knox's back, his arm, his hair. "It's all right. It's over now."

"Edward," Knox said in a dull voice.

"I'm here."

Knox raised his head, his eyes were puffy and red. There was something terrible in Knox's eyes, as if the heart of life had been ripped out, bloodied and still beating, in front of him.

"*Hush*," Edward pleaded, responding to the pain. "It's all right. You don't have to try anymore."

"Edward. What are the spores used for?" Knox's voice sounded dead.

"What?"

"The spores. What purpose do they serve?"

"They're... they're used for medicine. Life-saving pharmaceuticals. They—"

"Life-saving pharmaceuticals." Knox quoted the standard catchphrase, his voice bitter.

"That's right." There was something ugly in Knox's face. Edward swallowed.

Knox slowly shook his head. "No. They're used for terraforming. They're used to destroy worlds."

"What?" Edward drew back, not understanding but not liking the implication *at all*. Gods, the look on Knox's face! "That's n-not true. They're used for medicine, important medicine, they're—"

"Edward, I remember! I remember it all. We weren't *pirates*." Knox laughed in disgust. "And we weren't trying to *steal* the spores. We were trying to destroy them. I was part of a small rebel group, the only survivors of Nobira. The Federation destroyed our entire planet using the spores. The lichen took over, covered everything—killed our food supply and, of course, the spores were in the air. Millions breathed them in and died horrible deaths! We had no filters there, no systems in place to deal with them. *All of my people died.* And my planet too, the most beautiful place you've ever seen. The spores killed all the natural vegetation and all of the animal life. Oh gods, the waste! It hurts. It hurts! Why did I have to remember?"

Knox clutched his head as if grief were ripping him apart. Edward didn't doubt Knox believed every word he was saying. But it couldn't be true. It couldn't! It was some part of this sick aversion programming, putting nightmares into his head. It had no more substance than the imaginary horrors he'd recoiled from on the keyboard.

"Knox, listen to me! This isn't real. Why would the Federation do that? Why? It makes no sense."

Knox growled. "Because they can. They wanted astaturn, a radioactive element we had in abundance in our Clathean mountains. But that was sacred land and our leaders wouldn't allow the Federation to mine there, no matter how much money they offered or what they threatened. My people are—were—very stubborn."

"I still can't believe—"

"They tried blockading us—for almost a decade—denying us medicine, trade, information. But we were mostly self-sufficient and good at slipping past them when we had to, blocking their radar so they couldn't detect our ships. *I* was good at it. Pirates! Because we wouldn't submit. And then one day we came home from a trip and Nobira was dead. The spores had killed it all."

Edward shook his head. "No. No, I don't believe that."

But... something inside Edward niggled. It was as if there was a tiny thread inside him that, if pulled, could unravel him entirely, everything he ever believed to be true and everything that he was. He remembered the way Father used to shut himself up in this library anytime he was discussing spore business, Federation business, *private matters*. Edward remembered the night he'd seen his mother crying just before she'd left for good, her face devastated and guilty. He knew his father had done something bad, but what? He remembered the things his father used to say: *You're too weak, Edward. You have to be hard in this life. It doesn't do to give in to the female emotions, to pity. Nature has no pity.* He remembered the way the other farmers looked at him with speculation and distrust after he'd taken over the farm.

You'll never be one of us.

"Edward, think about what the spores do, even here! Think about what they are. Can't you see what would they do, let loose on a green world? Does it really make sense that they're used for *medicine*?"

Knox's voice was filled with hatred and disgust. Edward shrank back. He was starting to feel sick. "But… why… the spores *can't* live just anywhere. They only thrive on Kalan. If they could live on any planet, Kalan would be worthless. So what you're saying can't be true!"

"They're *terraformers*, Edward. They colonize, spread, and die. Only a few generations of the lichen can live off Kalan. That's why they're so goddamn perfect! The Federation dumps a load of the spores, then just goes away. A few years later, they come back—everything is dead, including the lichen and the spores. The planet is a blank slate. They can do with it whatever they want."

Bile rose in Edward's throat, bitter and caustic as sin. He couldn't breathe. He tore off his mask and swallowed the bile down. It burned, burned in his throat, in his heart.

It was true. He knew it was. He knew it in his gut. And his father had known, probably his brother too. And they hadn't cared, not when the Federation made it worth their while not to care, when their families were given such a privileged life. *World killers.*

He slumped down on the floor, spent. The mask slipped from his hand and rocked, like a discarded toy, on the floor. It didn't matter, not anymore.

His eyes raised and found Knox. The recon—no, *Trevellyn*—was still sitting on the floor, looking at Edward with an expression that warred between pity and hatred.

"I'm sorry," Edward whispered. "I didn't know. Please believe me."

Knox dug the heels of his hands into his eyes and let out an anguished groan. "Arrgggh!" He dove for Edward and grabbed the mask, shoved it at his face. "Put it on!"

"No!"

"Put it on!"

Edward obeyed.

Knox's face was still angry, but he pressed his lips tight and shook his head. "I… believe you. It's not your fault, Edward. Damn it! Keep that on."

Knox pushed himself up and went to the console. There was no hesitation, none, as his fingers attacked the keys, his eyes locked on the screen.

"Your aversion," Edward asked, wondering.

Knox laughed like a wild man. "By the gods, I broke it."

Edward watched Knox work, amazed at his speed and skill. Screen after screen flashed across the console. Abruptly, the alarm turned off. Edward's ears echoed. It had been on so long, he'd almost stopped hearing it. In the deafening silence, all he could hear was the rapid *click, click, click* of Knox's fingers on the keys. Then he heard the soft whoosh of the air system.

Edward slowly stood, not sure if he'd be welcome or not. "The filtration system is back on in the house?"

"Yes. But the sensors say the spore level is at 0.07. Keep that mask on. It'll take a while for the filters to clean the air."

Edward nodded. Knox was still typing furiously. "What are you doing now?"

"Saying hello to your neighbors. The underground grid lets me see their farms."

Edward said nothing more, just watched Knox work. And as he watched, he realized Knox was not Knox any longer. Edward hadn't realized how much fog had still obscured Knox's being; he had been intelligent but slow spoken at times. Now Edward could see how much had been *not there*, because now it was. Now that body was possessed entirely by Trevellyn. And he was scarily intense and prophetically intelligent. Edward would have been intimidated even if he hadn't just learned that he, and Parmeter Farms, was responsible for the deaths of all Trevellyn held dear.

"What temperature will kill the spores?" Knox asked sharply.

"What?"

"In the factory storage rooms. Can you kill the spores if the temperature is set too high or too low?"

Knox looked at him and waited. Edward knew what was being asked of him. He had to choose a side.

"Signis always said we should never put the heat above sixty in the factory. The spores don't like the heat."

"But will it kill them?"

"Yes, I think so."

Knox turned, his fingers a blur. "Eighty is the maximum temperature I can set."

"You can set the temperature in the factory from here?" Edward said eagerly, moving closer. "Our factory, you mean?"

"Any of them. Each farm's console system is connected to the grid. It's just a matter of slipping past a very simple gate to get in them."

"Oh," Edward said in surprise. Then, more firmly, "In this storm, no one will be in the factories, so they won't notice the high temperature. Unless they check the console, they won't notice it for days."

"And your factory?" Knox asked, pausing to look at him.

Edward hesitated. It was difficult to go against what had been ingrained in him his entire life—the importance of the spores, the demand to care for them, harvest them, wrap them up safely for shipping, to not waste them. But the revulsion he felt, the horror and guilt, were stronger yet. "Yes, do it," Edward said.

Knox hit them all. The Kalanese system was protected from outside, but once on the farm grid system, all the farms were linked into the main nav. Over two hundred farms, and Knox raised the heat on them all. By the time he was done, an hour had passed.

"The spore count is down to safe levels in the house. You can remove your mask."

Edward did, glad to be out of the sweaty rubber. "What about the spaceport?"

"I don't see it. It must not be on the underground grid system."

Edward hesitated. "You could turn off their air filtration systems too, couldn't you? On the other farms? Just as they did to me?"

"Yes."

"But you won't?"

Knox bit his lips. "No."

Edward was relieved. While he didn't mourn the loss of the spores, he didn't think he could handle killing the farmers and their families, even though they'd wished that death on him.

Knox sighed. "It's a childish gesture, killing the spores in the factories. They'll only harvest more."

"It's something," Edward said. And it was. Some tiny bit of payback for Trevellyn. "Will they know it was us?"

Knox shook his head. "They have no way to trace it."

Knox finally abandoned the console and turned to Edward. "When the storm passes and I can get back on the interspace, I'll send out some messages. I think I still have friends out there. I can get someone to pick me up. It may take a few months for them to get here."

"Oh." Edward tried not to show how much that hurt.

Knox gently touched Edward's face. "Do you think I would escape this place and leave you? You can't stay here, Edward. Tell me you don't want that."

Edward felt a pulse of hope at the words, but also anger. "Of course I don't want to stay! Do you think I'd continue to farm the spores now that I know? But... you can't want me to go with you. You must hate me now."

Knox smiled. That rakish corner of his mouth turned up, causing Edward to feel a sudden flush of longing. Knox pulled Edward to his chest and nuzzled his hair. "How could I hate you? You brought me back to life, Edward, reanimated my mind and my heart. And you forgave me the deaths of your family, something I did consciously. I'd be an empty soul indeed if I couldn't forgive you when you had no idea you were causing harm."

Edward clung to Knox, feeling the big, solid weight of him. He loved Knox in so many ways and for so many reasons, half of them a mystery even to himself. And now that he understood Trevellyn, it was as if the deep, buried heart of Knox had been revealed and Edward loved him even more—Trevellyn's courage, his brilliance, his tragic life and undeserved end. Edward knew right then where his loyalty lay and would always lay, and all else be damned.

"Come with me," Knox urged.

"Where would we go?"

Knox stroked Edward's back. "There's a place I've been to. It's a young planet and of no particular interest to the Federation. People there live simply off the land. It's not an easy life, but they're free. And it's green, so green, Edward."

Edward liked the sound of that. It sounded like a dream. He thought about it. "They expect me to be defeated, so I shall act the part. If I don't let on that I know about the spores, and I arrange to sell the farm after the next transport, they'll leave us be 'til then. No one here will be sad to see me go."

"Good." Knox kissed his temple.

"You won't go back to working for the rebels?"

Knox sighed. "I've seen too much death." He laughed bitterly. "Including my own. Let the worlds conspire and rage. Maybe I'm a coward, but I want none of it. I've been given a second chance and all I want now is *a loaf of bread, a jug of wine, and thou.* Will you come with me?"

Edward swallowed the emotion that threatened to spill out of him like an overfull glass. He put his arms around Knox's massive shoulders and held him tight. For the first time in his life, he was not alone. "Yes, Knox. I will."

ELI EASTON has been at various times and under different names a minister's daughter, a computer programmer, a game designer, the author of paranormal mysteries, a fanfiction writer, an organic farmer, and a profound sleeper. She is now happily embarking on yet another incarnation, this time as an m/m romance author.

As an avid reader of such, she is tickled pink when an author manages to combine literary merit, vast stores of humor, melting hotness, and eye-dabbing sweetness into one story. She promises to strive to achieve most of that most of the time. She currently lives on a farm in Pennsylvania with her husband, three bulldogs, three cows, and six chickens. All of them (except for the husband) are female, hence explaining the naked men that have taken up residence in her latest fiction writing.

Her website is http://www.elieaston.com.

Twitter is @EliEaston.

You can e-mail her at eli@elieaston.com.

By ELI EASTON

NOVELLAS
The Enlightenment of Daniel
A Prairie Dog's Love Song
Puzzle Me This
The Trouble with Tony

Published by DREAMSPINNER PRESS
http://www.dreamspinnerpress.com

Made for
Aaron
sue brown

To Jamie Fessenden, an amazing author I am thrilled to call friend.

Prologue
The Institution

AARON FOX flinched as an ice-cold drop of water ran down his forehead, closely followed by a second and a third. He moved away from the impromptu shower and tried to find a space that was dry, although that was nigh on impossible, as the roof had deteriorated to such an extent that much of the ceiling was dripping from the steady winter rain outside.

The gray light of the afternoon matched Aaron's mood as he looked around the large room, once a dormitory housing twenty men, including himself. Ignoring the drips, he walked to the spot where his bed had been—third window from the left, looking out over the gardens. Now there was nothing but overgrown grass and rubble from the decaying buildings. The asylum was due for demolition, and Aaron hadn't been here for years. He wasn't even sure why he'd come back, except that his world had unraveled and Aaron needed answers. This was the only place he could think of that might provide him with a clue, the institution where his relationship with Damon began.

He was wrong. There were no answers here. The buildings were just empty shells, ready to be leveled. The whole area was to become another building site, three- and four-bedroom homes for the middle classes. The road, once full of red brick buildings like this one, was now full of identical estates for families with money, ideal for commuters to central London.

He remembered what it was like before, with the shabby rooms filled with men and uniformed staff, always noisy even at night as the men snored and sobbed in their sleep. Aaron's mind was full of memories, bad and horrific. They haunted his dreams and defined the man he was. On his release, Aaron had sworn to Damon he would never go back, never have his life taken away from him again by his misguided parents. He had refused all contact with them, angry at what they had done to him. Instead Aaron had made his life with Damon, the gentle yet dominant man who had given his life validation and meaning. Eighteen years later, they were still together, married now with matching rings. They had taken their vows as soon as the law had changed.

Aaron looked out of the cracked panes of glass, smiling wryly as he remembered his first meeting with Damon by the hollow in the gardens. The matron had been a great believer in getting the men outside every day. There were tennis courts and football fields, and a running track painted onto the grass. In the summer, staff and patients played a weekly cricket game. Even if, as in Aaron's case, the patient hated sport, they weren't given an option. Aaron had loathed the enforced sport at school, and he had hated it even more at the asylum. He had learnt to sneak away early in the day and find a place to hide with his books and sketchpad. Others had done the same, and most of the staff turned a blind eye to the truants. There were enough participants to keep their hands full.

Behind the shed and just beyond the oak tree, there was a hollow dip. It had been Aaron's favorite place to hide, and read, and dream—of freedom from this place of rules and medication, dream of being able to be who he really was. He'd had no illusions. Aaron Guthrie, as he was, had been here for one reason and one reason only. He hadn't been mad, or simple, or dangerous to himself or another. He had been institutionalized because he liked men. He was a homosexual, and so his parents had hidden him away from the rest of society in case he infected them. That wasn't the official diagnosis, of course. It wasn't illegal to be a sodomite. But his parents were religious, and they knew people, who knew doctors, who weren't bothered by technicalities like legality. The furor surrounding his case was one of the reasons this place no longer existed.

Aaron picked his way amongst the rubble to the back of the sheds. They were little more than piles of bricks now, but the oak tree was still there, in the overgrown hollow. Aaron stared at the nettles and brambles in dismay.

He laughed harshly, startling a nearby crow. "What did you expect, dipshit? Damon to be waiting for you?"

He had been expecting, hoping, his husband would be there, just as he had been on the very first day that they met. Aaron had been dismayed to see someone already in his space, but Damon was so kind and gentle that Aaron had relaxed in his company. He had worried when he discovered Damon was staff, not an inmate, but after a few chance meetings, he had realized Damon didn't judge him for what he was. Damon hadn't cared he was gay, because he was also gay. Closeted, yes, because he hadn't wanted to end up like Aaron. Damon had handed Aaron a huge secret with that knowledge.

"You told me you were gay here," Aaron murmured. "Right after you kissed me."

Aaron closed his eyes as he remembered the love in that kiss. So soft and gentle, as if Damon didn't want to scare him. He hadn't been scared. Surprised, and more than a little turned on, but not scared.

Damon had drawn back, his eyes dark with passion, and licked his lips. "Now you know my secret," he'd said.

Aaron had pulled him down for another kiss. He hadn't wanted to talk secrets. He'd wanted the feel of Damon's body against his, in his. He had been almost eighteen and his dick had done his thinking. Damon had pushed him back against the grass and kissed him some more.

They hadn't gone further that day. He'd had to get back to the building for dinner. But he'd hugged Damon's secret to him like a child, giving him strength when he'd had to endure hours of disapproving therapy.

"How could you leave me?" Aaron shouted it up to the sky, making the crow flap away in alarm.

Damon was gone, vanished after a car accident. It had been a month since Aaron had been called to the hospital, only to find Damon had disappeared before he could be treated.

"I need you." Tears, always close, rolled down Aaron's cheeks, and he didn't bother to wipe them away. "I need you and you left me."

Damon had left him and Aaron's world was destroyed.

~1~

The Accident

AARON CURSED as his mobile phone rang just as he was negotiating his trolley out of the supermarket. He dug in his pocket for his phone whilst trying to get out of the way of a weary-faced woman with two small children and a screaming baby. His trolley wasn't cooperating. Three wheels were happy to go his way; the fourth had attitude.

Finally he managed to answer his phone. "Yeah?"

"Is that Aaron Fox?"

Aaron frowned, hoping it wasn't someone trying to sell him insurance or carpet cleaning. "Yes. Who's this?"

"My name is Tommy. I'm calling from St. Patrick's Hospital Accident and Emergency."

"Yes?" Aaron was confused. He couldn't think of any reason he'd get a call from Paddy's.

"Do you know Damon Fox?"

"He's my husband."

"He was admitted to A&E this afternoon. I'm sorry to tell you this, but he's been in a road traffic accident."

Aaron stopped in the middle of the pathway, ignoring the annoyed mutters from the people he was blocking. He struggled to get the words out. "Is he all right?"

"I think you should get here as soon as you can, Mr. Fox."

Aaron abandoned the conversation and the trolley before the end of Tommy's sentence. Damon would kill him for the waste of money, but Aaron didn't care. He heard someone shouting at him, but he sprinted for the rows of cars, only stopping as he frantically tried to remember where he left his Nissan Micra.

"Sir, you've left your trolley behind."

Aaron stared blankly at the security guard.

"Your trolley, sir?"

"I've got to get to Paddy's. My husband—he's in hospital."

The security guard nodded. "I'll take care of your shopping. Give me your name and come back when you can to collect it."

"I don't know where my damn car is." Aaron knew he was shouting—Damon wouldn't like that—but the man was holding him up and he couldn't find his car. He had to leave *now*.

The security guard nodded, his voice calm and soothing. "Tell me what we're looking for."

"A blue 2002 Nissan Micra." Afterward Aaron found it astonishing that he'd remembered the make and model of the car.

The guard walked with Aaron as he scanned the rows of cars. "How about that one," he said, pointing two rows along.

Aaron nodded tightly. "That's my car. Thanks." He ran off before the guard could respond.

"I hope your husband's okay," the security guard shouted after him as Aaron ran to the car.

As he drove away, Aaron realized he hadn't given the security guard his name. He banged the steering wheel. Nothing mattered. Nothing except Damon. His vision blurred, and he blinked back the tears furiously. The last thing Damon needed was for him to get into an accident.

St Patrick's Accident and Emergency was empty except for a white-faced kid holding his arm close to his body and a bored-looking adult with him, yet there was still a queue at the reception desk. Aaron joined the end, fidgeting from foot to foot until it was his turn to be seen.

The receptionist smiled at him. "How can I help you?"

"My name's Aaron Fox." When the woman still looked blank, he said, "My husband, Damon Fox, was brought in a short while ago. I got a phone call from Tommy to get here as soon as I could."

She nodded and tapped at her keyboard. "Damon Fox…. There he is. A car accident." Then she frowned, and the sick feeling in Aaron's stomach intensified. "Take a seat, Mr. Fox, and I'll get someone to talk to you."

"Where is he?" Aaron said, holding onto his control by a thread. "Can I see him? Whoever I spoke to told me it was urgent."

"Take a seat," she said firmly, "and someone will be with you shortly."

Aaron wanted to protest, but he wasn't any good at arguing with authority. He subsided onto the nearest plastic chair and waited to be called, sniffling and trying to hold back the tears. He wouldn't cry in public. He needed to know what had happened to Damon.

A door opened and a nurse in green scrubs called out a name. The pale kid and the adult went in. Just in time, from the sound of the puking as the door closed.

The hands of the clock ticked around unbearably slowly. He waited for nearly an hour before his name was called.

"Mr. Fox?"

"Yes." Aaron jumped up and ran toward the doctor.

The woman, wearing blue scrubs, a white coat, and a stethoscope around her neck, smiled at him. She was accompanied by a short, stocky police officer, a serious expression on his round face. "Hi, my name is Dr. Liu, and this is PC Collins. Are you here about Damon Fox?"

Aaron resisted the temptation to tear her head off. "I am. What the hell's going on? I was told it was urgent, but I've waited nearly an hour. Is he all right?"

"Come with me." Dr. Liu led him into a small room and indicated the only seat as PC Collins leaned against the wall. She waited for Aaron to sit down before she said, "I don't know how to tell you this so I'm just going to come out and say it. Mr. Fox disappeared just over an hour ago."

Aaron stared at her. "What? I was told he was seriously injured."

"He was. His car was completely totaled." The doctor looked at him seriously. "Mr. Fox, Damon shouldn't have been alive when he came in, let alone walk out an hour later."

"So what happened?"

"Firemen cut him out of the car." She rubbed at her forehead. "I know this isn't easy to hear. Damon wasn't breathing. He'd been crushed in the accident. The paramedics performed CPR all the way here but nothing; he was too far gone. All that was left was to call it when they arrived. *I* pronounced him dead at 3:45 p.m."

"But they rang me at four thirty. Told me to hurry."

"Hospital policy in these cases."

Aaron couldn't get his head around what she was trying to tell him. "So what's happened? Someone's stolen Damon's body?"

She hesitated, glanced at Collins, and said, "He got up and walked out."

"What? Dr. Liu, if this is some kind of sick joke, I'm not finding it very funny." This was sick. Someone was playing a sick joke on him.

The doctor gazed at him steadily. "I am telling you that at 4:35, just after we called you, Mr. Fox got out of bed and walked out without anyone seeing him."

"How do you know—"

The policeman spoke for the first time. "It was caught on camera. Someone came to get him and he left without anyone realizing. Mr. Fox, I need you to watch this tape."

PC Collins stepped forward and showed him an iPad. Aaron watched as a man, dressed as a doctor in the familiar scrubs and white coat, entered a cubicle that was completely enclosed by curtains. Nothing happened for a moment; then the doctor left.

Aaron looked up, but the policeman pointed to the screen. "Keep looking." Aaron noticed the policeman had smooth skin and manicured fingernails, just like Damon. Aaron's nails were ragged from constant biting despite Damon's gentle nagging.

A minute later, Damon walked out. His husband looked… destroyed; there was no other way to describe him: his face was a mess of bruising and cuts. Aaron forced back the tears to look past the injuries to his face and body.

"What is he wearing? He didn't leave with those clothes this morning." Damon had left wearing a charcoal-gray suit and mulberry shirt. Aaron had refused to let Damon leave the house until he'd shown his appreciation for what Damon was wearing—on his knees.

"They were cut off in the attempt to save him. He was naked, so we don't know where he got the joggers and T-shirt from."

"The other guy, the doctor, he didn't bring them in, did he?"

The doctor shrugged. "He could have been hiding them under the white coat."

Aaron stood up. "I ought to go home. See if Damon is there." That was all he cared about. Damon wasn't here, he must be back home.

"If he is, you need to bring him back," Dr. Liu said.

"Why?" Aaron asked suspiciously. "He's obviously fine now. Perhaps you just made a mistake."

Dr. Liu shook her head. "You don't seem to understand. Damon couldn't have survived the accident, and yet he gets up and walks out like nothing has happened. We need to find him, make sure he's not bleeding internally from the crush injuries."

Aaron smiled blandly and made a noncommittal noise, knowing the code. Damon had risen from the dead and therefore must be tested. Pain and indignity. He'd suffered under the endless tests that the asylum had subjected him to, and there was no way he'd subject his husband to the same torture. "I just hope he's gone home."

"We can give you a lift," PC Collins said.

"No need, I've got my car in the car park." He needed to get away now.

Dr. Liu touched him lightly on the arm. "Mr. Fox, I can't emphasize enough that he needs to come back here. Mr. Fox was clinically dead for over an hour. There's no way he should have… could have… got up and walked out on his own two feet."

"But he did, didn't he?" Aaron said, his voice strained. His lover had died and he'd known nothing about it. And then he'd risen, just like Lazarus, and walked out.

"Bring him back as soon as you can."

Aaron left the small room, almost running in his need to leave the doctor and police officer behind, the air of authority weighing down oppressively on him. As soon as he was out of the building, he called Damon's phone, cursing as it switched straight to voice mail.

"Damon, where are you? I'm at the hospital. They told me you were hurt. Call me as soon as you get this message."

He drove home, sick and anxious, one eye on his phone in case he missed a call from Damon. For a second he was surprised when he pulled up outside the house and Damon's car wasn't there. Then he remembered that Damon's car was wrecked. It wasn't going anywhere ever again. Damon would be annoyed at having to use their savings to buy a new car until the insurance paid out.

Aaron opened the front door and called out Damon's name, hoping he would answer, but he was only met by the soft meows of Ernest, their tabby cat. Aaron picked up the cat and rubbed his face into the soft fur.

"Where is he? Where's your daddy, Ernie?"

Despite the fact he was scared, and angry and so fucking confused, his brain was scrambled. Aaron went through his usual routine: feed the cat, make a coffee, look in the freezer for dinner, curse because he'd left the food behind at the supermarket.

Dammit!

Aaron hesitated, then picked up his keys. It would give him something to do rather than sit in an empty house, so Aaron drove back to the supermarket.

As he entered the supermarket, he was intercepted by the security guard he's spoken to before.

"How is he—your husband?" the guard asked.

Aaron stared at him, unsure what to say.

The guard looked at him expectantly; then as Aaron didn't speak, confusion covered his face. "Um, was it you? Your husband got taken to hospital?"

Aaron nodded slowly.

"How is he? He isn't...."

"He was. He got crushed and stopped breathing, but he's fine now. I need some food or he'll be angry with me."

The guard looked at him carefully. "I think you're in shock. Come over here and I'll get your shopping. Then you ought to go home."

Aaron nodded again. "Damon might be waiting for me."

"Sit down here." The guard manhandled Aaron into a plastic seat, ignoring the surprised squawks of a couple of old ladies already sitting there. "Wait there."

Aaron waited, pleased to be told what to do. After he left the institution, he'd found it hard to make decisions for himself, and Damon had naturally taken over that role. He ignored the bustle of the supermarket, his mind totally fixed on his missing husband.

Before long, the man came back with a loaded trolley. "Here we go. I'll take it to the car for you. Give me your keys."

Without a word, Aaron handed them over and led the way to the car. He watched passively as the guard loaded the car with the shopping and handed him the keys.

"I don't think you should be driving. Have you got far to go?"

"Not far."

"Okay. Drive carefully." The guard held onto the door until Aaron was seated and had put on his seat belt. "Concentrate." He closed the door firmly and stood back, not walking back to the supermarket until Aaron drove away.

There was still no sign of Damon at home, and Aaron went through the motions of putting away the shopping. He rang Damon's phone a couple of times, but it kept going to voice mail. He sat for an hour staring at the phone, willing it to ring.

How could a dead man walk out of a hospital?

Was Damon dead?

Why didn't he come home?

Why didn't he love Aaron enough to come home?

Aaron went to bed at ten o'clock, their normal time, burying his face in Damon's pillow. He inhaled Damon's scent, needing to feel connected to him in some way, because at the moment all he felt was fear and it was consuming him.

"Where the hell are you?" Aaron's control finally snapped, tears running down his face, wetting the soft cotton of the pillow. "I *need* you. You promised me you'd never leave me alone."

Damon had promised Aaron that he'd never have to survive by himself. Now he was injured or dead, and he was missing, and he hadn't come home to Aaron.

~2~
The Burglary

AARON WOKE up in a cold sweat, nausea clutching at his throat. He'd had a dream that Damon was running away from him, and the closer he got, the faster Damon ran. Gasping for air, Aaron sat bolt upright, waiting for Damon's soothing voice to calm him down, and then he remembered. He looked at Damon's side of the bed and broke down, crying until his eyes and throat were sore.

He went to work as usual because what the hell else was he meant to do with himself? Aaron knew Damon would be angry with him if he returned and found Aaron had been fired for not turning up, and he wanted Damon to come back and find how well Aaron had coped in his absence. His boss suggested Aaron take some time away to get himself together, but Aaron shook his head and returned to his desk, mechanically going through the motions and ignoring everyone's well-meaning condolences. In the end, they gave up and left him alone.

He arrived home from work to find two policemen on his doorstep. Aaron faltered with his hand on the gate. He found it difficult to deal with authority of any kind, any uniform triggering a painful memory of the torture to which Aaron had been subjected in the asylum.

The two policemen didn't notice him immediately, too busy chatting quietly to each other to see him at the gate.

"Can... can I help you?" he said.

They looked up and he saw one of them was PC Collins, who smiled at him.

"Mr. Fox, this is my partner, PC Lockhart."

The policeman nodded at him, his face grim. He was tall and slim with light gray eyes, towering above Aaron and Collins, and although he looked young to Aaron, he had an air of authority that Aaron had never managed to acquire.

"How are you?" Collins said.

Aaron resisted the temptation to make a sarcastic remark. Damon had always insisted that Aaron be polite to everyone. "I'm fine," he lied. "Have you found Damon?" Then he stilled. "Why is my front door open?" He peered closer and saw the wood around the lock was completely splintered. Someone had kicked in the door.

Aaron's feet were frozen to the spot. "What's happened to my home?"

"You've been burgled, Mr. Fox. Your neighbor spotted the open door, and investigated. She called us when she saw the door," Collins said.

"Why didn't you call me? I gave you my number yesterday."

Collins looked embarrassed. "I didn't connect you with this case until a couple of minutes before you arrived."

Lockhart coughed to attract Aaron's attention. "So it wasn't like this when you left?"

Aaron stared at him. "You think I'm stupid enough to walk out of my house, having just been burgled and leave the front door wide open?" He ignored Lockhart, who coughed again, and looked at Collins. "I want to go in."

PC Collins stepped back to let him through. "Be careful where you tread. I'm sorry, they've made a total mess."

That was a total understatement. As Aaron pushed open the door, he could see the shattered glass from the inner doors over the carpet.

"Oh my God." He couldn't breathe as he looked at the damage to his home.

"They've gone through the whole house, Mr. Fox." PC Collins laid a hand on his shoulder.

Aaron angrily shook it off. He didn't want to be comforted. "Where's Ernest?"

PC Collins frowned. "Who's Ernest?"

"Our—my—cat."

"I haven't seen him."

Aaron ran through the house, ignoring the glass crunching under his feet as he made for Ernest's favorite place. The cat wasn't to be seen. "Ernest? Ernest!" He looked in all the rooms downstairs for his elderly cat. He was looking in the understairs cupboard in case Ernest had been trapped in there, when PC Lockhart interrupted him.

"Mr. Fox, is this Ernest?"

To Aaron's relief, his cat was curled up in the policeman's arms, unharmed, if showing his annoyance at being held by a stranger by swishing his tail.

"Thank God." Aaron held out his hands for the cat, but the policeman said, "I think he ought to stay outside until we've cleared up. Otherwise the glass will cut his paws."

Aaron frowned. "Has the upstairs been trashed?"

"Not as badly as down here. You could leave the cat up there whilst we talk." Lockhart handed him over, receiving a sharp mew from Ernest. "I'll get some food and we'll put him upstairs."

Reluctant to give up his one certainty to home, Aaron clutched Ernest to his chest, but a nudge from the policeman and he went upstairs, obeying as he always did in the face of an order.

As Lockhart had said, the upper floor was covered in the contents of their wardrobes and drawers, but nothing was destroyed as it was downstairs. Aaron sat on the bed, trying to soothe Ernest, who was very obviously upset by the disruption to his routine as he stalked around Aaron on the bed.

Collins came in with two bowls, which he placed in the en suite bathroom. "Don't want to muck up your carpet," he said cheerfully. "Lockhart is making you a cup of tea."

Ernest jumped off the bed and headed toward the food bowls.

Aaron refrained from pointing out that trying to protect the carpets was like shutting the door after the horse had bolted. All the carpets would have to be replaced downstairs, as it would be impossible to get all the glass out. He would have to sweep and hoover the worst of it and lay something over them to protect Ernest.

"Do you think this is to do with Damon?" he asked Collins.

"What makes you say that?"

Aaron just looked at him, and the policeman shrugged.

"It could be. It might just be some little shits down the road. We don't know what they were looking for."

"What makes you say they were looking for something?"

Collins huffed as he sat down on the bed. "All your paperwork has been destroyed: bills, letters, personal documents. Whoever was here was interested in your life. The destruction of everything else could have been to cover up what they were actually after."

"So the little shits down the road are looking less likely."

"I really don't know, Mr. Fox. Anyway, we'll keep investigating. Have you got anywhere else you can go tonight?"

Aaron shook his head. He and Damon didn't have any friends or family.

"How about a hotel?"

"I can't take Ernest to a hotel."

"You could leave him in here with a little tray and some food," Collins said. "I don't think you should stay here overnight."

"Why not? I've got to get the placed cleared up." He'd rather be in his home than in a strange place without even his cat for company.

"Why don't you leave that to a cleaning firm?"

Aaron gave the policeman a sad smile. "It will give me something to do."

Collins looked dubious, but then Lockhart walked in with a mug, which he handed to Aaron.

"Do you want sugar in it?" he asked.

Aaron shook his head and looked at the contents of the mug. He didn't drink tea made with milk, and he wondered how he was going to be able to dispose of the drink without hurting the policeman's feelings.

"We had the crime scene people around before you arrived, so you are free to clear up whenever you want. You should ring the insurance people as soon as you can."

Aaron nodded. He'd have to make a list of things to do. Damon would expect him to handle all the paperwork.

"Mr. Fox, are you sure there isn't anyone we can contact for you? You've had two huge shocks in twenty-four hours." PC Collins looked genuinely concerned for Aaron's well-being.

"We don't have any family or friends. We kept very much to ourselves."

"If you're sure. I could contact someone from our victim support unit."

"And say what? Damon could have done this. He's walked out on me and now my place is ransacked. Perhaps this was him." Aaron's brain whirled at the sudden thought that his husband was responsible for the destruction of their family home. It wasn't like that was unheard of. Aaron had read the headlines of those rag mags when he'd been at doctor's surgery, to see some of the bizarre and evil things people got up to.

"Do you believe that?" Lockhart asked.

"No. I don't think he'd do that to me."

"Why do you think he hasn't returned?"

Aaron shook his head. "I have no idea. Maybe his head is banged up. Maybe he can't remember me or his life before the accident."

"Perhaps you ought to investigate."

"Isn't that your job?" Aaron asked wryly.

Collins and Lockhart snorted at his comeback.

Aaron ran his fingers through his hair. "I need to start clearing up," he said. "Unless you're here to help me do that?"

"I think that's our cue to leave," Collins said to his colleague.

Lockhart nodded. "I think it is. We'll need a statement from you. You could come down the station tomorrow or we could come here."

"I'll come down to the station," Aaron said hastily, anxious to get rid of the policemen. He needed a break from their presence in his home. They were pleasant enough, but Aaron could feel himself crumbling with each passing moment. He needed them gone—now.

"Don't forget to call the insurance company and a locksmith. You need to get the front door fixed," Lockhart said.

"I'll do it now." Aaron got to his feet. "That is, if they left me the insurance documents with the phone number."

He ushered the police officers out of the bedroom, shut the door behind him so that Ernest couldn't escape, and took a deep breath.

Collins looked at him shrewdly. "Are you sure you don't want to find a hotel for the night?"

"It will give me something to do. Keep me focused. I have no idea what's going on, but I need something to think about."

Collins hummed, although Aaron wasn't sure if he agreed, and walked down the stairs. Lockhart had gone ahead and was waiting by the front door.

"Call me if there are any further incidents," Collins said.

Startled, Aaron looked at him. "Do you think something else will happen?"

"We don't know. Better to be safe than sorry. I can give you the number of a locksmith."

"I know one, thanks." He and Damon had changed the locks on the doors when they had first moved in. Damon insisted they do it on every place they moved to. Aaron knew the number of the locksmith by heart, they had used them so many times.

"Okay, then. I'll call you tomorrow to see how you are."

Aaron really wished he wouldn't, but he didn't have the guts to tell Collins not to bother. He waited until they'd left, and then he contemplated the wreckage of his house. Tears prickled his eyes, but he blinked them back. This wasn't the time for crying.

He picked his way through the glass-strewn carpet to the kitchen so he could make a proper cup of tea, and as the kettle boiled, he called Joe, the locksmith.

"No problem, Aaron. We'll be there in an hour."

He knew them well enough to be on first-name terms and to be shown the family photos.

Then he called the insurance company as he drank the tea.

The hot black Earl Grey tea and the helpful girl at the insurance company restored a little equilibrium, and he swept up as much of the glass as he could, hoovering the carpets over and over to remove the small shards that could potentially hurt Ernest. Aaron looked at the broken glass still in the frames of the inner doors, not sure what to do with it. In the end, he knocked out all of the glass, bagged it up, and put it in the dustbin.

Aaron worked as mechanically as he had during the day, slowly working his way through the trashed remains of his house. PC Collins was right in his suspicions. The shattered glass was a ruse to cover up that the intruders were looking for something more specific. All their paperwork was over the floor, their passports and marriage and birth certificates taken. Whatever they were looking for, Aaron wondered if they had found it.

"Aaron, are you here, son?"

"In here, Joe."

Aaron was in the dining room, sorting out what was missing from his documentation. He did his best to smile as the fiftysomething gray-haired locksmith walked into the room.

Joe whistled as he took in the damage. "Christ, Aaron, have they left you with anything?"

"Not much. Upstairs is better than down."

"Do you need someone to deal with the doors?"

"Doors, carpet, furniture. They had great fun slashing the suite in the front room. The insurance company have promised to send someone over first thing in the morning."

"How about I get you a quote now, then you could get it all fixed tomorrow."

"Do they work that fast?"

Joe shrugged. "My cousin does carpets. He'll tell them you can't get all that glass up. My brother can repair the glass. It's dangerous to live with that." He pointed to the shards Aaron had missed in the frame. "We can give them a good quote. They'll be happy."

"And I expect you've got a sister who can supply me with a couple of sofas." Aaron was only half joking. He was well aware Joe came from an Italian family that extended forever.

"Her husband," Joe said, apparently missing the joke. "He can do you a good deal. I'll make a list of things you need."

He walked out before Aaron could speak, agree, voice a protest, cry on his shoulder. Aaron stared after him. He was being handled again, and the sad thing was, he really didn't care.

~3~

The Revelation

AARON'S WORLD had disintegrated with one phone call. He couldn't declare Damon was dead because there was incontrovertible proof that he had walked out of A&E on his own two feet. After the burglary, the police had questioned him extensively but he had a rock-solid alibi, both for Damon's car accident and the burglary. Not that he'd ever been a person of interest, they assured him, but he had to be ruled out of the investigation. Aaron got the feeling they didn't think he was strong enough to carry out either the accident or the burglary.

All of Damon's bank accounts had been frozen, so Aaron found himself short of cash, but he talked to the bank, the mortgage people, and the utility companies. He'd done everything Damon had told him to do in the event of an emergency. He had some savings, which wouldn't last forever, but it was a buffer. Damon had been insistent Aaron have money of his own, so he saved part of his wages every month.

He spent his evenings in bed wrapped up in an old rugby shirt of Damon's, burying his nose in his husband's scent. Aaron stopped eating. His appetite had disappeared from the moment he got the call. He put what food he could in the freezer and threw away the rest.

In the back of his mind, Aaron realized he was living his life around the belief that Damon was going to return. One day he would walk in through the front door and tell him that everything was fine, and life would return to normal.

He wasn't pleased to see PC Lockhart and PC Collins back on his doorstep a month after Damon's disappearance.

Of all the police officers he'd had to deal with, PC Collins had been the friendliest and the most gentle. It was hard for the others to understand that Aaron was fragile, that he'd never fully recovered from being institutionalized. They gave him the impression that he wasn't a "real" man. Somehow Collins had the knack of handling him that Damon had.

"Evening, Mr. Fox," Collins said. "We need to have a word with you."

"Why are you here?" Aaron left out the *again*, leaving his tone to say it for him. "What do you want?"

"We just need a chat. May we come in?"

Aaron looked at him suspiciously, but it was obvious that they weren't going to talk until they were in his house. He hated letting them over the doorstep, feeling they usurped what little authority he had. He led them into his front room, refurnished with a new suite and a new carpet since the burglary, and waited for them to talk.

"May we sit?" PC Collins indicated the sofas. At Aaron's grim nod, they both sat down.

He ignored Lockhart and looked at PC Collins, who cleared his throat before speaking.

"We have some news about Mr. Fox."

Aaron sat bolt upright. "You've found him?"

"Not exactly." PC Collins looked uncomfortably at his colleague.

"What then?"

"Mr. Fox...."

PC Lockhart intervened. "What PC Collins is trying to say is that Mr. Fox is proving to be somewhat of a mystery. How much do you actually know about him?"

"He's my husband," Aaron said icily.

"Where did you meet him?"

Aaron opened his mouth and shut it with a snap. That was a period in his life he never talked about.

For some reason, PC Collins nodded. "We know you met at Westmead Asylum. We know he was a nurse and you were a patient there."

"If you know that, you know why I was locked up."

Neither of them looked at him.

"I was locked up for being homosexual, even though it isn't illegal. Incarcerated by my loving parents." Aaron dripped every ounce of sarcasm he could into the words.

"They thought you could be cured," PC Lockhart said, and he sounded disgusted. Aaron wasn't sure what disgusted him: Aaron's homosexuality or the dangerous reparative therapy.

"ECT, ice baths, electrodes to my genitals. They forced me to have sex with prostitutes to cure me of the idea I wanted to sleep with men. My virginity was ripped away by a cheap hooker like it was nothing." He'd tried hard to forget about each time they'd forced him to penetrate a woman, replacing the pain with a memory of making love to Damon.

PC Collins looked as if he wanted to puke.

"They raped you," Lockhart said harshly.

"Over and over, only they didn't call it rape. They called it a cure for the disease inside me."

Aaron took a long breath, trying to cleanse himself of the agony of remembering the past. He licked his lips, his mouth dry of all saliva. "You said you had news of Damon."

"What do you know of Damon's past?" Collins asked.

Aaron frowned. "He's a nurse."

"What about his family? His friends?"

"He doesn't have any family and I'm his friend. We don't need anyone else."

"What about your parents? Have you seen them since you got out of hospital?"

"Never, and I never want to see their faces again."

"How did you get discharged?"

"Damon arranged it. I was eighteen, and I wasn't mentally ill. They had no grounds to keep me once I came of age."

"They did this to you as a child?" Lockhart sounded horrified.

Aaron shrugged. "It's more common than you think. Kids are locked away all the time by their parents. If the family's got money, then they can do anything they like. I don't know if it still happens but when I was there... let's just say I wasn't the only one."

Lockhart pursed his lips. "I thought that treatment was illegal."

"Not for queers."

The policemen were silent. Aaron wasn't bothered if they were shocked or not; his world was in tatters, and he had no empathy left for anyone else.

"When did you meet Damon?" Collins said eventually.

"You know when. At the asylum."

"The thing is… we can find no trace of Fox before he met you."

"He didn't work in the area. Have you tried his previous hospital?"

Lockhart shook his head. "We can't find any record of him working anywhere else except at the asylum."

"That's ridiculous," Aaron snapped. "He's a qualified nurse. I've seen his certificates from King's College."

"King's College nursing school have no record of a Damon Fox completing his degree," Collins said.

"They must be mistaken," Aaron said. "Universities make mistakes all the time. Check it again."

Collins leant forward, his gaze trained on Aaron. "There's no mistake, Aaron. Damon Fox, if that is his name, is a fraud."

"Why are you doing this to me?" Aaron whispered. "He is a nurse. He works in St. Joseph's Hospital in oncology, and I've seen him there."

"He does," Lockhart agreed, "and he's got a good reputation as a reliable nurse."

"Well then."

"It doesn't take away from the fact that Damon Fox appears out of nowhere to work at the asylum and his qualifications are fake. St. Joe's are furious. The repercussion for lawsuits if it gets out that an unqualified nurse has been working as a senior nurse on the oncology ward could be huge."

"No, you're wrong. I'm telling you he's a nurse, he's a nurse. Why aren't you finding him? He's missing and you're just making up lies about him." Aaron's voice rose angrily. He half stood, and then sat down, having nowhere to go.

"Calm down, Aaron," Collins said.

Aaron glared at him. "Don't talk to me as if I was a child. You come here telling me that my whole life is fake, that my husband is a fake, and expect me to be calm. Haven't I been through enough? He disappears and then my home is ransacked, and now you tell me he's a con man."

Collins held his hands up. "I'm sorry. I know this is difficult for you to understand."

The patronizing tone put Aaron's hackles up. "Do you have any more information about my husband?"

Collins shook his head. "Can you tell me some more information about him? Anything that might lead us to where he is? Mr. Fox, I've said this before, but his car was crushed. There is no way he could have survived the accident."

Aaron rubbed his temples. "What are you saying? Because Damon walked out of your hospital on his own two feet, and unless I'm mistaken, we haven't got to the stage of androids and robots yet." He expected them to laugh or snort, but they just stared at him. "Oh come on, you're not saying that, are you?"

"I know it sounds far-fetched—" Lockhart began.

Collins interrupted his colleague. "Have you got pictures of Damon before you met him?"

Aaron frowned. "No, he lost everything when his parents were killed in a fire."

"So you've never seen a single photo of him as a child?"

The blood thrummed in Aaron's head. "I can't believe we're having this conversation. This is the twenty-first century, not Star Trek. Just go please. I can't take this anymore."

Lockhart looked at Collins and stood, waiting for Aaron to stand before he held out his hand. "If you hear from him, you need to call us."

"You mean you aren't tapping my phones to see if he rings?"

Collins sighed. "We're local cops, not MI5, Mr. Fox."

"It's been a month, and there's been no sign of him. Don't you think if Damon was going to come back to me"—Aaron's voice cracked—"he would have been back by now? Maybe he *was* a con and he's moved on to the next sucker."

Collins squeezed Aaron's forearm. "I'm sorry."

"Me too." Sorry for being an idiot to have married a con man, sorry to have fallen in love with a fake, sorry to have given his heart and soul to a man who didn't exist.

They left him standing in the lounge. He didn't see them out. What was the point?

~4~

The Research

WORKING UP the courage took Aaron a few days, but eventually he rang in sick to work, even though he knew Damon would have been angry with him, and drove the short distance to St Joseph's where Damon had worked for the past ten years. It was raining the whole journey, the dull gray of the day matching Aaron's mood. He took the lift to the fifth floor and headed for the ward.

He'd rarely visited the busy oncology ward where Damon worked, but he knew a few of the staff. As he waited by the nurses' station, he hoped he'd see someone he knew, as they were permanently short-staffed and regularly used agency nurses.

"Aaron, what are you doing here?"

He breathed a sigh of relief as he saw Peter Hill, one of Damon's colleagues, coming toward him. Aaron smiled tentatively, not sure of reception he'd get after the news of Damon's fake nursing career was made public.

"I needed to know if it was true. Did Damon fake all his qualifications?"

Peter looked around. "Not a good thing to talk about around here. The matrons are steaming. Meet me in the café on the second floor. I'll see if I can get a break."

"Okay. See you shortly."

Aaron bought a black coffee and sat at one of the faux-pine tables waiting for Peter to join him. It was nearly half an hour before Peter slid into the chair opposite him.

"Sorry, we had a crisis just after you left."

"If you need to be on the ward—" Aaron started.

Peter shook his head. "It's fine. I told the sister I was talking to you. She's anxious to find out what you know. We loved Damon, and we're in shock. Damon's the last person you'd expect to be a...."

He trailed off awkwardly, and Aaron nodded. He understood. He was still in shock too.

Peter sipped his tea and pulled a face. "I don't know why I buy it. They make the tea like dishwater." He gave Aaron a shrewd look. "I was going to ask how you're doing, but it's obvious."

"That bad, huh?"

"That answers one question."

"Which is?"

"Whether you knew about Damon."

Aaron smiled at him sadly. "I thought I knew everything about him. Turns out I know nothing except his name. If it even was his name. Did you get any clue that Damon was a fake?"

"He was the best oncology nurse here. He was great with the patients, excellent with procedures. He knew about up-to-date research, better than some of the doctors."

"Sounds almost too good to be true."

Peter shook his head. "Now I say it out loud, yes, he does. We just thought we were really lucky to have him. Matrons fought handbags at dawn to get him into their departments."

"I.... Do you know what happened?"

"He was in a serious accident and then he vanished. That's what the police told us."

"He coded. They pronounced him dead, yet three quarters of an hour later he gets up and walks out of A&E."

"I spoke to one of the nurse at Paddy's. It's all over the hospital."

"Why didn't he come back to me?" Aaron whispered, so anguished that Peter caught his hand.

"Have you ever thought that maybe he can't?"

"Why not?"

"Amnesia, maybe he's ill elsewhere. Maybe someone's holding him."

Aaron snorted quietly. "Are you trying to make me feel better, because I have to say this approach isn't working."

Peter grinned at him, even if the grin was strained. "I guess it all sounds a bit melodramatic. I just want an explanation that makes sense. Damon was a logical person. He dealt with facts, not fanciful speculation. The one thing we all knew was that he loved you beyond anything. He wouldn't have left you without a good reason."

"Thank you," Aaron said quietly. "I needed to be reminded of that fact."

"So what are you going to do?" Peter asked.

"I don't know yet. I can't afford to keep the house on my wages, and I can't get the life insurance as Damon obviously isn't dead."

"You've got some hard decisions ahead of you."

Aaron swished around the last of the black coffee in his cup, now too cold to drink. "Yeah, and I can't leave it too long."

"Have you got any family?"

Aaron shook his head. "No, I was brought up in an institution."

It wasn't strictly true, but it usually stopped the questions.

"I'm sorry to hear that." Peter looked at the watch on his nurse's uniform. "Damn, I've got to get back to the ward. Listen, call me if you hear anything. No matter what everybody's saying, the ward loves Damon, and we want to know he's all right."

"If I hear anything," Aaron promised, although he didn't hold out much hope.

He got another coffee as Peter left the café. He had nowhere to be, but he did have a lot to think about.

BACK AT home, Aaron did a Google search for Damon Fox, but aside from a couple of celebrities, the results were thin on the ground. He couldn't find any links to his husband. He frowned, knowing there had to be at least a few references to him. Damon had been in the local paper a couple of times when the ward had received new equipment, or some local bigwig had opened a new unit. He typed in possible references to the ward but drew a blank.

Neither of them had bothered with social media; they didn't have anyone they wanted to connect with. Damon had been so scathing about such sites when Aaron had suggested it might be one way to make friends that Aaron had never raised the topic again. It wasn't like he wanted his family to find him.

Damon's rise from the dead and fraudulent behavior hadn't made the local press, which was a little surprising, but Aaron could understand them wanting to keep it quiet. There was a lot of money and prestige invested in that unit. The last thing they needed was for it to dry up in the wake of a scandal.

Frustrated by his lack of progress, Aaron put the laptop aside and encouraged Ernest onto his lap. The cat kneaded Aaron's thighs for a minute as he made himself comfortable, and then he settled down, purring happily. Aaron stroked behind his ears. "I don't know what to do next, Ernie. Any ideas?"

Ernest stretched out his claws, yawned, and fell asleep.

Aaron sighed. Maybe the cat had the right idea.

"MMMM, YOU'RE back." Aaron moaned contentedly as a warm body settled next to him.

Aaron hated it when Damon had to work late, and he spent the evening by himself. The house was so empty without the presence of his husband.

Damon murmured against Aaron's neck, a whisper of what he wanted to do to Aaron, who sighed and rolled over onto his back, his body lax and willing for whatever his lover had planned for him.

Aaron didn't make love to Damon. He'd never made love to Damon. Damon made love to him. Over the years Aaron had tried to take control, to love his man with the intensity that Damon showed him, but he knew that within minutes Damon would take over and he would be left gasping under Damon's skilled hands and even more skilled mouth.

Aaron kept his eyes closed as Damon straddled his hips and swept his hands down Aaron's body. Aaron wasn't aroused, not yet, but he was on the way to being persuaded.

"Did you have a busy day?" he asked.

"As always. I don't want to talk about it. I just want to concentrate on you."

Aaron hummed which ended in a gasp as Damon pinched his nipples. He arched up into the touch, his hands fluttering down Damon's arms.

Damon teased him with touches until Aaron was hard and leaking, needing more than soft caresses. Then he maneuvered them so that they were on their sides, Damon sliding with slick cock into his welcoming body. Aaron let Damon lead, his eyes closed as Damon filled him, body and senses. Damon picked up the pace, driving them toward climax.

"Not going to let you go again," Aaron whispered, holding onto Damon's thigh.

Aaron opened his eyes, sobbing as he climaxed. He was on his own in his bedroom. Damon wasn't there, had never been there. The sticky puddle of come beneath him was real, though, and it was going to get increasingly disgusting unless he got up and changed the sheet. He wept harder, harsh racking sobs that hurt his chest. He rolled over to the other side of the bed. Damon wasn't there to nag him. He could drown in his own come and no one would care.

Aaron indulged in his pity party for a few minutes longer, but he reached the nagging feeling he had hit the crux of the matter. Their life together had been so exclusive no one would know or care if he was dead or alive. He had never needed more than Damon to make him fulfilled and happy, and Damon had focused his entire life on Aaron from the moment they met. Others, acquaintances, had commented that their life wasn't healthy, but neither of them had cared. Faced with the reality of being on his own, Aaron had to concede maybe they had a point.

He rolled onto his back, trying to avoid the wet patch, and stared up at the projected figures from the alarm clock, the only light in the room. The numbers ticked by agonizingly slowly as Aaron thought long and hard about his situation.

As the light in the room changed from darkness to dawn, Aaron managed to catch a last hour of sleep.

~5~

The Distraction

EVEN THOUGH he'd barely slept, Aaron woke up strangely calm. For the first time since the accident, he knew that he couldn't go on like this. Damon was gone, even if he wasn't dead, but Aaron was still here. He could do one of three things: live, die, or fold. If he folded, then he'd be hospitalized again, taken into another institution. It was strangely appealing, knowing that he'd never have to make another decision for himself.

If he committed suicide, then there was nothing more to worry about aside from the method he used to kill himself. There were plenty of pills in the house, or the railway ran along the back of the garden. One step in front of a train and his troubles would be over. Except... the train driver. Aaron couldn't bear to bring trauma for the driver. He'd take the pills and call PC Collins when it was too late to save him. He didn't much care about the policeman's feelings. He was trained to deal with trauma.

That left the third option—living. Thirty-six years old and struggling to live. Pathetic, *he* was pathetic. The only reason Aaron was still alive was Damon had rescued his soul.

He wouldn't make a decision today on which of the three options he would pick. Today he would go to work as usual, maybe pick up some paracetamol, check out the times of the fast train just in case, and look up the local institutions. If he decided to be locked up, he'd need to know in which one he wanted to be incarcerated.

Aaron took a deep breath and relaxed. He had made a plan like Damon taught him to do in the early days after he had been released from the asylum and found it difficult to cope with the lack of rules.

Make a plan, write it down, schedule your day. Each minute accounted for... after he changed the sheet.

His planner was on the kitchen table. He made himself a cup of tea, sat down, and made a list of things he needed to do for options B and C. Option A, living, took more planning. He would deal with B and C first.

He sketched out a list for suicide and institutionalization. Either way, Ernest would need to be taken care of, and he made a note to look at animal shelters. By the time he finished his initial list, it was almost time to go to work. Aaron threw a cheese-and-cucumber sandwich (as always) together for his lunch, had a shower, and fed Ernest.

In a way, his administration job was comforting in its banality. Each calculation, each letter, gave him something to think about other than the fractured puzzle of his life.

After several weeks, his colleagues had stopped treating Aaron like he would fall apart at a single word and had gone back to ignoring him. He spoke when he was spoken to and got on with his work the rest of the time. Today was no different.

Aaron ate his lunch in the local park, sprawling out on the grass and reading his Kindle. He was addicted to thrillers and haunted the Amazon lists to feed his habit. He normally read a couple of books a week, but he hadn't finished the book he'd been reading the day of Damon's disappearance. Today he reread the previous three chapters, taking time to get back into the book.

As his lunchtime drew to a close, he closed up his Kindle case and gathered together the remains of his lunch to throw in the bin.

"What are you reading today?"

Aaron looked up to see a dark-haired young guy smiling at him. "Uh." He paused, and went to the cover, realizing he'd forgotten the name of the book.

The man peered over to look at it. "It's a good book. I read it a few weeks ago. I see you reading here most days."

"Do you like thrillers?" Aaron asked politely.

"Yeah, and crime novels."

"I prefer political novels to crime."

"I read those too. My name's Michael."

"Aaron. I've got to go. My lunchtime is up."

Michael pulled a wry grin. "Me too, sadly. I'm always desperate to finish a chapter before I have to leave."

Aaron chuckled. God, the first time he'd smiled in weeks. "Me too, I'm always a few minutes late back but they're good. My boss knows I'll make it up at the end of the day."

"You're lucky. My cow of a boss tells me off every day, but I can't stop reading."

Aaron nodded and smiled, feeling awkward and not sure what to say. He wasn't skilled at small talk, and he wasn't used to hot guys just talking to him. "I've got to go," he said eventually.

"Where do you work?" Michael asked.

"Horizon House."

"Oh, I work near there, in St. Martin's Close. That hideous concrete building."

"I know it."

"We can walk back together as far as the Lanes."

Aaron nodded again, feeling like one of the nodding dogs stuck in the backs of cars that drove him mad when he was stuck behind them. He didn't want to walk with Michael, because he wanted to concentrate on his suicide plans. Plan B needed careful planning. But he could hardly say that, and Damon had taught him to be polite to everyone.

He fell into step beside Michael and listened to his mindless chatter all the way to the Lanes. Michael loved books probably even more than Aaron, and at least he had something he could respond to. If he'd been talking about sport, Aaron would have been totally out of his depth.

At the Lanes they parted, Aaron to turn left toward Horizon House, a brick rather than concrete monstrosity, and Michael to carry straight on.

"See you tomorrow," Michael said.

Aaron hummed, noncommittal. It wasn't that he didn't like Michael; it was just he didn't figure in Aaron's plans for the immediate future.

"Am I coming on too strong?" Michael shuffled his feet.

"I... I'm not...." Aaron sought for the right words to say. "I'm not looking for a boyfriend." Then he panicked because he didn't even know if Michael was gay.

"Oh." Michael looked disappointed. "How about a friend? I could do with a friend as I'm still fairly new to the area."

"I might be… moving away," Aaron said, "but whilst I'm here that would be great." He smiled to cover his lie.

"Awesome." Michael beamed at him. "See you tomorrow, then."

Aaron walked back to his office knowing he'd have to find somewhere else to eat his lunch for the remaining days.

AT HOME, Aaron collected all the tablets he could find in the house and put them to one side. There was more than enough to kill him. He added the vodka to the bottles, and ticked his list.

Next was a local animal shelter for Ernest. He made a list from the Internet of all the local shelters he could find to visit at the weekend. Aaron wanted Ernest to be spoiled rotten for the rest of his life, and he planned to donate money to the shelter on the condition that they cared for his cat for his remaining days. At sixteen years old, Ernest was unlikely to find another home.

Aaron ignored dinner again in favor of googling for suitable institutions as an alternative for suicide. In the nearly two decades since he'd been out of Westmead, mental health provisions had changed in favor of care in the community. Aaron's lip curled as he read about that. He'd seen former inmates for years after he'd left the asylum, narcissists and pedophiles mixing with the thankfully oblivious general population. These were the people his beloved parents had locked him with: psychopaths and the bewildered mixing together in a closed community. Not so now. The asylums had long gone, and in their place were psychiatric hospitals and managed living. To get admitted to hospital, Aaron would have to escalate his symptoms. He could do that. Years of being at Westmead had taught him how to mimic symptoms of many mental health illnesses. Cold and calculating, Aaron made a list of illnesses and medication. He didn't want to be released, he didn't want to think; drugged and closed away suited him fine.

His lists complete, Aaron relaxed on the sofa, Ernest purring softly on his lap. He scratched lightly behind Ernest's ears, smiling as the purring deepened. Ernest loved attention, demanded it at every possible moment. Aaron would miss the cat. He'd spent hours on the sofa in Damon's arms with Ernest sprawled across them. The cat refused to move until he was forced off, usually as their cuddles turned into something more heated, soft kisses into panting need. Ernest was able to snooze in peace now. Sex was the furthest thing from Aaron's mind, even for a quick release.

Aaron closed his eyes, his mind filled with Damon's touch, his scent, the feel of his fingers splayed possessively across Aaron's belly. He opened his eyes again. Damon was the only thing that kept Aaron functioning as a human being. If he couldn't have Damon, then there was no reason to exist anymore. Option A, living, was not on the table. Option C, folding, had too many uncertainties. One could not simply walk back into another Westmead. Aaron wanted certainty. That only left option B. Aaron nodded to himself. He would sort out his finances and organize a home for Ernest as soon as possible. He had no reason to wait any longer.

~6~
The Decision

AARON SURVEYED the menu in the local coffee shop, although why he bothered he wasn't sure; he never changed his order. About to order, he startled as someone tapped on his shoulder.

"I guess you must be avoiding me." Michael smiled brightly at him.

"No, no," Aaron said, lying through his teeth. He stepped away from the counter so he didn't hold up the queue behind him.

Michael guided him to an empty table. "Then you've suddenly changed your routine and developed a love for the coffee shop?"

"You do realize that sounds very stalkerish."

"Aaron, I've been watching you for months in the park before I had the courage to approach you."

Aaron chewed on the inside of his lip. Michael was a nice man, young and hot in his own way with dark curls and bright blue eyes, but he wasn't interested. "Michael, I like you, but I said I wasn't interested in a boyfriend. I'm married."

Michael laid a hand on his forearm. "I'm still interested in just being a friend."

"I'm sure you're a lovely man, but life is complicated at the moment. I think you'd be better looking elsewhere for a friend."

"I think you might need a friend," Michael said.

Aaron shook his head. "I don't need anything, Michael. I've got to go. Excuse me." He stood, but Michael blocked his way.

"Just one drink, that's all I ask."

Aaron looked at him doubtfully. "One drink and you'll leave me alone?"

"I promise. What would you like?"

"Black filter coffee."

Michael raised one eyebrow. "You took ten minutes staring at the board to pick that?" He laughed as Aaron blushed. "Don't worry, I'll get that for you."

Damon had never laughed at him or questioned his choices. Damon had got him a black filter coffee every time without him even having to think of what he wanted.

As soon as Michael's back was turned, Aaron headed for the door.

"Hey, where're you going?" Michael caught Aaron around the arm.

"I've got to get back to work," Aaron mumbled.

"Before your coffee?"

"I need to go." Aaron tugged his arm, but Michael wouldn't let go.

"Hey," Michael said softly, no trace of the amusement on his face. "Just stay for a drink. Please?"

Despite Aaron's flight response, he could see the sincerity in Michael's expression. "Why are you bothering with me?"

"I think you need a friend, and I need a friend."

"Couldn't you find someone less screwed up than me?" Aaron asked, a touch exasperated now.

Michael huffed out a laugh. "Definitely. But you're stuck with me until the end of lunch. Now let's get those coffees."

He coaxed Aaron back to the counter and placed their order. Aaron felt trapped, his heart pounding as Michael led him to a table.

Aaron perched on the edge of a wooden seat. "I haven't got long."

"I know," Michael said calmly, sipping at his coffee.

"Do you always kidnap potential new friends?"

"Only the ones who need me."

The breath caught in Aaron's throat. "I... I don't need you. I don't need anyone."

"Everyone needs someone," Michael said.

"I have my husband."

"Then why have you looked like the living dead over the past month?"

Aaron stared at him, knowing Michael would catch him in any lie. "He's missing."

Michael didn't gasp or look shocked. He just nodded, saying, "How long for?"

"Nearly a month."

"Tell me what happened."

"What do you want to know?" Aaron clasped the coffee cup with both hands, the warmth of it steadying him.

"What was his name?"

"*Is* his name," Aaron said. "He isn't dead."

"I'm sorry, what is his name."

"Damon Fox."

"How long have you been together?"

"Twenty years, and we've been married for ten."

Michael looked impressed. "Wow, that is a long time. You must have been a kid when you met."

"I was sixteen."

"When I first met you, I thought you about my age."

As Michael looked a good ten years younger than him, Aaron took that with a pinch of salt. "How old are you?" he asked.

"Twenty-eight, twenty-nine next month."

Aaron gave a polite smile, not particularly interested.

Michael slurped more of his coffee, a habit which used to infuriate Damon. Aaron looked at the table so Michael didn't see his smile.

"What happened to Damon?" Michael asked.

"He was in a car accident. He got taken to St Paddy's, then he walked out of the hospital, and I've not seen him again. I don't know any more than that."

"Jeez, that's harsh."

Aaron snorted. Yeah, harsh was one way of looking at it. Crucifying was another.

"So you know he wasn't injured badly. That's one good thing," Michael said.

Aaron made a noncommittal noise before he finished his coffee. "I've got to go," he said, pushing his chair back and standing. "Thanks for the coffee."

Michael leaned back in his chair to look at him. "Will you be here tomorrow or are you going to find somewhere else to have lunch?"

Caught on the hop, Aaron opened and closed his mouth a couple of times because of course he'd planned to just stay in the office.

"I thought so." Michael stood up, sweeping up the two cups to return them to the counter.

Aaron waited for Michael to join him before leaving the coffee shop.

"Thanks for waiting," Michael said as they walked out.

Aaron shrugged. "There seemed little point in running away now," he admitted honestly.

"Have you ever thought about a private detective?" Michael asked as they walked back to their offices.

"If Damon wanted to come back to me, he knows where I am."

"Don't *you* want to know where he is?"

"You don't understand." Aaron didn't understand himself, so how could he expect a stranger to comprehend the workings of his mind?

"Try me."

"Damon… he was mine, like he was made for me. He was everything I needed. I thought I was all he needed. It was bad enough knowing that he'd been injured, and then they tell me he was dead. But seeing him walk out of the hospital and he didn't come back to me." Aaron drew a shuddering breath. "He's destroyed everything I loved, the fabric of my life." He walked for a while, unable to speak for the thick lump in his throat. "I wasn't enough."

Michael was silent for a while, and they reached the corner where they parted ways.

"I hate this phrase," Michael started as Aaron turned away. "But Damon's not the only fish in the sea. There could be another man out there that's just right for you—in time."

Aaron shook his head. "He was the one—the only one. I don't want anyone else."

"So what are you going to do?"

"Go back to the beginning."

~7~
The Facility

AARON HAD planned to "fall asleep," as he was now euphemistically calling it, in the hollow behind the oak tree, but it was so overgrown that it was impossible to find anywhere to lie down.

Angry at his plans being thwarted, Aaron tore at the brambles and nettles with his bare hands, adrenaline driving him forward until he was left bloody and in pain, his hands wrecked and long deep scratches up his arms. It shouldn't have mattered; he would be dead in hours, but watching the blood trickle from his wounds made him even more distressed. He was soaked to the skin and in considerable pain, but he managed to clear a small enough patch to lay his blankets. Aaron topped out the contents of his rucksack onto the blanket: a bottle of vodka and enough pills to kill him. He'd researched it carefully, combining the pills that he thought had the best chance of succeeding. He'd planned to take paracetamol until he'd looked at the effects of a paracetamol overdose and realized the agonizing death he would put himself through. He wasn't brave enough to put himself through that much pain. He just wanted to fall asleep and never wake up. He'd already crushed some of the pills into the vodka to speed the effect and because he'd read somewhere that people tended to fall asleep before they'd taken enough tablets.

The rain had penetrated his clothes to the skin, leaving him cold and clammy, and his torn and battered hands still bled in places. The image Aaron had in mind of drifting off to sleep under a moonlit sky retreated further away. He was cold, wet, in pain, and miserable. He wanted it to be all over.

Aaron fumbled with the bottle, struggling to open the childproof bottle. "Open, damn you, just open up." Angry tears spilt onto his cheeks at the frustration of not being able to open the bottle. He threw the bottle in anger and then had to search a patch of nettles, getting stung as he retrieved it.

He took a short swig of the vodka, knowing it would do little more than make him sleepy, and curled up on the blanket, too exhausted and angry to tackle the bottle of pills again.

"Damon, where are you? Why don't you want me anymore?" He cried out his pain into the silence of the evening.

During his time at the asylum, Aaron had spent many hours in this exact spot, waiting for Damon to visit him. The nurse had promised him a visit every day to check on his well-being after seeing the treatment inflicted upon him by the medical staff at the hospital. Damon had been a junior nurse at the time, unable to protect him from some of the more extreme treatment methods, but he had made Aaron a promise that he would get him out of Westmead, and in the meantime Damon would protect him, every day, even on his days off. For two years, until Aaron reached eighteen, he'd met Aaron at the hollow, to check over him: a detailed inspection of his injuries both to his body and his psyche. Aaron wanted more, wanted to be touched and loved, but Damon wouldn't take it further than kissing until the day Aaron walked out of Westmead and into Damon's arms.

Damon had taken him home and slowly stripped Aaron's clothes, piece by piece, until he was naked and exposed, as vulnerable as he had been to the medical staff but safe in Damon's care.

It was his eighteenth birthday, and Aaron had lost his virginity. In reality, he'd lost that with the first rape by the whores, but in Aaron's mind, that first time with Damon was the first time he'd been involved, both mind and body. He'd fallen asleep in Damon's arms, safe for the first time in his life.

Damon hadn't told Aaron that he called the authorities on Westmead months previously, almost as soon as he met Aaron, but twenty years ago, the police and social services were as corrupt as the doctors, easily bought by hard cash. The asylum had stayed open for months after Aaron left, and then an inmate died in horrific circumstances—Damon would never tell Aaron the full details—and the media picked it up, slashing it across the tabloids. Suddenly, the parents who had friends, who knew doctors, who didn't care about the legalities, discovered exactly what happened to the children they'd locked away. Some of them cared enough to call in the authorities and make enough noise until they were heard. Not Aaron's parents, but he didn't know and neither would he have cared. In his eyes, Damon was his family, the only person he gave a shit about.

Just once Aaron had met his father in the street. Fortunately he was with Damon, and as soon Damon discovered why Aaron had frozen, unable to move from fear, he had stood in front of Aaron, blocking his view, and kissed him in front of Aaron's father, the street, and the whole damn world. No one screamed; no one called the cops. The world was changing even if bigoted arsewipes like the Guthries hadn't evolved. By the time they'd finished kissing, Mr. Guthrie had disappeared and the day was a brighter place.

As he curled up on the blanket, despite the fact he was still getting wet, Aaron dozed off.

"WAKE UP, Aaron, you've got to vomit. Here, roll over on your side," PC Collins shouted loudly in Aaron's ear, but the act of being manhandled more than the words penetrated Aaron's stupor.

Drowsy and confused, Aaron flailed his arms, protesting at the rough handling that was trying to force him away from the cozy slumber, but the attack was relentless, two fingers stuck down his throat. Inevitably he gagged, unable to stop the retching and the vomiting. Aaron tried to push Collins away, but every time he stopped, he was forced to be sick again, until he was curled up in the fetal position, wrung out and empty. Aaron wasn't sure how long he lay there, weeping helplessly as Collins stroked his hair, pushing back the damp, sweaty fringe.

"I didn't take them. Leave me alone, dammit. I didn't take them." He flapped his hands weakly in case Collins tried to attack him again.

"Aaron, I'm sorry, the bottle was half-empty, and I couldn't take the risk," Collins said firmly. "I had to make you vomit."

Aaron opened his eyes and looked at PC Collins. "Why?" He coughed against the raw harshness of his throat. "There's nothing left for me here. Why did you try to stop me?"

"Because...." Collins huffed. "Dammit, why do I have to do this?"

Aaron frowned because he had a feeling Collins wasn't talking to him. "I didn't want you to do anything."

Collins sighed and rubbed at his temples. "Aaron, there's something you need to know. It's... bizarre and you probably won't believe me, but you need to hear it. Perhaps then you can move on with your life."

"What are you talking about?" Aaron coughed again, grimacing at the foul taste in his mouth.

"Here, drink this. It'll help your throat." PC Collins handed him a bottle. When Aaron didn't take it, he said, "It's just water. It will make you feel better. Sip it slowly."

He was right. Aaron took a mouthful, swished it around his mouth, and spat; then he drank, cool water sliding down Aaron's sore throat. For a moment his stomach threatened to rebel, but he held on with grim determination.

"I couldn't do it. I wanted to, but each time I tried to take a tablet, I just couldn't." Tears spilled over onto Aaron's cheeks. "I should have stepped in front of the train."

Collins pressed his lips into a thin line. "Thank God you didn't. There's something that you need to know."

Aaron waited, his arms wrapped around his knees. He was so cold now, his teeth chattering, but Collins didn't seem to notice.

"Damon Fox isn't dead."

His heart beat faster, but Aaron just nodded; he already knew this.

Collins chewed on a hangnail. "Fox has been away, recovering from the accident."

"In a hospital? He was injured? If you knew where he was, why didn't you bring me to him?" Aaron's eyes pricked with tears at the thought of Damon sick and injured without Aaron to help him.

"Not exactly a hospital. He's been in... a facility which deals with people like Damon."

"What do you mean people like Damon?"

"Nonhumans," Collins said in a rush, as if saying the words quickly would make them more comprehensible. "Damon isn't human."

Aaron stared at him. "What are you saying?"

"Damon is a mader." He pronounced it "madder," which Aaron thought was appropriate in the circumstances, for he surely was crazy. "He's not human. He was made for you."

"Made for me?" The words stuck in Aaron's throat.

Collins nodded. "They recognized you probably wouldn't survive in the outside world by yourself, so you were given a mader who would help you to function and become a useful member of society."

"Who are they?" Aaron said harshly. "My parents? Are they the ones who did this?"

"Your parents had no part in this. Fuck, why do I have to do this? There are people trained to do this. Look, there is an organization… I'm not telling you who they are, so don't ask, but they're rich and powerful beyond your imagination. They look after homosexuals when they hear they're in trouble. Your case came to their attention. They needed a way of getting you out of the asylum, but you were weak and needed support. They organized for Fox to be made, and to support you."

"An organization?" Aaron frowned, not understanding. "Like what? Like the Masons or the Mother's Union?"

Collins's lips twitched. "Not quite. Think a private organization with endless supply of money, and resources that would make MI5 cry."

"But—"

"Aaron, these people could bring down governments, yet they pour all their resources into helping people like you."

"So why don't they bring down the governments and stop them hurting people like me?" Aaron cried.

"I don't know. They have to keep things secret in case the government get hold of the technology. Can you imagine what they'd use the technology for?"

Aaron stilled. "The burglary at my house. Was that the government?"

"We suspect it was. They've been looking for evidence of maders for years. It's no coincidence that I was assigned to your case. I had to protect you from government interference."

"Bollocks! This is all lies. Damon's a human. He's warm, he bleeds. He farts, for God's sake."

"It's all true. The technology is beyond anything that's publically known."

"So what is he, an android, a robot, Frankenstein's monster?" Aaron waited for someone to jump out of the bushes to tell him this was a stupid, sick prank and he'd been followed around by cameras for the last month, because this couldn't be true, any of it.

"Fox is a mader. I don't know how to describe us. A human body created in a laboratory, for one purpose. More than anything you can think of. We are created as adults, we don't go through childhood."

Aaron heard the emphasis. "Us? You're a mader too?"

Collins nodded. "I was made about five years ago for Lockhart."

"You two are together?" Aaron hadn't caught a hint of that.

"Not like you and Fox. We're partners. I was made to help Lockhart as he progressed through the police force. Gay police officers face huge challenges and I'm there to support him. They think he could go all the way to the top."

"So he's human?"

"Yes, and he's only just found out about me, and he's still struggling with it."

"Where is he?"

Collins hesitated, then said, "He's with Damon. He's as shocked and angry as you are."

"You knew Damon was alive all along?" Aaron said slowly.

"The minute I saw the tape in hospital I knew what he was, but we don't know each other. We are just made for one person. I am made for Lockhart, Fox was made for you."

"And all that crap about his fake nursing qualifications?"

"I needed to know how much you knew."

"Why didn't you ask Damon?"

"He was virtually destroyed in the accident. They sent a man to retrieve him, but he needed to be rebuilt from the ground up. Aaron, he's like a factory edition."

"What?" Aaron stared at him in horror.

"His memory is wiped clean. He has no record of your life together."

"You're lying. Damon is human and he's somewhere, but he remembers me."

Collins shook his head. "To remake him they had to wipe him. He's not made for you anymore. They'll reassign him when he's ready.

The techs made a new man, someone different, someone more appropriate for you now."

"More appropriate?" Aaron's voice rose up a register. "Damon is everything to me, all I've ever needed. I don't want a new man."

"You like him," Collins said.

"What?"

"You've met him and you like him."

Light dawned. "Michael."

"They thought he was what you need now. Less of a mentor and more of a partner. They think... they think it's time you grew up. Damon's kept you as a child."

Aaron snorted, a harsh, unamused sound. "They know nothing about me."

"They know everything about you," Collins contradicted. "They've been watching you since you were sixteen."

"You'd think they know me better then," Aaron said snidely. "I don't want Michael. I want Damon."

"He's gone, Aaron. Your Damon is gone."

"I want to meet him."

"That's not possible."

"It wasn't a request."

Collins laid his hand on Aaron's arm. "Forget him, he's gone."

Aaron shook his head. "Show me him. You tell me he's gone. I want to see it." He tried to get to his feet, but his legs wouldn't hold him.

"They didn't tell me you were such a stubborn shit," Collins muttered as he propped up Aaron with his arms.

"Told you they didn't know anything about me. Damon knew it, he still loved me."

"Yes, he did, and hang onto that, Aaron, because you're going to need it."

Aaron ignored the cold chill that Collins's words engendered and concentrated on bearing his own weight. That was a more immediate problem.

AARON SLEPT as Collins drove. He wasn't sure if he was still affected by the drugs in the vodka, but he didn't wake up until Collins cut the engine. He blinked, his head muzzy, and looked around. "Where are we?"

"I can't tell you that," Collins said.

They could be on any industrial estate in England. He couldn't see any clues of their whereabouts as he looked around, not even a road name.

Aaron stared at the bland office building in front of him. "Is my Damon here?"

Collins nodded. "He is, but this is the time to back out, Aaron. You're not meeting your boyfriend. You're meeting a factory model mader. No identity, no life, no clue who you are. He's been stripped of everything that made him Damon Fox. You should move on and forget about him."

Aaron pressed his lips together. "Do you have a lover?"

"I'm a mader, remember? I'm made for one purpose."

"To support Lockhart."

Collins nodded again.

"Do you love him?"

"Who?"

"Lockhart. Do you love Lockhart?"

Collins furrowed his brow. "I'm not here to love him."

"Are you sentient? Does your programming evolve or is it static?"

"I adapt as time goes on."

"What do you feel for Lockhart?"

"I…." Collins stopped. "I… care for him."

"Perhaps you ought to tell him that sometime. You never know when it might be your turn for the factory settings."

Collins looked deeply unhappy as they got out of the car. He knew it was childish, but Aaron felt he deserved some payback for hiding the fact he knew Damon's whereabouts all the time.

"Are you ready?" Collins asked.

Aaron swallowed hard and stared up at the building. Which floor was his love on? "No, but I need to do this. Need to see him if I'm to move on."

Collins glanced at him suspiciously. "As long as moving on doesn't mean another suicide attempt."

Aaron smiled at him blandly, because if Damon wasn't around, he wasn't going to make any promises. He followed Collins into the building.

The male receptionist smiled at them as they approached the desk. "Lee, good to see you, and this is Mr. Fox?"

"Hi, Steven. Yes, this is Aaron Fox. They're expecting us?"

"Fifth floor. Mr. Fox just needs to sign in here."

Aaron signed the tablet and accepted the visitor's badge, fixing it awkwardly to his sweater. He was conscious of the aroma of alcohol-laced vomit that clung to him, and he looked at his companion. "Could I clean up somewhere?"

"Sure. I'll take you to the bathroom on the third floor. Nicer than trying to clean up in the gents."

Collins led the way to the lifts. "I could do with a cleanup too."

"I'm sorry you had to stop me," Aaron said quietly. "I never meant you to discover me until it was too late."

"I realize that. And if I hadn't been looking for you, your plan would have probably worked."

"You were looking for me?"

"Michael was worried he couldn't find you. He never thought about you visiting the old asylum."

Aaron snorted gently. "I wondered why he was so persistent when I didn't give him any encouragement."

"He's been made for you, Aaron. Give him a chance."

"Damon is all I need," Aaron said, refusing to look at Collins.

"Damon is…."

"Gone. Yes, I know that. So you keep saying. But I don't need Michael. Damon was it for me."

The lift doors opened, and he followed Collins into the glass-and-chrome cage.

Collins waited until the door closed before he spoke again. "Humans need people, need companionship."

Aaron burst out laughing. "Is that what 'they' tell you?"

"It's a fact."

"People live by themselves all the time, Collins. Who lives with you, with Lockhart?"

"He still has friends."

"I had Damon. I didn't need friends."

"Now you will."

The lift doors opened, and Aaron followed Collins into the lobby area. He didn't bother to respond. They, whoever "they" were, had no clue what they had done in giving him Damon. For twenty years, he'd been the sole focus of Aaron's life. Take that away and Aaron Fox didn't exist anymore. Giving him what he needed may have seemed like a good idea, but perhaps he'd have been better off to fold under the weight of his own fragility.

Collins stopped outside the bathroom door. "Would you like fresh clothes?"

Aaron shrugged, not caring one way or the other.

"You have a shower and I'll get the clothes."

"Okay." Aaron functioned better with a direct order. He pushed open the door to find a plush bathroom fitted with three showers.

Uncertain, he hesitated in the doorway, until Collins said, "Towels are stacked up on the left, and shower gel and shampoo are in the cubicles. I'll get a toothbrush and toothpaste for you."

"I only wanted to wash my face. Aren't they waiting for us?"

"They can wait a bit longer. You'll feel better once you are clean. I'll be back in a minute." Collins pushed Aaron gently through the door.

Alone in the bathroom, Aaron grabbed a towel and went into one of the cubicles. He was functioning on automatic, doing what he was told until someone told him something different. He closed his eyes as the hot water ran over him. Physically he was exhausted, wanting only to sleep, but he had to see Damon with his own eyes. Then he could accept that his life was over.

~8~

Damon

AARON WRAPPED a towel around his waist and stepped out of the cubicle. Collins had obviously returned because the shower was on in one of the other cubicles, steam billowing over and under the door, and two piles of folded clothes lay on the counter, including socks and boxer-briefs. Collins had thoughtfully stuck a Post-it note on one of the piles with Aaron's name on it, next to the toothbrush and toothpaste.

He got dressed quickly, unsurprised that the long-sleeved T-shirt and joggers were his size. It was probably on record somewhere along with his shoe size and dick length.

The other shower stopped as he was cleaning his teeth, and Collins stepped out, a towel around his waist.

"Good, you found the clothes."

"It was easy enough," Aaron said, after he'd spat out the toothpaste.

Collins grunted, using the towel to dry himself off.

Aaron looked away, embarrassed at seeing the other man (mader) naked. After years of enforced communal living, Aaron had refused to change in any communal locker rooms.

Collins didn't seem to notice his discomfort, throwing the towel on the floor and getting dressed.

"How can I tell?" Aaron said suddenly.

"Tell what?"

"That you're a mader."

Collins stepped closer and raised the back of his hair, near the nape of his neck. "Feel here."

Embarrassed at touching another man, Aaron hesitantly ran his fingers where directed, feeling a soft bump under the wet hair. "Damon had that," he said.

"All maders do. It's the final part of us."

"Damon said it was a cyst."

"It's easier than the truth."

"He could have trusted me." That hurt more than anything. He thought he knew everything about Damon, and it turned out he knew nothing.

"We're not allowed to. If they had found out he would have been taken away immediately."

"You told Lockhart."

"He found out and I told them immediately."

"You haven't been taken away."

Collins pressed his lips together. "Not yet."

Aaron stared at him. "They wouldn't do that to you."

"I'm a mader. We aren't human. We have no choice."

"And Lockhart? What choice is he being given?"

"It's not as simple as that."

"Yes, it is. It really is." Aaron laced up his trainers and waited for Collins to finish getting dressed.

Collins shut up in the face of Aaron's stubbornness.

Before he left the bathroom, Collins said, "Leave the clothes here. I've got someone who'll clean them, but you'll need your visitor's badge."

Aaron clipped it to the neckline of the T-shirt and followed Collins back to the lift. His stomach churned at the thought of what was to come, and he was a heartbeat away from a panic attack. He grabbed Collins's arm before they went into the lift. "You're not going to leave me, are you?"

"I'll stay with you all the time and make sure you get home," Collins promised.

Aaron let go of him with a force of will and looked out of the window of the lift cage, waiting for its inevitable rise to the fifth floor.

Three people were waiting for him in the lobby area, one of whom he recognized.

"Aaron." Michael stepped forward, "You scared us," he chided gently.

"Michael." He allowed Michael to kiss him on the cheek.

"You know about what happened?" Aaron glanced at Collins, who shrugged.

"I had to tell them."

"He'd warned us that he thought you were going to try and commit suicide weeks ago."

Michael stroked Aaron's cheek. "You should have asked for help."

Aaron clasped Michael's thin wrist. "I don't need help. I need Damon."

He stepped back to get away from Michael's touch and looked at the other two, a man and a woman dressed in white coats. He had an immediate image of Dr. Frankenstein in his laboratory.

"And you are?" he asked them.

"Jill Francis and Bob Lomax. We're…. I guess you could call us the handlers for Damon," the woman said.

"He needs a handler?" Aaron raised his eyebrows because in his world, Damon was the one who did the handling.

"We're the link between the Facility and the mader. We don't normally get involved unless the mader unit is damaged, as in Damon's case."

"I'd like to see him."

"Of course." Jill smiled at him, and he could see the sadness in her eyes.

Aaron took a deep breath, relieved when Collins and Michael fell into step on either side of him, Collins guiding him with one hand on his back.

Jill stopped outside a room. "Damon is in here. He knows you are coming, but he knows you have a history together. We felt we had to warn him. But he doesn't remember it. Mr. Fox, be under no illusions: he does not remember you and he isn't coming home with you. Damon is to be reassigned to someone else."

Aaron nodded, and she sighed. "Come on, then."

The room was a small laboratory, but the only thing Aaron focused on was Damon who was standing by the window, PC Lockhart next to him.

Aaron stared at Damon, his eyes soaking him up greedily, unable to believe after eight weeks he was standing in front of him as though nothing had happened. Not nothing. Everything had happened.

"Damon," Jill said, "this is Aaron Fox."

Damon smiled politely at Aaron. "Pleased to meet you, Mr. Fox."

And Aaron learnt that his heart could not only fracture but dissolve into pieces. He'd been warned by everyone, but it was still a shock to see Damon's face, Damon's body, but not Damon standing in front of him. He looked perfect, about Aaron's age, his skin a little worn. How the hell did they manage to do the aging process?

"Pleased to...." Aaron swallowed against the lump in his throat and tried again. "It's good to see you again, Damon." He was grateful for Collins's hand, strong against his lower back, and Michael lent his support by grasping his shoulder.

To his surprise, Damon came over to stand in front of him. "They told me what happened to you. I'm so sorry."

Aaron couldn't help the tears, so ready to fall these days. "I'm sorry too."

"They tell me we were together a long time."

"Almost twenty years."

"I don't remember."

Aaron wanted to fall at his feet, beg him to remember something, anything, of their past life together.

"I wish I did."

"You were made for me."

Damon nodded, his dark hair falling in his eyes. "So they tell me."

Unable to stop himself, Aaron reached out and pushed back the wayward curls. *His* Damon would have leaned into the touch; *this* Damon stood still but didn't pull away. Perhaps they were indifferent to being handled.

"That feels nice," Damon said.

"Your hair always does that," Aaron chided. "I keep telling you to get it cut."

"Mr. Fox, step away from Damon."

Jill tried to step between them, but Damon put out his hand to stop her. "Leave him alone, Dr. Francis."

"He's here to see that you have recovered and been stripped of your memories. That is all, Damon. It's time for him to leave."

Damon shook his head. "I don't think so. I don't think your factory setting has fully worked. I may not remember my life with Aaron, but there is a pull inside me for this man."

"That's impossible," Jill snapped.

"She's right. You were fully stripped down and rebuilt, Damon. There is virtually nothing left of the original Damon Fox," Bob said.

"Nevertheless, there is something inside me, something telling me I belong to Aaron."

"You were made for me." Aaron repeated his words from earlier, a tendril of excitement running through his veins. Damon wasn't acting as they had anticipated. He was breaking their programming.

"Yes, I was. I was made for you."

Aaron and Damon stepped forward, almost simultaneously, pushing Jill out of the way.

Damon looked down at Aaron. "I wish I could remember us, our life together."

"You don't have to," Aaron said. "I can show you our life at home. Oh my God, Ernest!"

"What's happened to him?" Damon said.

Aaron stared at him. "You remember Ernest?"

"Who's Ernest?" Jill said.

They both ignored her.

Damon tucked a knuckle under Aaron's chin to force him to look up. "What did you do with the cat?"

"I put him into a shelter because I...." Aaron didn't want to admit what he'd just tried to do.

Damon enfolded Aaron into his arms, and for the first time in weeks, Aaron felt at home. "We'll talk about that when we're on our own. I hope we can get him back."

"Damon, you cannot leave the Facility," Jill said. "This has never happened before. We need to conduct tests. Find out what went wrong."

"No." Aaron hung onto Damon. "You aren't taking him away from me again. I know what you're going to do. You'll have another attempt to wipe him clean."

Damon didn't let go of Aaron. "Nothing's gone wrong, Jill. I've evolved. I'm the longest-paired couple, and obviously that's made a difference to my programming. I'm beyond your programming now."

"That's impossible." Jill's face was white.

"Isn't that what they wanted all along?" Bob said suddenly. "Up to now each mader"—he pronounced more like mader than Collins did—"has had its limitations, problems that need to be fixed with tweaks and patches. Damon is the first one that has gone beyond his original intention."

"No, he's not," Aaron said, looking at Collins.

Collins looked frightened. "Aaron, don't."

"Damon is not the only one," Aaron said.

"What do you mean?" Bob asked.

"Collins loves Lockhart."

"What?" PC Lockhart stared at his partner. "Is this true?"

"Collins was designed to look after Lockhart and support him in his career, no emotional involvement at all, but he's fallen in love with him."

"Lee, is this true?" Lockhart was so pale Aaron worried he was about to pass out.

Collins bit his lip, and then he nodded.

"Thank Christ for that." Lockhart walked across the room and yanked Collins into his arms so that he could kiss him. Beyond a startled squeak, Collins just subsided into his embrace.

"Come on, Jill, we need to let them know about the maders. We're going to have to tear up the manuals."

"They can't leave," Jill hissed. "What if the humans tell other people?"

Aaron squinted at them. "Are you both maders?"

Bob nodded. "Aye, some of the first made as was Damon. We live at the Facility because we were paired with scientists here."

"What happened to your partners?"

"Mine died and Jill's found someone else."

"They don't need to know that," she said.

Aaron could see the pain in her eyes, and he broke free from Damon to go over to Jill and take her hands. "Damon and Collins aren't the only ones, are they? You're still hurting."

Jill said nothing, but she didn't tug her hands away.

Bob steered her away, looking over his shoulder as he reached the door. "I think we need to talk to them about the success of our program, Jill. Let's leave them alone. Damon, Lee, we'll be in touch as usual."

"What about us?" Lockhart asked. "We know your secret."

"And you're going to have to carry it for the rest of your life, son," Bob said. "Can you do that?"

"Is that an *or else*?"

"Yes." Bob was totally serious. "We cannot risk this Facility or our mader couples."

"We understand," Aaron said, back in Damon's arms.

Lockhart grunted, holding Collins close.

When the scientists had gone, Aaron turned to Damon. "Take me home?"

Damon looked at Collins. "Can you take us?"

"With pleasure."

Damon turned his attention back to Aaron, pushing his damp hair back from his face. "I know very little about our life together."

"You know me. That is all that matters. Other couples survive amnesia."

"I won't be able to work until I retrain as…." He frowned. "What the hell was I before?"

"You were a nurse. You won't be able to do that again. Shit, what happens if the hospital gets wind of his return?" Concerned, Aaron turned to Collins.

"The Facility will take care of it. They will reprogram him. It will be a simple clerical error. The university records will be found and Damon will be fine. They'll be pleased to see him back."

"And what about you?" Aaron looked at Michael, silent during the proceedings.

Michael shrugged. "I'll be factory stripped and reassigned to another man."

"I'm sorry," Aaron said softly.

"I haven't had time to evolve. It's okay."

Aaron nodded, sad for the mader's fate. Then he looked at Damon, and his world settled back into focus.

"Come on, Aaron, let's go home." Damon smiled at him.

Aaron burrowed into Damon's arms. "Home," he agreed.

SUE BROWN is owned by her dog and two children. When she isn't following their orders, she can be found plotting at her laptop. In fact she hides so she can plot, and has gotten expert at ignoring the orders.

Sue discovered M/M erotica at the time she woke up to find two men kissing on her favorite television series. The series was boring; the kissing was not. She may be late to the party, but she's made up for it since, writing fan fiction until she was brave enough to venture out into the world of original fiction.

Sue can be found at her website, http://www.suebrownstories.com/;

her blog, http://suebrownsstories.blogspot.co.uk/;

Twitter, https://twitter.com/ suebrownstories

and her Facebook, https://www.facebook.com/suebrownstories.

By SUE BROWN

NOVELS
Final Admission
The Isle of... Where? • Isle of Wishes
Nothing Ever Happens

THE MORNING REPORT SERIES
Morning Report
Complete Faith
Papa's Boy

NOVELLAS
Frankie & Al
The Night Porter • Light of Day
The Sky Is Dead
Waiting

THE MORNING REPORT SERIES
Luke's Present

Published by DREAMSPINNER PRESS
http://www.dreamspinnerpress.com

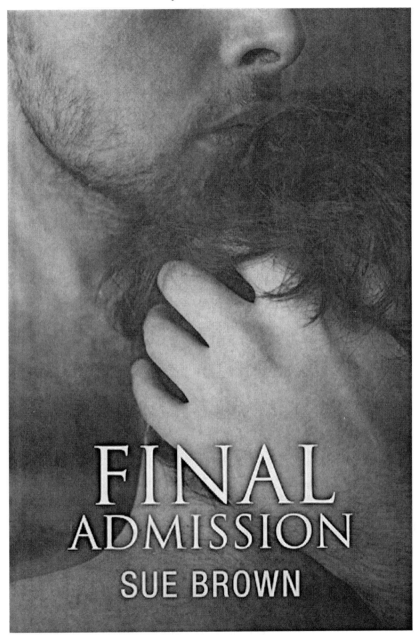

FINAL
ADMISSION
SUE BROWN

The Morning Report Series by SUE BROWN

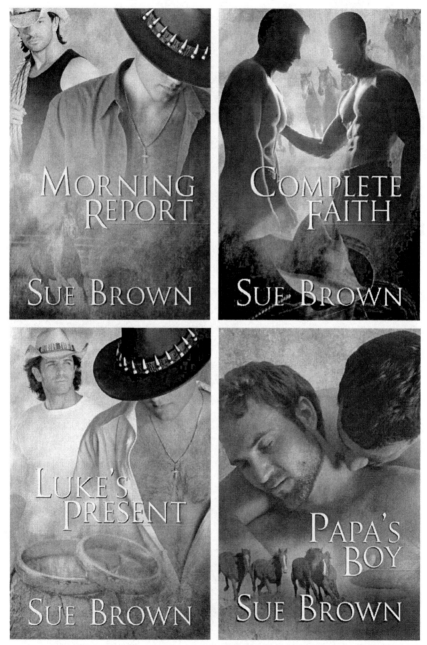

Also by SUE BROWN

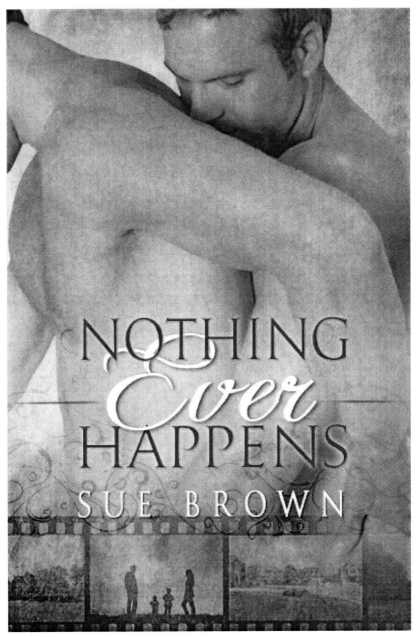

http://www.dreamspinnerpress.com

The Isle of... Series by SUE BROWN

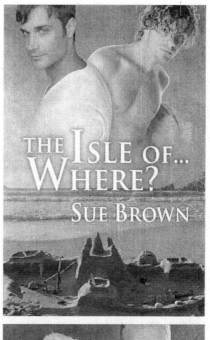

http://www.dreamspinnerpress.com

The Sex in Seattle Series by ELI EASTON

http://www.dreamspinnerpress.com

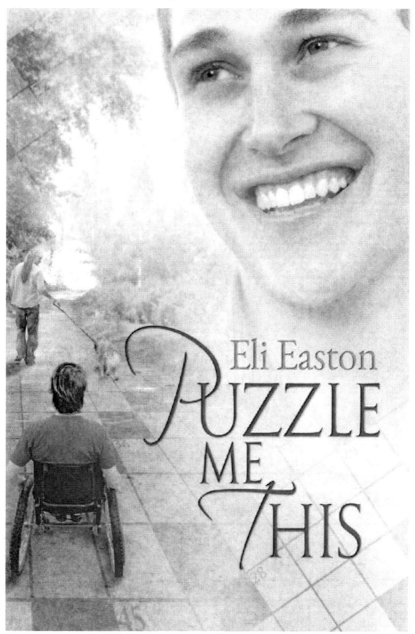

Also by ELI EASTON

http://www.dreamspinnerpress.com

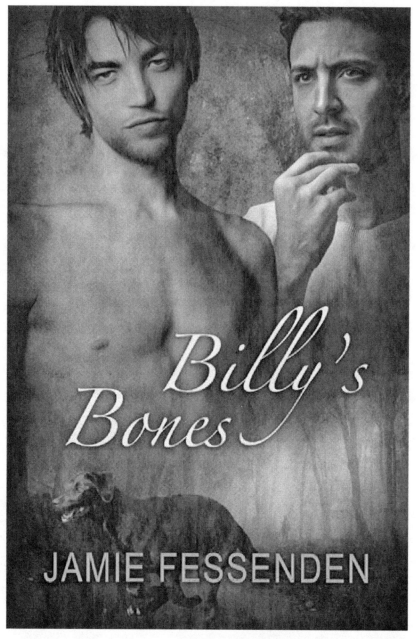

Billy's Bones

JAMIE FESSENDEN

Also by JAMIE FESSENDEN

Jamie Fessenden

Murderous Requiem

http://www.dreamspinnerpress.com

Also by JAMIE FESSENDEN

Screwups

JAMIE FESSENDEN

http://www.dreamspinnerpress.com

Also by KIM FIELDING

http://www.dreamspinnerpress.com

Also by KIM FIELDING

KIM FIELDING

The
Tin
Box

http://www.dreamspinnerpress.com

Also by KIM FIELDING

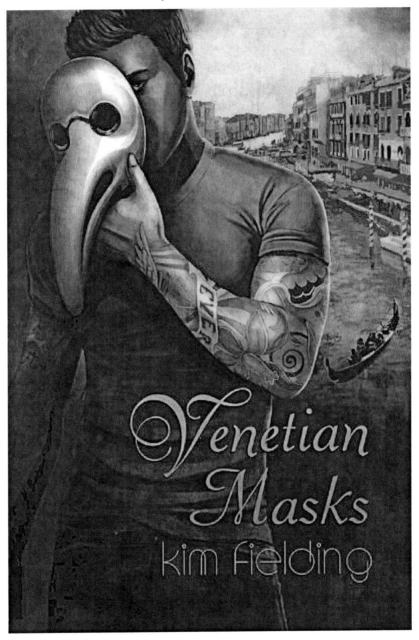

http://www.dreamspinnerpress.com

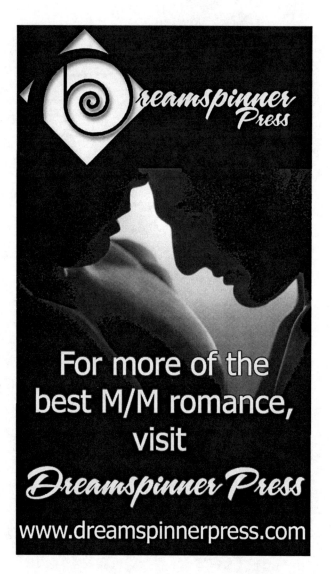

CPSIA information can be obtained
at www.ICGtesting.com
Printed in the USA
FFOW01n1950101017
40907FF